Daughters
of the Silk Road

Also by Debbie Rix

The Girl with Emerald Eyes

Daughters

of the Silk Road

DEBBIE RIX

bookouture

Published by Bookouture

An imprint of StoryFire Ltd.
23 Sussex Road, Ickenham, UB10 8PN
United Kingdom

www.bookouture.com

ISBN 978-1-78681-010-6
eBook ISBN 978-1-78681-009-0

For my mother
Margaret Rix
Architect, artist and amateur historian

Thanks to:

My family, as always, for their understanding as
I disappear to my 'shed' to write

My publisher – Claire Bord, Kim Nash and the rest of
the team at Bookouture

My agent, Rowan Lawton, for her enthusiasm and support

All the wonderful readers, reviewers and bloggers
who have provided so much encouragement

"Their god, named T'ung, was once himself a potter. In former times during the Ming Dynasty, after the large dragon fish bowls had failed in the baking year after year, the eunuchs in charge inflicted the most severe punishments, and the people were in bitter trouble. The god, throwing away his life for the rest, leaped into the midst of the furnace and died there, and the dragon-bowls were afterwards taken out quite perfect. His fellow-workmen, pitying him and wondering, built a temple within the precincts of the government manufactory, and worshipped him there under the title 'Genius of Fire and Blast', so that his fame was spread abroad. The potters offer annually reverent sacrifice, just as others worship the gods of agriculture and the land. In my day, when the people are content and trade brings success, when work is well paid and life is easy, the fame of this genius should not be forgotten."

T'ang Ying's words from the *T'ao-shu*

PROLOGUE

The girl looked up at the soft blue sky, glimpsed through the bars of the high window. A cloud blew in from the lagoon, its shape swirling and changing. Was it a snake, its scales mirrored in the high cirrus cloud? The form changed with the high winds; it grew a leg, then two, floating down from its body. She heard the rustle of trees in the unseen garden below as the wind gusted suddenly. The cloud continued its journey past her window until she saw now that it had metamorphosed into something quite different. Her hand scrabbled at the rough-hewn stone wall. She eased a section out and laid it silently on the floor; there stood the vase hidden in a small niche. Her fingers touched the dragon that snaked its way around the centre and she looked again at the cloud. The head – for there was indeed a head now – gazed down at her with benevolent eyes, before a sudden gust of wind blew it onwards and out of her eyeline. The dragon had been looking down on her...

PART ONE

CHAPTER 1

Sheen, London
Late September 2015

The vase stood on the hall table. A pair of dusty dried hydrangea flowers jutted awkwardly from its narrow neck. One had been a bright pink when Miranda had first brought it inside in the last dying months of summer. Now its petals took on a dusty greenish tinge. The other had been white, but had long lost any resemblance to the clear sparkling flower that had glowed out that late summer evening when Miranda went out with her secateurs in search of something to 'cheer up that vase'.

Slam. The door juddered as it closed. Its base, swollen by a particularly wet summer, caused it to catch on the mat, so that whoever was trying to open or close it had to use extreme force, shoving it hard, sometimes kicking it, sometimes leaning their entire body against it, or even, on one particularly wet day, taking a sledgehammer to its base.

The slamming sound reverberated around the empty hall. The vase wobbled imperceptibly on the narrow console table.

'Hi Mum, it's just me.' Georgie flung her coat onto the Shaker pegs that had been inexpertly screwed into the wall a few months earlier. Miranda had found them in a car boot sale and was rather pleased to have discovered something so chic for just a few pounds. She had made an attempt at hanging them correctly – DIY being just one of the many things she had had to 'take on' over the years, but her skills with a drill were adequate at best and the wall on which the pegs hung was made of old lathe and plaster and simply did not have the resilience for something as heavy as a wooden coat rack. The pegs strained under the weight of Georgie's damp army surplus wool coat. The coat's grey edge grazed the side of the vase; a fine spray of dust flew out from the flowers. A pale green petal fell onto the console table.

'In here,' Miranda called out to her daughter. Miranda sat at the kitchen table, bills spread out all around her.

'What are they?' Georgie asked as she casually opened kitchen cupboards.

'Trouble,' her mother replied.

'Oh?' Georgie hovered anxiously near her mother, before she returned to her searching, finally slamming the door of the cupboard under the sink with a dramatic flourish.

'There are no biscuits. I mean nothing.'

'Well you won't find them in there,' Miranda said curtly, gesturing towards the sink.

'Well where are they?' Georgie asked irritably.

'What?' Miranda asked distractedly.

'The biscuits?'

'Oh. There aren't any. I've not done a shop. Sorry. Why don't you make some? I've got flour and stuff.'

'Never mind.' Georgie mooched across the kitchen and, grabbing her heavy school bag, clattered up the stairs. Halfway up she turned round and leapt back down onto the hall floor, landing heavily, before reaching over to her grey coat and feeling in the pocket for something. She brought out a crumpled packet of gum, knocking the dried hydrangea with her elbow as she did so. The vase trembled.

Miranda filled the kettle and gazed out at the wintry garden. Frost clung on late in the day, carpeting one side of the lawn and the adjacent flowerbed with a fine film of white ice. The other side, the sunny side, lay green and damp, the earth of the flowerbed dark brown and crumbly. The hydrangeas on the shady side of the garden drooped sadly, their leaves turning brown as the frost did its work in the late afternoon light.

She switched the kettle on and sat back down at the table – ninety-five pounds, forty-three pence for electricity; eighty-four pounds for gas; thirty pounds for the Internet; seventy-five pounds for council tax. Her bank statement bore witness to the necessary expenditure at the garage for fixing the ancient Volvo's exhaust pipe. That and a few meagre presents she had bought the previous month for Georgie's fifteenth birthday were the only 'extravagances' she had allowed herself. She totted it all up on her calculator. In all, it was more than her ex-husband Guy paid her in child support each month.

She heard Georgie clump down the stairs. She heard the struggle with the door.

'Where are you going?' Miranda called out.

'To Cassie's.'

'Why?'

'They've got food there.' And she was gone. The door juddered behind her as she yanked it closed using the letterbox. The vase rocked, before settling once again on the console table.

Miranda opened the fridge and peered into its interior, hoping to be surprised by some previously overlooked delicacy. The near-empty fridge stared back. It yielded only a few strips of bacon, three eggs, and the edge of what had once been some quite good cheddar that she had bought the previous week at the farmers' market. She took flour and a little butter that was left in the dish and rubbing it together made some pastry. She rolled it out on the kitchen table and lined an old rather discoloured flan dish, one of several domestic items she had inherited from her mother's Aunt Celia.

The old lady had lived in the tropics for many years with her engineer husband, but had ended her days in a romantic vicarage near Cheltenham. Miranda had had to guard against disappointment when she received a letter from a solicitor earlier in the year, informing her of her great aunt's bequest. Ripping the letter open she had initially hoped that the huge house and its splendid contents were to be hers, but reading on, she discovered that her aunt, who had been childless, had left the majority of her estate to be divided between the local donkey sanctuary, the Ghurkha's association, and prostate cancer research – the condition that had taken her beloved husband from her. Delighted for the splendid Ghurkhas and the sweet donkeys in equal measure, Miranda was about to throw the letter in the bin when she read on. It appeared that her aunt had left her a selection of "domestic" items that she hoped Miranda might find both "useful and aesthetically pleasing".

When the large removal chest was delivered a couple of weeks later, she had to stifle the desire to send it back where it came from, marked "not known" next to her name and address. Instead, she dragged the box into the sitting room and taking the contents out, tried to decide if she found any of them either useful or pleasing.

There was a set of ancient French flan dishes decorated with yellow and green flowers that would, she decided, look attractive on the kitchen dresser. So, both useful and aesthetically pleasing. There was an early Victorian carriage clock, that she remembered admiring one afternoon when visiting Celia. It was sweet of Celia to remember that she had liked it. Miranda had a fleeting thought, quickly dispelled, that it might even be worth something - as she thought of the gas bill that had landed on the mat that morning. There was a leather-bound set of Dickens novels and a complete set of Walter Scott – neither of which were exactly unique, but nice to have. She placed them on the bookcase in the sitting room. There was an early edition of Jane Austin's *Pride and Prejudice* that was in good condition and might be worth taking to the bookshop where she worked three times a week. Jeremy, who owned the shop, would be able to tell her if it had any value. In the corner of the chest, wrapped in an old patchwork quilt which now lay across her bed, was the vase. Blue and white porcelain, it featured an angry dragon chasing around the centre, its face staring ghoulishly ahead, its back decorated with what looked like the sharp teeth of a buzz saw.

Incredibly, given its mode of transport, it appeared to be completely undamaged. Miranda took it out and wandered around the sitting room trying to decide where to put it, before finally settling on a central position on the mantelpiece. But Georgie had pronounced it 'spooky' when she came home from school, declaring that she couldn't concentrate on the telly with 'that thing' staring down at her. So Miranda moved the vase to the hall table, and there it had stayed – a useful receptacle for dried flowers, unwanted keys and unpaid bills.

She put the flan dish lined with pastry in the fridge to chill and turned on the oven. Rummaging in the drawers of the ancient dresser she found the baking beans wrapped in old and much-used greaseproof paper. She laid the paper and beans over the chilled pastry case and put it in the oven to bake blind. She inspected the vegetable basket. There were a couple of elderly potatoes, two large onions, a slightly manky leek and a tomato – already beginning to wither. She put the tomato in the fridge, hoping to save it for another day, and then carefully sliced a large onion. She washed and trimmed the leek and cut that up too. She took the three strips of streaky bacon and snipped them into small pieces before frying them off a little. Once the pastry case had been baked, she removed the paper and sprinkled the cooked bacon over its base. She added the onions and leeks to the bacon fat and cooked them delicately until the onion was almost translucent before transferring them to the tart shell. Then, mixing the eggs with the old cream – slightly off, she noted, but no less useful for that – into a thick batter, she poured it into the tart, topping it off with salt, pepper and grated cheese, and placed it in the oven to bake.

She washed the potatoes and put them into the oven next to the tart, then sat back down at the kitchen table to study her bank statement. It revealed an alarmingly small amount of money, barely enough to get her through to the next payday. On the back of the statement she wrote a list of all the bills that would need paying before that date and deducted the total from her available balance. It did not make comfortable reading. The phone rang. It was Georgie.

'Mum, I'm going to stay at Cassie's for supper. I'll see you later.'

'But darling, I've made a…'

The phone clicked before she could tell her daughter of the culinary delights awaiting her at home.

Resisting the temptation to cry, Miranda picked up the pile of unpaid bills and dumped them back in an old rattan tray that served as her office on the kitchen dresser, and laid the table for one.

CHAPTER 2

'Georgie!' Miranda yelled up the staircase to her daughter. It was eight minutes past eight and if they did not leave in the next twenty seconds, Georgie would miss her bus and Miranda would be forced to drive her to school, making herself late for work.

'Georgie, I am leaving in ten seconds!' She heard the loo flushing and finally her daughter appeared at the top of the stairs with a toothbrush ensconced firmly in her mouth.

'I'm mumming,' she mumbled, toothpaste escaping from the sides of her mouth and splashing onto her school jumper.

'You are going to miss your bus and I really do *not* have time to take you today!'

Her daughter disappeared into the bathroom and Miranda heard her spitting violently into the basin.

The house rattled as Georgie slammed the bathroom door and descended the staircase in two giant leaps, landing heavily in the hall.

'Georgie – please don't do that. You'll go through the floor one day. I'm sure that floorboard is cracking,' her mother said exasperatedly.

'Do you want me to hurry or not?'

'Oh, for goodness sake. Where's your bag?'

'Here.' Georgie grabbed the bag from the Shaker pegs so violently they teetered on the edge of their rawl plugs. The bag grazed the side of the vase.

'Careful!' Miranda steadied the vase on its table.

'I hate that thing. Who cares if it gets broken?' said Georgie.

'I would. It was left to me by…'

'I know, I know. Come on.' Georgie yanked open the front door. 'Let's go.'

Miranda arrived at the bookshop on Barnes High Street just before nine o'clock. She took the shop keys out of her basket and unlocked the door. A pile of envelopes were stacked up on the other side, which made opening the door tricky, but she managed to reach round its base and move the pile of mail out of the way.

Most of it, she knew, would be rubbish, but once inside, she nevertheless dutifully sorted through it, laying it out on the owner's desk in three piles: urgent, probably rubbish, definitely rubbish. The urgent ones were fairly obvious; they normally had a see-through window and the words 'final demand' in red. The rubbish were predominantly begging letters and the odd charity fishing expedition; the definite rubbish consisted of catalogues for office equipment that they simply didn't need and couldn't afford anyway.

Miranda worked at the shop on Tuesdays, Thursdays and Saturdays. It was a convenient arrangement that enabled her to earn enough money to cover bills, and allowed Jeremy – her boss – two days off per week. On her days away from the shop Miranda was working hard to establish a small knitting business. It was just a fledgling enterprise – something she had started as her marriage fell apart. She had built up quite a following amongst friends and acquaintances for her colourful Fair Isle scarves and hats, and had a long list of orders that kept her busy. She had even considered selling to a couple of local boutiques, but it was hard to build up sufficient stock and the profit margins were lean. It made more sense for the moment to continue selling direct. Like many artisans, she was at a crossroads. She had a product that customers wanted, but her profit margins made any kind of expansion impossible. She had an old pine chest in the sitting room crammed with balls of wool, arranged in colour co-ordinated groups. Boxes of finished garments were stacked neatly in the hall, next to the console table. She spent any spare time designing packaging, and had a simple website. But when she had explored the possibility of making it transactional, the costs had been prohibitive. And so she continued to work at the bookshop, and fitted in her knitting where she could. Both she and Jeremy worked on Saturdays to cope with the 'rush', although Miranda could not actually remember the last time either of them had been exactly busy on a Saturday. On Jeremy's days away from the shop, he was supposed to be writing the *great novel*, but Miranda suspected that he actually spent the time mooching around in his flat above the shop, judging by the creaking floorboards she could hear as he wandered back and forth between kitchen and sitting room.

Sitting at Jeremy's desk at the back of the shop, Miranda heard the loud jangle of the shop's bell, alerting her to the arrival of her first customer.

'Damn,' she muttered under her breath. Checking her watch, she saw that it was just nine-fifteen, and the shop was not due to open until ten o'clock, a time that she and Jeremy had arrived at based on their mutual loathing of early morning starts and the necessity to plough through paperwork uninterrupted for an hour before opening time – something that had become increasingly superfluous, as the shop had fewer and fewer visitors and customer orders had shrunk over the years.

'I'm sorry,' she called out to the invisible customer, 'but we're not actually open yet. It's my fault; I must have forgotten to lock the door behind me when I came in. We open at ten o'clock if you'd like to come back?'

Her question hung unanswered in the air. Irritated at this apparent rudeness, she got to her feet and walked round the large desk and out into the shop. Standing at the rare and second-hand book section, one of her recent initiatives, was a tall fair-haired man wearing a dark grey suit. He turned slowly to look at her.

'Oh I see. That's a shame. I don't have very long, I'm on my way to Hampshire and just spotted your shop and thought I'd come and see what little gems you might have here. But if I must go…'

'No, no, that's all right,' she relented. 'I'm sorry, do please have a browse, and let me know if there is anything I can help you with.'

She was on the phone to the distributor, trying to order a book for a regular client, when the man appeared in front of her desk. She gestured that she would be a few minutes more. He stood patiently, gazing down at her and she found herself feeling rather self-conscious. Her impatience with Georgie that morning had caused her to skimp on her own appearance. She wore a rather inelegant combination of a loose-fitting cheesecloth shirt and blue jeans. She was vaguely aware that she had not actually brushed her dark blond hair at all that morning, and found herself smoothing it down awkwardly with one hand, the phone hooked under her chin as she wrote some numbers in her order book with the other.

'Thanks Mavis,' she said to the distributor at last. 'Look I've got to go. I've got a customer; if you could email me a confirmation of the order that would be great. Bye.'

'Now…' she said at last, gazing up at the man. 'What can I do for you?'

He was tall; his hair was…. What? Blond? No. Red? No. Strawberry blond.

'You have lovely hair,' she said suddenly, and then blushed scarlet. 'Oh I'm sorry! How embarrassing… I just meant that it's a rather unusual colour.'

'That's all right.' He smiled at her; his grey eyes crinkled at the corners. He had a deep voice, reassuring, posh. He reminded her of the young men of her youth. The sort of men her mother would have liked her to marry.

'Right, so what do we have here then?' She attempted to sound business-like and stood up to look at his pile of books. 'Oh, that's a good choice,' she murmured appreciatively. 'That's a particularly lovely early edition. Are you a fan of Lewis Carroll?'

'Not especially,' he muttered.

'Oh, I just wondered if you were buying it for your daughter perhaps?'

'No, I have no children. It's more a professional thing. I'm an auctioneer and I've got an early edition of *Wonderland* already; this one of *The Looking Glass* might make up a good lot.'

'Oh, how interesting,' said Miranda as she wrapped the book in brown paper.

'It's quite expensive, but I imagine you're used to high prices in your business.'

'Yes. Do you take cards?'

'We do, yes. Now let's just add it all up. The Lewis Carroll is fifty-seven pounds fifty. The other items add up to…' Miranda totted them up on her calculator; 'another forty-eight pounds and thirty pence. So that's…'

'One hundred and five pounds and eighty pence,' he replied swiftly.

'Gosh, yes. That's quite right. Thank you.'

An awkward few minutes followed, while Miranda tried and failed to get any sort of signal on the credit card machine.

'I'm really very sorry. It does this sometimes. We're in a bit of a black hole here. I do keep asking Jeremy – he's the owner – to sort it out, but technology is not really his thing. You don't have a cheque I suppose?'

'A cheque?' the man asked with surprise. 'Yes, I might have somewhere.' He rooted around in his leather briefcase before finally bringing out a chequebook.

'Here.' He ripped one out with a flourish and handed it to her.

'Perfect. If you could just put your card number and your address on the back? I'm sorry to ask, but the bank get a bit huffy if we take cheques over a hundred pounds with no other information.'

'No problem,' he said.

'Well,' he said finally, as she handed him his brown paper parcel, 'this has been most enjoyable. I shall remember your shop, but I'll try to come after ten o'clock in future.' He smiled again; the pale grey eyes twinkled. Guy's eyes had been brown; a very dark brown. She always felt that she could not quite work out what he was thinking, as if his eyes were too dark to read. But this man's eyes were like cool pools of water.

'Yes. Do come again; we'd like that.' She glanced down at his cheque and noticed his name for the first time, 'Mr Davenport.'

'Charles, please. Well, Charlie really.'

'Charlie,' she said lightly, 'and I'm Miranda.'

'Delighted, Miranda.'

CHAPTER 3

Miranda was never quite sure what made her keep a note of Charlie's address before she banked his cheque. But she was glad that she had. Two weeks after his first visit, a dealer came into the shop and offered them a rare and beautiful edition of both Lewis Carroll books bound in one volume dating back to 1898.

'Can you leave it with me for a day or two?' Miranda suggested. 'I might have a buyer for this. I'll keep it in the safe, I promise.'

The dealer agreed to return the following week and Miranda lost no time in tracking down Charles Davenport. She had made a note of his address on a post-it and stuck it onto her computer: The Manor, Chattleton, Hants. When she checked with enquiries, he appeared to be ex-directory. So she put his name and address and the words 'antique dealer' into a search engine and discovered the auction house he worked for. She rang them and asked to be put through.

'I'm afraid Mr Davenport is not in today,' said the girl at the other end.

'Oh that's a pity; I have a rather wonderful rare book that I think he'd appreciate. In fact I know he would; he asked me to keep my eye out for just such a thing the other day when he bought something from me.'

The receptionist sounded dubious, but was finally persuaded to part with Charles's mobile phone number. She dialled.

'Hello.' The voice sounded familiar… Deep.

'Hello, Charlie? It's Miranda.'

'I'm sorry?'

'Miranda Sharp – the woman in the bookshop the other day?'

'Oh yes, of course! Forgive me, Miranda, I had a momentary lapse. How lovely to hear from you.'

She felt a wave of relief that he had remembered her. 'Look, I hope you don't mind me calling you like this?'

'Not at all.'

'It's just that I've been shown a first-rate early edition of *Alice* – the two novels in one edition dating back to 1898, and I wondered if you might be interested.'

'How did you get hold of it?'

'Well, a dealer we do a bit of work with brought it in this morning and I just wondered…'

'Well yes, of course. It does sound interesting. How much does he want for it?'

'I don't know really – I think it's a matter of negotiation. But he's open to offers.'

'Well, depending on the price, I'd be keen to come over and have look at it? I could come tomorrow; how does that work for you?'

Knowing that would be her day off, Miranda told a small lie. 'Oh, I'm not sure we can do that, we're closed you see? How about Saturday?'

'No can do, I'm afraid; bit busy on Saturday.'

'Yes, of course. What about next Tuesday?'

'Yup, I can do that. You'll be able to look after it till then?'

'Oh don't worry. I'll take care of it. It'll go in the safe right now.'

'OK, well I'll see you next Tuesday, sometime after ten. '

'Ha… Yes. Thank you for remembering our strange opening hours.'

Miranda felt a sense of rising excitement over the next few days. Jeremy, who was not particularly bothered about Miranda's second-hand book venture, didn't seem remotely interested in the valuable book stored in his safe.

'It could be worth a fortune Jeremy,' said Miranda enthusiastically. 'I've been doing a bit of research and it could be worth as much as a thousand.'

'Really?' said Jeremy distractedly, as he totted up their profits for the previous month.

It did not make edifying reading.

'And I've asked Malcolm, the dealer, for at least twenty percent of any profit, as a finder's fee,' she said with satisfaction.

'Well done, well done.'

'Jeremy! That could be as much as two hundred pounds if we're lucky. That's more than we take in most weeks isn't it?'

Jeremy looked up from his hand-written list of figures. 'Well, yes, if you put it like that.'

'So?' Miranda said with exasperation.

'Well let's hope that this chap wants to buy it then.'

On Tuesday morning, Miranda was more than usually interested in her appearance. Georgie watched her with suspicion as she modelled three outfits for her over breakfast.

'Which one, G? I think the first one. The others are a bit 'buttoned up'. What do you think?'

'Mum – you're only going to work. What the f… is going on?'

'Language, Georgie,' her mother said with mock ferocity.

'I didn't even say the word, Mum; anyway, why all the fuss about what you should wear? What's going on, Ma?'

'Oh, just an important client is coming to the shop and I want to look nice. That's all. So which one do you think?'

'I think the black dress looks professional,' said Georgie reluctantly.

'I don't want to look professional,' said her mother, gazing at herself in the small mirror she had hung from the dresser's hook.

'I thought you were seeing a client!?'

'I am. I just want to combine professional with elegant,' her mother said quickly.

'Oh, I don't care. Wear what you like. I'm off to do my teeth.'

They left the house with Miranda wearing an old but nevertheless well-fitting wrap dress that her friend Sasha had given her during one of her annual 'chucking out' sessions. It was a shade of blue that brought out the colour of Miranda's eyes and suited her rangy figure well. 'God, Miranda, it never looked that good on me! Take it. You look fab.'

She arrived at the shop just before nine o'clock and sorted the mail as usual. Then she tidied Jeremy's desk and put out a tray with two cups and saucers and a plate of biscuits that she had bought on the way in. She stapled the receipt for the biscuits to the petty cash book and took out the one pound twenty-nine they had cost her. It was a 'necessary' expense, she reasoned to herself. And then she waited. Ten o'clock came and there was no sign of him. Customers wandered in and annoyed her with their irritating questions and requests.

At one o'clock she was just considering turning the shop's sign to 'closed' and popping next door to the café for a sandwich when he sauntered through the door.

'Hi Miranda,' he called out as he came in. 'Sorry, I'm a bit later than I had expected to be – traffic was murder on the M3 this morning.'

'No problem,' Miranda said, crossing the shop to greet him. She shook his hand rather awkwardly before darting behind him to turn the shop's sign to 'closed'.

'I think it would be best if we weren't disturbed,' she said by way of explanation.

She went to the safe and removed the book, laying it carefully on the tidied desk for Charles to examine.

'Tea? Coffee?' she asked.

'Coffee, thanks.'

'Biscuit?' she offered as she handed Charles his coffee.

'No, thanks. The book is in excellent condition; very nice indeed. Could you find out how much your dealer wants for it?'

'I've asked him already and he's happy for me to negotiate on his behalf; but it would need to be in the region of a thousand.'

Charles looked at her with his cool grey stare. 'That's quite steep.'

'Yes, but, as you say, it's in excellent condition and as you probably are aware, it's really rather a rare edition. We've done a bit of research and we think it's a fair price.'

'Well, I might need to think a bit about that; would you mind if I slept on it?'

Disappointed that she had not secured an instant sale, Miranda nevertheless said, 'No, of course not, and feel free to come back to take another look.'

They drank their coffee and Charles finally relented and took a chocolate digestive. He was very slim, Miranda noted, and didn't look like the kind of man who ate unnecessary calories. As he left, he turned round to her. 'Look, I hope you won't think me too forward, but I'd love to see you again, outside of work.'

She felt herself blushing. 'That would be lovely.' It had been so long since anyone had asked her out, she felt strangely elated.

'Well, I don't know what you're up to over the next couple of days, but perhaps when I come back to view the book again, we could go out for a drink afterwards?'

'That would be great.'

'I'll do a bit of research on the *Alice* book and call you... Tomorrow? And we can arrange something.'

'Great.' She struggled hard to keep the excitement out of her voice. 'Until tomorrow then.'

Their 'date' was simple enough. He arrived just before closing time and agreed to buy the book for a 'bargain' price of seven hundred and fifty pounds. She was annoyed with herself for not holding out for more, but he could be very persuasive. Wrapped in brown paper, it was laid carefully in the boot of his Audi car. They then walked to a wine bar a couple of shops down from the bookshop. They sat at a small table in the window and drank white wine, and ate olives and pistachio nuts out of little Moroccan bowls. The conversation flowed easily. He was amusing and attentive, but revealed little about himself. He somehow deflected all personal questions, insisting on learning as much as he could about Miranda. And so she told him about her divorce, and Georgie.

'It must be hard, bringing up a child on your own,' he said sympathetically.

'Yes, and no. In many ways, I'm relieved that Guy doesn't show much interest; it means I don't have to pass every decision by him. He ran off with our nanny, did I mention that? I came home early one day from work – I worked at an art gallery in those days – and found Georgie alone in front of the telly; she was about two. I noticed Guy's briefcase in the hall, and went upstairs to look for him. On the landing I thought I heard some weird noises. I pushed open the door and there they were…'

'That must have been terrible!'

'Yes, but I should have seen it coming. He had obviously fancied her for ages. She was tall and blonde with legs up to her armpits. She cooked like a dream and was very, very organised. Eastern European, you know – very together. I left him there and then. The sight of them at it was the last straw. I just picked up Georgie and drove off to my mother's. Anya – that was the nanny's name – actually said "do it to me, big boy," can you believe that? I mean, does anyone actually say that outside of porn films? To be honest, I wouldn't be surprised if she'd been in a porn film. Anyway, they're married now and he and Anya have twins – typical of her to be so efficient about having an instant family! He does see G occasionally and sends her birthday cards and so on, but he's *so* moved on – this year for her fifteenth birthday he gave her a cheque for twenty-five quid. Can you believe that?'

'That does sound a bit mean.' Charlie's grey eyes flickered momentarily to his watch.

'I'm sorry,' she said. 'I'm boring you.'

'Not at all, it's fascinating. And I was just thinking, I'd love to buy you dinner, but I really ought to get back to Hampshire tonight; I've got a sale down there first thing and there's still lots to do…'

'Oh dear,' she said. 'I've been wittering on, haven't I? I'm sorry. Jeremy's always telling me off for it. He's the owner of the shop and a dear friend – a platonic friend.' She blushed slightly. 'He saved my life really, after the divorce, giving me a job here. And he's great with G too.'

'He sounds wonderful,' said Charlie. 'Perfect husband material I'd have thought.'

'Oh, he is great, yes. But not husband material – no. He's gay – and adorable. He's a very old friend. I've known him since we were kids. We were virtually brought up together. Then we rather lost touch for a while – he went to university, and I got married. But we met again, by chance, just outside the shop here. I was house-hunting after I'd split up with Guy. Dear Jeremy… He's hopeless with the shop though. He really wants to be a writer, but can't seem to get it together. He bought the shop after his parents were killed in an accident. It was all a bit of a tragedy. You'd love him. Oh God, here I go again – chattering too much and you've got to go.'

'It's fine. I just wish I had more time. And if you want my opinion, I don't know what that husband of yours was thinking of, leaving you for a leggy blonde called Anya. She sounds very hard work.' He smiled and their fingers just touched across the table.

'Yes, she is rather. Still, she keeps him out my hair. Thank you, for the drink. And don't worry at all about dinner. I need to get home and make sure G is OK anyway. She's not used to me being out in the evenings.'

Miranda had a sudden frisson of anxiety that she had yet again revealed far too much about herself. She didn't want to give the impression that she had no social life.

'I mean, I do go out, obviously – to yoga and a book club. It's just that I didn't tell G I'd be late.'

'It's fine. Let me drop you off anyway.'

'You don't have to. I have my car.'

'Oh.' He sounded genuinely disappointed. 'Well perhaps we could have dinner another night, maybe next week?'

'That would be lovely. I'd like that. Thank you.'

They stood up and an awkwardness descended, as each tried to decide if it was 'too soon' to kiss the other goodbye. Finally, he leant down and kissed her fleetingly on the cheek.

'Look,' she said as she turned to walk back to her car. 'Why don't you come to me next week for supper? It won't be anything special and Georgie will be around, but…'

'Thanks… I'd love to.'

'Great. Well, shall we say Wednesday? I don't work in the shop that day, so you might actually get something worth eating. I'll text you my address, shall I?'

He smiled in acknowledgement.

'Seven-thirty? '

'Perfect.'

As soon as Charles's cheque for the book had cleared safely through Jeremy's account, he generously gave Miranda seventy-five percent of their finder's fee.

'Oh Jeremy, that's so kind of you. You're such a pal. That will be over £100!'

'I know. Well you deserve it Manda. It was all your idea – the second hand area; and it's turning out to be rather a good one. Enjoy it; fill the fridge for that starving daughter of yours.'

The following Wednesday, Miranda drove Georgie to her bus stop.

'G, darling, I've got a friend coming to dinner tonight, just thought I'd mention it.'

She tried to sound as casual as she could.

'Who?' Georgie asked, 'one of your yoga people? Oh God, it will be veggie hell for supper.'

'No G, not one of my yoga friends. It's a man if you must know.'

'A man!' Georgie spat the words at her mother. 'What man? God, Mother... Do you have a boyfriend?' This was hurled at her mother with such an air of disdain that Miranda felt quite hurt.

'No G, he is not my boyfriend. Just a good customer and I like him, that's all. But if he were my 'boyfriend' would that be so terrible?'

Georgie fiddled with the buttons on her army coat and stared sullenly out of the window, avoiding her mother's gaze.

'Oh G, darling, don't worry! He's just a friend. Now get out of the car and go to school. I'll see you later.'

Miranda's 'share' of the book deal was undoubtedly a boon to her finances, but she still had bills to pay and so was careful, as always, when purchasing food. She bought a whole frozen chicken, the cheapest she could find. Once defrosted and jointed she would use it to make her 'chicken with tarragon and bacon,' one of her most reliable supper dishes. If she were careful when serving it, there would be enough for the next night too. She bought lemons to make a tart and a small pot of double cream for pudding. At the cheese counter she anguished over a piece of Stilton, before finally giving in and buying a slim piece – just enough for two people to share.

When she got home, she went out into the wintry garden and picked a few late dahlias for the table. She looked around for a vase before remembering that Georgie had broken her only glass one. She wandered into the hall and removed the dusty hydrangeas from the blue and white vase on the hall table. She took it into the kitchen and ran it under the tap to remove the dust, knocking it slightly against the side of the stone sink as she did so. She dried it carefully before filling it with fresh water and arranging the dahlias in it, and set it in the middle of the kitchen table. She had already decided to feed Georgie early, as a treat in front of the television, and so laid the table carefully for two. She put out some blue and white napkins that she'd had since the Guy days, and set out two of her four crystal wine glasses – another thing she had rescued from their wedding presents.

Then she set about making her chicken tarragon and the lemon tart. It had been quite a while since she had cooked a meal for someone other than Georgie and Jeremy, and it felt good to be chopping and frying and grating.

At four-thirty, she drove to the bus stop to collect Georgie, who threw her bag into the back of the car as she leapt into the passenger seat.

'God I'm starving,' said her daughter.

'Good; I've made a nice supper of chicken tarragon; you can have yours in front of the TV if you want?'

'What?' her daughter exclaimed. 'You never let me do that. What's going on?'

'My friend is coming to supper and I thought it would be better if you were banished,' Miranda said with a smile.

With Georgie settled happily with a tray on her lap, Miranda went upstairs to change. Not wishing to appear to have made too much of an effort, she put on a pair of clean jeans and a black t-shirt. But she also put on a little make up and brushed her hair up into a chignon. She hoped Georgie wouldn't notice and make something out of nothing. She had a bottle of white wine chilling in the fridge and at seven-fifteen opened the bottle and poured herself a glass.

The doorbell rang at seven thirty-five. Georgie beat her to the door, and yanked it open to reveal Charles Davenport, wearing a dark suit and brandishing a bottle of wine and a bunch of peach-coloured roses.

'Charles!' exclaimed Miranda as she shepherded Georgie out of the way. 'Georgie, this is Charles Davenport – the gentleman who bought that beautiful book about Alice that I mentioned the other day; Charles, this is my daughter, Georgina.'

Georgie, who had been scowling at Charles, guffawed as her mother introduced her. 'Georgina! Since when do you call me that?'

'Very funny G, now toddle off and let me get Charles a glass of wine. Oh, you brought some, how kind, and flowers too; that's so thoughtful!' Taking his gifts, she led the way to the kitchen.

'I'd better put these in water,' Miranda said, frantically opening cupboards in search of another vase. 'My daughter broke one the other day. I'll put them into the one on the table. It's not really a vase, but it's all I have.' She unwrapped the roses and cut the stems before laying them on the draining board and bashing the bottoms with a rolling pin. She arranged the roses in the vase; their colours blended well with the dark reds and oranges of the dahlias. 'I'm never sure that roses mix with other flowers really,' she muttered, 'but they look rather jolly all mixed in together.'

Charles smiled and offered to open the wine.

'Let's have that with dinner, I've got some white already open in the fridge, will that do?'

She poured and they clinked the crystal glasses.

They made small talk, about the house, the kitchen, the garden, what they were having for supper, but Miranda was aware that Charles seemed slightly distracted. As they sat down at the table and she ladled out the chicken tarragon he said casually, 'The vase here, that's rather nice, isn't it?'

'Oh, that, yes, my aunt left it to me. It's just some replica or other that I suspect she picked up in Hong Kong. She and her husband were there for twenty or thirty years. Georgie absolutely hates it.'

At the mention of her name Georgie appeared at the kitchen door, carrying her empty plate. 'Thanks Mum, that was nice. Is there pudding?'

'Yes, lemon tart; but can you wait till we've finished this first?'

'OK, and what do I hate?'

'The vase. You say it scares you, don't you?'

'Yeah, I think it's spooky.'

Charles smiled. 'Well, I could take it off your hands if you wanted?'

'Really? Oh no, I couldn't do that. I know G hates it, but Aunt Celia left it to me and I'd feel a bit guilty really. Why? Do you think it's worth something? I'm sure I saw one very like it in a car boot sale the other week.'

'Well, I'd have to take a closer look, but it's a very nice copy. Nicely painted and fired, you know. We've got a sale of porcelain coming up at the auction house soon. It could be worth as much as a hundred pounds if you're lucky, maybe more.'

'Gosh! Well that is tempting, I must say.' Miranda refilled their glasses.

'Well,' said Charles, 'think about it. The offer is there. But don't wait too long – the sale is at the end of January.'

'Yes, well, thank you; I will think about it.' She touched the petals of the peachy rose that stood in the vase. A thorn pricked her finger and a small drop of blood dripped onto the pale white porcelain. It ran down the vase, colouring the fiery breath of the dragon that circled its centre.

'Ow,' she said licking her finger. She looked at Charles and followed his grey gaze. He was transfixed by the dragon.

High in the mountains of Ching-te-Chen white clay is dug from the ground. The clay is not clay as you or I would know it – sticky, heavy and malleable – but solid, hard stone that has to be hacked from the earth. It is backbreaking work. Relays of men carry the stones down the mountain in panniers – baskets hanging on either side of a long stick that rests across their shoulders. The stick digs deeply into their flesh leaving permanent wounds. The men vary in age; some as young as fourteen or fifteen, others grey-haired, bearded, and weary from years of carrying the heavy loads. They form a human chain of misery. Their clothes – short tunics, knee-length breeches – tattered. Their feet are protected only by sandals laced around their stocky shins with leather bindings. On their heads they wear straw hats to protect them against the fierce sun in the summer months. In the winter the work is indescribably brutal, as the workers battle against the frost and snow.

CHAPTER 4

The Adriatic, off the coast of Venice
1441

Maria dei Conte struggled up the ladder of the galley, her skirts caught up between her legs in a practised fashion to make the climb easier. The storm of the previous night had departed as swiftly as it had arrived, and with the dawn had come a stillness that left the ship almost becalmed. Well used to ocean travel, she rarely suffered any form of seasickness, but had succumbed the previous night. As the ship heeled and tossed, she had several times been thrown bodily up into the air, her nose almost colliding with the cabin's low ceiling. Now, as she hauled herself up the ladder, the muscles in her stomach ached from retching and her mouth tasted sour.

Up on deck all was quiet. The sun was just beginning its ascent on the horizon and a gentle breeze blew in off the sea. She reached into the bucket of fresh water that was kept on deck and ladled some into her hand, sipping it gently. The sun warmed her face as she sat, her mouth a little refreshed, her stomach settling, gazing across the water.

Up above, on the bridge, the captain, Marco, shouted instructions to one of the crew.

'Throw up that mainsail; the wind's coming up behind us.'

The young sailor paid out lengths of rope and the huge mainsail began to flap feebly as it unfurled. It continued its pointless dance with the wind until a sudden gust filled the sail, causing it to bloom outwards like a belly filled with child. Two crewmen formed a tug of war with the sail's 'sheet' – the rope that would be used to make the sail fast. The sheet tied in securely, Maria felt the change of speed instantly as the boat began to crest across the waves.

'When do we make land?' she yelled up to Marco.

'Not long now,' he replied. 'Keep your eye on the horizon over there; we should see a first sight of Venice anytime.'

Maria felt excited at the prospect of finally, aged seventeen, seeing the place of her father's birth. Niccolò dei Conti had left his home twenty-five years before. He had travelled far and wide – all through the Middle East, as far as India and further east still to the land of 'further India', as China was known. And now he was to return, at last, to the land of his fathers. He had left as a twenty-one–year-old with a thirst for knowledge and adventure. And adventures he had had, aplenty. Now, aged forty-six, he had decided that his duty lay in Italy. He would write of his adventures, and his experiences would serve as a vital tool for future travellers. He brought with him a precious cargo to trade on his return – spices, silver, and other precious metals from India; carpets from Damascus, and lengths of silk and damask from the lands east of India. And porcelain – buried deep in the ship's hold – the palest, most translucent porcelain that dei Conti had ever seen. Some pieces were in delicate shades of pale celadon, their glaze crackled, like the veins of a leaf. But most were pure white, their surfaces painted in bright cobalt blue with flowers, fruit and courtly scenes, or with dragons – the symbols of good fortune. He had watched as these pots and plates were decorated in the porcelain workshops on the banks of the Yangtze River; he had witnessed the delicate hands of the artists who created such beauty.

He had purchased much of what lay now in vast wooden barrels in the bowels of the Venetian government ship. But one or two pieces had been gifts, presented several years before by Admiral Zheng He, the military leader and favourite of the Emperor of China himself, Emperor Xuande.

Admiral Zheng He was a eunuch, and as such had been promoted by his master to a position of absolute trust. He was free to enter the private quarters of the Emperor, to mix amongst his many wives and concubines. He was also a brave and adventurous explorer and military leader. Since the age of ten, he had been in the employ of successive Chinese Emperors, and at the impressive age of sixty-two was in charge of his seventh and what was to be his final expedition, travelling as far as the eastern coast of Africa, commanding a vast fleet of two hundred and fifty ships and twenty-seven thousand men. Sixty vast treasure ships, supplied by one hundred and ninety 'support' ships, carrying horses, troops and a month's supply of fresh water.

Like many of his Mongol forebears, Zheng He was an exceptionally tall man, measuring almost seven feet in height; he sported long moustaches, and was resplendent in silken robes decorated with the Chinese dragon motif, with a jewelled belt wrapped round his vast stomach. He had arranged to meet dei Conti during his final expedition, on the island of Sumatra. There, they had feasted on board Admiral He's ship. Dei Conti liked and admired the Admiral.

'*We dined in some style with the Admiral,*' he wrote in his diary late that night. '*The people of further India lead cultivated lives, far from all barbarity and savagery; for they are courteous people and extremely rich merchants. We ate at a table laid with a fine cloth, on plates and dishes made of silver.*'

The Admiral returned dei Conti's admiration. He recognised a fellow adventurer and enjoyed dei Conti's educated mind, acquired through years of study, travel and careful observation. They shared an interest in religion and other cultures too. The

Admiral, who had been born in Yunnan province, was of Mongol and Arab ancestry, and as such had been born into the Islamic religion. In his later life, he had embraced other religions – especially Buddhism – but he nevertheless worked hard to develop relations between China and Islamic countries. Dei Conti had been brought up as a Catholic, but he had huge respect for the customs of other religions and in all the years he had travelled through the Middle East and India, he had often taken the disguise of a Persian merchant, concealing his true faith and embracing Muslim customs. So, the two men had much in common, but with one obvious difference: Niccolò was free to enjoy a loving relationship with his Indian wife Roshinara, and the Admiral was not.

The Italian had married whilst travelling through India. He and Roshinara had four children, Maria, Daniele, Dario and Magdalena. The family travelled together at all times, with the parents educating their children along the way. As a eunuch, Zheng He could only dream of such private fulfilment, but he also knew that it was his status as a eunuch that had enabled him to have such a privileged life, and he did not regret the sacrifice. Nevertheless, he was intrigued by the Italian's easy and loving relationship with his wife and young family, for it was in stark contrast to the marriages of his own acquaintance, in particular those of the Emperors he had served. His most recent master, Emperor Xuande, had three wives. The first, Empress Shunde, was deposed from her position when the Emperor elevated his favourite and most senior concubine to the role and created her Empress Xiao Gong Zhang. They were soon joined by a third wife, Empress Xiao Yi. In addition, the Emperor had thirteen concubines, all meticulously arranged in order of significance from Imperial concubine through to noble consort and down to ordinary consort level. These relationships were based on subservience and control. The concubines in particular were destined to die alongside their Emperor so they could be buried with him in his tomb.

The dei Conti's marriage, by contrast, appeared to be based on a sense of equality and mutual respect. The Admiral was in no doubt that it was also a relationship filled with love; for the couple were scarcely ever apart and when together found opportunities to touch hands, or stroke the other's cheek, or embrace. Born in the north of India, near the border with Persia, Roshinara (which means bright dawn light), had long dark hair and extraordinary turquoise eyes that wavered between blue and green depending on the sari she wore, or the colour of her surroundings. Her eldest daughter Maria had inherited these beautiful eyes – although hers had a translucent quality that reminded the Admiral of the sea in mid-summer – changeable from the brightest blue to the darkest green when storms threatened. The sea was the foundation of the Admiral's existence. He was a believer in Mazu, the Goddess of the Sea who protected sailors. He had asked Emperor Xuande to build a temple to her, and his emperor had been happy to indulge his favourite admiral. Zheng He would pray to Mazu faithfully before and after each sea voyage to protect him.

When he met Maria and Roshinara in China, he was bewitched by Maria's pale aquiline eyes, as if they were possessed of some kind of supernatural power. He was so taken with the beauty of mother and daughter that he asked dei Conti for permission to paint them, seated beneath a blossom tree, with their dark hair trailing down their backs and both wearing a shade of blue that perfectly matched their eyes. He had shown the painting to the Emperor, who had been equally fascinated. A talented artist himself, the Emperor had also expressed a desire to paint the mother and daughter, and so Roshinara and young Maria sat patiently for him too, throughout one warm spring, allowing him to record their beauty forever. It occurred to dei Conti that the Emperor might be minded to take his beautiful daughter for one of his own concubines, but fortunately the Emperor had only recently acquired a new consort, and his Empress was already jealous and proving difficult. Another young girl in the household, especially one with turquoise eyes, would be nothing more than trouble.

Shortly afterwards, the family left the Emperor's court and made their way overland and thence by sea to the island of Sumatra, where they were to rendezvous with the Admiral and say their farewells.

After dinner in his impressive private cabin on board the lead vessel of his fleet, the Admiral clapped his hands and a stream of servants brought in a selection of precious items, which were then set out in front of the dining guests and displayed ceremoniously on tables. There was a golden casket; a pair of paintings featuring little monkeys at play, painted by the Emperor himself; a dark red writing desk – a popular colour in the Emperor's court; and lastly, a blue and white vase, decorated with a dragon which chased around its centre.

'My friend,' the Admiral said with due reverence to his dining companion. 'My Emperor would be honoured if you would take these items back to Italy with you. They are a gift for the Doge from my Emperor. He sends his good wishes to his trading partner and wishes him long life. The vase, or jar, in particular will bring good luck; it is decorated with the most powerful of all symbols – the dragon.'

He clapped his hands once again and a young man entered the cabin holding the painting of Roshinara and Maria that the Emperor had painted before they left. 'He would like you to take this picture too; it is not a gift for the Doge you understand, but a personal gift to you.'

Dei Conti bowed deeply. 'You must tell your Emperor that I am deeply honoured that he has seen fit to bestow this beautiful painting on me and my family. As for the other items, I shall guard them with my life and they will be presented to the Doge as soon as I arrive in Venice.'

When the diners finished their meal, the gifts were carefully packed, wrapped in paper, and then again in silken cloth, placed in sturdy wooden chests, and winched from the Admiral's vast ship onto dei Conti's smaller vessel.

The pieces had travelled by sea and overland with the family since that time. In the eight years that it took them to return from Sumatra to Italy, via India and Arabia, they had hardly left dei Conti's sight. But trouble struck as they attempted to enter Egypt. Niccolò's plan was that they would sail up the Red Sea and make land there. They would then take their goods overland, following the path of the Nile, to Cairo and thence to Alexandria, where they would join with other merchants and passengers on a boat that could sail them through the Mediterranean and back to Venice. But at the border with Egypt, all sorts of difficulties erupted. It was forbidden for any European to trade with Persia or India at that time, and Niccolò had long ago adopted a disguise when travelling – passing himself off as a merchant from Persia. He had learnt the language many years before, when he first studied in Persia; it was almost a second language to him and he was confident in it. His Indian wife lent some veracity to this deception and they were used to playing the part of Persian merchant and wife. But at the border, the guards suspected something was not right and began to open and inspect the various crates and trunks that Niccolò had so carefully protected on their long journey. His goods were seized and the family thrown into gaol. Terrified, Niccolò nevertheless remonstrated with the guards to, at least, release his beloved wife and family. They languished for over a week in the filthy gaol, with its appalling food and surrounded by people with all manner of illness and suffering.

On the eighth day, Niccolò demanded to be seen. He offered goods as part-payment to get the family out of trouble. Some of his precious cargo of spices was taken. But still they would not allow the family to leave. Finally, he was presented with an ultimatum: convert to Islam, and you will be allowed to go. It was not a difficult decision for him to make. By the following evening he and his family were safely out of gaol and they had been reunited with most of their possessions. Spices and some lengths of cloth were missing, but the vast collection of porcelain that he hoped to trade back in Venice and, most importantly, the items he had been presented with by the Admiral, were secure.

The family, along with their retinue of servants, followed the path of the Nile all the way to Cairo. But on the outskirts of that city, little Dario became ill. Roshinara was desperate that they rest for a few days and take care of the child.

'Niccolò, we cannot look after Dario whilst we are travelling; he is sick and is struggling to breathe; he needs to rest; please let us stop somewhere and care for him.'

Niccolò was concerned that he would be unable to keep their goods secure in Cairo. Warehouses were hard to come by and he had no agent in that city to manage the situation. And so he made a decision, later regretted, to send a young apprentice on ahead to Alexandria with their goods, accompanied by most of his household. The young man was instructed to make for the port of Alexandria and meet with Niccolò's agent who would then stow his precious cargo in a warehouse at the port under the watchful eyes of paid guards. Niccolò watched the caravan of goods and men snaking out into the dark night with a sense of foreboding.

The family took rooms on the outskirts of the city. Roshinara cared for Dario with the help of the two servants who remained with them – a Sumatran couple that had been with Niccolò for many years. The man, Chahaya, and his wife, Kade, were not quite as old as Niccolò, but had been with the family for so long, travelling wherever they went, that they were almost like alternative parents to the children. The two older children stayed together in another room. Little Magdalena spent much of her time curled up at the end of her little brother's bed. Niccolò had business in Cairo, and whilst Dario appeared to be suffering from no more than a slight illness, he busied himself meeting old acquaintances and making arrangements for the next leg of their journey on to Alexandria.

On the second morning, Dario appeared to rally and Niccolò began to believe that they could perhaps set off the following day and, with luck, catch up with their caravan of goods. But later that night the child began to vomit violently. As the night wore on, he struggled for breath and soon was coughing up blood. His fever raged and in spite of Roshinara's best efforts to lower it, nothing would bring it down. The next morning he was no better – coughing blood, vomiting. It was almost impossible to get any water into the child, for as soon as he drank he either brought it back up or it raced through his body, causing him to curl up with pain.

Towards the middle of that second afternoon, when the heat of the day was almost at its zenith, and the room in which Dario lay was like a furnace, the poor child's lungs finally collapsed and he stopped breathing.

Roshinara was in despair, begging her husband to help the child. But there was nothing Niccolò could do. He knew what had taken his child. He had seen the symptoms many times. It was a form of the plague – and he knew too, that his wife, servants and daughter were all now at risk from the same disease. Those who nursed the sick were almost certain to catch the illness.

Within hours, his fears were realised, as both Roshinara and little Magdalena, and then Chahaya and Kade, all began to vomit, while struggling for breath, and bringing up blood. Magdalena, who was only ten years old, went first. She barely lasted a full day before the illness took her.

Niccolò refused to allow his other two children anywhere near the sick members of the family.

'You are not to come in', he said to Maria and Daniele. 'I will cope with it. And if it takes me too, you are to go on to Alexandria, meet the shipment and go to Venice as planned; do you understand, Maria?'

'Yes, Papa, of course. But I must nurse *Mamma.*'

'No! I will not lose you too.'

Once, when Niccolò had been living in Damascus, he had observed that the nurses who survived the epidemic kept their headscarves wrapped around their faces. They believed the illness was carried on the air, and so Niccolò unwrapped his turban and wound the length of cloth tightly around his face while caring for his patients. His two beloved servants only lasted another few hours. They were both dead by nightfall. But Roshinara fought the illness hard. She drifted in and out of consciousness, and in her lucid moments she wept for her lost children and gripped Niccolò's hand. 'God help our other children. Niccolò; do not let them in here... You must keep them safe.'

'I promise, Roshinara; they will go on, whatever happens to us, back to Venice.'

Roshinara slept fitfully through that night. Her coughing became worse, and she struggled for breath. Niccolò tried to make her comfortable, soaking a rag in water and squeezing it into her mouth. She too began to vomit uncontrollably, until there was nothing left but water and bile. She curled up in agony as the illness scorched its way through her bowels. Blood projected from her mouth with the bile, as her lungs collapsed. And finally, late on the third night, while holding her husband's hand, he felt her energy simply evaporate; her grip loosened and he was left clutching her small lifeless hand in his.

The fear of the plague was such that anyone who had been taken by the illness had to be buried as soon as possible. Respectful always of other religions, aware that his servants were both devout Muslims and that his own wife had been born into the Islamic faith, Niccolò bathed the bodies of his beloved wife and children, along with Chahaya and Kade, before wrapping them in cloth, as is the Islamic custom. Then he carried their bodies out into the night and loaded them onto a cart. He drove out into the desert and buried them by the light of the moon. He prayed most earnestly for their eternal souls, initially falling back into the Catholic practices of his youth and mouthing the *Requiescat* over the grave of his wife and beloved children. He said the Muslim prayer for souls – the *Janazah* prayer – over the graves of Kade and Chahaya. He did not mark his family's grave with a cross, not wishing it to be desecrated later, but simply brushed the sand over the place where they lay. As he climbed into the cart, ready to drive back to Cairo, he thought better of it, and found a few stones and laid them in a pile over the area; one for each person who rested beneath.

Desperate and exhausted, he returned to Cairo, and retreated to the room where his wife's body had lain just a few hours before. There he slept the dark, deep sleep of those for whom unconsciousness can provide the only respite for despair.

He was woken by a soft hand brushing his cheek. The room was suffused with a golden glow, as the sun cast sharp shards of early morning light through the unshuttered window. For a moment, as he lay between sleep and wakefulness, the traumas of the previous days were obliterated.

'Roshinara,' he murmured, taking the hand and kissing it.

'Papa,' whispered Maria.

He opened his eyes, blinking against the bright light, and looked around him. The beds where his wife and children had lain just a few hours earlier were now just a pile of crumpled, soiled linen.

'Papa, where is *Mamma*? Oh, please tell me she has not gone.'

The memory of the previous night flooded back, accompanied by deep despair. He looked up at his daughter's sweet, frightened face.

'I'm afraid she has, *cara*. God took her in the night. She is sleeping now with the babies.'

'You should have woken me.'

'No,' he said, sadly. 'It was better this way. You will remember her as she was in life… The plague is a vicious and unforgiving master. I could not risk you coming near.'

'And Magdalena and Chahaya and Kade…?'

'All gone…' He turned his face away from her, towards the wall, anxious that she should not see his tears.

'But you were with them all the time… What about you? What if it takes you too?' She began to cry, and reached out for her father, desperate for him to hold her.

'Don't worry about me,' he said, sitting up; he was determined to be strong for her. 'I was careful; the nurses in Damascus showed me what to do many years ago. You must not breathe the same air. I wish with all my heart that I had realised what was wrong with Dario sooner, perhaps I could have saved Magdalena and your mother as well as Chahaya and Kade. But they are all gone… Due to my stupidity. I will never forgive myself.'

His determination to contain his emotions evaporated suddenly. He buried his head in his hands and wept.

His daughter attempted to comfort him. 'It is not your fault, Papa; they must have become ill when we were in gaol.' She reached out once again and tried to wrap him in her arms.

'No!' he said, recoiling from her. 'You must not come close to me. Not till we are sure that I do not carry the illness. I will keep apart from you all. Now you must wake Daniele and tell him what has happened. We must get on to Alexandria as quickly as possible; go now.'

They left their lodgings as the sun rose over the city. The sound of the Muezzins calling the faithful to prayer filled the air.

'Papa, please. You must take us to their grave before we leave,' begged Maria.

Reluctantly, Niccolò retraced his steps and the family said prayers for their mother and young brother and sister. Maria, who had taken a few rose petals from the garden of their lodgings, sprinkled them over the stones. Then, with the sun beating down, they set off for Alexandria; Niccolò up ahead leading the way, his scarf still tightly wrapped round his mouth, the children following on behind. As they journeyed on towards the Mediterranean, dei Conti cursed his bad luck. Somewhere in his distraught, exhausted mind, he began to believe that he should never have allowed the dragon vase to be sent on to Alexandria with his other goods. It was a talisman of good fortune and he had recklessly sent it away at the time he needed it most. Perhaps if he had kept it close he might not have lost his beloved Roshinara and children.

The journey took fifteen days. By night the family camped out in the desert, the children huddled together for warmth in the cold desert nights; Niccolò slept fitfully alone, desperate not to pass on any illness to his remaining children. But by the time they were approaching Alexandria, he began to believe that he had, perhaps, been spared. He removed his scarf and allowed the children to hug him once more.

Once reunited with his possessions, he hardly let them out of his sight. The ship they were due to board was already loaded with a vast cargo to be taken back to Venice. It was one of three thousand merchant ships sailing regularly between Venice and Alexandria. The captain Marco was a man of great experience. He warmly welcomed the family on board, and their goods were stowed in the great bowels of the ship. But the barrel containing the precious vase was not kept with the other porcelain in the hold. Instead, dei Conti had it placed in his own cabin. A tiny space, with scarcely enough room for the bare necessities of life, it made getting into his bed difficult, but he was determined that he would keep the vase close in order to protect his family from further disaster.

Their journey through the Mediterranean was uncomfortable. Rats scuttled between the decks. Fleas and lice were commonplace. The sleeping quarters were cramped and insanitary. There was a stench below decks that pervaded the whole ship, and the passengers spent much of their time up on deck, in all weathers. Food was sparse and repetitive – salted fish, a small ration of water each day, and dry biscuits. They docked in Crete for fresh supplies and watched with delight as fruit and olives were brought on board.

Niccolò, as an experienced traveller, knew that the major threat to a ship such as theirs was not insanitary conditions or bad food but pirates. The eastern Mediterranean was under constant threat from bands of pirates seizing ships for their valuable cargo and passengers. If the ship were taken, the older passengers would almost certainly be killed. But young girls like Maria were more likely to be taken into slavery and face a desperate future serving the needs of a pirate captain, or even to be sold off to the highest bidder. Their ship, however, was part of the Venetian government's fleet, and as such was safely escorted through the eastern Mediterranean by a military escort. The journey passed, miraculously, without any confrontation, and by the time they reached the tip of Italy, Marco informed them that the risk of capture was over. In spite of the devastating events in Egypt and the hardships they had encountered along the way, the dei Conti family found some kind of peace on this final leg of their journey. The weather, for the most part, was kind to them and when they were not eating together, Niccolò spent much of his time writing, while the children sat up on deck watching the horizon, chatting to the other passengers, or singing songs they had learned on their travels.

Up on deck, Maria wrapped her shawl around her shoulders. The breeze was refreshing, but the previous night's illness had made her chilly and a little weak. Daniele, her younger brother, wrapped his arms around her and kissed her cheek, before taking his place beside her.

'I heard you last night. You are unwell.' The anxiety in his voice was palpable.

'It was nothing darling – just sea sickness.' She looked deeply into his dark brown eyes. 'Honestly.'

'It's just that it reminded me… You know? Hearing you like that… Of *Mamma* and…' he broke off.

'I know, but it was just seasickness. Not the same thing as the others had… Really.' She took his hand in hers and kissed it. 'Look out there – keep your eyes on the horizon. We will soon see the home of our beloved father.'

Venice, when it came, did not disappoint. A young sailor high up in the crow's nest saw it first.

'Look,' he called out to the passengers below. 'Venice! Over there…'

Brother and sister stood eagerly and, at first, could see nothing. Just an expanse of blue sea below, flecked with the spittle and foam of white horses, mirrored by the blue sky above, streaked with high wispy clouds. A mist separated the two, like a mirage, ethereal and shimmering in the morning light, concealing and revealing at the same time. As the ship sailed closer, a thin sliver of land emerged through the mist; it appeared to be almost suspended on the surface of the sea. As they drew closer, a tall tower could be seen rising up at its centre; next to it, a dome appeared, sparkling in the morning light. Leaving the open sea, they sailed towards the islands and entered the curtilage of the lagoon; other boats, fishing vessels and smaller galleys – all making for land – emerged from the mist. Some of them were close enough to call out to:

'Where've you come from, then?' shouted the captain of one nearby galley.

'Alexandria,' Marco replied.

A flurry of tiny boats rocked towards them, carrying goods and people offering services, who called up to the passengers: 'Fresh milk here, and delicious fruit – lemons and limes!' A young boy, no more than seven or eight years of age, held up lemons in a basket, showing them off to the passengers now assembled on deck.

Maria's mouth watered as she contemplated the sharp, zesty lemons. It had been some time since she had tasted something so fresh.

They were now close enough to see the colours of the city: rose-coloured roofs; the opalescent grey and white of the Doge's Palace, like the inside of a mollusc's shell; the apricot campanile of St Mark's Cathedral rose high above its lowlier neighbours. And then another, smaller tower appeared on the horizon. Their father joined them.

'So children, what do you make of my city?' he asked with pride.

'It is beautiful Papa. What's that tower there…?'

'The campanile of San Giorgio Maggiore; and the bigger one there is the campanile of the city's cathedral – San Marco.'

'There are so many of them. They remind me a little of Damascus, Papa. Are they Muslim here?' asked Maria.

'Ah, no. They follow Jesus here, child. Mohammed is not for them. But the people of Venice have traded for hundreds of years with our friends in the east and the buildings here bear testament to that influence. You will see when we land.'

'If they are not Muslim here, Papa, will we be allowed to stay, after what happened in Egypt?' Maria sounded anxious.

'Oh yes, don't worry about that. The people here are used to Muslims, and Jews. There should be no problem.'

The nearer the ship came to Venice, the more crowded the seas became, until Marco found himself almost jockeying with other ships and smaller boats in order to get into a favourable position to drop anchor. They passed a small island with a large square building, a church, and yet another campanile.

'What is that one called, Papa?' asked Maria.

'That is the island of Poveglia,' replied Niccolò.

'It's so small; just enough room for the large house and its church. Do a family live there?' Maria continued cheerfully.

'It's the plague island. It's just for people who have the disease and the nurses who care for them.'

Daniele looked up at his father, questioning, anxious.

'It's a good idea,' their father continued matter-of-factly. 'It helps to keep the illness at bay and stops it spreading into the city. There was a terrible outbreak twenty or so years ago.'

'So if there had been an island like that in Egypt... Would *Mamma* and the little ones still be with us?' asked Daniele quietly.

'It's impossible to say. They don't have such things in Egypt and the plague runs like a fire through a community. One day you are well, the next...'

'So this island,' Daniele continued.

'Daniele, please, can't you see you are upsetting Papa?' Maria interjected.

'Let him speak,' said Niccolò. 'What do you want to know?'

'How do they decide who should go there?'

'Well as soon as someone shows the symptoms of the illness, they are taken there.'

'And can they make them well there?' the boy asked.

'Who knows…?'

Their father turned away in search of the captain. He needed to discuss where the ship would dock.

Daniele slipped his arm through his sister's and rested his dark head on her shoulder.

The pair gazed at the island as they slipped by, their ship carving a snowy outline through the dark emerald waters, both reflecting on the terrible last illness that had taken their mother and little brother and sister from them. The main hospital building was a large square shape, its walls faced in stone, with high windows criss-crossed with strong iron bars. Smoke snaked into the pale blue sky from a chimney.

'It looks nice,' Maria said encouragingly. 'Maybe they do get people better there…'

'It looks like a prison,' said Daniele darkly.

Their father Niccolò joined them.

'So, Maria – are you packed and ready?' His voice was brisk and light, always positive.

'Yes, Papa…'

'You were sick last night… Are you feeling better this morning?' He sounded calm and cheerful, as he always tried to do, but she could sense the anxiety behind the question.

'Yes, Papa; I have told Daniele. I am fine. It was nothing, really.'

'Good.'

Marco called for the sails to be lowered. The ship would be rowed to its final docking position at Malamocco. The family stood gazing out at the city wrapped around the lagoon.

'It must be hard for you, Papa – thinking of *Mamma* and all that we had to leave behind in Egypt.'

'Yes.' Niccolò said nothing more, but took his daughter's face in his large hands and kissed her forehead. 'But having you and Daniele here with me now is a huge joy. I am glad to be back.

I am tired. My travelling days are over. Our first task is to find lodgings and a place for our merchandise to be stored. Now come, children, come to the prow and I will show you your new home.'

'And how does it feel, Papa,' said Maria, tucking her arm through her father's, 'to see your Venice again after all this time?'

'It is wonderful. It is the most beautiful city in the world. And after all these years, and all that has happened, now that I smell the sea in the lagoon and watch as the morning sun glints on the roof of San Marco, it is as if I had never left.'

CHAPTER 5

Castello, Venice
1441

The house that Niccolò found for the family was in the district of Castello, east of the Piazza San Marco, site of the Doge's Palace and the Cathedral. Although it was just minutes away from the religious and administrative heart of the city on its western boundary, Castello spread eastwards out towards the lagoon. It was the first point of contact for anyone arriving by sea and its mixture of industry and commerce, alongside inhabitants from many nations, lent the area a bustling, cosmopolitan atmosphere, in contrast to its regal, more straight-laced neighbour.

On its northern boundary was the area known as the Arsenale, which for hundreds of years, had been the heart of the Venetian naval industry – supplying boats, ropes and munitions. The yard spread across one hundred and ten acres and was divided into separate areas, each producing different elements of the ships, which were then finally assembled in as little as one day. The thousands of *Arsenaletti*, as the workers were described, lived cheek-by-jowl with their workplace in a jumble of houses that rose up out of the waters of the lagoon. A little to the south and west of the Arsenale, in an area called Riva degli Schiavoni, lived settlers from Greece and the Dalmatian coast. They were predominantly fishermen and sold their dried fish and meat along the edge of the lagoon. Merchants from Turkey, northern Europe and North Africa lived alongside their Greek and Slav counterparts selling their wares.

Niccolò settled his family on the western edge of Castello. The house was less expensive than if it had been in the San Marco district, but close to the Doge's palace and the Rialto Bridge. And if he missed life in the Middle East, he was just a few minutes' walk from a cosmopolitan hubbub of people that reminded him of his time in Damascus.

Their house fronted onto a canal called the Rio dei Greci and was arranged over four floors. There was a serviceable kitchen and a dining hall; a large reception room that ran the length of the house, a study at the back for Niccolò, bedrooms overlooking the canal for the family, and at the top of the house, rooms for their servants. A cook, Alfreda, was appointed, who was helped in the kitchen and around the house by a maid called Bella who, at eighteen, was just one year older than Maria. From the start Maria liked her and the pair began to form a close bond. The household was completed by the presence of a young man called Andrea, who brought in wood for the fires, served at table, and helped with the heavier jobs. Several weeks went by and they settled into a happy routine, exploring the city with their father, studying each day, and were able to start the long process of grieving for their lost mother, brother and sister. The goods Niccolò had brought with him from the East were installed in the customs warehouse in Punta, opposite San Marco. Here they would stay while the value was assessed and duty could be applied and paid. Only then could the porcelain, spices and silk be sold on. The vase, casket, paintings and desk that had been given to him by the Admiral as a gift for the Doge were safely installed in Niccolò's study. He would have to deliver them soon, but there was important business to be dealt with first.

Niccolò's apostasy – his conversion to Islam – had reached the ears of Pope Eugenius IV. He summoned dei Conti to Florence, where he was to meet one of the Pope's senior advisors.

'Oh Papa, what will happen to you? Please do not leave us here alone. We've been so happy here together.'

'And will be so again. Besides, you will not be alone, Maria. The servants will be with you.'

'But I am fearful… We have lost *Mamma* and now you must go too.'

'I am only travelling to Florence, my dear child. I will be a way a few weeks – two months at most. By the time I return, I shall be able to sell our goods and we can truly begin our new life here in Venice.'

'But why must you go? Is the Pope angry with you? He might put you in gaol…'

Dei Conti could see how fearful his children were. Their experience in Egypt had left its mark. 'My darlings, the Pope has written to me and asked that, in penance for adopting the Muslim faith, I meet with his secretary, Poggio Bracciolini. He is a great scholar and man of learning, and the Holy Father himself has asked that I tell him all that I can of our travels. He wishes to record it and to publish it to the world. Bracciolini believes that my knowledge will help others who come after me to understand the lands of India and the East. I have told you, have I not, of the travels of the great Marco Polo, who also came from Venice?'

The children nodded.

'Well, this great scholar, Bracciolini, is keen that I provide new information and help to create new maps of the world where we have been, for up until now we have relied on maps and accounts made by the great Marco. But they are two hundred years old. It is a huge honour for me to be asked to do this thing. Trust me my darlings, all will be well. I shall tell this man all that I know and then I shall be allowed once again into the faith of my birth. I shall soon return and we shall live happily here. You will see.'

Three days later, dei Conti set off on horseback, accompanied by two servants. Before he left, he held Maria and Daniele to him.

'Maria, I expect you to take care of Daniele for me.'

'I do not need looking after,' Daniele exploded indignantly.

'Well then, I expect you to care for your sister,' said Niccolò magnanimously. 'Continue with your studies – I have arranged for a tutor to come in each day – and Maria, you will manage the servants for me. '

'I will, Papa. Oh, but I do so wish I could come with you.'

'No, you will be safer here. You have the vase with you, remember? Keep it safe for me.'

Maria nodded. 'Perhaps you should take it with you, Papa?'

'No, I leave it here to protect the two people I love more than life itself,' said Niccolò. 'Work hard, take care of the house and continue your discovery of Venice. You could live here your whole life and never see everything. Try to walk a little each day and explore.'

'You will write to us, Papa?'

'Of course!'

Niccolò left for Florence early one morning, accompanied by his personal servant, Mattheo, and secretary, Vincenzo. The children missed him desperately, but both were resilient and determined to be positive for the sake of their father, if not for each other. Maria, as her father had instructed, ran the house, ordering supplies and managing the staff. She was a gentle mistress, much as her own dear mother had been with their own servants Chahaye and Kade, but efficient and capable. Daniele, whilst only two years her junior, seemed to her to need special care and she took it upon herself, just as her father had asked, to ensure that Daniele kept up with his studies. This was their only point of conflict, for Daniele hated the school room and struggled with formal learning. But when he was despondent and sad, she would construct a game they could play, or suggest that they put on some kind of charade for their household's amusement.

Their house had windows onto the canal at the front, and this was where the main entrance was placed, with steps that led down to the water and a small landing platform to allow visitors or members of the household to step safely on and off a gondola. At the back of the building they looked out onto the Church of San Zaccaria. There had been a church on the site for six hundred years and eight Doges were buried there. But the Gothic façade was being re-built under the watchful eye of the architect Antonio Gambello, and there was a stream of workmen filing onto the site each morning. Maria and Daniele were intrigued by the constant activity visible from the upper storey windows. Next to the church stood a convent. The nuns were mostly daughters of prominent noble families, and Maria was fascinated by this closed community of women. In some ways it reminded her of the Chinese Emperor's household except, of course, in the palace there had been many children too. In the convent there was no sound of childish laughter. Instead there was the distant chorus of singing at regular intervals during the day. When the nuns were not praying or singing they appeared to spend most of their time tending their large vegetable garden. If Maria peered out of the rear window of her father's study, she could see into the convent's vegetable garden and observe as the nuns, dressed head to toe in black, weeded and dug and picked, their sleeves pushed up over their elbows. It struck her that their clothing looked uncomfortable for such hard, hot work. Occasionally, one or another would stand up and stretch her tired limbs, or wipe a little sweat from her brow with the back of her hand. One evening, as the sun was setting, casting long shadows across the garden, a young nun caught sight of her; she smiled and waved. Maria waved back just as an older nun came over to the novice and appeared to reprimand her. She looked up at Maria and frowned. The younger woman bowed her head and continued her digging. But Maria couldn't help but notice that she cast her eyes back up towards Maria's window one more time and broke into a broad grin as the older nun turned her back. Not wishing to get the girl into further trouble, Maria merely smiled in reply, before retreating once more to the safety of her father's dark study.

The children's bedchambers were at the front of the house and overlooked the canal. The proximity of the water was a novel experience for them and they grew to love the sound as it lapped against the walls of the house, slapping against the landing deck, as the gondolas slipped through the dark water.

Each morning they would throw open their shutters and lean out to see who, or what, was being ferried down the canal. The gondolas at that time were decorated in various colours, some with little cabins in the centre where couples could flirt unobserved or goods could be ferried in secret. Over time, the pair began to recognise certain gondolas, and would wave at the *gondolieri.*

'*Bon giorno, gondoliere.*'

'*Bon giorno, regazzi,*' the gondoliers would shout up to the pair.

'*Cosa ce li dentro?*'

'*Qualcosa per mercata!*' they would shout back. And the children would watch as the *gondolieri* steered their gondolas through the water towards the Grand Canal. Once there, they would deliver their goods to the markets on the Riva degli Schiavoni, or travel onwards to the shops on the Rialto, or unload them nearby at the Fondaco dei Tedeschi – a large building that combined a warehouse with lodgings for German merchants trading in the city. Here the *gondolieri* would offload the cargo at the portico, overlooked from an airy loggia above by the merchants and their families. The goods were then shipped out of Venice to the East, or to northern Europe – Germany, the Low Countries and England.

One morning, as Daniele slept on, Maria opened her shutters and gazed as usual down onto the canal hoping to catch sight of one of the familiar *gondolieri*. A pair of seagulls swooped down the canal, snatching a piece of bread that had been cast into the water. Within moments, she heard the familiar slip, slop of a gondola. This one was painted a brilliant shade of red and she knew the *gondoliere* by name.

'*Bon giorno, Fabio,*' she shouted down to him.

'*Bon giorno, Signorina. Come va?*'

'*Bene grazie.*'

A young man with fair hair emerged from the little cabin in the centre of the gondola. He gazed up towards Maria's window. Embarrassed, she ducked out of sight, before reappearing once more as the gondola slipped past. The young man, she noticed, had remained on his feet and as she peeked out of her window once more, he waved at her before disappearing onto the Grand Canal.

The following morning, as she took up her familiar position at the window, Fabio's gondola appeared once again. But this time the young fair-haired man was seated next to the *gondoliere* in the open part of the gondola. He waved up at her and smiled. He had long straight hair, a broad face and a kind expression. She waved back nervously. He called up to her.

'*Bon giorno, Signorina.*'

His accent was unfamiliar; he was certainly not Italian. She ducked out of sight again, and sat on the window seat from where she could see but remain unobserved. She spent the rest of the day wandering between her bedchamber and her father's study, musing on the young man with fair hair. Having been brought up in the Middle and Far East, she was fascinated by people with fair hair. Her family's travels had occasionally taken them to parts of the Middle East where people had fair hair, or blue eyes. She herself had blue-green eyes. But she had never seen hair that resembled fine gold thread. His skin too was pale, far paler than her own olive skin. Since their arrival in Venice, her father had explained that many of the people who lived in the city came from lands far to the north, and they were more likely to have fair hair and skin. On her walks to the market and Piazza San Marco with Daniele, they came across people of all different races, and she enjoyed listening as the merchants bartered and argued over the cost of goods in a hurly-burly of different languages. But without her father to interpret, she had no idea where they came from.

She yearned to discuss all this with her father. She missed his company so badly. She wondered if he would have been shocked that the young man had called up to her. He would probably have invited the fair-haired man to meet them; he was always interested in meeting new people. She went into her father's study and sat down at his desk with paper and pen to write him a letter. She thought of the young nun who had waved at her a few days before, and wondered if she was in the garden. She stood up from her father's desk and peered out of the window.

Directly beneath her stood the nun, gathering pears from a large tree that had been trained against the wall.

'*Buona sera*,' she called down to the young nun. 'Those pears look lovely.' She pointed to the large basket filled with fruit at the young nun's feet.

'*Buona sera*,' the nun replied. 'Would you like one?' And she made to throw one up to Maria.

'You'd better not, you might get into trouble. Are you allowed to speak to me today?'

'No, not really,' said the nun, 'but there's no one else around. What is your name?'

'Maria, and you?'

'Polisena.'

'How are you Polisena?' asked Maria kindly.

'Rather lonely… Ooh, I had better go,' she said suddenly, as an elderly nun appeared on the opposite side of the garden. She cast a last, longing look up at Maria and threw a pear up to her; she caught it, and as she did so whispered, '*Grazie. A domani.*'

Polisena smiled back before she picked up her basket and retreated into the cloisters.

Maria went to her father's study every day after that; partly in case Polisena wanted to see her, but also because it helped her to feel close to her father. She tried to pretend to Daniele that she was strong and capable, but in reality she felt very alone and missed her father desperately. Sitting at his desk, fingering his pens and touching the box of seals that he kept there made her feel close to him. Once or twice she even took down the vase and placed it tenderly in the centre of his desk in order to study the painting, gazing intently at the dragon's face. She wondered how such a fierce creature could be considered a symbol of good luck. It seemed curious to her, and yet there was something about the dragon – about its intent, beady blue stare. If she placed the vase so that the dragon's face was towards her, its eyes would follow her around the room, tracking her as she crossed from one side to the other. She would stroke the porcelain, feeling it cool and smooth beneath her fingers before placing it carefully back on the shelf. In some strange way, it made her feel closer to her father. He had believed in its power and had been desolate that he had allowed it out of his sight when his son became ill. And he was a wise man, the wisest man she had ever known. If he believed in its power to protect them, then it must be true. She pondered sadly on the fact that it was intended not for them but one day would have to be handed over to the Doge. She hoped that her father might have a rare moment of forgetfulness once he returned from Florence, and somehow the vase would be allowed to remain with them forever.

The following day, she sat again at her father's desk, the vase placed before her. She was writing to her father telling him about the little nun she had befriended.

'*I think she must be one of those nuns who are there because their families have no dowry for them. She seems rather jolly and occasionally I catch sight of her beautiful red hair poking out from her wimple. I only speak to her when she is alone in the garden. The older nuns do not approve of the younger ones speaking to people outside the order. It must be so sad and lonely for her…*'

She remembered what he had told her about the nuns in Venice and how so many of them were in the convents against their will.

'Why are they forced to live there?' she had asked him, horrified, when he told her.

'They are often the daughters of good families, but perhaps their parents have died, or they are unable to find them a suitable marriage partner, or they cannot afford a dowry. The authorities in Venice demand that any girl must have a dowry in order to marry, and that does create problems.'

'But that is terrible,' protested Maria. 'Does that mean that if you have no dowry, you cannot marry?'

'It does,' said her father.

'But *Mamma* did not have a dowry did she? And you married her.'

'Ah, little one, that is because I am not interested in rules, and I go my own way.'

'Well I shall follow my own way too,' said Maria enthusiastically.

'Good,' said her father, 'let us hope that will be possible.'

'So all these girls are in the convent against their will?' Maria continued.

'Well, not all, no. There are girls who have a vocation and a love of God. Sometimes a girl might be a little slow… You know?

Not very bright, and her parents think the convent will provide a refuge from the demands of ordinary life. And there are prostitutes, of course.'

'Really!' said Maria, in horror. 'In a place of God?'

'Yes. The church here can be very broad-minded. Sometimes they have had enough of their life and retreat to the convent. And on occasion, I'm sorry to say, some are there at the invitation of a priest.'

'No!' said Maria. 'Surely not here? At our church of San Zaccaria?'

'No; our church and the convent here are very respectable. The nuns here are all from very noble families. It means they come with a certain amount of money which keeps everyone, even the Bishop, very happy.'

'Oh, Papa! You are such a cynic,' laughed his daughter.

'Oh, they do some good work, you know. There are over thirty convents here in Venice – some on the tiny islands in the lagoon; a sort of physical manifestation of their separation from the 'ordinary' world. There is just enough space for the convent building, a church and a garden on which to grow produce.'

'It must be terrible,' said Maria. 'They must be so bored!'

'Ha, ha, yes, I think you are right. But they care for the sick on the *lazzaretti* that are dotted around the lagoon; it's important work.'

'Like that island we passed when we arrived?' asked Maria.

'Yes, like that one, and others.'

'What was it called again?'

'Poveglia. But you needn't worry about it. They only take victims of plague and lepers there.'

The following morning, she found Daniele weeping in his room.

'Little one, what is the matter?' she asked tenderly, wrapping him in her arms.

'I miss *Mamma* so much,' he replied.

'I know. So do I.'

'And now Papa; he has not written for over a week.'

'Yes. I shall write again to him today and perhaps we will hear from him soon. Darling Daniele, shall we go out? I need to order some provisions and we have not had a walk for a few days, and Papa did instruct us to continue to get to know Venice. We could take a gondola and go down the Grand Canal. We could go all the way to the Rialto Bridge and then walk back. Or perhaps, the other way around: walk first and then a gondola. What do you say?'

The house on Rio dei Greci had two entrances. The 'front' door was situated on the canal, and entailed arriving and departing by gondola from the small wooden deck that jutted out onto the water. The family had a gondola of their own, decorated with a pair of dolphins at either end, tethered to the dock. Niccolò had encouraged Andrea to learn how to operate it, but he had proved a poor student. On his first attempt to navigate the long dark boat he had jutted up against a neighbour's jetty and damaged their gondola. Since that time, he had been nervous of attempting the task again. Daniele was desperate to be given the role of *gondoliere* for the family, but Niccolò was uncharacteristically reticent. Whilst a modern man in many ways, and open to new ideas, he was reluctant for his son, the son of a good family, to be seen in charge of the family's gondola. And so it stood rocking in the breeze, unused, much to Daniele's frustration.

'We could take our gondola,' said Daniele, showing some enthusiasm for the first time that morning.

'No,' said Maria. 'I do not think Papa would be pleased with me if I let you do that.'

'But he would never know,' reasoned the boy.

'No, Daniele. We will walk there, and then get a *gondoliere* to bring us back. We shall take Andrea with us, in case I purchase anything that needs to be brought back home with us.' Frustrated, but aware that this was an argument he could not win, Daniele agreed.

The three young people let themselves out by the side entrance that opened into a narrow alleyway running alongside the perimeter wall of the convent. From there it was just a short walk to the hustle and bustle of Piazza San Marco. They walked in single file up the narrow alleyway. To their right stood the convent, the high wall and terracotta roofs of its cloisters shielding the nuns from the watchful gaze of passers-by. No sound came from behind those walls as the three slipped past. Maria had heard the nuns singing mass earlier that morning, but as the sun rose high in the sky, the ladies of the San Zaccaria convent were involved in their daily tasks, undertaken with a minimum of chatter or conversation. Housework – sweeping the marble floors of the cloisters, polishing the gold candlesticks and cross on the altar, preparing food and gardening – all took up the hours during the day until evening vespers, when they would file silently into the chapel and fill the air with their singing and prayers. She thought of Polisena and wondered what she was doing. It seemed so sad that she was unable to come out of the convent and join them on their walk.

As the young people made their way along the dark alleyway, the heat of the day radiated from the high stone walls. It gave off a strong scent, which Maria could never quite identify – dusty, a little dank, sour. After a few moments they emerged into the brilliant, bright light of Piazza San Marco.

'Let's walk to the Rialto,' said Maria. 'Then perhaps, we could take a gondola back home.'

Leaving the heat and bustle of the Piazza behind, they turned into Merceria, a lane which ran all the way from the Piazza to the Rialto. It was lined with shops selling all manner of luxurious goods such as silk, tapestries, carpets and spices. As they got nearer to the Rialto, the crowds grew denser. Maria caught hold of Daniele's hand. 'Stay close to me, *caro*,' she murmured. But her brother pulled his hand away. 'I'm fine. I'm fifteen. You don't have to treat me like a child.'

Andrea watched the pair out of the corner of his eye. He was fascinated by them, or at least by Maria. He was originally from the Dalmatian coast and had arrived in Venice at the age of twelve, in search of a better life. He had an uncle, a fisherman, who had offered him bed and board in return for helping to man the fishing boats that he ran from the Riva dei Schiavoni. But Andrea had ambitions for something other than the brutal life of a fisherman, and besides he had no head for the sea. He suffered terribly from sickness when on the water and had no intention of living the seafarer's life. He had acquired some education before he left home and was determined to continue with it in Venice. He had already worked in several fine houses when he encountered Niccolò. He had been serving at the table of one of dei Conti's friends and Niccolò, being egalitarian by nature, interested in everyone he met, had slipped into conversation with the boy. He sensed his desire to improve himself. When he established his own household, Niccolò had asked his friend if he might spare the boy to work in his own house. He had offered to tutor Andrea a little each day and was impressed by how quickly he had mastered the written word. He earned his keep and his education by helping the staff in the kitchen, serving at table, bringing in wood, and generally fetching and delivering for the household. But Niccolò sensed the young man's ambition, and had hopes that, one day, the boy might amount to much more and perhaps become a secretary in his household. When, as was the custom in Venice, one of the great moral speakers of the day gave a public lecture on logic, philosophy or theology, Niccolò would, from time to time, allow the young man to visit Piazza San Marco and listen to the lectures.

Andrea was grateful for Niccolò's kindness and the opportunities he had afforded him, but this kindness also served to create a sense of confusion in the young man's mind. For at times he was required to behave like a servant – to fetch and carry and do the family's bidding. At others, he was encouraged to improve himself, to imagine a future free of the shackles of service. Niccolò even allowed him to join in with the lessons of his own children. Andrea was a quick learner, and soon outstripped Daniele in his understanding of mathematics and his love of reading. Niccolò's son appeared to have little enthusiasm for learning, preferring more energetic pastimes. Maria, however, was a different matter. She had a huge desire to learn, and was an exceptional student. Andrea would watch her as she worked, fascinated by the way her long dark hair fell in a river down her back, or occasionally draped casually over one shoulder, revealing her neck – soft and inviting – on the other side. Her eyes, of course, were beautiful, remarked on by everyone who saw her. But she seemed to find any sort of compliment embarrassing and would brush such comments aside; this only served to add to her allure. For Andrea had fallen desperately in love with the daughter of his master.

Maria was completely unaware of the young man's feelings and would have been horrified had she known. She did not dislike Andrea but saw him as one of her father's household. As far as she was concerned, he was simply a polite young man in the service of her father – nothing more.

The three arrived at the Rialto just before lunchtime. There were stalls set up nearby selling all kinds of food and drink. Maria took it upon herself to order some meat and vegetables. She went from stall to stall discussing the produce and bartering the price like an old hand. She had watched her mother through the years as they travelled in the East, and had a good eye for both a quality product and a bargain. She chose some Tuscan mutton, but argued the price. 'I will not pay three *soldi* for that. I will give you two.'

'But *Signorina*,' the stall-holder implored her, 'you do me an injustice.'

'Two *soldi* is all I will pay.'

The deal was done and the meat was wrapped. It would be delivered later that day, along with a selection of fresh vegetables.

'Daniele, are you hungry? We could eat something here if you like?'

The three chose a little taverna called the *Cantina do Mori*, next to the Fondaco, the German merchant's warehouse. They settled themselves at a table near the window overlooking the canal and ordered some wine and food.

Maria was not quite sure when she became aware of the blond man staring at her. She was spooning mouthfuls of '*risi e bisi*' – a mixture of rice with peas that was popular in Venice and which reminded her of the rice dishes she had eaten in the Middle and Far East, and giggling at one of Daniele's childish jokes. As she laughed, a few grains of rice flew across the table, and at that precise moment she looked up and realised that the blond man from the gondola was gazing at her, smiling wryly. He was sitting at a table almost next to theirs.

She covered her mouth in embarrassment, and blushing, looked down at her plate. Andrea noticed instantly that something was amiss.

'Are you well?' he asked Maria.

'Quite well, thank you,' she responded curtly, taking a large gulp from her cup of wine.

Having composed herself, she looked up again; the man was still smiling at her. She smiled back briefly and continued to eat her food and chat to her brother and Andrea. Their meal finished, she stood and gathered her cloak around her ready to leave.

'Come along, Daniele; we should be getting back.'

As she passed the blond man's table, he stood up and barred her way.

Andrea pushed himself between this interloper and Maria. 'Out of the way of my mistress,' he said firmly.

'Forgive me,' said the blond man. 'I merely wished to give the lady something.' And he took out from his doublet pocket a delicate lace handkerchief.

'It is Bruges lace, my lady. I hope you will accept it.'

'My sister cannot accept any gift from a stranger.' Daniele spoke loudly and clearly and now inserted himself between Andrea and the blond stranger. 'She is a lady and you show her no respect.'

'I assure you, I wish the lady no harm, nor do I mean her any insult.' The young blond man seemed utterly self-assured and stood his ground. He was a good head taller than either Andrea or Daniele, and Maria had the impression that he was mildly amused at the young men's attempts to protect her reputation.

'Thank you,' she spoke at last. 'I would be delighted to accept your gift; it is beautiful. I have never seen such fine work before.'

Daniele cast her an angry glance, and Andrea stood back dejectedly.

'The lace-makers of Bruges are famous for the delicacy of their workmanship,' said the young man. 'You will not find a finer example anywhere in Venice. I import it myself. I have the monopoly.'

'Then I am grateful to you,' said Maria, tucking the handkerchief into the pocket of her gown.

'May I know your name?' she asked the young man.

'Peter,' he replied, 'Peter Haas. And yours?'

'Maria dei Conti. My father is Niccolò dei Conti – merchant and traveller. We are recently returned from the East.'

'I am honoured to make your acquaintance,' said Peter, as he bowed low.

'I think we should leave now,' said Daniele anxiously.

'May I call on you?' asked the young blond man.

'You may…'

'Maria,' interjected her brother.

'Please do, but when my father has returned. I think you know where we live,' Maria continued.

And with that she shepherded her brother and Andrea out of the *cantina* and home.

CHAPTER 6

Peter Haas

Peter Haas was twenty-seven years of age and had lived in Venice for nine years. He was the son of a well-respected German merchant, Franck Haas from Nuremberg, and Beatrix van der Beke. Her family were merchants in Bruges and their marriage, and consequent unification of their two businesses, had enabled the family to dominate trade in a significant belt stretching from Bruges in the north – with its monopoly of the northern sea routes, through Nuremberg, at the centre of twelve of the major trade routes in Europe – to Venice in the south, with its firm grip on trade to the East.

Peter had spent his young life travelling between Bruges, where his mother's brother Tobias ran the family business, and his father's home city of Nuremberg. Linens, paper, ironwork, brass, armour and printing were that city's major exports. Together, the family prided themselves that the extent of their mercantile territory, which also stretched from Venice to the English Channel, was unsurpassed by any other German merchant. They were ambitious, industrious and courageous. They were prepared to take financial as well as physical risks. Peter in particular was a young man of huge determination and with a strong sense of adventure. He had two brothers who had remained in the north: one based in Nuremberg with their father and the other working with Tobias, who had no sons of his own.

Peter had first come to Venice aged just eighteen, to trade on behalf of his family business. Having spent time in Bruges he was familiar with canal life and felt at home instantly in his adopted city. Germans had traded and lived in Venice for hundreds of years, and his native tongue was widely spoken, or at least understood amongst the merchant class. But Peter was bright and enthusiastic and determined to mix fully in his adopted city, and soon mastered Italian. He lived in the German *fondaco* – the lodging house reserved for German merchants – and revelled in the freedom of being away from his family. He was a young man with a fondness for beer and wine, in a town filled with ladies of uncertain virtue, and he took full advantage of all that the city had to offer. Each Sunday he would make his way to the church of San Bartholomew alongside his fellow German merchants. There he would worship and mix with the respectable German families who lived and worked alongside him in Venice. But by the evening, he would be in a *taverna* near the Rialto – a bright, high-spirited young man enjoying his life to the full.

His father tasked him with purchasing goods that could be shipped north and sold either in Germany, the Low Countries, or in England. He bought woollen and silken cloth manufactured in Venice; he purchased spices from the Near East, carpets from Damascus and porcelain from the lands of further India. He imported goods into Venice too – many originating from Russia and the Baltic – furs, leather and metals, including gold and silver. Through his uncle Tobias came lace from Bruges and raw wool from England, which was considered the only wool of choice for Venetian fabric manufacturers. Business was good and the family prospered.

In spite of their long association with the Venetians, German merchants were forced to live and work under certain restrictions. They were not permitted to conduct their own business in the Adriatic and beyond, or to run ships to Alexandria and trade directly. Instead they had to buy their goods from Venetian traders, and conduct their business under the watchful eye of the authorities, paying taxes and duty for goods they wished to purchase and transport on to northern Europe. In return, the Venetians agreed not to do business directly with Germany, although Venetians did trade with Flanders and England.

The Germans were obliged to live and work in the Fondaco dei Tedeschi. This large building on the Grand Canal served as trading centre, warehouse and lodgings. One hundred and twenty guests were housed there and leased rooms from the authorities of San Marco. Apart from their rent, they paid for extra services such as meals and cleaning. In return, the authorities provided security for their goods, but also applied a curfew on the residents, locking them up in the residence at night.

For the most part, the merchants coped with these regulations. For they understood that Venice was the most important trading route to the Middle and Far East, and the advantages outweighed any personal disadvantages or irritations. But occasionally, frustrations erupted to the surface, usually in the guise of rivalries between different groups of German merchants. The citizens of Cologne and Ulm fell out and refused to dine together. They insisted on separate kitchens, cooks and ovens. The authorities' response was conciliatory, but firm; they must share a kitchen, but would be allowed to retain separate cooks and ovens.

Peter's attitude to this squabbling was one of mild amusement. His nature was cheerful and optimistic, and he refused to allow his compatriots' irritations to spoil his life. He was not particularly anxious about the curfew either, and found ways to escape at night, with one or two other bold young men in the *fondaco*, to meet with prostitutes who frequented the streets and brothels near the Rialto. Prostitution in Venice at that time was widespread. It was said that there were eleven thousand prostitutes amongst a population of one hundred thousand people. But it was carefully regulated by the city's authorities. Prostitutes had to live and work within the *Castelletto*, near the Rialto, and as long as they followed the rules, conducted their activities discreetly and paid their taxes, they were allowed to play their part in society. It was not exactly encouraged, but was seen as a necessary part of a healthy social mix. The reasons for this were complex. All patrician and high-born women in Venice were required to offer a large dowry in order to marry. This often led to younger sisters being left with no dowry at all, and consequently no possibility of marriage. The only future for them was to take the veil. And as the pool of suitable brides diminished, many of the young men of the city were forced into a life of permanent bachelorhood. Added to which the needs of a large population of unattached merchants and travellers in the city had to be satisfied and prostitution was considered the answer. The alternative, in the minds of the Church, was for these young men to seek pleasure amongst one another and that was considered a worse sin. Better that they visit a woman of ill repute than they take pleasure in sodomy.

Peter had made frequent use of the brothels in *Castelletto* since he had lived in Venice. It was rather fortunate that they were within a few minutes' walk of the *fondaco*, next to the Rialto Bridge. Prostitutes were forbidden from forming lasting relationships with their clients. As a young man, Peter had impulsively fallen in love with several of the ladies at the *Castelletto*. His head was full of their beauty and generosity. On more than one occasion he would arrive at the brothel begging to be allowed to visit one particular girl, only to be refused by the madam and sent in to visit another girl altogether. Sometimes, late at night, when he had indulged in more wine than was good for him, he was inclined to take advantage of one of the unregulated ladies of the night that lurked in dark corners of the street – an experience that he usually regretted seconds later.

Tiring a little of these unsatisfactory liaisons, he was introduced by a friend from the *fondaco*, to the nuns of the Sant' Angelo convent. The convent had a rather racy reputation, populated as it was with beautiful young women from good families who were there, quite frequently, against their will. They were young, charming, accomplished and artistic. Many were daughters of the nobility who had been forced to take the veil when no dowry was forthcoming, and as such were completely without religious conviction, and refused to wear either the garb of a nun or practice their rituals. Their clothes were extravagant and colourful, and their dresses cut low over the breast. They were fond of dyeing their hair blond, a craze that had swept through the ladies of Venice for some time. And rather than passing their days in prayer and good works, they spent their time painting, playing music and sewing. Their parties were legendary gatherings filled with music, laughter and fornication. It was to one such occasion that Peter was taken by his friend Jacob.

Jacob had recently become the lover of a particularly pretty red-haired nun named Elena Marcello, otherwise known Sister Angelica. He had seen her one day as she sat in her window that overlooked the Campo Sant' Angelo. He had smiled at her and she had begun a conversation with him. He visited her window several times before she invited him into the convent one afternoon. There he had met a number of other young men who had been invited by like-minded 'nuns'. The women had sung and danced, sharing wine and sweetmeats with their guests. Before long, he and Elena were lovers – a state of affairs that appeared to be overlooked, or even condoned by the abbess of that establishment. Elena suggested that Jacob bring along a friend to their next evening's entertainment and so Peter was invited. Fascinated and not a little horrified at the implications of what he was doing, he and Jacob were silently let in through a side door into the convent garden. They walked along the cloisters past several older nuns who appeared to be engrossed in conversation, their prayer books resting in their laps; religious music escaped through the door of the chapel. But at the far end of the cloisters, they were shown into a brightly lit room filled with young women wearing colourful gowns, their hair elaborately coiled, who danced, sang and laughed gaily. In the middle of the room, playing the harp, sat a beautiful blond girl wearing a low-cut scarlet velvet dress. As she sang a sad love song, her eyes fell on young Peter. By the end of the evening, after much wine, food and song, she had taken him to her room, where she proved a more than able guide and mistress, enthusiastic in her desire and appetite for sex. He was bewitched by her and came to visit her regularly after that. They formed a strong attachment, and spoke from time to time of how he might 'rescue' her and take her from the convent. But in his heart, Peter knew that his parents would never countenance such a relationship being formalised. The risks to any young man who eloped with a nun, even a nun who had been placed in a convent against her wishes, were severe. A prison sentence was almost guaranteed, fines would be imposed and his family's reputation would be destroyed. As a visiting merchant in Venice he was bound to suffer a more severe punishment as a deterrent to others. With a heavy heart and a sense of guilt that he had never felt before, he had put a stop to the affair. It was rumoured that he had broken poor Sister Theresa's heart.

At twenty-seven, Peter was growing weary of this dissolute life and in truth had begun to yearn for a wife. His father had suggested much the same in his last letter to his son.

My dear Peter,

Your mother, uncle and brothers send you their best. We have been thinking of you and hope you may be able to visit soon – perhaps you might travel north with the next consignment of cloth and carpets you mentioned in your last letter. I hope so, for we have someone we would like to introduce to you. She is the daughter of a respected member of our community, Friedrich Drenyn. The family are from Nuremburg. Her name is Agnes and she is a God-fearing girl, and strong and sensible. We believe she would make a most suitable bride and partner for you. Her father's business would be a good association with our own. Write soon, my boy, and tell me when you intend to travel north. I will make the arrangements.

It was, of course, quite natural for families at that time to arrange marriages for their children. And it was important that those marriages would benefit the families involved. Uniting two big mercantile dynasties through marriage was something that Peter had long been led to expect. And yet, he felt uneasy and not a little distressed at the prospect of being introduced to his future wife in this way. Her name alone filled him with anxiety. Could he really love a woman named Agnes, however 'strong and sensible' she proved to be? And while he could see the advantages of marrying such a woman, his time in Venice had taught him that he would prefer a wife who was soft, yielding, amusing, beautiful and exotic.

He had been reading this letter and considering the implications while working his way through a large flagon of wine when his eye fell upon the beautiful blue-eyed girl he had espied the previous day in the window of the house on the Rio dei Greci.

He had been spellbound by her eyes then; were they blue, or green? It was impossible to say, but either way, they contrasted wonderfully with her long dark hair and olive skin, and together created a vision of exotic beauty that he was quite sure was unsurpassed in Venice. He had forced the *gondoliere* to row past her house twice and had been delighted to see her on both occasions;

he had then spent much of the following twenty-four hours musing on how he might manage to actually meet her. To find her sitting not a few feet away from him in the *taverna* on the Rialto was an extraordinary coincidence – or perhaps a sign?

He had loved her uninhibited laughter and he had smiled at her subsequent blushing embarrassment when she saw him. When she rose to leave, he could not allow the opportunity to introduce himself pass. And she had liked the handkerchief, he could tell. Perhaps she even liked him too, a little. He was amused by the two young men who had sought to protect her. She was obviously a lady of some standing and respectability. But there seemed to be a spirit and freedom about her that he did not normally find in the well-born but dull young northern women of his acquaintance – this girl was different.

When she had left, he resolved that he must be bold and find his way to her house on the Rio dei Greci. Perhaps if he could be introduced to her father he would be admitted to her presence and they would be allowed to spend time together, chaperoned of course. Perhaps, he might never have to marry the unappetising-sounding Agnes.

And so he began to plan his seduction, with the skill and cunning that he normally reserved for sourcing a particularly fine example of silken cloth or a beautiful carpet. He must learn all he could about her family; he must discover her father's profession and endeavour to meet him. He was a young man filled with energy, a characteristic that made him a talented trader. For he was able to convince almost anyone to do business with him – that he offered the best deal, the best product, or the best market. But now the prize was not a beautiful carpet from Damascus or some fine porcelain from the land of further India. The prize this time was a girl of such beauty that he could not displace her from his mind. This girl, with blue eyes and shining black hair, with the wild laugh and the confident look, was destined to be his bride.

CHAPTER 7

Peter and Maria

It did not take Peter Haas long to find a way to meet Maria dei Conti again. The family had only recently moved into the house on Rio dei Greci, and Niccolò's large shipment of goods that stood in the warehouse at Punta were already causing quite a stir amongst the merchants of Venice.

'It is said that he has one of the largest shipments of porcelain ever brought into Venice,' said Wilhelm Rumlin, a trader from Munich, over dinner one evening in the *fondaco*. 'I have tried to get in touch with him and his agent to discuss a price, but it seems the man has disappeared.'

'He has been excommunicated, or so I have heard,' said Friedrich Ditterichs from Ulm, as he gnawed at a mutton bone. 'He took the Muslim faith whilst abroad. He was married to a savage.'

'Really?' gasped Willhelm. 'What kind of savage?'

'An Indian woman. He is clearly a man of no moral substance at all.'

'Well perhaps we can do a good deal with him when he returns from wherever he has gone,' muttered Friedrich. 'I am not interested in his soul, but his porcelain interests me greatly,' he chortled, as he took a large gulp of wine, causing it to dribble down his pockmarked chin into his silken doublet.

Peter listened to the conversation in silence, not wishing to reveal anything about his meeting with the beautiful Maria. He was fascinated and appalled in equal measure at the cynicism and hypocrisy of his fellow merchants.

Slowly he pieced the story together. Maria and her brother were alone in the house with their servants while their father had travelled to Florence to seek some kind of reconciliation with the Catholic Church. It would be difficult to visit her with her father abroad. But it might just be possible to meet her in some other way.

His friend Giovanni, an Italian merchant, mentioned to Peter one day that he had fallen in love with a nun who lived at the convent of San Zaccaria, the convent that stood directly behind the Rio dei Greci. Peter realised that Maria's house must over-look the convent gardens. The nuns at San Zaccaria were selected almost exclusively from the nobility of Venice, and were more respectable than their sisters at the convent of Sant' Angelo. In fact, their record was unblemished. But Giovanni Valler had met a young lady named Polisena Cavorta who had recently been forced to enter the convent against her will. Hopelessly in love, he had been writing to her regularly and begged her fervently to marry him. But she had no dowry and the situation was hope-less. She was also a girl of great virtue and had, until now, been reluctant to break the convent rules.

'I have written to her every day,' he told Peter one night, as they sat in a *taverna* on the Rialto. 'But she will not see me. I think I shall go mad for love.'

One day, as Peter sat musing on how to get to see Maria once again, Giovanni rushed into the *taverna*.

'Peter, I am so glad to have found you. I have some wonder-ful news. Polisena has agreed to meet me. I must break into the convent of course; there is no way that the Abbess will allow us to enter through the door.'

'Us?' queried Peter.

'Yes, us. I thought you would help me. Please Peter. I am des-perate. I must see her, or I will go mad.'

'And how do you propose to make this break-in, may I ask?'

'I will climb over the wall, of course. There is a strong vine on the convent side, she says, but I will need your help to get up there. Say you will help me?'

'Yes, of course I will help you. But don't blame me if the Abbess finds you and you are arrested by the authorities!'

'I knew I could count on you.'

The assignation was arranged for a few days hence. On the appointed evening, the pair lingered in the narrow alley that ran beside the convent. Peter realised that the alleyway ran down as far as the Rio dei Greci itself, and that Maria's house was just a little further on. Leaving his friend waiting for Polisena's call, he wandered down the lane until he came to a door that led to one of the houses on the canal. It was without doubt that of Maria dei Conti. The urge to knock on the door or even to try the handle and enter was overwhelming, but he restrained himself. He wandered back up the lane, and soon the young men heard Polisena's whispered call.

'Giovanni – are you there?'

'I am *cara*... I am here.'

'Climb over the wall… There is a strong vine on this side that you can climb down. Is there someone there to help you?'

'Yes. My good friend Peter is here.'

'Thank him for me.'

Peter lifted Giovanni up until he was standing on his shoulders. Giovanni could just reach the top of the wall. Peter lifted him by the ankles just long enough for him to grab hold of the top of the wall and pull himself up. In a matter of moments, Giovanni was up and over.

The following evening, he begged for Peter's assistance once more; and again, the next day. In fact, the young man secretly entered the convent every night for the next two weeks. He and Polisena would wander together in the moonlit cloisters of the convent, safe in the knowledge that the virtuous nuns slept soundly in their cells. He professed his undying love to the girl, and begged her to marry him, and eventually, to his great delight, she allowed him to take her to her cell and make love to her.

Peter had been a kind and patient accomplice. And one evening, as they waited for Polisena's call, he mentioned that he had fallen in love himself.

'A nun?' asked his friend.

'No. She is the daughter of a merchant. They live just over the wall of the convent there, in a house that backs onto the canal.'

'Why do you not present yourself?' asked his friend.

'I have met with her once, in a local *cantina*, but I cannot visit her house; her father is away on business and her brother is very protective. But I wish desperately to see her again.'

'Maybe Polisena can help us,' said his friend.

The following evening, when they met in the *taverna*, Giovanni had news for Peter.

'Polisena knows the girl. They wave to each other when she works in the convent gardens. She is beautiful I hear, with dark hair and startling blue eyes.'

'That's her!' said Peter excitedly.

'Polisena has offered to help you. She says that she will endeavour to speak to the girl tomorrow, when she is in the garden. If Maria comes to the window, and she often does, she will tell her to meet you tomorrow night.'

The following evening, Peter lifted his friend up and over the wall, before walking a little further on to Maria's door. Polisena had sent word that Maria would be waiting for him. He was to tap three times on the door and she would on the other side. He tapped as directed and within moments, he heard the bolts of the door being delicately slid back. At last the door opened and Maria stood before him, her hair braided and falling in a long dark plait down her back. She wore a simple green velvet dress over a white linen *camicetta*. It was as much as Peter could do to stop himself embracing her there and then.

'You are here,' was all he could say.

'Yes. I am here,' she whispered. 'I cannot ask you in. I'm sure you understand. But we could walk a little way up the alleyway if you like.'

The pair walked up and down together, their fingers just touching. They were lit by the sharp light of a new moon, a slender arc that hung over the dome of San Marco.

'Tell me everything about yourself,' begged Peter.

'There is so much to tell,' replied Maria.

'Then tell it.'

And so her story unfolded. Of her family's life spent in the East; of their travels in India, and further India. She told him of the Emperor and the Admiral, and of the tragic loss of her beloved mother and little brother and sister in Egypt; she even told him about the vase, and how it was supposed to bring the bearer good luck.

'My father always blamed our mother's death on the fact that he had let the vase go on to Alexandria without him.'

'And where is the vase now?' asked Peter.

'It is in my father's study. Because it is supposed to be a gift for the Doge, there is no duty to pay. He was not required to leave it in the *Punta* with his other merchandise. But when he gets back from Florence, I suppose he will have to pass it on. I wish he could keep it though.'

They talked all night, until the arc of the moon had long since faded from the sky and the glow of the sun began to spread up from the lagoon. The birds in the convent garden were beginning their dawn chatter when Peter heard his friend's soft leathered tread on the alleyway.

'Peter, we should go,' Giovanni whispered.

'Yes. Maria may I come again?'

'Of course. Tonight if you like. I shall wait for you.'

The pair met each night for the next week. They walked and talked. He told her of his life in Bruges and Nuremberg. She told him of life at sea, and in the Emperor's palace. She talked of Damascus and of Persia. She was, without doubt, the most exceptional person he had ever met. He knew – had known almost from the first – that he was in love with her. But did she share his love?

One evening, as they strolled near the church, he held her hand and turned her to face him.

'Maria … you must know that I love you.'

She smiled a little to herself.

'And that I wish to marry you…'

'Oh, Peter! But my father…'

'I know – I must wait until I can meet him.'

'I do not know if there will be any dowry. He has goods to sell when he returns, but how much they will bring I do not know. I am not a rich woman, Peter.'

'I do not care if you are the poorest woman in Venice,' he said. 'I am going to marry you, Maria. When your father returns, I shall pay him a visit and everything will be well; you will see.'

Maria smiled up at him. 'Well, you should know that I love you too. I'm sure my father will love you just as I do. I will write to him tomorrow and beg him to come back to Venice.'

'I am the happiest of men,' he said, as he leant down and kissed her.

Standing in the shadows of the convent just a few yards away from the couple was a man who also loved her; a man who had shared her house since her arrival in Venice. A man who had adored her from afar, but was – he could see now – of no consequence to her. Andrea watched her kiss the blond stranger and felt such rage and jealousy that it was as much as he could do to stop himself rushing over to them and striking the man.

He could not allow this love to continue. He would stop it in any way that he could, and the sooner the better. She would soon see that he only had her best interests at heart.

CHAPTER 8

Andrea's revenge

Maria wrote to her father the following day. She did not mention Peter's proposal, of course, but told her father that all was well, that Daniele was working hard at his studies - a slight exaggeration - and that they yearned to see him again. As an aside, she also mentioned that she had some interesting news for him and that he must come home as soon as possible.

She handed the letter to Andrea that afternoon.

'Could you see that this is sent to my father as soon as possible,' she asked. 'I am taking Daniele to San Marco for a walk and then we shall visit the apothecary. He is feeling a little melancholy this afternoon and I think he needs some fresh air.'

Daniele had recently developed a skin condition; the skin on his elbows and knees had become rough and raw. Maria had acquired a herbal remedy from the apothecary but it had not worked as well as she had hoped and she intended to take her brother to meet her that afternoon to discuss an alternative.

As soon as the pair had left the house, Andrea broke the seal on the letter and read its contents. He had done this before and knew that he could easily re-seal it once Maria had gone out. She was trusting and never locked her seals away as she was supposed to do.

He read the letter with a beating heart; he realised that he must act quickly. If Niccolò returned to Venice, the German would present himself at the house and ask for Maria's hand. He had no idea if Niccolò would agree, but he knew his master well enough to know that he could refuse Maria nothing. He was not like other well-born men. He did not set as much store by the customs and practices of his class. It would be no surprise at all if Niccolò gave Maria permission to marry her German merchant.

Andrea considered destroying the letter, but he knew that when Niccolò next wrote to Maria, she would expect him to mention her request. So the letter would have to be sent, and he must find another way. Somehow he had either to remove the merchant or Maria – and so, an idea began to take shape.

Andrea had recently become acquainted with one of the two men who patrolled their *sestiere* investigating possible plague cases. Since the great plague of 1347, Venice had been in a state of alert. There had been occasional slighter outbreaks in recent years and the authorities understood that a city which had as much foreign trade and as many visitors as Venice must be constantly vigilant to the possibility of plague arriving in their midst. He knew that quite often people were taken from their homes mistakenly. A young man of his acquaintance had only just recently been sent to the plague island because he had a bad case of acne. Another suffered from psoriasis and he too had been removed. Both were now languishing in the Lazzaretto Vecchio on the island of Poveglia, where they must endure a minimum of forty days' quarantine. Forty days was widely recognised as the length of time it would take to discover if someone was suffering from the disease or not. If they recovered, they would be sent for another thirty days to the Lazzaretto Nuovo on an island nearby before finally being returned home, where they would be quarantined for a further ten days. Of course, some of the patients really did have the illness, which made the quarantine of the unaffected even more dangerous – for they would be liable to actually catch the disease from infected patients at the hospital.

Andrea knew that if Daniele were suspected of carrying the disease, he would almost certainly be taken to the island. The house would be evacuated and the residents sent away, usually to the island where patients recovered in the Lazaretto Nuovo. If this were to happen, he and Maria would be quarantined together, and he would have a chance to show Maria how much he cared for her. She would see that he was brave and dependable. She would, he felt sure, forget her German merchant and perhaps, when Niccolò returned, he – Andrea – might be able to ask for her hand in marriage. He gave little thought to the predicament of Daniele, whose life would be put in danger in the plague hospital. He had little regard for the young man, thinking him a fool with little ability. If he died, perhaps it would be as well. Then he and Maria would be married and he would become the important, learned figure that he had dreamed of becoming, a surrogate son to Niccolò with a beautiful and intelligent wife by his side. And so he set in motion a sequence of events that once begun could not be undone.

Maria returned from the apothecary later that afternoon with a salve made of carline, which was known to be helpful with skin conditions. She applied it carefully to Daniele's affected skin. She noticed that the eczema had spread a little and he had developed a small patch near his hairline. His forehead was also developing spots – painful and puss-filled. She applied a little of the salve to those to.

'Ow,' he said, pushing her hand away.

'I'm sorry Daniele, but this will help. The apothecary said it was the best thing.'

'Well, there's no need to rub.' Daniele's eyes filled with tears.

'Oh darling brother,' said Maria sitting down next to him and holding him closely. 'I'm so sorry that this has happened. But the apothecary was certain that we would be able to make it all go away. You need to get out in the sunshine as often as possible and

I shall make you a nice tisane each day to purify your liver. You'll see. You'll soon be better.'

'I am a monster,' muttered her brother.

'You are not a monster, my darling. You are a beautiful, handsome, brave boy.'

'I am an idiot,' said the boy.

'That is ridiculous, Daniele. Why would you say such a thing?'

'I am no good in the schoolroom. Why, even Andrea is quicker at learning than I am. Why am I so stupid? I cannot even read properly. I am fifteen, nearly sixteen. I would be better away from here. I belong on the sea, or travelling. I hate Venice; everyone here is interested in art or books. And I am no good at either.'

'Oh Daniele, when Papa gets back we will talk to him. Maybe you could be apprenticed to a merchant here. Would you like that?'

'Yes, oh yes, Maria! That would be the best way for me to live. I am not stupid, Maria.'

'I know that! You are bright and brave, my dearest brother. Don't be sad. I'm sure that we will make you well and everything will work out. You will see.'

The following morning, there was a loud knock on the door in the lane. Bella the maid went to the door. Before her stood two men dressed in dark cloaks. They wore masks over their mouths.

'We are here to see the master of the house.'

'He is not at home. He is abroad.'

'Who is in charge here?' asked the taller of the two men.

'My mistress, the master's daughter, Signorina Maria dei Conti,' replied Bella with as much dignity as she could muster. She did not like the tone of the two strangers. Besides, it was unusual for guests to arrive by the side door. It was customary for anyone of note to arrive by gondola at the front of the house. The side entrance was for tradesmen and the servants; she was understandably suspicious.

'Take us to her,' demanded the shorter of the two men.

'I will first go and ask if she is receiving visitors; wait here please,' said Bella and she attempted to push the door closed. But the taller man stuck his leather-clad boot between the door and the frame and pushed past the girl.

She chased after the men as they ran up the large oak stairs two at a time. They pushed open doors until they found Maria and Daniele sitting quietly on the window seat overlooking the canal.

'Mistress, I am sorry; these men just forced their way in,' gasped Bella, arriving a few seconds later.

Maria stood up to greet them, and Daniele leapt to his feet, ready to protect his sister. 'It is all right, Bella, thank you. Gentlemen, can I ask if you would like to sit down? I'm afraid my father is not at home.'

'So we understand,' said the taller man. 'I believe it is this young man that we are here to see.' He pointed at Daniele, who blushed and took a step back.

'My brother? Why should you be interested in him?' asked Maria.

'It has come to our attention that you are recently returned from the East. Is that correct?'

'Many weeks ago now, yes. We travelled from Alexandria with Captain Marco.'

'You were in Egypt, we understand.'

'Yes, that is correct. But who are…?'

'Where your mother, brother, sister and servants died… Of the plague.'

A flicker of alarm and comprehension seeped into Maria's mind.

'That is correct. But they passed away many, many months ago now. They were buried in Egypt.'

'Your brother…'

'Daniele?' said Maria, glancing anxiously at her brother.

'Yes, your brother Daniele would appear to have the marks of plague. We are here to remove him for examination.'

'What!' Maria exploded. 'What nonsense is this? My brother has a mild skin condition, which the apothecary is treating. He does not have the plague.'

'Are you a doctor?' asked the man imperiously.

'No, but …'

'Then you cannot know if he has the plague or not. I have with me a plague doctor.' He indicated the stocky man at his side. 'He will now examine your brother for signs of the illness.'

The examination was brief. The doctor, his mouth covered by a mask of dark cloth to prevent the *miasma*, or bad air, affecting him, turned Daniele's head this way and that studying the spots and the rash on his forehead. He asked the boy if he had other 'marks'. Daniele showed him his elbows. The doctor tutted and sighed before finally declaring to his companion:

'I cannot be sure, but there are sufficient signs here for alarm. He should be removed now.'

'What are you saying?' shouted Maria, standing between her brother and the two men.

'You will not take my brother anywhere. He is perfectly well. He just has a mild skin condition.'

'We have had the plague here for hundreds of years, *Signorina*. We know the signs. We had an outbreak just six years ago. You have recently returned from a plague area. Your own mother and family died of the disease. We have rules here in Venice that have enabled us to limit the spread of this disease for half a century. Your brother will be sent to the Lazzaretto Vecchio. If he survives for 40 days, he will then be moved to the Lazzaretto Nuovo to recover. He must take all his personal belongings with him. This house must be evacuated and all your goods must be quarantined at the Lazzaretto Nuovo, where they will be aired each day to ensure that any trace of the illness is removed. How many of you are in the house?'

'Myself, my brother, and our three servants.'

'You must all leave. I suggest you go and stay with friends or relations outside of Venice.'

'I have no relations or friends here – we have been brought up abroad.'

'Then you must come with us and must stay at the Lazzaretto Nuovo until you can be reunited with your brother.'

The rest of the day was a blur. Maria, distraught but endeavouring to be strong, begged the two officials not to separate her from her brother, but they were adamant that the rules could not be broken. The doctor cursorily examined Alfreda, Bella and Andrea and declared that they appeared to be disease-free.

'They may leave and go outside the city and stay with relatives, if they are able,' he declared at last. 'Otherwise they must come to the island with you.'

Bella began to sob. 'I will stay with you mistress. It is my duty,' she said bravely.

'No, Bella. You, Alfreda and Andrea must all go elsewhere. Daniele and I will be fine. We shall all be reunited, I am sure of it.'

'I will come with you,' said Andrea.

'No, Andrea; that is not necessary,' said Maria.

'Like you, I have no one outside Venice who can take me in,' he persisted. 'Besides, it will be my honour to come with you. I will protect you.'

The tall man, irritated by these protracted arrangements, sighed deeply. 'Well make your decisions quickly. You and your brother and this young man must go now. Your staff must pack up all your goods; they will be sent on after you, then they must leave. The house will be inspected and closed up once they have gone.'

'Please,' said Maria desperately, 'I must do something first. May I at least write to my father and explain what has happened?'

'Yes, very well. But be quick about it,' said the taller of the two men.

Maria rushed to Niccolò's study, where she wrote a note to her father.

My dearest Papa,

Something terrible has happened. Men have come to the house and have accused Daniele of having the plague. It is not true – but they believe it to be so. He and I are to be taken to an island – perhaps the island we saw as we arrived here that first day; do you remember? Oh, beloved father, please help us. Bella and Alfreda are to return to their homes in the country. But Andrea insists on coming with me. Papa, I shall take the vase, to help us. Do not be angry with me. Please rescue us, dearest father.

Your loving daughter, Maria.

Maria sealed the letter with wax and replaced it in the box. This time, she was careful to lock it, and hid the key at the back of a drawer of her father's writing table. It was pointless, really, given that all their goods were to be removed. She stood at his desk, and opened the large drawer in the centre where her father kept a cache of money. She took it all and stashed it in her pocket. She might need it for bribes on the island. Looking momentarily out of the window, she caught sight of Polisena working in the garden. She was picking artichokes and putting them into a large basket. Maria opened the casement and leant out.

'Polisena,' she called down, for once not caring if the older nuns heard her. 'Polisena…'

The nun looked up and ran across the garden to the window. 'Maria, I cannot be long.'

'I know. I'm sorry, but I have some terrible news. Please, will you find a way to tell Peter for me? I am to be taken with Daniele to the plague island.'

Polisena recoiled visibly, a look of horror on her face. 'Oh no!' she cried. The nuns were familiar with the hospital islands. Even those who were not directly involved in the care of the sick understood how dangerous they were.

'But you are not unwell, are you?' she asked.

'No, and neither is Daniele; it is a mistake, but we are powerless. I have written to my father, but please tell Peter. I do not wish him to think I do not care – that I have just disappeared. Tell him… Tell him that I love him.'

'I will tell him. And I will pray for you both Maria – with all my heart.'

Maria heard footsteps outside the study door.

'Hurry in there; time is running out,' the man spoke gruffly.

'I'm coming,' she called out. 'Just one moment, please.'

She crossed over to the shelf where her father kept the Ming vase. The dragon's blue eyes stared back at her as if to say, 'I will keep you safe. The dragon will protect you.' She took it down carefully, feeling it cool and comforting beneath her trembling fingers, and wrapped it in a rug that her father kept on the back of his chair. She took it to her bedchamber, where Bella was rapidly packing some clothes into a bag.

'Here, Bella – put the vase into the bag. Hide it under my clothes.'

The girl did as she was told, and tearfully bid farewell to Maria.

CHAPTER 9

Poveglia

'The Lazzaretto Vecchio seemed like Hell itself. From every side there came foul odours, indeed a stench that none could endure; groans and sighs were heard without ceasing; and at all hours clouds of smoke from the burning of corpses were seen to rise far into the air. Some who miraculously returned from that place alive reported, among other things, that at the height of that great influx of infected people there were three and four of them to a bed. Since a great number of servants had died and there was no one to take care of them, they had to get themselves up to take food and attend to other things. Nobody did anything but lift the dead from the beds and throw them into the pits... And many, driven to frenzy by the disease, especially at night, leapt from their beds, and, shouting with fearful voices of damned souls, went here and there, colliding with one another, and suddenly falling to the ground dead. Some who rushed in frenzy out of the wards threw themselves into the water, or ran madly through the gardens, and were then found dead among the thorn bushes, all covered with blood.'

From an account of the plague epidemic of 1575-7
by a Venetian notary, Rocco Benedetti, 1630

As the small boat set off from the pier at San Marco, Maria looked back at the beautiful Piazza, rose-gold, apricot and pink in the early evening light; she made a silent promise to herself. 'We will survive, and we will see this place again.' She clung tightly to Daniele's hand. They sat in the prow of the boat and gazed towards the city, their backs to the tiny island of Poveglia, somewhere out there, unknown, threatening in the lagoon. They could not bring themselves to face it; not yet. Gradually the city transformed into a thin sliver hovering on the horizon; the sea became choppy and the boatman struggled to hold the boat steady. On any other day Daniele would have leapt up cheerfully to help the man, delighted to be able to demonstrate his strength, grateful for the exercise. But he sat, paralysed with fear at what was unfolding.

Andrea sat opposite the pair, looking towards their destination. He too felt fear, but it was more of an anxiety of anticipation, mixed with a curious excitement. Would his plan work? Would Maria be grateful to him for his loyalty? Would she, could she, be made to love him?

The journey took longer than they had expected; the island was several miles out into the lagoon, beyond Malamocco. The sea became rougher as they travelled on; the boat rocked and bucked as the billowing water broke over the bow, leaving a fine sticky film of salty dampness on the passengers' clothing. Maria and Daniele began to feel nauseous.

'I feel sick,' said Daniele to his sister.

'I know,' she said helplessly. 'Try to take a deep breath of air.'

As she attempted to breathe through the nausea, Daniele leant over the side of the boat and vomited. He tasted fear mixed with the salt of the sea, bile and bitterness. His mind was numb. He could not understand how such a terrible mistake had been made. He knew he did not have the plague. He had watched as his mother, brother and sister had suffered with it, and knew what they went through as they died. He felt sure that he did not have this terrible illness. Somehow this nightmare must come to an end. He could not, surely, be taken to this dreadful island and left to die.

Maria clutched his hand in hers and spoke gently to him throughout the journey. 'You will be all right, little brother. You are strong. Remember to do as Papa did and cover your mouth at all times. Here, let me show you. Take the end of your turban like this and tie it across your face, as Papa did. I asked Bella to put two clean lengths of cloth in your bag. Change them often and try to find some way of washing them. Do not breathe the air of another person if they are unwell. Do not share food with anyone. Do you understand? Alfreda packed some food in your bag. Eat that. Do not eat anything they give you. Oh my dearest, I would do anything to be with you and protect you.'

Daniele sat mute, listening and yet unable to hear. He began to weep, silently.

Maria turned to the boatman. 'You – boatman. Do you know where each of us is to be taken?'

The boatman took his eyes off the horizon for a second and took in the beautiful girl, her blue eyes almost a match for the incongruously clear blue sky above.

'Two of you for the *Nuovo*, one for the *Vecchio*,' he said matter-of-factly. 'The lad, there – he's for the *Vecchio*.'

Daniele's weeping turned to sobbing.

'My brother… He is not strong. I would like to go with him, to look after him.'

'You'll not be wanting to do that,' said the boatman, keeping his eyes steadfastly on the sea ahead. 'You're to go to the *Nuovo* with this other here.'

'There has been a change of plan. It cannot matter to you where I go. It is my choice. I wish to go with my brother.'

'I'm not sure about that,' said the boatman. 'My orders is to take two of you to the *Nuovo*.'

Maria reached into her pocket and removed six ducats; it was more than six months' wages to the boatman. 'Here take this; does that make it easier to forget your orders?'

The boatman looked at the money suspiciously. Maria laid the coins carefully at his feet in case he was fearful of touching her hand.

He picked them up and slipped them beneath his cape, revealing a dagger in his belt. He was clearly under orders not to let them escape.

'Two for the *Vecchio* then,' was all he said.

Andrea, on hearing this exchange, was in a blind panic. This was a disaster. This was not part of the plan. Maria must stay with him on the other island, where there was no illness. Daniele alone must be taken to the plague island. His mind was struggling with how to deal with this development. Finally he said, 'Maria... I do not think this wise.' He spoke quietly, his voice almost drowned out by the wind. 'The boatman might take you, but surely they will not let you stay there. You are to go to the other island with me. Once Daniele is free of the disease he will be sent to join us. That is the plan.'

Maria stared at Andrea. 'Plan? What do you mean?'

'Oh, well that's what the doctor told us at the house. That is what he said must happen.'

'Well, I do not care what the doctor said. I do not believe he was even a doctor. I intend to stay with my brother. That is my duty; to protect him. You must do as you see fit, Andrea.'

'But Maria... You might catch the illness. Surely you will not take that risk?'

'My brother might catch the illness. You know as well as I that there is nothing wrong with him. This is all a terrible mistake. If he must take the risk, then so will I. I would do anything to protect my brother,' she said firmly.

Daniele gazed at her bewildered. 'But Maria, Andrea is right. Please, remain on the other island and protect yourself. I could not bear for you to get ill. Please.'

'*Cara*, did our father desert our mother in her last hour? Did he leave Magdalena and Dario? No, he was with them to the end. But remember this: he took precautions and survived. And so will I, and so will you.' She held Daniel's face between her hands and kissed his forehead.

Andrea knew that he should offer to stay with the pair. His plan depended on Maria understanding how much he cared for her. But when faced with the prospect of almost certain death, his courage faltered. He sat silently, staring out to sea, nausea rising in his throat, as the realisation of what he had set in motion enveloped him like a dark, terrible storm.

The boatman steered the boat expertly towards the island. The sun shone brightly and the hospital and its neighbouring church glowed rose-red against the sparkling blue sky. The gardens of the house were wild and unkempt, but Maria took some comfort that there would be berries to eat there perhaps, or a shady corner where she and Daniele might shelter. But as they drew closer, she saw that the garden was, in fact, just a tangle of thorny bushes and scrubland.

The boatman was paid well to transport patients to Poveglia. However, he would not risk touching his passengers, and so could not help them from the boat. But he was not a cruel man and took care to bring his boat up alongside the stone jetty and threw a rope fore and aft to hold the boat steady.

Andrea, filled now with a mixture of fear and remorse, was the first to speak. 'Is this it? The Lazzaretto Vecchio?'

'It is.'

'And the Lazzaretto Nuovo?'

'Over there. It is the smaller island of the two. I shall take you there once these two have been left here.'

Andrea unloaded the bags onto the jetty for Maria and Daniele, all the while agonising as to how to proceed. To stay, or go? He felt sick with indecision, appalled at the prospect of remaining in this hellhole, but equally distraught at the missed opportunity of convincing Maria of his undying love. Maria stepped gracefully off the boat first, climbing determinedly up the stone steps and onto the jetty. She got to the top and held her hand out to Daniele.

'Come, brother. Come with me.' He followed her obediently, in a daze, still struggling to understand how they had come to this.

As the two stood on the jetty, their bags at their feet, she looked down at Andrea.

'Well, are you coming? Or going?'

She had sensed his despair as they travelled from the city and was perplexed by it. There was no need for him to remain with them.

'I... I...'

'Andrea – go the *Nuovo*. With luck we will see you there in forty days. Maybe you can get word to Papa; that is the best way you can serve us now.'

And with that, the boatman released the ropes and pushed off from the jetty with his oar. The boat floated round in front of the main building. Andrea looked back at the pair as they picked up their bags and walked the twenty yards towards the studded oak door of the hospital. Maria stood erect, her brother weeping slightly. She put her arms around him and he saw her say something to the boy, but their voices were drowned out by the wind. Andrea held his hand up to wave, but Maria was not looking in his direction. She was gazing up at the hospital. He saw her cross herself, and within minutes she was out of sight as the boatman steered their boat round the side of the island and out into the open sea towards the smaller island that housed the Lazzaretto Nuovo.

CHAPTER 10

Niccolò meets Peter

Niccolò received Maria's letter six days after she had sent it. He had been in Florence for over five weeks, and his work with the scholar Poggio Bracciolini was nearing completion. He had dictated a long and thorough memoir – although Bracciolini chose neither to enquire about, nor record Niccolò's perceptions of the places he had visited, nor his motivation. He was interested solely in the facts: the countries he had visited; the length of rivers; the animals he had seen; the customs he had witnessed. The memoir would be published under the title '*Historia de Varietate Fortunae*' (A History on the Vicissitudes of Fortune) and dedicated to Pope Nicholas V.

Later, this work would be the inspiration for the Genoese map maker Fra Mauro, who depicted the old world as a beautiful ovoid shape, much like an eye, who took many of the location names and descriptions from dei Conti's account, describing him as 'a trustworthy source'.

Referred to by subsequent writers as 'The Man from Cathay', dei Conti wrote of the vast Chinese junks that were two thousand tons, with five sails and masts, and three decks separated into different compartments. He impressed with tales of the beauty and industry of the people of further India, and of the marble bridges that straddled their rivers and their great wealth from gold, silver, gems and spices. He suggested that the 'Latins' should visit this country and experience for themselves the impressive nature of their philosophy, astrology and art.

'*Civility increases the more one moves inwards,*' he wrote, *'the inhabitants of the further India being, by repute, most polite, wealthy, humane and refined.*'

When he read Maria's letter he was filled with dread. He went at once to visit Bracciolini. 'I must leave Florence, my friend,' he said. 'I have troubles at home and must travel to Venice to make arrangements. God willing, I shall return and we shall continue our work.'

Bracciolini wished him Godspeed, and accompanied by his servants, Mattheo and Vincenzo, Niccolò rode out of Florence that night. Their journey was one hundred and sixty miles. If they managed twenty-five miles a day, it would take them nearly a week to get back. Desperate to rescue his daughter and son, Niccolò was determined to get to Venice as soon as possible. He drove the horses and his servants hard. They arrived in Venice barely five days later, to find the house locked and deserted.

He went at once to the Council and demanded to know what had happened and where his children had been taken.

'What evidence was there of plague?' he asked.

'The boy had marks on his face, arms and legs – suppurating sores, they appeared to be.'

'And my daughter?'

'She appeared well, and was taken to the Lazaretto Nuovo, with one of your servants, I believe.'

'And how did you come to notice my son and his "suppurating sores?"' Niccolò asked.

'It was reported; that is all I can say. Someone told us that they had their suspicions. We sent our inspectors and they confirmed it.'

Niccolò racked his brains, trying to work out who amongst their acquaintances would have 'reported' such a thing.

'And how long will they remain there?' Niccolò asked the official.

'Some forty days in the *Vecchio*, and then another thirty on the *Nuovo* – seventy in all – as long as they stay alive, of course.'

'You know as well as I do that if he was not ill when he arrived, he almost certainly will be by the time he leaves... If he ever gets to leave at all.' Niccolò sat, his head in his hands. Finally, he stood. 'I need to get into my house,' he said.

'No, the house is quarantined – also for forty days. You may enter once again in a little over a month's time; as soon as we are sure that any trace of the disease has been eliminated.'

Niccolò wanted to argue with them, to shout and scream, 'My children are well, and you are probably going to kill them with your meddling.' But he knew well enough that nothing could be achieved by arguing. The decision had been taken and he must abide by it. He would have to find some other way of helping Maria and Daniele.

He found temporary lodgings in a *taverna* near the Piazza San Marco and slept fitfully that night. The following morning, he walked to his house down the lane that led past the convent. He stood at the side door and pushed, more in hope than anticipation, wishing it to open. But it was locked, and there were strong wooden barriers nailed across the door barring entry. A tall young man with blond hair, who had been hovering in the lane nearby, approached him.

'Excuse me, *Signor*,' he said to Niccolò. 'Forgive me, but do you know the family that live in this house?'

'I do – and well. I live in this house – or at least I did. Why?'

'Are you Maria dei Conti's father?'

'I am.'

'Sir, I am a friend of your daughter... A good friend. She sent me a message telling me what had happened to her. I presume that is why you are returned? She told me that you were in Florence.'

Niccolò looked up at the man in some surprise.

'You appear to know much of my business and that of my daughter.'

'Sir, please. I mean no harm. I am a merchant too, as you are. I come from Nuremberg. I was recently introduced to your daughter.' The young man paused.

'Go on,' said Niccolò.

'Sir, I seek only to help her and her brother. I know that they have been taken in error. I am sure there is nothing wrong with Daniele. It is all a terrible mistake. I am here to help you, Sir. To offer you any assistance.'

The two men retreated to the *taverna* on the Piazza and Peter told Niccolò all that he knew of Maria and Daniele's predicament.

'I know she wrote you a letter. She has become friends with a young nun in the convent over there.' He gestured towards San Zaccaria.

'Yes,' said Niccolò. 'She mentioned her to me in one of her letters – Polisena, isn't it?'

'Yes, Polisena. She is the friend of a friend of mine. She is there against her will, if you understand?'

'I do Peter. I understand well. But what of her?'

'Maria spoke to her as she was being taken away, I understand. It was fortunate that she was working in the garden that day. She said it was all a terrible mistake and asked Polisena to make sure that I knew, so that I could help her.'

'Maria must have great faith in you,' said Niccolò.

'I certainly hope so. Sir, I am willing to try to rescue her – if you will allow it.'

'That surely would be impossible,' said Niccolò darkly.

'No, I do not think so. I have been making enquiries about this island.'

'Poveglia?'

'Yes. It is a boat ride away. I can row a boat. Surely we can rescue them both.'

'Well, I admire your bravery. But even if we could rescue them, and I am doubtful, what then? They will be tracked down in Venice and returned to the island immediately. The authorities take any suggestion of the plague very seriously.'

'Yes, well, I agree that it is a complex problem. But I have a solution.'

'Go on.'

'Sir, I love your daughter, and I believe she loves me. I give you my word that I have not dishonoured her in any way, but just a few days ago, we discussed marriage. She was concerned that she has no dowry, or at least was not sure if she did. But I do not care, Sir. She is the most remarkable woman I have ever met. I am a merchant from Germany. My family – we do not require any dowry. We are successful. Besides, I'm sure my father would be delighted to know that you are also a merchant. He has always wanted our family to be united with another great mercantile family. I am sure I can persuade my father. And if you would allow us to marry, I would take her straightway to live with me in the north, far from here. I would take her brother too – if you would allow it. She has often mentioned that he yearns for a more active life. I could take him into my business, Sir, and care for him.'

Niccolò sat quietly through Peter's speech. 'You take a lot on your young shoulders, Peter Haas.'

'I am ready for it, believe me.'

They sat in silence for a few minutes, before Niccolò spoke again. 'I have spent the last twenty-five years travelling the world. I have seen and done many things – things that would amaze you, Peter. I have met Emperors and Princes: men of extraordinary wealth and power; who married hundreds of wives – women who must be burned alive when their husband dies. I have seen all manner of wild animals and strange creatures. I have travelled by sea, and on land. I have studied languages and religions. And

I was married to a beautiful woman from the land of India. I had four children with my wife and lost two of them, and her, to plague in Egypt. I returned to Venice hoping to live peacefully until my death with my two remaining children. But the truth is that my children are travellers, as I have been. They have lived all over the world and travelled from the moment they were born. They have only known adventure. They are both brave and capable. If my daughter truly loves you and wishes to marry you, then who am I to prevent it? And as for my son, I know that he struggles with life here in Venice. He misses his active life on the road.

'Of one thing, I am certain. If I leave him on Poveglia for forty days, he will almost certainly die. Maria will probably survive on the quarantine island, if she is there. But I know my daughter, and what I fear is that she will have gone with Daniele. She would not let him face that on his own. So, young Peter Haas, let us rescue them, for they will not survive on that island, full as it is of illness and depravity. But I beg you, do not betray me. If we do this, you must take them away from here. If you go back on your word, I will never forgive you.'

'We will not fail; and I will not betray you, sir. You have my word – my merchant's bond.'

CHAPTER 11

The Island

Maria and Daniele knocked on the old oak door of the hospital. After a few minutes, they heard a rasping, rattling cough, as a woman – grey-haired and dishevelled, in filthy clothes – opened the door.

She took in the two well-dressed young people standing on the doorstep. Both were tall and attractive; neither showing any signs of illness. The girl wore a long dark blue gown over a linen *camicetta*. Her dark hair was covered by a turban of rich dark red silk and, over it all, a dark cloak of the finest wool cloth. The boy, a head taller than his sister, also fashionably turbaned, was wearing dark red hose, with a sage green *coppia* held in place with a narrow leather belt.

'Well, you're a fine sight,' said the woman, looking the young people up and down.

Maria and Daniele glanced nervously at one another.

'You'd better come with me,' was all she said, before leading them up two flights of stone stairs to the top of the house. Judging by her appearance, she was neither a nurse, nor a nun; she was simply a serving woman who had survived more by luck than judgement, and now appeared to be in sole control of over two hundred sick and dying patients.

As the old woman opened the door to the ward, Daniele gasped. Rows of beds stretched away from them, with two or three patients to a bed. The bed linen was filthy; the patients' clothing in tatters. The stench of humanity was overwhelming, in spite of the fact that several of the high, barred windows had been opened. The bedlam on the ward was so at odds with the glorious sunny day outside that Maria could hardly take in what she was seeing.

'These people are in a terrible state,' she said sharply to the woman.

'So they are, and what did you expect?'

'And where are we to sleep?' Maria asked incredulously.

'There's a bed there – in the middle. It's just been emptied,' said the woman.

'Emptied?' said Maria.

'They were taken away an hour or more back.'

Maria cast an anxious glance at Daniele. 'And you expect us to sleep in that bed, in those sheets, where people have just died?'

'It's there, or the floor,' said the woman.

Maria took a coin out of her pocket and showed it to the woman. 'There is more where that came from if you find us a bed next to the wall and remove all the sheets. I have brought our own bed linen and will change it myself.'

The woman eyed the coin and snatched it from Maria's hand before marching into the ward. She dragged the bed down to the far end, and tore the soiled linen off it, throwing it onto the floor.

'There… Happy now?' she asked.

Maria and Daniele walked down the centre of the ward. As they passed each bed, bony hands reached out to them begging for help.

'I am cold… Help me?' asked one.

'Water… Please…' pleaded another.

A young man clutched at his stomach before vomiting violently. He tried to lean over the edge of the bed, but the putrid mess spewed over the sheet and onto his flimsy nightshirt. He sank back onto the soiled mattress, apparently unaware of the filth in which he was now lying.

The patients were in various states of sickness. Most appeared to be suffering from the bubonic form of the disease; the skin on their necks, armpits or groins erupted with vast boils the size of eggs; boils that appeared to be black but were actually due to bleeding beneath the skin. In spite of herself, Maria was revolted at the sight of these poor unfortunate people.

At their allotted bed, Maria took out the sheets that Alfreda and Bella had thoughtfully packed for them. She made up the bed, fighting back tears, desperately trying to remain in control for Daniele, who stood, his back to the wall, staring in horror at the people with whom they would spend the following forty days.

'Daniele,' she said to him, 'look out of the window. You can see the sky from our bed. The clouds are beautiful today. Look… See?'

But he could not hear her. He stood quite transfixed, unable to move.

The bed made up, she guided him to sit on the edge, facing the wall.

'Look Daniele. . . at the sky. . . out there. That is what you must concentrate on. Would you like something to eat? Alfreda has packed some delicious cheese and bread.'

He shook his head.

The serving woman returned to the ward with a bowl of water and began, ineffectually, to mop up the vomit on the floor. She muttered as she worked. The young man who had been sick raised his head from his soiled pillow and begged her for water to drink.

'I have water, but it's not for drinking, you filthy devil. Look at this mess you've made.'

Daniele, overhearing this exchange, rose indignantly to his feet. 'Get that boy some water,' he demanded. 'He is sick, he cannot help it.'

The woman looked at Daniele with such hatred that he physically recoiled. He sat back down on the bed next to his sister. But he found his courage again. 'Where is the water?' he demanded. 'I shall bring him some.'

Maria clutched at his arm: 'Daniele, no!'

'I cannot sit here and watch this,' he said.

He strode decisively between the row of beds and down the stairs. On the floor below, he passed two other wards, one on either side of the staircase, each containing as many sick and dying people as the ward above – all of them begging for help, crying, vomiting. He ran down the stairs two at a time now, and rushed over to the front door, yanking it open. He inhaled the clean, salty air that blew in off the lagoon, breathing in deeply.

Returning to the house, he found what passed for a kitchen: a dingy space at the back with a large fire in the grate – long since extinguished. There was a well in one corner with a pump. He took a wooden bowl from a shelf and pumped the water out of the well, filling the bowl. He grabbed two small ceramic cups and returned to the ward, where he ladled water into the mouths of the thirsty patients.

Maria, overwhelmed by his generosity of spirit and bravery, rushed across to him and quickly tore the turban off his head and wrapped it around his mouth. She did the same with her own turban, freeing a length long enough to tie around her face; she also took a cup and went round the ward, helping the patients to drink.

Returning to the kitchen, the pair searched for provisions. There was a crust of bread on the table, blue with mould. A pot of what might have once been gruel lay solidifying near the fire. In a cupboard near the fireplace, Maria found a sack of rice and another of barley. There were a few onions, but little more.

Daniele went outside into the garden and found some pieces of wood to light the fire. An old man appeared as he gathered the wood into his arms.

'What are you doing there?' he demanded of the young man.

'Gathering wood of course – to light a fire,' Daniele said defiantly. The man was frail, older even than his own father. He was bent over with arthritis. He was no threat to the tall healthy boy who stood boldly before him. 'What is your job here?' he asked the old man.

'I bury them,' said the old man darkly. 'Over there, behind the hedge, in the pit.'

Daniele swallowed hard and turned his back on the man.

The old serving woman returned to the kitchen and stared at the two young people, as Maria pumped water from the well and attempted to clean the kitchen whilst Daniele laid wood in the fireplace.

'What are you doing?' demanded the woman indignantly.

'I am trying to cook some food for those poor people up there,' replied Maria.

The woman stared at the pair suspiciously. 'Why are you here? You don't look sick.'

'There has been a mistake,' answered Maria. 'Now pump that well and fill that bowl with water. And light that fire. We need to get some hot water and cook some food for the patients who are well enough to eat.'

The woman shrugged her shoulders and did as she was told, apparently grateful to be relieved of the responsibility of caring for two hundred sick people.

While Maria cleaned the kitchen and cooked up some of the rice with a little of the onion, Daniele went from bed to bed offering water and comfort where he could. He found that he was quite unafraid. He clung to the belief that the turban wrapped round his mouth would protect him. It had protected his father and it would do the same for him.

Once the patients had all been offered water and food, Maria suggested to the serving woman that they begin to wash the linen. 'If a patient dies, their sheets should be removed and boiled up over the fire, ready for a new patient.'

The old woman looked doubtful, but did as she was told. As sheets hung on a line to dry, Maria and Daniele went outside into the garden and sat on the edge of the jetty looking longingly out to sea. As they removed their masks and allowed the sunshine to warm their faces, they could see distant fishing boats, even the occasional galleon sailing towards Malamocco.

'Why can't we just leave here?' said Daniele. 'Perhaps we could attract attention somehow, and get one of those boats to come and rescue us.'

'*Cara*, they all know this is the plague island. Who would come to help us? No, we are here until the boatman comes and take us to the Lazzaretto Nuovo. We must resign ourselves to that and just endure it. But Daniele, I am proud of you for standing up to that horrible old woman. You were right. If we must be here, then at least we can try to help. But we must be vigilant, and keep our faces covered at all times in there. Do you promise me?'

Later that night, their work finished, they returned to their ward and lay down exhausted on their bed.

Daniele was asleep within seconds. Maria lay gazing at the moon, dreaming of Peter, and of their home on the Rio dei Greci. She was startled from her thoughts by the appearance of an old woman patient who had been in the bed near the door and asleep when they arrived. She shuffled towards Maria.

'What do you want?' she asked the old woman, grabbing her mask and pulling it up over her face. She tried to pull Daniele's mask over his face too, but he moaned in his sleep and turned away from her towards the wall.

'We are trying to sleep. Please leave us alone.'

The woman didn't move. 'How did you come to be here?' she asked. 'There's nothing wrong with either of you. You must have made some terrible enemies.'

'There has been a mistake,' said Maria. 'But I'm sure it will be rectified and with luck we will be leaving soon.'

'Ha! Don't bank on it,' said the woman. 'I've been here forty days. I had the pestilence, but it's gone now and I'm off to the *Nuovo* tomorrow. But there's many who don't manage it. I've seen over a hundred people die while I've been here.'

'That's terrible,' said Maria.

'Do you know what they do with them?'

'What do you mean?' asked Maria.

'When they die?'

Maria shook her head.

'They throw them in a pit – out there in the garden – there's no burial for 'em. No priest comes near. Hell and damnation, that's all they can hope for.'

'I'm sure you must be mistaken,' said Maria.

'I'll show you if you like? Before I leave tomorrow – if you don't believe me.'

'No,' said Maria. 'Thank you. Now please, leave us, we need to get some sleep.'

'You've got some nice clothes,' said the woman, eyeing Maria's bags that lay at the end of the bed.

'We really don't have much with us,' said Maria, pulling the bags closer to her. 'Just some spare underclothes.'

'Hmm,' said the woman as she shuffled back to her bed.

Unable to sleep, Maria lay with her hand clutching at their belongings. She had no real interest in whether the woman stole her clothes, or even some of their food. But she was in terror of someone stealing the vase. It was their talisman, their only protection. If they lost the vase, they themselves would be lost.

Earlier that morning, Maria had discovered that there was a loose stone in the wall near their bed. She had pulled it aside quietly and found a void behind. Maria waited until the old woman had finally fallen asleep and was snoring loudly, her dress pulled up over her naked body. She then began to chip as quietly as possible at the wall. She removed a second stone, and then a third. At last, she had a space large enough in which to hide the vase. She took it out of the bag, still wrapped in her father's blanket. She held the blanket to her face and inhaled the heady scent of wool mixed with leather from his chair. She placed the blanket back in the bag and then pushed the vase into the void. She put the little bag of money she had taken from her father's desk in there too before carefully replacing the stones. They were not quite as flush with the wall as they had been, which worried her. Someone might be clever enough to work out that they had been moved. She took an old wooden chair that sat in the corner of the ward and silently moved it in front of the hiding place.

Exhausted, she closed her eyes and fell into a deep sleep.

She woke in the night and was instantly alert. Perhaps it was the light of the full moon gleaming brightly through the high barred window, or the scuffling sound as the old woman from the far end of the ward crouched beneath their bed, rummaging amongst their belongings.

'What are you doing there?' demanded Maria.

The woman leapt back, clutching a piece of cheese in her grubby fist, stolen from Alfreda's picnic. 'I'm hungry,' the woman whined. 'I've not eaten for days, and you've got all that food.'

'Take it and go,' said Maria. 'But do not think you can steal from us again. I shall be watching you.'

The woman took her prize and retreated to her bed, where she stowed it at the foot beneath her foul sheet.

Her heart pounding, Maria lay watchful and wide awake for the rest of the night. She was grateful that she had hidden the vase, but fearful that the woman may have seen her. Slowly, as the moon descended, the few birds that survived on Poveglia began their morning chorus. A blackbird took up its position on a tall chestnut tree just outside her window. He broke into a song

– so beautiful, so full of longing, that Maria lay for a few moments, her eyes closed, imagining herself in Peter's arms, as her father smiled down upon them.

She must have slept for a few minutes, or perhaps longer. When she woke again she looked up at the soft blue sky, glimpsed through the bars of the high window.

A cloud blew in from the lagoon, its shape swirling and changing. Was it a snake, its scales mirrored in the high cirrus cloud? The form changed with the high winds; it grew a leg, then two, floating down from its body. She heard the rustle of trees in the unseen garden below as the wind gusted suddenly. The cloud continued its journey past her window until she saw now that it had metamorphosed into something quite different. Her hand scrabbled at the rough-hewn stone wall. She eased a section out and laid it silently on the floor; there stood the vase hidden in a small niche. Her fingers touched the dragon that snaked its way around the centre and she looked again at the cloud. The head – for there was indeed a head now – gazed down at her with benevolent eyes, before a sudden gust of wind blew it onwards and out of her eyeline. The dragon had been looking down on her...

CHAPTER 12

Rescue

Confined to the Lazaretto Nuovo, Andrea was in a state of utter desolation. Surrounded by a motley crew of recovering patients, he was unable to rid himself of the realisation that he had made a terrible mistake – firstly by setting the plan in motion, and secondly, by not accompanying Maria to the Lazaretto Vecchio, however terrifying a prospect that was. His fear of death now seemed pathetic and pitiful compared to the lost opportunity of remaining with Maria and proving how much he loved her. The family's goods had been sent over the morning after he had been deposited and were now 'airing' in a large warehouse on the island. Andrea had been allotted a bed on one of the wards for recovering patients. It was not full. There were approximately fifty beds, but less than half were inhabited. Clearly, not everyone made it to the Lazaretto Nuovo. The hospital generally appeared to be quite well run; food was provided once a day and the sheets on which he slept appeared tolerably clean. There were quite a number of staff living and working there – the warehouseman, guards, two nurses – and a doctor had made a visit earlier that morning; he had been brought over by boat from the mainland, but had left by the afternoon.

Andrea thought constantly of Maria and wondered if she ever thought of him at all. He was permitted to exercise in the hospital gardens and went there most days. They were not well kept, but there were some large trees, a patch of scrubby grass and even a few flowers near the hospital building. One morning, as he went for his daily walk, he encountered an old man tending to a rose bush, deadheading the spent flowers and cutting back long trailing branches.

'Have you been here long?' Andrea asked the old man.

'Nigh on twenty years,' said the man.

'Really! All that time, here?' Andrea was amazed.

'I was a patient on the *Vecchio* during the last bad bout of pestilence. I was sent here to recover and never left. It suits me here. I've got no family of my own.'

'Do they have a boat here?' asked Andrea as casually as he could.

'No,' said the old man firmly. 'So don't you be getting any ideas of leaving.'

'No, no I wasn't,' said Andrea hurriedly.

'You must wait till the boatman comes. The doctors will tell you when you can go back.'

'Yes, of course they will.'

He wandered off, battling his way through the woodland, until he came upon patch of scrubby grass that led down to the shoreline. He was now at the back of the hospital and as he gazed out to sea, he realised he could see the other island that housed the Lazaretto Vecchio. The islands were nearly a mile apart, but the hospital was still visible. He could see a faint trace of smoke drifting up from the chimney on the roof. So a fire had been lit. A guard walked towards him. 'Don't get any ideas,' he said.

'What do you mean?'

'Of swimming off. If you go that way you'll only land up on the plague island. And trust me, you don't want to go there. If you go in the other direction, you're miles from anywhere. No one has ever managed to swim away from here. A few have tried, but they've all drowned.'

'Oh, don't worry about me,' said Andrea hastily. 'I can't swim anyway... Never have been able to.'

The guard walked off saying, 'Just mind you don't try it. The water's treacherous here.'

It was laughable... Even the idea of Andrea trying to swim away. He recalled his uncle guffawing at him when he first arrived in Venice as a young boy, sent by his father to be apprenticed.

'You can't swim?' his uncle had said. 'How do you expect to be a fisherman if you can't swim?'

He cuffed the child around the head and went back to his nets.

Andrea knew then that he would never be a fisherman. He had no interest in anything to do with the sea. He despised fish, and loathed his uncle. He was appalled at the prospect of spending his life trawling for fish, cleaning them, gutting them. He was a boy with ambition. He was interested in study, in science, mathematics and philosophy. He should have been born to a man like Niccolò dei Conti – a man of learning and imagination – who could see his potential. Not for the first time, he felt a kind of fury that he had been born to the wrong family. He deserved to live with Niccolò and Maria. They were his destiny, he was sure of it.

But now, standing and staring at the island where the woman he loved languished, he wished most fervently that he could swim. If he were able to reach Maria and show her how much he cared, she would be bound to love him.

Peter and Niccolò had arranged to meet in the late afternoon at the *cantina* near the Rialto. The sun was setting, creating a dark amber glow that reflected off the water of the Grand Canal, and the market stalls were beginning to pack up their produce for the day. Peter was keen to introduce Niccolò to someone who could help them.

'Giovanni is a friend of mine. He's a merchant too; and he is in love with Polisena.'

'I intend to marry her,' said Giovanni firmly to Niccolò.

The older man smiled faintly.

'Yes, yes,' said Peter impatiently. 'We don't have time to hear about your love for Polisena. We are here to plan how to rescue Maria and Daniele.' He spoke quickly and quietly, anxious not to be overheard.

'Yes, of course, Peter,' said Giovanni hurriedly. 'Forgive me, sir. But Peter helped me so much – in my pursuit of Polisena – I would do anything for him.'

'Good,' said Niccolò. 'I believe that he is about to ask for that favour to be returned.'

It was obviously impossible to hire a boatman to simply take them to the island and rescue Maria and Daniele. Poveglia was well known as the Plague Island, and no boatman would deliberately flout the law and take people there. Not only would they risk imprisonment, but they were too fearful of what they would catch if they went ashore. The only solution was for Peter and Niccolò to row their own boat out into the lagoon.

'I have a gondola moored at our house,' said Niccolò. 'We can use that. But it will take at least two men to row the boat that distance. I am not as strong as I once was, and I fear that we need some help.'

'Then I am your man,' said Giovanni immediately.

'It is not without risk, my friend,' said Peter. 'What we are doing is illegal. And the boat is not large. It is just a normal domestic gondola. The sea can get rough out there in the lagoon.'

'My friend,' said Giovanni to Peter, 'you have helped me to visit Polisena for the last four months, and she has finally agreed to run away with me. I owe you my entire happiness. How on earth could I desert you now?'

'It will be complicated when we get there too,' said Peter. 'We do not know what we will find, or where Maria and Daniele are being held. Maria may well be on the other island – the Lazaretto Nuovo. I am pretty sure that their servant Andrea is there, but we will have to see when we arrive. I do not know how the patients are guarded either. We must be prepared for anything. And we must go tonight. We cannot risk leaving them for a day longer than we need to. They have already endured two weeks in that terrible place.'

The three men took a small stock of provisions and armed themselves with two daggers and a sword. They walked along the back streets until they arrived at the lane that led down to the Rio dei Greci. As they passed the high walls of the convent of San Zaccaria, Giovanni blew a kiss to his beloved Polisena. At the bottom of the lane, a barrier had been erected, preventing anyone from getting round to the front of Niccolò's house via the jetty that protruded into the canal. Giovanni lifted Peter up and he jumped over the barrier before deftly leaping onto the jetty and from there onto the dei Conti gondola. He unhooked the ropes fore and aft and pushed the gondola off, sailing it down the canal in the moonlight. Niccolò and Giovanni then walked swiftly back up the lane and down onto the Riva degli Schiavoni. As soon as they saw Peter, they leapt aboard the gondola and together Giovanni and Peter fell into a rhythmic motion, rowing the gondola out into the moonlit lagoon.

It was a still night, at the end of September. The autumn storms had not yet rolled up from the Adriatic. As they rowed out, past the Isola di San Giorgio Maggiore, the sea became rougher, the waves breaking over the prow of the gondola. The dolphin attached to the prow dipped and bowed in the waves as the two men rowed firmly on. Niccolò looked back at the city.

They were making slow progress. At this rate, they would take many hours to reach the island.

Andrea lay wide-awake in his bed, the moonlight streaming in through the window. He had been unable to sleep and all around him men dozed, snuffling and snoring. One of the three women in his ward moaned slightly. He had come to a decision that afternoon. He must try to get to Maria, however fearful he might be of the sea, and of the plague. She was across the water from him; he could see the island from the window near his bed, and it tormented him to think of her imprisoned there, with no one to protect her but her pathetic brother. He could not swim across to her, so a boat was the only possible answer. The gardener had told him there were no boats on the island, but Andrea was convinced that there must be some form of transport. How else could they collect provisions?

He slipped out of bed and, holding his boots in his hand, padded along the ward. He paused at the door to check that all was quiet before running down the stairs. Once outside, he put on his boots and went in search of a boat. He had explored the gardens that day, but had not completed a full circuit of the island's shoreline. The warehouse guards were normally patrolling during the day, making a thorough reconnaissance impossible, but he was certain that they would be asleep now, or at least dozing, and not expecting any visitors.

By the light of the moon, and moving as silently as possible, he walked down onto the rough, stony beach intending to search the island's shoreline for some kind of boat. Jagged rocks and stones cut through the soft leather soles of his boots, causing him to cry out. He considered removing the boots and walking in the water, but the stones continued into the sea. It would be as painful in the water as out of it. He came upon a large matted mass of bull rushes that barred his way. He had to walk inland twenty feet or so, to avoid them. As he did so, he caught sight of a strange shape in the midst of the rushes. He walked towards it and touched it. It was a canvas cover of some kind, and as he pulled it aside, revealed a small rowboat. His heart began to beat loudly. He had never rowed a boat alone in the open sea before and had no idea if he was capable, but Maria's beautiful face rose up before him, filling him with determination and courage. He pulled the boat out of the rushes and dragged it onto the beach. Then he pushed the boat out into the water, raced after it and jumped aboard.

It was harder to row than he had expected. As he pulled at the oars, the little boat remained steadfastly in the same position. In fact, the tide began to draw him further back in towards the shore. Amid a sense of rising panic, Andrea dug the oars deep into the water and pulled back fiercely. The boat moved imperceptibly out to sea. Little by little, he got further away from the island. He looked around, frantically searching for the Lazaretto Vecchio, but he had become disoriented and could not see it. He realised that it must be on the other side of the island. He would have to row round, hugging the shoreline all the way. As he rounded the island's northern tip, the hospital island loomed up in the moonlight. He set his boat towards it and began to row.

Peter and Giovanni were making good progress towards the island in the gondola.

'Not long now my friends,' said Niccolò. 'Shall I take over from one of you for the last section?' he asked.

'No, sir. We are fine; you stay there and keep your strength. God knows how we will get them out of there once we arrive,' said Peter.

They spotted the jetty in the moonlight and set their gondola in that direction. It rocked up against the stone steps and Giovanni deftly leapt ashore and tied the gondola fore and aft.

The moon was still hanging low in the sky, but there was a pale apricot glow on the horizon.

'We must be quick,' said Niccolò. 'Daylight will be upon us before we know it.'

The three moved silently towards the hospital and pushed at the door. It was unlocked. Inside the hall, they paused. They heard a faint snoring to their left. Peter crept after the noise and spotted the old maid asleep on her little cot bed in the kitchen, the remains of a fire in the grate. He held his finger to his mouth and gestured to the others to creep upstairs. On the first floor Peter and Giovanni each inspected a ward, searching for Maria and Daniele. They met again on the landing and shook their heads. The three went up to the top floor and Peter, alone, began to search the long ward. The old woman near the door woke suddenly, and sat up in bed.

'What are you doing here?' she asked in a gruff voice.

Peter rushed over to her and said quickly, 'Be quiet, old woman.' And removing a dagger from beneath his cape, he held it to her throat.

She made as if to scream, but he pressed the blade against her crepey flesh and held her gaze.

Niccolò, meanwhile, crept down the ward until he found his children. He woke Maria with a kiss on her forehead. She gasped as she saw him, and shook Daniele awake. He broke into a broad grin when he saw his father. But Niccolò held his fingers to his mouth and whispered, 'We must hurry.'

Maria grabbed their bags and was about to run down the ward when she remembered something. She rushed back to the bed, moved the chair away from the wall and eased out one of the stones, followed by another. At last, she removed the vase and the leather pouch of money and placed them carefully in the bag.

Giovanni had stayed on the landing keeping watch and now the five rushed down the stairs towards the door. As they reached the bottom flight of stairs, they crashed headlong into the old grave-digger who had just come upstairs from his bed in the cellar.

'Oi!' he shouted. 'What goes on here?'

Giovanni held his sword against the man's chest. 'You say another word and you will be joining those poor bastards you bury out there.'

Peter and Niccolò ushered Maria and Daniele outside and into the gondola. Then Peter came back for his friend.

'Come Giovanni. We are done here.'

'You say a word, old man, and I will come back for you – understand?' shouted Giovanni as he and Peter ran out of the hospital, along the harbour wall, leaping aboard the gondola as Daniele expertly pushed off from the jetty and steered it out into the lagoon.

Maria sat in the prow of the boat, laughing and crying, with tears streaming down her face.

'Papa, I cannot believe what you have just done!'

'I couldn't have done it without Peter here, or Giovanni.'

Giovanni and Daniele steered the boat out into the choppy waters. It would be hard work getting the boat back to the city.

Suddenly, Maria called out. 'Oh no! What about Andrea? He was taken to the Lazaretto Nuovo. It's over there, I think. We cannot leave him there.'

'No,' said Niccolò. 'Maria is right. We must find a way of rescuing him too.'

'Not now,' said Peter. 'It is already daylight. We cannot risk it now.'

'No, you are right,' said Niccolò. 'We will have to go back for him tonight.'

Peter's heart sank. 'Niccolò – they will have raised the alarm by then and be looking for Maria and Daniele all over the city. I need to get them out of Venice as soon as possible.'

As the impossibility of the situation began to dawn on them, Daniele called out. 'Over there – a boat.'

Peter drew his dagger and Giovanni handed him his sword.

'It might be someone coming after us,' he said to his friend.

They watched as the boat drew closer.

'It's Andrea!' said Maria. 'Andrea, over here!'

Andrea turned around and stood up as his name was called. When he saw Maria surrounded by her family in the gondola, he dropped his oars in surprise and one floated off into the sea, before sinking into the depths.

Daniele and Giovanni steered the gondola towards him and Peter leant over grabbing hold of the boat.

'What are you doing?' he asked Andrea.

'I was coming to rescue you,' Andrea said to Maria.

'Thank you Andrea, but as you see, I have already been rescued.'

With Andrea safely on board, they abandoned the small boat in the lagoon, and rowed back towards the city. To avoid suspicion, they split the party up, dropping Andrea and Giovanni at the Isola di San Giorgio Maggiore from where they would pick up a gondola back to the main island.

Meanwhile, Peter, Niccolò, Maria and Daniele rowed back to the pier at San Zaccaria. The sun was quite high in the sky as they arrived, and the Riva degli Schiavoni was filling up with stalls, merchants and customers. As they fought their way between the rough tables laid out with fish and meat, one of the stallholders recognised Niccolò. 'Hey, Signor dei Conti! How are you? It's been a while since we last saw you.'

Niccolò raised his hand to acknowledge the man before shepherding his family hurriedly towards the Piazza. Within minutes they arrived at Niccolò's lodgings; desperate not to be spotted, they crept up the back stairs to his room. Word had already spread of the plague that had affected the house of dei Conti, and they could not take the risk of being found now.

'Damn,' said Niccolò, shutting the door. His children, exhausted and exhilarated to have been liberated, threw themselves on their father's bed and laughed.

'You must keep your voices down. It is unfortunate that we were seen down in the market. Word will soon be out that I am back and someone is bound to remember that I had you two with me.'

'What are we to do?' asked Maria anxiously.

'Peter and I have a plan.'

There was a knock on the door.

'Who is it?' asked Niccolò.

'Giovanni and Andrea.'

Niccolò opened the door and pulled the two men inside.

'We must act fast. I have been seen at the market. First, let me say this to Andrea. Thank you, for attempting to rescue Maria.'

Andrea blushed and looked down at his feet.

'I understand that you tried to persuade Maria to go with you to the quarantine island. You should have known her better than that. She would never have deserted her brother.'

Niccolò s dark eyes bored into Andrea, unsmiling. Andrea began to feel discomforted.

'You are a runaway, like my children,' Niccolò continued. 'But you were not suspected of having the illness, or so I understand; the authorities will be content if you simply disappear. They want anyone who has been in touch with a possible case just to get out of the city.'

'I have nowhere to go,' said Andrea, beginning to understand the full import of Niccolò's words.

'I realise that. I have friends in Chioggia where I grew up. I shall write to them and ask them to they take you in. You must be inconspicuous for a long time.'

'But Master, I do not wish to leave you… Or Maria, or Daniele, of course.' Andrea said.

'I'm afraid it is the only solution,' said Niccolò firmly.

'And what of Maria?' asked Andrea.

'She is no longer your concern. Now, I suggest that you leave us straight away. Here is the address of my friends. I have written a letter for you to give to them on your arrival. I wish you luck, Andrea, and Godspeed.' Niccolò shook the young man's hand. 'Just one more thing – I do this as a favour to you – do you understand?'

Andrea nodded uncertainly.

'If any word should reach the authorities,' continued Niccolò sternly, 'of what happened to Maria or Daniele, of how they were rescued, I shall ensure that your part in this is known.' And with that, he opened the door and ushered Andrea down the stairs of the *taverna* and out onto the Piazza.

'Papa,' said Maria, 'there is something curious about Andrea's part in all this.'

'Yes,' said Niccolò.

'What do you know?' asked Maria.

'Only that someone in our house told the authorities that Daniele was ill. I cannot think of anyone who would do such a thing; certainly not Alfreda or Bella, except…'

'But why would he do that?'

'I think he is a very confused young man,' said Niccolò.

'I did feel, as we were rowed over to Poveglia, there was something he wasn't telling me. He was very upset that I wouldn't go with him to the Lazaretto Nuovo. It was almost as if he had decided what was going to happen and was cross with me when I didn't go along with it…' Niccolò said nothing, but gazed out of the small window that overlooked the Piazza. He watched as Andrea walked unsteadily away, looking back just once towards the *taverna*. He held Niccolò's letter in his hand. Tears streamed down his narrow face.

'I don't think we shall see him again. Now Maria, we have more important things to discuss.'

'Yes, Papa?'

'Yes, such as your wedding to young Peter here, and the fact that he is going to take you and Daniele out of Venice and back to his family in the north.'

The two young people looked at one another in amazement. Then Maria burst into tears. 'But Papa, I cannot leave you. I have just got you back after all these weeks.'

'I know, my darling, but you and Daniele are in a serious situation. I couldn't leave you on that island and risk you catching that terrible illness. We had to rescue you; but having done so, you must now get out of Venice. You must see that?'

'I understand,' said Daniele. 'But Peter, do you really want me with you? I could go off on my own,' he said bravely.

'No!' said Maria. 'If I am going, you are going with me, little brother. We cannot be parted. But what about you, Papa, and Giovanni?' asked Maria. 'Will you be punished? What will happen to you?'

'To me? Nothing,' said Niccolò. 'The authorities will ask me if I know what happened to you both, and I shall deny all knowledge. Then I shall go back to Florence and finish my work there. It is important work, I believe.'

'And I shall marry Polisena,' said Giovanni cheerfully, 'and we will go abroad.'

'But can we marry, so quickly?' asked Maria anxiously. 'What of my dowry?'

'That is all arranged,' said Niccolò, smiling at Peter.

'Really?' said Maria.

'Peter and I have drawn up the contract already. You will take the vase as your dowry. It is worth a great deal of money.'

'But you are supposed to give it to the Doge.'

'I do not think the Doge will miss it. I have many other pieces of porcelain that he can have. Take the vase, daughter. It will bring you luck all your life. Look! It has already rescued you from Poveglia and provided you with a husband.'

Maria and Peter were married later that evening in the garden of the convent of San Zaccaria. Their witnesses were Giovanni and Polisena, who stood with her hand resting happily on her swollen belly. Maria and Peter then stood witness for their friends, as they too were married. Peter gave his wife a gold ring, set with a diamond. It glinted in the moonlight.

'Where did you get such a thing?' she asked as he slipped it onto her finger.

'I bought it from a merchant I know... The day I first saw you. I knew then, that one day we would be married.'

There was no time for a feast. No opportunity for the bride to wear her finery. Instead, Maria, Peter and Daniele rode out of Venice, their way lit only by a waxing moon, heading for Bruges and a new life in the north – three young people with a sense of adventure, and a Ming vase for company.

The mountains are blessed with streams that flow from the summits down onto the plains below. The water is of particular clarity and it is this which helps to create the pure white porcelain that is the feature of this region. At the base of the mountain, large wooden water wheels are erected to take advantage of the fast flowing stream. The kaolin stones are tipped into bowls and pounded into a fine powder by a simple mechanical crusher, powered by the water wheels. This powder is then washed clean and reshaped into clay bricks called pai-tun. The job is overseen by a high official, who observes the activity of the workers from horseback. The horse's harness is of great beauty. His stirrups are made of silver, and the saddle of a beautiful silken fabric. He is accompanied by coolies; one holds an umbrella over the overseer's head to protect him from the sun, while the other carries his luggage.

CHAPTER 13

Christmas is coming
Sheen, London
October 2015

Miranda loved Christmas. She knew that it was a tawdry, commercial waste of time, but nevertheless she began to get excited at the prospect as soon as Georgie broke up for half-term in October.

Of course, Christmas involved a huge amount of work and potentially a lot of expense, but Miranda took huge delight in making cards and creating gifts – some food-related, but also knitted or sewn. Her necessary frugality was the mother of invention as far as Christmas was concerned, and as soon as her daughter broke up from school she would sit with Georgie at the kitchen table and make a list of all the people who needed gifts. She would then create a second list of all the items they could produce between them.

It was a far cry from her time with Guy. He had always been so keen to appear extravagant at Christmas, a characteristic at odds with his parsimony towards his ex-wife and daughter since the divorce. It was all about 'show' for him, she supposed. His parents and sisters were all quite wealthy, and she always had the impression that he struggled to keep up with them all financially. But although most of the presents were for his family, he'd made it clear from the start that the responsibility for buying them was hers. 'I'm far too busy with work to flog round the shops. You do it. Girls love shopping.'

And so, in the weeks leading up to Christmas, Miranda rushed out each lunchtime, from the art gallery in Mayfair, to do battle with the crowds in Selfridges or Liberty to buy a cashmere scarf or an expensive pair of leather gloves for his mother. It had been a source of friction, even in the early days of their marriage.

'Couldn't we just give them a nice bottle of wine?' she'd argued one year. 'I could pick something up at Fortnum's – so it would look smart. Or I could make them something?'

'Make something? What are you thinking of? My mother doesn't want some god-awful knitted scarf. Your friends might think your homemade accessories are in some way chic or right-on, but my mother has slightly better taste. God, Miranda,' he'd said with irritation. 'What on earth will they think if we turn up with a cheap bottle of plonk or pair of knitted mittens? You know how generous they are with us.'

'Yes, and I'm sure we're very grateful, but they aren't behind on the mortgage payments, are they?'

He had glared at her and left the room.

The mortgage payments had become something of a running sore in their relationship. When they first married, Guy had a small flat off the Fulham Road. It was charming, if a little cramped. But Guy was determined that they should move to something more substantial. The chosen house was a villa nearby with five bedrooms. It was far too large, and certainly more than they could afford. But Guy convinced Miranda that a promotion was just around the corner.

Two years later, with Miranda now six months pregnant, the promotion had failed to materialise, whilst the mortgage payments had increased with the interest rates.

Any hopes Miranda might have entertained of taking a few years off to look after her first child had to be shelved. It had been a double blow, because Miranda had hoped to take advantage of the time caring for her new baby to explore other work opportunities. Working in the art gallery had been a temporary job that had become permanent. It was not something she loved. It had not even been particularly well paid. She had fantasised that while her new baby lay sleeping peacefully in her cot in the pretty Fulham house she might develop a plan for a business or kick-start some kind of creative career. She was in the habit of knitting Fair Isle scarves and hats as presents for friends, and had built up quite a following. Guy had hated it; he would scowl when he came in from work and found her sitting at the kitchen table in the large house, surrounded by the builders' detritus and 'clattering those needles.'

'God! Have they still not finished the kitchen? How long is this going to take? Do you have any idea Miranda what these pirates are costing us? Knitting again, I see; is there nothing for supper?' He had looked around the dust-covered kitchen despairingly.

'Yes, Guy, I do know what it's costing, although I hate to point out that it was you who wanted a new 'top of the range' kitchen. I'd have been quite happy with something from IKEA. And yes, there is supper – it's in the oven.'

In fact, her food was one of the few things that Guy had not complained about. But he had refused to contemplate her starting up a 'knitting' business.

'Miranda, you don't seem to understand. We are on the edge financially – until my promotion, of course. In the meantime, I would appreciate it if you forgot these ridiculous fantasies of starting up a business. Your job at the gallery may not be brilliantly well paid, but it covers quite a lot of our expenditure, and we need it. We'll have to get a nanny and you'll have to go back to work as soon as you can.'

'But by the time we've paid a nanny, I might as well have stayed at home,' argued Miranda.

'Nonsense. I've done the sums and you really have to go back. I'm sorry, but it's the way it is.'

The end of their marriage had come almost as a relief. The expensive house was sold and she and Georgie had moved to a much smaller house in Sheen, with a deposit provided by her parents and a lump sum from Guy – a final payment on their marriage together. He had agreed to pay some child maintenance, but nothing else. She accepted the 'deal' with alacrity, so grateful was she to be finished with the relationship and to have a roof, however tiny, over her head. A chance meeting with her old friend Jeremy as she wheeled Georgie in her pushchair down Barnes High Street had resulted in her job at the bookshop. And she was slowly building up her network of customers for the knitting business. The problem was, Guy had been right. It didn't really bring in a huge amount of income. She covered her costs, but barely made a profit.

Miranda and Georgie sat at the kitchen table making their Christmas lists.

'Blackberry jam I think, for my godmother,' said Miranda, 'or maybe some marmalade? She loves marmalade. As long as the Seville oranges get into the shops in time. Or do I have some left from the last batch; can you look for me, G?'

Georgie rummaged in her mother's 'larder'; in reality it was just a big pine cupboard that had been built in with the Victorian house. The glazed top cupboards held Miranda's hotchpotch of china. The solid cupboards beneath were filled to bursting with jam jars of all shapes and sizes.

'There's no marmalade, Ma, but there's heaps of that Damson chutney.'

'Really?' said Miranda, looking up from her notes. 'No marmalade. That's a shame. Never mind, the chutney will do. I've been thinking, G, I've talked to Jeremy about it and I've decided to take on some extra work.'

'Oh? What sort of work?'

'Well, you know my friend Suzanne, Jenny's mum at school?' Georgie nodded. 'You know she's the editor of a local magazine, rather glossy, aimed at the yummy mummy brigade round here. It's full of fashion and make-up tips and house interiors. Lots of adverts from estate agents, you know? They give it away in cafés, and restaurants, and at the station; in fact, we stock it at the shop. They make their money through advertising really. Anyway, she bought a couple of scarves from me last Christmas for her kids, and really liked them. And we got chatting, and she's asked me to come up with a couple of column ideas for her magazine. I don't know if she's just being kind, but she suggested that I could mention the knitting company, so it would be a bit of promotion for that.'

'What sort of column does she want – knitting patterns?'

'No, not that, although she is thinking of doing an article herself on 'great knitted accessories' and she'll give me a mention. No, she seems to think I might be quite good at a recycling, make-do-and-mend sort of column.'

Georgie laughed. 'Well she's right there. You're brilliant at that!'

'Oh, so you think I could do it then?'

'Mum, you'd be great. Just tell them what we have for supper each evening.'

'Cheeky! OK, I'll give it a go. I love going round boot fairs, and I could find some bits and pieces and do them up, take pictures and so on. Or I could do homemade preserves, homemade presents, that sort of thing. And who knows, maybe something will come from it. She wants me to blog about it as well, to sort of drive interest. The problem is I'm not sure I know how to set up a blog, if I'm honest.'

'I can show you. We set up a blog at school a couple of years ago. It's really easy.'

'She'll pay, of course – Suzanne. Not heaps, but enough to make it worth doing. It will mean a bit less time for the knitting, but will make a nice change. I should be able to fit it all in. And who knows, it might lead to other work.'

Georgie banged a couple of jars of damson chutney on the table.

'That could be your first blog,' said Georgie. 'Christmas on a shoestring…'

'That's a jolly good idea,' said Miranda. 'So, damson chutney, OK. We might need to make up some new labels for it. And I could get some pretty fabric from the little shop in the High Street to make nice tops; what do you think?

'Yes, sure. And you could take lots of photos and put them on your blog.'

Georgie felt a little frisson of pride for her mother. They had been together and reliant on one another for so many years. She knew it hadn't been easy for Miranda after the divorce, but her mother was always cheerful and, apart from the odd anxiety about bills, was relentlessly optimistic. As the child of divorced parents, she was not alone; nearly a third of her classmates were in the same position. Over the years, as she had listened to her friends swapping stories of arguments and unpleasantness between their parents, she felt lucky that her mother always managed to maintain a positive view of the world. She saw her father occasionally; not as often as she'd like, but that was no fault of her mother. She had never stood in his way. It was just one of those things. And she had Jeremy of course. He wasn't a father, but had long ago appointed himself as her 'honorary godfather', a role that pleased them both.

The lists written and pinned to the notice board in the kitchen, Miranda took some potatoes from the vegetable basket.

'So what are we going to do this half term, sweetheart?' she said, as she began to peel them at the kitchen sink. 'Just think, a whole week off school! I've asked Jeremy for an extra day off so we can do things together if you like. I will have to go to work on Thursday and Saturday. You could come with me if you want to, or you could stay here if you think you'll be OK.'

'Mum, I'm fifteen, of course I'll be OK!'

'Yes, of course you will. I just wondered if there was something you'd like to do.'

'No, I've got work anyway. We've got a project I've got to get on with.'

'Ooh,' said Miranda, in her most annoying helpful-mother voice. 'Anything I can help with? You know how much I love glueing and sticking.' She put the peeled potatoes on to boil.

'No, but thanks. We've gone a bit beyond glueing and sticking these days. Besides, sounds like you'll have enough to do with your own project. Do you mind if I go and watch telly for a bit before supper?'

'No darling, off you go. It won't be long.'

Miranda took some mince out of the fridge to make a shepherd's pie. If she added lots of vegetables she could probably make it last for two nights. She peeled two onions, a couple of carrots and a sweet potato and chopped them all in the ancient blender her mother had given her years before. She fried them all off before adding the mince and browning it a little. She added a bit of Lea & Perrins followed by a tin of tomatoes and salt and pepper. She considered taking a picture of it for the blog. Surely everyone knew how to make shepherd's pie – didn't they? She took a picture anyway. Then she pushed the saucepan onto the cooler side of the cooker before sitting back at the table. She opened her laptop and wrote: *Austerity Blog: how to live for virtually nothing by Miranda Sharp.*

The phone rang. It was Charles. 'Hi Miranda, how are you?'

'I'm good. How are you?'

'I'm very well. Darling, I'm sorry it's been a while. I've been away on business as you know. But I'm back now, and would love to take you out for dinner. What are you up to this coming week?'

'Well it's G's half term, so not a huge amount. We're just here, you know..'

'How about tomorrow?'

'Yes, OK, that would be lovely. I'd ask you here but…'

'No, I'd like to take you out.'

It had been two weeks since she had last seen Charles. They had been out together four times in all – twice to the Curzon cinema in Richmond, an art house cinema that showed not just the latest movies but also filmed theatrical performances. He'd managed to get two tickets for them to see the latest production of *Hamlet*, which had impressed her. They'd also been out for dinner. Once to a chic restaurant on the edge of Kew Green, which Charles had declared 'rather a find.' And the second time to Bocca di Lupo – a bustling Italian restaurant in the heart of Soho. The food on both occasions had been delicious and Miranda enjoyed their evenings out enormously. Charles was handsome and charming and Miranda felt herself melt a little each time he called her 'darling'. It made her feel special; as if he really cared for her. It had been so long since anyone apart from Jeremy or her mother had called her by any sort of endearment. She had been surprised at how disappointed she had felt when Charles announced an urgent business trip that would take him away for a couple of weeks.

'I've got to go away, darling,' he'd said during their supper in Soho. Miranda had been spooning chocolate mousse into her mouth, luxuriating in its sheer indulgence. Charles had watched her with a combination of amusement and affection. Charles didn't eat puddings.

'Some interesting things are on sale in Hong Kong, and I really need to get there. Normally I'd do my buying on over the Internet, you know? But I ought to see the stuff for myself.'

On the way home, he had held her hand in the car as he drove – a romantic but tricky manoeuvre that involved them changing gear together, his hand over hers on the gear stick. Until that evening, their kissing had been a relatively innocent affair: a kiss on either cheek when they parted, just once a kiss on the mouth. But that night, as they sat in his expensive, leather-lined car outside her house in Sheen, he had kissed her properly, his tongue exploring her mouth, his hands slipping beneath her coat and caressing her breasts through the silk of her blouse. The windows had steamed up and she found herself hoping he would let his hand drop down between her thighs, as boys had been wont to do in her youth, their hands sliding up and up until... But he stopped at her waist and pulled away slightly.

'I ought to go,' he said abruptly. 'I'll be back in a couple of weeks, and I'll call you, OK?'

Miranda had to admit that she had been slightly disappointed and surprised that he had not suggested they go into her house together to finish what they had started. They were both adults, and she thought she had made it clear enough that she fancied him – wanted him. Perhaps he was an old-fashioned sort of guy. Perhaps he had an early start. To be fair, she hadn't suggested it either, but mostly because she was at a loss to know how she could sleep with anyone with Georgie in the next room. It was unimaginable. The thought of her daughter either hearing them having sex or finding them together the following morning was so appalling, that she had not encouraged it. Sex was something that had effectively been turned to 'off' since she had split up with her husband, but her desire for Charles was becoming harder to control. She only had to see him cross the road to her house from his car to feel the familiar surge of longing. His body was perfect: tall and angular; his voice was low and strong. When they sat together having dinner, she was mesmerised by his forearms – long, lean, covered in fine gold hairs that matched the hair on his head. When he spoke, he used his hands quite a lot in an expressive way. He often had his shirt-sleeves rolled up and she loved those arms. His watch was elegant and expensive. He dressed beautifully, but not in a mannered way. Always blue shirts. Nice cufflinks. Smart suits.

But she did wonder why he hadn't mentioned the sex thing to her. Why, for example, had he not taken her to his house? She knew he lived a little way out of London down the M3, but she didn't know any more than that. Sometimes, in her darker moments, she wondered if there was a wife somewhere in the background, managing the M3 life. Elegant and beautiful, just like him. But she couldn't bring herself to ask. Besides, how do you ask?' Oh Charles, lovely dinner. By the way, do you have a wife?'

She'd discussed it with Jeremy, of course. In fact, Jeremy had become positively obsessed with her love life.

'So,' he'd say when they arrived together at the shop on a Saturday, 'tell me *all*. I want to know *every* detail.'

'Oh Jeremy, there's nothing to say.'

'What do you mean, there's nothing to say? Have you slept with him yet? Why not? Do you love him or is it just a physical thing? Do you think he loves you? What do you mean, he calls you darling? That means something, surely!'

'Oh Jeremy, you call me darling, and that doesn't mean anything at all, does it?'

'It means I love you, just not in that way.'

'I know, but maybe he's just a bit theatrical,' said Miranda.

'No. I know his sort. I think he's an old fashioned romantic. It's all those antiques he deals in. He's like some wonderful Edwardian gent, don't you think? Miranda, I think maybe he's the one. And you not sleeping with him is probably the best thing you could do. You'll drive him wild with desire.'

'I think you're a little bit in love with him yourself, Jeremy,' said Miranda, laughing.

Jeremy blushed. 'And for the record, I'm not avoiding sleeping with him,' she continued, 'I just don't know where we can do it. I mean I can't do it at home with G there, can I?'

Miranda sat musing on this last conversation after she hung up the phone to Charles. She dialled Jeremy's number.

'Jeremy, darling,' she said in a sweet, almost unctuous tone.

'What do you want?'

'Oh Jeremy, really, you are so cynical.'

'I am not cynical. I'm realistic.'

She outlined her plan. She was having dinner with Charles the following evening, and might Jeremy possibly take pity on her and have Georgie for the night? Perhaps they could have an 'unsuitable movie' extravaganza and sleep-over at his house?

'My God,' he protested, 'how old do you think I am? Fourteen?'

She laughed.

'Oh, of course I will – anything for my goddaughter. I can't have her despoiled by the sound of rampant sex going on in the next bedroom can I? It might scar her for life.'

'Oh Jeremy, thank you…'

Miranda nervously suggested the idea to G over supper.

'So Jeremy wondered if you'd like to go there tomorrow. He's got a plan to take you to some madly risqué movie or something and then to his flat. You'd like that wouldn't you?'

'Oh, I don't know, Mum. I was thinking of asking Cassie over; we've just been on Facebook.'

Miranda felt a wave of disappointment, followed by the familiar feeling of resignation.

'Oh. Well, OK, if you don't want to.' She spooned shepherd's pie onto Georgie's plate.

'But,' said Georgie, gazing intently at her mother's face, 'it would be nice to see Jeremy. And I do like his idea of an unsuitable film. So yeah, tell him, yes.' She noted how her mother flushed with excitement and felt pleased that she could make her so happy quite so easily. She wondered what plans her mother had in her absence. 'Don't you want to come with us?'

'No,' said Miranda a little too hurriedly. 'I thought you might like some time with your godfather alone.'

'Really?' asked G.

'Oh, all right; Charlie has asked me out and…' She trailed off.

'You want to come back and shag each other's brains out,' said Georgie.

'Oh Georgina!' Miranda said sharply. 'That's a disgraceful thing to say.'

Georgie laughed. 'It's all right, Ma. I do understand; as long as you know what you're doing. And as long as you think he really likes you.'

Her mother paused mid-forkful and gazed lovingly at her daughter. 'Since when did you get to be so bloody wise?'

'Since I had you for a mother,' said Georgina.

CHAPTER 14

The date

On Saturday morning, Miranda woke early, drowsy and with a sleepy sense that something important was supposed to happen that day. As she emerged into wakefulness, she remembered what it was. She and Charlie were going on a date that night. And what was more, she had managed to engineer it so that Georgina would be at Jeremy's house. She swung her legs over the side of the bed and sat staring into space for a few moments. She felt nervous. It didn't take long to identify the reason. Was this the night that she and Charlie would end up in bed together? If she was honest with herself, she felt acute anxiety at the mere idea of having sex. It had been so long – almost thirteen years. The number thirteen struck her as symbolic. Unlucky for some? Or lucky for others?

She wandered into her tiny en-suite bathroom and looked at herself in the mirror. Her hair needed washing and she looked tired. She peered down inside her nightie and decided that things needed a bit of a tidy up 'down there'.

'Oh God,' she said aloud as she squeezed toothpaste onto her toothbrush. Maybe it was just all a bit too much effort – love. Maybe it would better if she just cancelled the date and instead spent a jolly afternoon with Jeremy and Georgie.

She washed her face and applied a little moisturiser. She was thirty-seven years old. She had not had a boyfriend since her marriage had ended. Surely it was time for her to embrace life, and Charles too, with open arms and see what might ensue? She'd played it safe for so long that she had really forgotten how to take risks. And there was no doubt that sleeping with Charlie would be a risk. She didn't know him that well. He was deliciously handsome of course, and entertaining and charming. But there was a private core to him that appeared pretty inscrutable. Could she be comfortable having sex with someone she didn't know that well? She had never been a one-night-stand sort of girl. But, she had known him for a few weeks now; they had been on four dates; he was not really unknown and, she reasoned with herself, it was just sex, after all. What was the worst thing that could happen?

She brushed her hair and tied it back into a ponytail before taking off her nightie and putting on some old tracksuit bottoms and a t-shirt. 'Shit,' she said out loud. 'I'm not on the pill!' She had not been on the pill for years. She might actually get pregnant. 'Shit, shit,' she said again putting on an old cardigan that had once belonged to her father – large, moth-eaten cashmere, but comfortable. How on earth could she suggest to a new boyfriend that he might actually have to use a condom? It was really all too complicated and embarrassing. Maybe, she thought to herself, as she peered under the bed for her slippers, maybe he wouldn't want to sleep with her anyway. Yes, that's probably what would happen. And who says she had to sleep with him? Just because G wasn't there didn't make sex automatic. Maybe they would just cuddle and have coffee and if she felt that he was keen, she could go to the doctor on Monday and get the pill sorted out. Then she would be ready the next time.

Her mind was a whirr of conflicting ideas and emotions as she descended the stairs. Georgie's coat had been thrown onto the pegs in the hall the previous evening, and the hem was draped over the vase. She moved it to another peg and adjusted the vase so that it stood in the centre of the table. As she looked at the face of the dragon snaking its way around the centre, a comment her aunt had made to her on one of her last visits to the house in Cheltenham came to her: 'Life, Miranda, is either a daring adventure or nothing at all.'

She went into the kitchen and turned on the kettle. The sound of morning television blared through from the sitting room next door. 'Georgina,' she shouted, 'do turn that down a bit; they must be able to hear that telly in Richmond.' She made a mug of tea and surveyed the kitchen. It was a mess from the previous evening. Jeremy had given her the day off work to get ready for her date. She might as well give the house a bit of a spring-clean. Whether she slept with Charlie or not, at least he would find her house clean and tidy.

'Mum,' said Georgie as her mother forced her to lift her slipper-clad feet from the floor in the sitting room so that she could push the hoover closer to the sofa. 'Mum, he won't be looking for dust under there – unless you get up to some seriously kinky stuff on the floor.'

Georgie changed channels and turned up the volume while slurping cereal from a large soup bowl.

'I do wish you would stop focusing on the *possibility* that I might actually be a little intimate with my boyfriend this evening, G. Besides, I always clean the house; I just don't usually get a chance to do it on a Saturday. I do normally work on a Saturday if you remember!'

'Intimate – yuck!' exclaimed Georgie, shovelling in another mouthful of cereal.

Miranda yanked the hoover round the coffee table, bumping Georgie's arm as she did so, causing her daughter to spill Coco Pops over one of seat cushions of the cream sofa.

'Oh no!' screamed Miranda. 'Oh look what you've done.'

'What *I've* done?' retorted her daughter. 'You're the one who pushed my arm.'

'Oh never mind who did what to who – run and get some paper towels from the kitchen – quick!'

Georgie slowly put the bowl, dripping with chocolate milk, down onto the clean coffee table before ambling to the kitchen.

'Oh, G, I've just polished this table.'

Georgie wandered back into the sitting room with the roll of kitchen towel. Her mother snatched it from her and began to mop furiously at the cream upholstery.

'I cannot believe you did that,' muttered Miranda furiously. 'I think we're going to have to have a new rule in this house; no cereal, and particularly no bloody awful chocolate cereal, to be eaten anywhere but the kitchen.'

'How about we have a new rule about not hoovering while people are trying to eat their blinking breakfast?' said Georgie before stomping upstairs.

Miranda went into the kitchen and filled a bowl of water from the kettle, adding some cleaning powder. She returned to the sitting room and began scrubbing at the sofa cushion frantically. The brown stain appeared to be indelible. She simply managed to spread it in ever-increasing circles. She sat down, finally, on the damp, sticky coffee table; tears began to roll down her face.

Georgie reappeared at the doorway.

'Mum,' she said. 'I'm sorry. I know you're a bit on edge. And I'm sorry about the Coco Pops. Is the sofa all right?'

'Thank you, G. I'm sorry too – for shouting. It *was* my fault. But I'm just a bit upset. The sofa was the nicest thing we had. I only finished paying for it last month, and now it's ruined.'

'No it's not,' said Georgie brightly. 'We can take the cushion cover off and put it in the washing machine.'

'Oh, yes. I suppose we can.'

'Worth a try?' said Georgie hopefully.

'Yes, worth a try.'

Together they removed the cover and Miranda stuffed it into the washing machine with a cupful of every cleaning product she could find.

Georgie magnanimously turned off the TV and went in search of a can of furniture polish.

Miranda had arranged with Jeremy to drop Georgie at the shop around three o'clock. She drew up outside the bookshop at the allotted time and kissed her daughter on the forehead. 'Have a great time, sweetheart. I hope he takes you to something good.'

'I will. I expect it will be something political and challenging. That's his normal idea of a fun night out.'

'Oh Lord, is it? He is a funny guy isn't he? Well, I hope there will be a great supper then.'

'Yeah, that should be OK. He's promised me pizza.'

'Oh, good. Well, darling, have a lovely time and tell him I'll pick you up tomorrow morning at about eleven.'

She watched as Georgie climbed out of the car in her old army coat, dragging her sports bag filled with her overnight things out of the back seat.

'Oh, and Mum,' she said before she slammed the car door, 'stay safe.'

'Oh G, I'll be fine, but thank you.'

She blew her a kiss before pulling out into the busy Saturday afternoon traffic in Barnes High Street. In her rear view mirror she could see her daughter standing anxiously on the pavement watching her mother drive away. Little did Georgie know that Miranda felt just as anxious as her daughter about the impending 'date'.

When she got home, Miranda threw herself into her preparations. The house now tidy, she hung up the damp cushion cover on the line outside. The mark had gone, but she feared the cover was a tad smaller than when she had put it into the washing machine. She would have to put it back onto the sofa cushion slightly damp in order to stretch it back into position.

She dashed upstairs and ran a bath, and added some bath oil that Jeremy had bought her for Christmas and which she kept for special occasions. She bathed, and washed her hair, then, wrapped in an old towelling dressing gown, unpegged the cover and did battle with it. It had definitely shrunk, but she finally managed to squish the unyielding cushion back into its cover.

Back upstairs, she dried her hair, painted her toenails and put on her make-up. She wore the blue wrap dress that Sasha had given her, and a turquoise locket that had been a present from her grandmother for her twenty-first birthday. By six forty-five she was ready. She looked at herself in her bedroom mirror. She didn't look at all bad.

She wandered into the sitting room and laid an old paisley throw over the sofa and rearranged the cushions. It looked quite elegant. Earlier, she had picked some bright blue hydrangeas from the garden, which matched perfectly the cobalt blue of the dragon vase. She had taken a close-up picture of the flowers and vase and posted it on Facebook. It already had twelve likes.

Miranda sat down at the kitchen table to wait. It was exactly seven thirty when the doorbell rang. She checked her reflection in the hall mirror above the table, and then opened the door.

CHAPTER 15

The morning after

Miranda woke the following morning alone. The house was eerily quiet. She looked at the clock; it was twenty minutes past eight. She went downstairs and filled the kettle. Standing at the sink, she gazed out onto the autumnal garden. She made a cup of strong tea, sat at the kitchen table and thought about the previous evening.

Charlie had taken her to a 'celebrity chef' restaurant in Grosvenor Square. The diners had an air of money about them – overly made up, ultra-skinny women who looked as if they never actually ate anything, men in slim dark suits pontificating with wine waiters about vintages, and a sprinkling of celebrities intent on having a good time. Miranda felt distinctly out of place. But Charlie was charming and told her that she looked beautiful. They ate seafood and drank a very good bottle of white burgundy. Charlie took control of the ordering; in fact, he took control of the whole evening. They talked of course, but mostly about her. Once again, Miranda tried to draw him out about his personal life. He seemed elusive, but finally she persuaded him to part with a little information. His first love had been a girl he'd met at university. They split up soon after, and she worked in PR, he thought. Another girlfriend was a Scottish landowner's daughter, who now ran the estate for her father. When she asked why they had broken up, he seemed vague. 'We just drifted apart

I suppose,' was all he would say. Either way, they both sounded out of Miranda's league.

At one point, emboldened by the wine, Miranda asked him if he had ever been married.

He looked at her with his clear grey gaze. 'Married? No…'

'Why not?' she probed.

'Never met the right girl, I suppose. And I'm busy, you know – travelling.'

'But lots of people travel for work, don't they, and they manage?' she had suggested.

'Just not lucky in love, I guess. Now – pudding?'

It seemed that particular conversation was at an end.

On their way back to the car he had put his arm around her shoulders and drawn her close to him. She timidly wrapped her own arm around his waist. As he opened the car door for her, he held her to him and kissed her. A long, tender kiss that left her breathless for more. She slid into the expensive leather seats and reached out to hold his hand. He held it to his mouth and kissed it, placing it back in her lap.

'So – no Georgie at home tonight,' he said. 'Shall we go back to your place?'

There was an almost tangible energy between the two them as they sat in the dark in the car in Grosvenor Square. She sensed it and so did he.

'Yes,' she found herself saying.

He drove carefully out of town, crossing Barnes Bridge and turning towards Sheen. As he parked outside Miranda's house, he turned to her and said, 'Are you sure? There's no pressure, you know, Miranda. I'm very fond of you – very fond – and I'm not messing around, you know? I'd love to take you to bed. But if you're not ready, I do understand. I know you've had a hard time bringing G up on your own. It's bound to be a big step, letting someone into your life.'

The emotion she felt was one of overwhelming relief. 'Oh, I *do* want to sleep with you!' she blurted out. 'Oh, that sounds awful! What I mean is, I do really love being with you, fancy you, but you're right. It is a big step.'

He kissed her again and stroked her hair.

'Look,' she said. 'Come in, OK? I cleaned the house specially; you might as well see it!'

He laughed and they went inside holding hands. They made coffee in the kitchen and he kissed her again as she reached for the coffee pot. They took their coffee into the sitting room and as she put the tray down onto the table, he kissed her once more; this time it was longer, deeper and he held her closely to him, stroking her hair, breathing into her ear, 'You smell delicious.'

They sat on the sofa and took one sip of coffee before he kissed her again.

At last, she said, 'Come on... Let's go upstairs.'

They almost ran up the stairs and into her bedroom. He lifted her dress high over her head; she unbuttoned his shirt, pulling it away from his smooth chest.

'I'm not on the pill,' she blurted out, blushing.

'That's OK,' he said, fishing a condom out of his pocket.

'Better safe than sorry,' he murmured into her hair.

The sex was intense, good. He was passionate, loving, tender and yet strong. When they had finished making love for the third time, she said weakly. 'You won't believe how nervous I was about that.'

'Oh, I think I would,' he replied. 'I was a bit nervous myself. you know.'

'What, you? But, you're so... Together.'

They fell asleep in each other's arms, but he slipped out of bed very early and she woke up as he was putting his shirt on.

'Where are you going?' she asked sleepily.

'Got a flight to New York later today. I need to get home and pack.'

'Oh? You didn't say.'

'Well, I won't be away long; just a couple of days.'

He sat down on the edge of the bed and put on his shoes, before turning and kissing her again.

'Have a lovely day, and I'll see you in the middle of the week; supper on Wednesday?'

'Oh, I'd love that. Thank you. Come here. I'll cook. G will be here, of course.'

'Great. It's no problem for me that she's here you know. I think she's a lovely kid.'

'Do you? Well, yes she is. And I'd love you to get to know her.'

'Well, let's do it. Now, don't move. Go back to sleep. I'll let myself out.'

All things considered, she reflected, it had been pretty perfect. She began to hum to herself, as she tidied up the coffee cups from the night before.

On the way out of the house, just before eleven, she noticed water on the hall table. The hydrangeas were somehow different; as if they had moved themselves into a different arrangement during the night. 'Odd,' she thought.

Jeremy was waiting for her at the door to the shop. 'Darling. G is glued to crap TV upstairs in the flat. I want to hear everything. Let's go for a coffee next door.'

'So – how does it feel to finally get laid?' he asked, grinning at her over their lattes.

'Rather good, to be honest. I'm just amazed that it all seems to be in working order… You know?'

'So it was good then?' he asked.

'Stop being so bloody nosy. But yes, it was good.'

'And are you seeing him again?'

'Sure am. This Wednesday. He's having supper at ours, with Georgie.'

'And staying the night?'

'Not sure… Probably. Do you think he should? I don't want to upset G.'

'Manda, we had a long chat about that yesterday – your girl and me. She's unbelievably mature, you know. I think she understands that you are lonely and need a man in your life, apart from me, that is. I think she'll handle it OK. At least that's my opinion.'

Miranda and Georgie spent an amicable afternoon snuggled up on the now dry sofa watching old films. Miranda cooked a roast chicken for supper, something of a treat. As Georgie went upstairs to bed that night, she leant over the banisters. 'Ma?'

'Yes,' called Miranda from the kitchen.

'I'm so glad you had a nice time with thingummy.'

'Charlie.'

'Yeah, with him. Love you…'

'Love you too darling.'

At breakfast on Wednesday, Miranda mentioned that Charlie was coming for supper that night. 'I'd like you to meet him properly and vice versa.'

'OK,' said Georgie.

'That sounds a bit qualified,' said her mother.

'No, not qualified. I just don't know him, that's all.'

'Well, hopefully you'll know him better by this evening,' said Miranda.

She cooked a fish pie for dinner. Not one of Georgie's favourite things, but it was easy enough to prepare in advance and would give her time to monitor any conversation between Charlie and her daughter.

They sat in slightly awkward silence at first in the sitting room. Charlie asked Georgie questions – how she liked school, what were her favourite subjects, what she wanted to do when she grew up – predictable questions that adults often relied on when talking to young people. Miranda was impressed that Georgie managed to answer politely without resorting to her usual sarcasm. Interrupting, she suggested they go into the kitchen to eat. Both looked relieved. Walking with her arm wrapped round her daughter's waist to the kitchen she whispered in her ear, 'Well done, darling.'

Charlie opened a bottle of wine over dinner, and rummaged in a drawer to find the corkscrew. This simple act of domesticity did not go unnoticed by Georgie. Miranda seemed to relax after a glass or two of wine and they ate their dinner in convivial enough fashion. Pudding cleared away, Miranda suggested they played cards together.

'Oh Mum, I'd love to, but I've got homework to do.' Georgie rose from the table, put her plate into the dishwasher and kissed her mother on the top of the head. She turned as she reached the kitchen doorway.

'Nice to meet you properly, Charlie… See you.'

They heard her leaping up the stairs two at a time.

'So, ' said Miranda, 'that wasn't too bad was it?'

'No,' said Charlie. 'I was probably a bit boring for her, wasn't I?'

'Not at all,' Miranda said, a little too hurriedly. 'Look,' she said, 'teenagers are not the easiest people to get to know. But she likes you, I can tell. And if I'm happy then so is she.'

The following morning Charlie left early. He was conducting an auction down in Hampshire and had to be on the road before six thirty. Miranda was relieved that she did not have to endure the sight of her daughter and boyfriend together over the breakfast table.

Georgie shuffled into the kitchen at seven forty-five and opened the larder in search of cereal.

'No Charlie then?' she asked.

'He had to go early,' said Miranda, before adding, 'thanks for being so polite last night. It wasn't so bad, was it?'

'No mum, it was fine, really. Like I said – if you like him then that's all that matters.'

Before long, Miranda realised, she couldn't count their dates anymore. She was just 'going out' with Charlie. He came and stayed three or four nights a week. He helped to cook; he stacked the dishwasher; he even hoovered the house occasionally. One evening, he arrived for supper to find Miranda fighting with a plunger in the sink and failing to unblock the drain. He simply rolled up the sleeves of his expensive shirt and fixed it by unscrewing the pipework in the sink cupboard. He watched TV in the sitting room with Miranda and played board games on occasion with Georgie. One weekend, he turned up unannounced and asked if they could watch an international rugby match between England and Wales. He and Miranda sat together on the sofa, she resting her head on his chest. She felt utterly content, she realised, as he roared at the television. He picked up a take-away curry that night from the local Indian restaurant and the three sat together in the sitting room eating it on their laps.

'Mum *never* lets me do this,' said Georgie, struggling to hide her admiration. 'And curry too; better not spill on the dreaded sofa or you'll never hear the end of it.'

He had laughed and smiled fondly at Miranda.

'And quite right too,' he'd said. 'It would be a terrible thing to do and I promise to be extra specially careful.'

And so it continued, until Miranda began to believe that her relationship with Charlie could become something really important. She had realised several weeks before that she had fallen in love with him. She daydreamed about him at work. She planned their meals together. She thrilled to the sound of his car drawing up outside. Two weeks before Christmas she took Georgie down to the local garden centre to pick their Christmas tree.

'I want a really big one this year, G – something rather stunning.'

They selected the tree and managed to shove it into the Volvo. At home that evening, Miranda brought down the decorations from the attic and she and Georgie decorated it together.

'I think it's going to be a lovely Christmas this year, G,' said Miranda, pinning the fairy on the top before standing back to admire their handiwork.

'Why?' said Georgie. 'Because of Charlie?'

'Yes – because of Charlie; is that so odd?'

'No,' said Georgie. 'Is he coming here?'

'I don't know yet,' said Miranda. 'We've not had a chance to talk about it.'

The next time they met, she broached the subject. 'Charlie, I just wondered what you were doing for Christmas this year?'

'Oh,' he said. 'Not sure. Seeing you, I hope.'

She smiled. 'Of course! That's what I was hoping.'

'I'll have to visit my parents, of course, but only for one of the days. Let me sort a few things out and we can discuss it next time.'

The following week, he had to go abroad. 'It's a bit of a last minute thing,' he said to Miranda when he rang her from the airport. 'But I've got a bit of a treat for us on 23rd December. I remember you saying that Georgie liked pantomimes. Don't make any plans for that evening, OK?'

On the evening of the 23rd, Charlie had arranged to collect them at six-thirty; at six-fifteen, Georgie jumped down the staircase and stood with her coat on in the hall. Miranda came through from the kitchen, pulling on her own coat.

'My God. You're ready,' she said to her daughter.

'Yeah, well, don't want to miss the beginning do we?' said Georgie.

'You're excited,' teased her mother.

'No, I'm not,' said Georgie, chewing gum. 'Well maybe a bit. There's something about panto, isn't there? Maybe it's because we couldn't really afford it when I was little. I never really grew tired of it. Don't tell any of my friends though, will you?'

'Darling, of course I won't! Although you have nothing to be ashamed about. I'm quite excited too. I love pantos, and circuses come to that, and I'm sorry we couldn't spare the money when you were little.'

Georgie hugged her mother.

As they climbed into Charlie's car, Georgie said, 'Thanks Charlie for this. It's my guilty secret, my love of pantos.'

'I know,' he said, smiling back at her in his rear-view mirror. 'Your mother told me. Your secret is safe with me.'

Richmond Theatre was a hive of activity as the three battled through the crowds of excited children in the lobby. Charlie bought a programme for Georgie and a box of chocolates for them all to share. He'd booked a box to one side of the stage and once Georgie and Miranda were in their seats, he brought out a bottle of champagne from beneath his cashmere coat. He had a small hip flask in his pocket with a silver cup and as the panto-mime began, he quietly uncorked the champagne and handed the first sip to Miranda.

'You are naughty,' she whispered.

'Well, not sure I could get through the whole thing without a drink. Besides, I wanted to treat you,' he whispered back, kissing her briefly on the cheek.

The pantomime was Cinderella. It was full of the usual cli-chés: a beautiful Cinders played by a famous soap star; comedi-ans dressed as dames over-acting as the ugly sisters; a sweet but hopeless Buttons and a fine performance by a well-known game show host who played Prince Charming and turned out to have a magnificent singing voice.

On the way home, Georgie played one of her favourite games of assigning real people to the characters in the production.

'Mum obviously is Cinderella – the beautiful girl trapped in a house doing all the work.'

Her mother laughed. 'So who are you then?' asked Miranda.

'Not sure yet,' said Georgie. 'Jeremy is definitely Buttons – good-natured, loyal, but ultimately useless.'

'Oh G, that's too unkind,' said Miranda, stifling a laugh.

'And Charlie, of course, is Prince Charming. Tall, handsome and here to save Cinders.'

Charlie fell silent. Miranda blushed. 'Oh G, you do talk a lot of nonsense.'

They arrived back at Miranda's house just after half past nine. She threw her coat over the banisters and rushed into the kitchen to check on a casserole she had left in the oven.

Georgie went upstairs, turning round at the top of the landing and calling out, 'Thanks Charlie, for the panto; it was great. And don't take my silly game too seriously, will you? I didn't mean anything by it.'

'You're welcome G, no problem,' he said.

In the hall, Charlie removed his coat and hung it up carefully on a peg by the door; he wandered into the kitchen holding the blue and white vase in his hands.

'Miranda, darling,' he said as he walked into the kitchen. 'Do you want me to flog this for you? You remember that sale I was telling you about? It's on in the New Year. I could take it down to the sale room tomorrow and log it into the catalogue.'

'Oh,' said Miranda, setting the casserole onto the table, 'I'd forgotten about that. I'm not sure. I feel a bit guilty about selling it really.'

'Well, if you don't want to, that's fine. I just thought I'd mention it,' he said, smiling and wandering back into the hall.

'How much do you think it would fetch?' Miranda called after him.

'Not sure – could be fifty pounds, could be a hundred and fifty. It's a nice thing, probably forty or fifty years old. Hard to say.'

'Not sure it's worth selling for fifty quid, is it really?' said Miranda, laying baked potatoes on the table as he came back into the kitchen.

'Tell you what,' he said, 'how about I buy it from you now, then you'll know exactly how much you're going to get and can spend the money accordingly.'

'Oh, that's nice of you.'

'Well, call it a bit of an early Christmas present. I'll give you two hundred for it.'

'Oh, Charlie, that's too much. You said yourself it might only get fifty.'

'Well I wasn't sure what to get for Georgie, so why don't you give her the extra money and say it's from me.'

'You don't have to give her anything,' said Miranda.

'Yes I do. Oh, and… Well, I was going to give this to you tomorrow, but you might as well have it now.'

He handed her a beautifully wrapped box, turquoise blue, with Tiffany written on the lid.

'Oh my God,' said Miranda, untying the ribbon. Inside, nestling in the white satin lining was a silver bracelet. 'Oh Charlie, it's so beautiful,' she said slipping it onto her wrist.

'No more than you deserve,' he said, lifting her wrist to his lips and kissing it.

'And I've got something for you,' she said, a little shyly. She went through to the sitting room and brought out a present that had been lying under the tree. 'I hope you like it… I made it myself.'

He unwrapped the present carefully. Inside was a Fair Isle scarf in shades of dark green, navy, coral and grey.

'That's fantastic, Miranda. It's really beautiful. I know you mentioned you made these, but I had no idea they were so good. I mean you could sell this in a shop.'

'I do sell them… I told you.' She smiled. 'So you like it?'

'I do! Thank you.'

He wrapped the scarf elegantly round his neck and the three of them ate supper in a cheerful mood. But at half-past ten, when Georgie had gone up to bed, he stood up and said, 'Look love, I ought to be off really. I've got a long day of cataloguing tomorrow for the New Year sale. Would you mind if I didn't stay tonight?'

'Oh, yes, sure. If you need to,' said Miranda, trying hard to hide her disappointment. 'We've not really sorted out what we are doing over the next few days, have we?' she asked, a little anxiously.

'No. I think I mentioned I've got to see my folks in Devon for Christmas Day, and I ought to head off there tomorrow night. But I'll be back on Boxing Day evening. How about I come up to see you both then and we can have a re-run of Christmas to-gether – just the three of us?'

Her disappointment lifted as she realised that they would be spending at least part of the holiday together. 'Oh, that would be lovely, Charlie. What shall I cook? Anything but turkey, I presume.'

'Whatever you like, darling.' He kissed her: a long, lingering kiss. As he left, he picked up the vase.

'I'll take this, shall I? I've written a cheque for it. I'll just put it on the hall table.'

Before Miranda could say anything, he had gone. She wandered over to the table and picked up the cheque. It had been written, or at least dated, a week earlier. All that was left of the vase was a watermark where it had once stood. The hall felt curiously empty, as if some important force of nature had simply evaporated.

The clay bricks are thrown into a large pool of water, where they are stirred with iron shovels. The workmen are assisted by a pair of sturdy buffaloes. One man beats the animals with a rod, to encourage them as they walk round and round the pool, kneading and trampling the clay bricks. While the buffaloes rest, a thick cream floats to the surface of the pool. This is scraped off and stored in a vase of water. The process is repeated, until there is nothing left but coarse pieces at the bottom of the pool.

When the clay is finally free from all impurities, workmen carry large wooden tubs of the creamy substance to a low building by the side of the river. Here ladies sit on green and blue porcelain stools beneath an arbour of vines. They pass the cream through a fine horsehair sieve, then into a large bag made of two layers of silk. They sit and drink tea, and sieve. This is women's work. Once the paste is clean, it is solidified, wrapped in fine cotton cloth, and laid, one brick on top of another. In this way, all remaining water is absorbed into the cloth. Before it is completely dry, the kaolin is pressed into wooden moulds, and sliced neatly with a wire cutter, before being stamped with the mark of the manufacturer. These white clay tiles, known as 'pai tun', are then dried in the sun on large low tables, before they are stored in warehouses.

PART TWO

CHAPTER 16

Bruges
1469

Margarethe ran down the impressive oak staircase of her family's house on Groenerei, her little dog Spitzke at her heels. She leapt the last two stairs, holding her skirts up to avoid tripping. At nineteen years of age, she was on the cusp of womanhood, but craved the freedom of her childhood. Her leather mules clattered onto the black and white tiled floor as she landed. Spitzke barked excitedly and danced around her feet, her intelligent currant-black eyes sparkling in the candlelight. It was a dull day, and Margarethe's mother had ordered wax candles to be lit in all the downstairs rooms. The flickering light bounced around the hall, refracted by the tall, latticed windows that looked out over the canal.

That evening, the family was to host a grand party to celebrate Margarethe's betrothal to Cornelius van Vaerwye, a merchant from one of the most significant families in Antwerp. Her parents, Maria and Peter Haas, had invited over one hundred people to their home overlooking the 'Green' canal. Her Uncle Daniele, who had recently returned from a lengthy period of travelling in Sweden, was also to attend, along with her three sisters, Beatrice, Caterina and Katje. The household staff had been busy since dawn cooking and baking, arranging chairs and covering tables with crisp white linen cloths. Crystal sparkled, silverware had been polished, and a collection of exquisite and rare Chinese porcelain was laid out on the tables and filled with spectacular arrangements of crystallised fruit.

The gown Margarethe was to wear that evening had been laid out on the bed in her room by her maid. Delivered a few days earlier by the dressmakers, it was made of silk brocade in a shade of blue-green that perfectly matched her eyes. The sleeves were lined with sable, a fur normally reserved for the nobility or royalty which had been specially sourced by her uncle Daniele; her headdress would be made of the finest Italian linen edged in Bruges lace.

A painting had been commissioned by her parents to commemorate their eldest daughter's forthcoming wedding. Margarethe and Cornelius had spent many hours 'sitting' for the artist. The composition had been the subject of much discussion. Every last detail had been artfully constructed: the vividly coloured silk of Margarethe's dress; the colour and style of her husband-to-be's coat and hat. Even their positions had been carefully considered. The artist had decided they should both be standing, Cornelius gently holding Margarethe's right hand. Between the pair lay Spitzke, Margarethe's little Brussels griffon; a bowl of oranges sat on the dark oak chest next to the bride, symbolic of the family's great wealth and a nod to her mother's Italian heritage; and on the mantelshelf above the great fireplace in the drawing room, positioned exactly between the couple, stood a Ming vase.

The painting had been hung above that same fireplace the previous day, and Maria had wept when she had seen it. She had told Margarethe that she was determined that her betrothal would be the most splendid celebration in Bruges since the wedding the previous year of Charles the Bold, the Duke of Burgundy, to Margaret of York.

'My own betrothal to your father was not quite so elaborate. Things were done differently in those days,' she had said mysteriously to her daughter, alluding to her rushed nuptials in a Venetian convent.

Maria had never revealed to her children the nature of her and Peter's sudden departure from Venice. The fear of plague was so powerful, the pair had agreed to conceal their brush with the terrible disease all those years before. All the girls knew was that their parents had met in Venice and had moved to Bruges on their marriage.

Maria and Margarethe sat now on either side of the fireplace in the tall leather-backed chairs gazing up at the painting.

'He has caught you very well,' Maria said to her daughter. 'The light catches your hair so beautifully.'

'I love that look on Spitzke's face. He looks so naughty,' said Margarethe.

'Yes, he is adorable. And the vase looks good, don't you think?'

'It does, Mama,' said her daughter.

'I had not mentioned this to you before, my darling, but your father and I want you to have the vase as part of your dowry.'

'Oh Mama, no! I couldn't take the vase from you. I know how you love it so.'

'Yes, I love it. It's a part of our family history; we brought it back from the East with Papa all those years ago. It came with us on board ship, as part of caravan as we crossed the desert. And it was my dowry when I married your father. But I have always told you that it would be handed on, and your marriage seems the most opportune moment.'

'But Mama, are you sure? I know what it means to you.'

'I know you do. But it's not just that it's been in our family for many years. I truly believe it has a mysterious power. You know – I have told you before – that the one time we let it out of our sight we lost our darling *Mamma*.'

'Mama, you don't really believe that, do you?' asked Margarethe, slightly incredulously.

'I know it sounds ridiculous, but trust me, Margarethe; it has brought us luck all our lives. Look at how successful we have been here in Bruges. Your father is one of the most important merchants in this city. We have been very fortunate. I want that fortune to be handed on. I have four daughters and sadly I cannot split the vase into four pieces. So we have decided that you shall have it, as our eldest child. I'm sure Cornelius will make his own luck. He seems a bright and industrious young man. But I want you to have it nevertheless. You are sensible, Margarethe, and careful. I know you will value and protect it. It came all the way from the court of the Emperor of China. Remember that. Promise me that you will look after it.'

'I will take it with me to Antwerp and keep it safe, I promise.'

'And one other thing,' said Maria. 'I have written a brief history of the vase, here on this paper. I shall put this note into the vase and I would take it as a kindness if you could carry that history on for me, and if God wills it and you have a child, ask them to do the same.'

'If that's what you wish, Mama, yes of course,' said her daughter, kissing her mother's soft cheek. 'Now, I must go upstairs and get ready; our guests will be here soon and I want to look my best for Cornelius.'

Maria watched her daughter leave the dark, panelled drawing room; she was proud of her eldest child – of her thoughtfulness, intelligence and beauty. Margarethe's betrothal had proved a great comfort in recent weeks. Two months earlier she had received the sad news that her beloved father Niccolò had died, quite peacefully, in his sleep. It had come as a terrible shock to Maria. Despite his seventy-four years of age, he had appeared to be in good health, writing regularly to his daughter and keeping her abreast of his work and life in Venice. It had been many years since she had seen her father, and she felt his loss keenly. She had hoped he would travel from Venice for Margarethe's wedding, and had been looking forward to it enormously. As soon she heard this news of her father, she wrote to her brother Daniele and begged him to return to Bruges.

My darling Daniele,

I trust all is well with you in Gothenburg. I am writing with some very sad news. Our beloved father has passed away. I hear from Mattheo – who was with him at the end – that it was very peaceful. It seems that he went to bed after a fine dinner and the following morning, when Mattheo went to wake him, he appeared fast asleep in his bed. He was, however, quite departed from this world.

His will is to be read next week. I shall be unable to attend; Margarethe's wedding is taking all my attention. But his notary has promised to send details to me here in Bruges.

Write to me soon, and let me know if you are able to return to us here.

Your loving sister,
Maria de' Niccolò Haas

Maria's mood had lifted when she had received a letter from Daniele, dictated to his servant, informing her that he would be returning to Bruges in time to celebrate his niece's betrothal.

I am so saddened to hear of Papa's death. He lived a good and long life, and we should be grateful for it. But it has been too many years since we were all together. I see now that I have been living the bachelor life too long. It is time for me to put down roots, sister. And so, I too have some news, my dear Maria. It seems remarkable, I know, but at the age of forty I am finally to be married myself. I hope to bring my betrothed with me when I visit you next. She is the daughter of a Swedish merchant, Lars Petersson and is called Annelise. I know you will love her.

Maria was delighted when she read Daniele's letter. She had worried about him in the last few years. He had travelled widely since she had brought him to Bruges with Peter; he was always itching to be on the move. He had proved an able enough merchant, although too trusting, her husband said. 'Always ready to take the first price he is offered – not wishing to bargain hard. But he has a good eye and has improved our supply of furs from the north.'

Daniele had based himself in Gothenburg, and when not purchasing and exporting furs such as sable, mink, or arctic fox, to be sewn into sleeves of a man's *coppia*, or a woman's gown, he spent his time hawking and hunting. He was at his happiest galloping through the woods chasing deer, his bow or sword at the ready, his beloved greyhound Freya at his heels.

Just two weeks before Margarethe's wedding, Daniele arrived. Annelise was not with him; she had resolved to remain at home in Sweden with her father until after she was married. Maria was delighted to have her brother back with her and was secretly relieved that he had not yet brought his fiancé to meet the family. She was keen for him to make a marriage and settle down, but she was keener still to spend time with him alone. It reminded her of the early days of her marriage to Peter, when she was newly arrived in Bruges. While Peter was out having meetings with the League or making deals at the Bourse, she and Daniele would curl up in front of the fire in the house on Groenerei and tells stories, or read one of the new books that Maria had purchased. She had made a home in Bruges and Daniele had been a part of that. When he was eighteen and Peter had suggested that he be the family's representative in the north, she had been heartbroken at the thought of him leaving. But she knew that Daniele needed to make his own way. She had suggested to Peter that he might return to Venice to act as their agent there and live with his father, but Daniele had insisted that he would not go back to Venice. The memories of their escape had never left him. Instead he was delighted at the prospect of striking out into new, unknown territory in the north.

The day of his arrival in Bruges lifted her from her sadness at their father's death. She sat in the small sitting room overlooking the cobbled road that ran alongside Groenerei, scarcely able to concentrate on her needlework. Several times the needle caught her finger and a tiny drop of blood had marked the piece she was working on. She would have to work some red silk into the design to cover the stain. It was over ten years since she had last seen her brother, and she tried to imagine how he would have changed. He was forty years old now, and when they had last met he had still been a young man – tall and dark, with their father's dark brown eyes. Might his hair now have a little silver running through it? Might he have eaten too many excellent dinners, causing his stomach to swell? Suddenly, there was a clatter of hooves on the cobbles outside and the barking of a dog. She leapt to her feet, her needlepoint falling to the ground, and rushed to the large latticed window. Leaping from his horse was her brother. He was still tall and handsome, and his hair, escaping from the fur hat, was long and dark. He looked well and ruddy-cheeked as he bent down to pat his dog. The servants opened the sturdy studded oak door and Maria rushed down the steps to greet him.

'Daniele, darling Daniele,' she sobbed into his heavy woollen cloak. 'You are here, safe and well.'

'I am, *cara*…' He held her by the shoulders and looked deeply into her tearful blue-green eyes. 'You look well, sister, if a little tired. Don't cry. I am here now.'

'I am well,' she said, laughing, 'and I am not sad now – just happy and all the better for seeing you.'

She dragged him up the steps to the house and his trunks were unloaded into the hall. At the top of the steps, he turned round and snapped his fingers, calling 'Freya'. The greyhound leapt up the steps and into the house. She lay obediently in the hall, her dark eyes watching her master intently. Finally he said, 'Good girl. Come and meet my sister.' The dog leapt to her feet, her tail wagging, and her paws clattering on the tiled floor as she rushed at Maria, who knelt down and took the dog's fine long-boned head in her hands, scratching her ears.

'She's a beauty, Daniele – a real beauty. Have you had her long?'

'Five years,' said Daniele, glowing with pride. 'She's the best dog I've ever had – the most responsive, the most intelligent, and the most obedient.'

'Well, we must make her a comfortable bed for her stay,' said Maria kindly.

'She'll be fine with me,' said Daniele. 'She warms my feet at night.'

They spent the following days rediscovering each other and talking incessantly. Maria took huge delight in her brother and they laughed and joked from morning till night. On their first evening together, as the family assembled in the large dining room, Daniele went from one niece to another, expressing his admiration for their beauty and elegance.

'They are more than just pretty girls,' said Maria with pride. 'They all speak several languages – French of course, Italian, Flemish and German. They paint and they play the spinet. They are the most talented young ladies in Bruges.'

'Oh Mama,' said Margarethe, 'you embarrass us.'

'Well, I look forward to witnessing all your talents whilst I am here,' said Daniele. 'The last time I was here, you were just little girls. Adorable, but noisy, I seem to remember!'

The girls laughed and each one found herself just a little bit in love with their tall dark uncle.

Peter was keen to introduce his brother-in-law to their business partners as soon as possible. But Maria begged him to be patient.

'Just give us a little time together first, Peter – please? It has been so many years since we last were together.'

On their walks round Bruges, Maria took Daniele to visit the hospital of St John, of which she was a patron. Since their experience on the island, she had been pleased to be involved in the support of the sick and dying in Bruges. She was proud of the high standards of the hospital and the care that the patients received at the hands of the nuns.

'It is nothing like the island, brother,' she said when she took him there.

'We take good care of our patients here. They are well fed, warm and comfortable. And many of them get well. I hope you will be impressed.'

Maria took great delight in showing Daniele all the little hidden byways of Bruges. One morning, she took a large basket from the hall table and asked him to accompany her to the fish market.

'He doesn't want to go there,' said Peter irritably. 'He's not come all this way to buy fish, for goodness sake.'

'I just want him to see it.'

'I shall go with her, Peter. I shall enjoy it,' Daniele said amicably.

The day was sunny and the brother and sister walked happily along by the Groenerei together. Maria took Daniele's arm.

'I wanted to live near here when we first moved to Bruges. It reminded me of the fish market in Venice. Do you remember?'

'Of course I do,' said Daniele. 'How could I forget? That last walk through the market nearly did for us – the fishermen recognizing Papa like that.'

'Yes, that was unfortunate. But it was a friendly place and I loved the noise and bustle of it all. Our little fish market here is much the same. And if I need other things – to order meat or vegetables for the house – it is just a short walk to the main market square, just beyond the Burg.'

'It seems you have everything here,' said Daniele.

'We do, and we are very content.'

'But Margarethe is to move to Antwerp; how do you feel about that?'

'It will be a wrench, that is for certain,' said Maria sadly. 'But I am happy for her. Cornelius is a good man and has a good business. He is interested in developing a porcelain import business. They are to have the vase. I hope it will provide inspiration for them.'

That evening, after dinner, the family sat as usual in the drawing room. The girls played cards. Maria sat at her needlework and Peter and Daniele stood with their backs to the fire, drinking a glass of wine.

'I am glad to see you here, brother. My own brothers hardly come to Bruges anymore. My uncle passed away several years ago. To be honest, I feel in need of some male company!' And he gestured at the five women sitting near them. 'I live in a female household.'

'It seems to me that you are a fortunate man,' said Daniele, smiling.

'I am,' said Peter. 'Nevertheless, it is good to have you here. If my wife has finished showing you around, I shall take you to the Burg tomorrow and introduce to you to my fellow counsellors.'

It was but a five-minute walk from their house on the Groenerei to the Burg. Peter was one of an exclusive group of twenty-six town councillors who were also magistrates. These twenty-six also formed the guild of the Holy Blood – a fraternity dedicated to protecting a holy relic held at the Basilica, the richly decorated church that stood next to the Burg. The relic was said to be a vial of 'holy blood' taken by Joseph of Arimathea from Jesus Christ after his crucifixion. It was brought to Bruges, according to legend, during the second crusade in 1150 by the Count of Flanders.

The fraternity were tasked with its protection and on Holy Blood Day would take part in a procession through the town wearing the guild livery, during which the vial would be displayed to the townspeople before being safely returned to its sanctuary in the Basilica behind a heavy iron grille.

Peter had become an elevated member of Bruges society and he revelled in it. But it created stresses and strains. He spent at least half of his time on town or guild business and worried constantly about the development of the family's enterprise. He hoped, when Daniele arrived in Bruges, to convince him to return to the city and help him to run the business.

After their day on the Burg, he took his brother-in-law to the bathhouse. Sited in a large building on the edge of the square, this was a convivial place for merchants to meet and discuss business. It was also a convenient place for assignations of other kinds; couples were regularly to be espied bathing together in dark corners, lit only by candlelight. Unlike Venice, prostitution was actively discouraged by the straight-laced burghers of Bruges; but they would turn a blind eye to an unmarried couple, or a visiting merchant seeking comfort in a lady of lesser virtue in the bath house.

Peter and his family were able to take baths regularly at their house on the Groenerei. Large wooden tubs would be brought into the bedchambers and lined with linen before being filled with water from the kitchen. It was a laborious process, but served its purpose. But Peter enjoyed the bathhouse. He had never quite forgotten the easy lasciviousness of Venice, and relished the opportunity to espy beautiful naked women as they climbed into a bath in a dimly lit corner. He adored Maria, of course, but had been tempted once or twice during their long marriage by these ladies at the bathhouse. He felt some guilt about it, but reasoned that it was a small reward for his hard work over the years.

The bathhouse, however, was not just an opportune place to meet women; Peter relished it for its warmth on a cold winter's night; for the steam, which cleared his sinuses; and most of all, for the opportunity the bathhouse afforded for relaxed conversation. Deals could be struck more easily with a merchant from Genoa or Nuremberg if you sat in a bath with them drinking a large glass of wine.

Daniele was used to bathhouses of course. They were common in the Nordic countries too, although there too any drinking or 'loose' behaviour was actively discouraged.

'Does Maria know you come here?' he asked his brother-in-law as they lay back in the deep hot water.

'Yes, she knows. She wouldn't come here herself, of course – it wouldn't be seemly. But she knows that a lot of business gets done here and she understands. She is a good woman, your sister.'

The following day, Peter took Daniele for a meeting at the international exchange on Vlamingstraat, the Herberg ter Buerse, to discuss prices for their goods. Daniele had arranged a large shipment of furs to be delivered to Bruges the following week. After lunch Peter had arranged for them to visit the loggias of Venice and Genoa, which stood either side of the Buerse, where the talk drifted easily to their shared experiences of Italian life. Peter relished these meetings. He had enjoyed his time in Venice and fell easily and naturally into the language. And he enjoyed the reminiscences. He was happy to be in Bruges, of course; it was the most important city in northern Europe at that time, and he was proud of his success there, but his time in Venice would always hold a special place in his heart.

Daniele, by contrast, felt uncomfortable around people from his father's home city. He lived in dread of someone revealing how he and Maria had left Venice. But the story had long been forgotten. If there had ever been gossip amongst the merchants of Venice about the sudden disappearance of dei Conti's two children, it appeared to have faded with the years, and no one he met in the loggias connected either him or his sister with the plague, or with the island on which they had been briefly incarcerated.

Daniele was impressed by how Maria and Peter had grown in stature in the city. They were clearly at the centre of business and courtly life. Preparations for Margarethe's betrothal party were nearing completion and the house was humming with activity. Greenery was delivered – picked from the Haas's country estate – to decorate the ballroom and drawing room. Baskets of fresh flowers arrived daily. Haunches of venison were unloaded from carts on the cobbled street outside. Boxes of fruit and vegetables arrived on an almost hourly basis. From dawn till dusk staff were polishing, baking, cooking and arranging.

'You have done well, sister,' Daniele pronounced the evening before the party, as he sat with his sister in front of the fire in her small sitting room. 'I like this room, Maria. It reminds me of my own little wooden house in Sweden. My life there is much simpler than yours here in Bruges. I have only two servants and I prefer it that way. I like to be outside, in the woods. I love the clear air, and the snow, when it's thick on the ground. I love nothing more than to be outside hunting with Freya at my side.'

'And will Annelise be satisfied with just two servants, do you think?' asked Maria, her eyes firmly on her needlepoint.

'Yes, I think so. Why? Do you think she might prefer something a little grander? I do hope not. She seems a sensible, straightforward girl.'

'Well, when you are married, you must bring her here to meet us, Daniele. Then perhaps I can judge her needs. But if you require a larger house, brother, you just have to say. The business is doing well and you are entitled to more of the profits if you need them.'

'Ah, you are kind, sister. I doubt we will need more; certainly nothing like your house here on the Groenerei. It is so splendid; it's almost like a palace. I wonder what our father would have thought of it all? I am glad for you, though, and I am proud of my nieces. They are all beauties, your girls, *cara*. But you must have yearned for a son, I think?'

'I love my daughters so much,' said Maria. 'I don't say that we wouldn't have liked a son. I'm sure Peter would have done – to carry on the business. But Margarethe is very intelligent and sensible. She is marrying a wonderful young man and I know they will be successful in Antwerp.'

'And the others?' asked Daniele.

'They are all remarkable in their own way. I'm sure they will each find suitable husbands in time.'

Upstairs, as Maria chatted with her brother, Margarethe's younger sister Caterina sat at her dressing table in the window of her room overlooking the canal. She was sixteen, and the third daughter of Maria and Peter Haas. Her elder sisters, Margarethe, Beatrice and 'baby' sister Katje, had all inherited their mother's dark hair and blue eyes. Margarethe's eyes were the most startling – a blue green that shone out from her pale face. But Caterina, the only daughter to be given an Italian name after their mother's family heritage, was blonde. Her hair was the softest gold, much like that of their father, Peter. Her eyes matched his too; they were grey, like the cool water than ran through the canal outside their house on the Groenerei.She had retreated to her bedroom earlier in the day, in part to escape the frenzied activity in the house below. Margarethe's betrothal party would take place the following evening, and Caterina had to confess that she was jealous: of the party itself, and of the fuss being made of Margarethe.

But there was another reason for her ill humour. The man Margarethe was to marry, Cornelius van Vaerwye, had caught Caterina's eye the previous year, when they had taken part in the celebrations for the sumptuous wedding of the Duke of Burgundy to Margaret of York. The Duke's father had set up court in Bruges some years before and the town was proud of its royal associations. The marriage itself was conducted in the Church of our Lady at Damme, near Bruges, and was followed by twelve days of banquets, pageants, masques, processions, jousting and tournaments. The great families of the town were all involved – hosting parties, attending the banquets and tournaments.

On the day of the marriage itself, the royal couple arrived in Bruges to find the streets decked with ribbons and bright banners. A spectacular procession took place through the streets, in which the new Duchess was carried on a litter to her Ducal Palace. Tableaux were performed all along the route; the first was of Adam and Eve in paradise; the second depicted Cleopatra being given in marriage to Alexander. English and Burgundian nobles, accompanied by their yeoman and men-at-arms, led the procession. Minstrels and trumpeters, playing as they marched, followed them. Ambassadors, knights, bishops and clerics came next. Then the merchants of all the loggias of Bruges processed, led by the Venetians dressed in crimson velvet; they were followed by the Florentines, with the Medici banker Tomasso Portarini leading the way; his merchants were all dressed in black satin with crimson doublets. After them came the Spaniards, followed by the Genoese, led by a beautiful girl on horseback representing the virgin saved from the dragon by St George. Finally, one hundred and eight German merchants, including Peter Haas, dressed in violet cloth and grey fur, made a spectacular finale to the procession.

The new Duchess arrived at the Ducal Palace at midday. The wedding breakfast was to take place in a wooden banqueting hall complete with glass windows, which had been prefabricated in Brussels and erected on the Duke's tennis court. In the afternoon, the wedding party moved to the Market Square to watch the first of many jousts. Peter and his family joined the crowd watching the spectacle from the upper rooms of the Burg. As one of the leading merchant families in the city, Peter, Maria and their daughters had been invited to a banquet at the Palace that evening. Maria had insisted on new gowns for their four girls. Margarethe, Beatrice and Katje had chosen silks in shades of green and blue. But Caterina, with her fair hair and grey eyes, had selected a dramatic cloth of red silk, embroidered with black thread. It was cut in a low 'V' at the front, revealing a little décolleté, with a belt of black silk just under the bust and sleeves edged in fur. Her hair would be pulled back, as was the fashion, and she would wear a tall *hennin* headdress with a delicate veil. The dress was delivered the day before the grand banquet and Caterina could not wait to try it on. She hoped it would create a magnificent impression.

On the evening of the banquet, Peter Haas ushered his beautiful wife and four daughters into the Duke's Palace. The entrance was dominated by a vast tableau painted in gold and azure blue depicting two lions, the Duke's coat of arms. On either side were painted two archers; created in relief, they appeared almost real to the observer. But behind their wooden facades, newly constructed fountains had been erected that flowed with wine. It spouted and gushed from the archers' arrows: Beaune from one and Rhenish wine from the other. It fell into large stone vats from which guests could take their fill.

Inside the large banqueting hall, two gargantuan mechanical chandeliers had been suspended from the ceiling. They looked like mountains, with paths winding round their bulk, decorated with life-like flowers and trees. Models of people and animals ascended the paths, climbing towards a castle that stood at the summit of each mountain. At the base of each chandelier were seven mirrors which were arranged so that anyone glancing up could see everything that happened in the vast space beneath; the walls were hung with rich tapestries made of gold and silver thread and a large stage had been erected for dancing and tableaux. The food was served on silver plates and guests were seated at long wooden tables on which stood seven-foot-long wooden ships painted in gold and azure blue and each carrying the name of one of the Duke's lordships. They were perfect in every detail – with ropes made of gold thread and miniature models of sailors. Into each ship was placed the food for the banquet. Beside them stood tall pies made to look like castles, also decorated in gold and azure blue. And surrounding each one were little dishes of olives and capers and lemons.

The girls gasped when they sat down at their places. 'What extraordinary imagination the organisers must have,' said Beatrice. 'Look up there,' said Katje. 'You can see your face in the mirrors. And the little sailors… They're so sweet.'

Caterina refused to be drawn by her sisters' excitement. Her attention had been taken immediately by a handsome young man seated on her right-hand side. Carlo Cavalcanti sold silks on behalf of the Medici family, who were bankers to the Burgundian Court. His manager, Tomasso Portarini, had been intricately involved in the wedding arrangements. He had supplied the cloth of gold worn by the Duke on his wedding day along with a large proportion of the clothes worn by the Duke and his family throughout the twelve days of feasting and jousting. The Duke owed Portarini over fifty thousand pounds, and young Carlo, who had arranged for the fine cloth to be imported, had been rewarded with a place at the Duke's feast.

'So, madam,' he said to Caterina, gesturing towards the royal couple at the top table, 'what do you think of the Duke's fine cloth of gold?'

'It is stunning,' said Caterina. 'Why do you ask?'

'I brought it into the country, from Florence. The Medici were tasked with supplying all the wedding clothes.'

'I'm very impressed,' said Caterina politely. 'And what do you make of my dress? My father had the silk brought in from Venice.'

'I recognised it. It's beautiful – as are you, lady.'

Caterina giggled. There was no doubt that Carlo was a handsome man; he was also amusing, and well connected. At fifteen, she was keenly aware that she should find a husband soon. The Duke had the power to compel unmarried or even widowed women from merchant families into marriages with his friends and acquaintances if he thought the alliance would be helpful. Caterina had recently overheard her mother discussing the plight of a young widow who had been persuaded into a marriage against her will. Her husband, a furrier named Jean Pinte, had died suddenly and even as he was being buried his widow was forcibly engaged to another furrier named Willeret de Noeuville. He had the virtue, at least, of being a young man, aged just twenty, but nevertheless, the woman was forced to consummate the marriage the day after she buried her first husband. Had she been a rich widow, her family could perhaps have paid money to prevent the marriage, which was the only way to avoid it. This was not a predicament Caterina wished to find herself in. Her parents were rich, of course, which would afford her some protection. But Caterina didn't want to take any chances; she had already asked her father to help her select a suitable husband as soon as possible, and he had promised to do so. She wondered now if Carlo Cavalcanti might be the man.

'How long have you worked with the Medici bank?'

'Some five years. I speak French and so it makes sense for me to liaise with the court here in Bruges. I have a good position.'

'They are powerful, the Medici.'

'Yes, very. We do well here.'

'And will you stay – here in Bruges?'

'I think so,' said Carlo. 'At least for now. I like it here. The people are wealthy, the ladies are beautiful, and I am good at what I do.'

'You are full of conceit,' said Caterina playfully.

Opposite Carlo sat a dark-haired young man. He had pale blue eyes and a long nose, which he rubbed from time to time between thumb and forefinger. He was not classically good looking, but he had a gentle countenance. Perhaps he was shy, Caterina thought, for he had not yet spoken to anyone around him.

Wishing to tease Carlo a little, Caterina turned away from him and spoke instead to the young man.

'Do you like it here, in Bruges?'

The young man blushed a little and looked slightly surprised to be so addressed.

'I do,' he said quietly.

'I do not believe we have been introduced. I am Caterina Haas, the daughter of Peter Haas the merchant; he is sitting down there.' She gestured towards her father, who was laughing loudly at a friend's joke.

'Cornelius van Vaerwye, from Antwerp.'

'Antwerp – is it nice there?'

'It is. I have lived there all my life. I like it.'

'And what do you do in Antwerp, Cornelius van Vaerwye?'

'I am a merchant too. My family has been there for many generations.'

'And are you successful?'

Cornelius blushed. He was slightly shocked at the young woman's impertinence. 'I am, madam. I mean, we are.'

Margarethe, who had been seated next to Cornelius, glared at her younger sister.

'Cornelius,' she interjected, 'what did you make of the wonderful tableau as we arrived? Was it not astonishing?'

The young man smiled and appeared to relax a little. He and Margarethe began to chat easily. Not for the first time in her life, Caterina felt a pang of jealousy. Her elder sister appeared to have an easy way with conversation. Caterina preferred a combative style. Her father often chastised her for it, but secretly he admired his daughter's quick wit and sharp tongue. She made him laugh and he saw himself in her – cool and fair-haired on the outside, but fiery and hot within.

Caterina spent the rest of the meal chatting with Carlo. He was charming and intelligent and appeared to enjoy her company. But she could not help glancing across the table towards her sister. Margarethe and Cornelius appeared to be in deep conversation about something. They kept their voices low and it was impossible to decipher what they were saying.

When the meal was finished and the tables cleared away, the room was prepared for dancing.

A group of performers displayed the latest dances on the stage. The audience all applauded. Then the musicians struck up a familiar tune and the guests were invited to take to the floor.

Carlo invited Caterina to dance. She accepted, but noted with irritation that Cornelius had asked her sister Margarethe. They lined up next to one another. There was something in Caterina's nature that caused her to chase after anyone who failed to show an interest in her. It was as if she was determined to have whatever she set her mind to. She resolved to persuade Cornelius to fall in love with her.

The first dance was the *basse danse*. It was popular at the Burgundian court. The couples processed gracefully in an elegant gliding motion. Caterina found it rather dull. She preferred dances where the participants were required to leap or hop from the floor. She and Carlo moved elegantly around the room, his hand just touching hers. He was tall and graceful and smiled at her from time to time. But she was unable to take her eyes off her sister who appeared to be quite entranced by Cornelius. The pair moved together so perfectly, in such unison, that they were almost like one person.

The *pavane* came next. Much like the first dance, it involved slow graceful processional movements. Caterina suggested to her partner that they went for a glass of wine. She stood at the side of the great hall watching her sister with Cornelius. Carlo leant down and whispered in her ear.

'You watch your sister with great interest, Caterina.'

'Yes, I think she is making a fool of herself with that boring merchant from Antwerp.'

'Shall we break them up?' asked Carlo, smiling.

'Can we?' asked Caterina.

'I shall ask her to dance, then he will be forced to dance with you. I am envious of him already.'

'Why would you do that?' asked Caterina.

'Because it would please you.'

As the *pavane* came to its stately close, the couples began to disperse. Cornelius and Margarethe walked back towards their table.

The musicians struck up a *saltarello*. This was much more to Caterina's liking as it was faster than the earlier dances and involved the dancers hopping on each second beat. Carlo went at once to Margarethe and asked her to dance. Cornelius looked around and saw Caterina gazing at him. He was powerless to avoid her.

'Would you care to dance the *saltarello*?'

'I would,' said Caterina. She threw herself into the dance, laughing as she leapt into the air, twirling around her partner. Her pale skin flushed a little, her fine gold hair escaped from her hennin.

Cornelius danced well; he appeared more handsome than at first sight. As the dance came to a close he spun her round; he put his hand on her waist and she felt herself shudder with excitement.

The two couples walked back to the table. Caterina chattered gaily to her companion. But Cornelius seemed impervious to her; his eyes, she noted with irritation, followed Margarethe around the room.

The family arrived back at their house on the Groenerei well after midnight. Maria kissed the girls as they went upstairs to bed.

'You were all beautiful tonight.'

Her daughters smiled: 'So were you, Mama.'

'I think perhaps one of you might have met your husband tonight?' said Maria, smiling up at Margarethe.

'Mama! What makes you say such a thing?' said Margarethe, blushing.

'Just something about the way you were together. I spoke to him a little, as did your father. He is from a fine family of merchants in Antwerp.'

Margarethe smiled. 'So, did you like him?'

'We did. We have invited him to dine with us next week.'

Margarethe was delighted. 'Oh Mama, thank you. I should very much like to see him again.'

'He will be here throughout the Duke's celebrations. I thought it would be a good opportunity.'

'I thought him rather dull,' said Caterina spitefully. 'I can't imagine a worse person to marry than that.'

'Oh Caterina,' said Maria, 'don't be so silly. He is delightful. He would not be right for you perhaps, but Margarethe has a much gentler disposition.'

This cut Caterina to the quick. Her mother professed to love her daughters equally, but she could not avoid the feeling that her eldest sister had more of her mother's love and affection.

'So who am I to marry?' she asked petulantly. 'Someone with a violent disposition? I will not be forced to marry some man that the Duke chooses for me.'

'Oh Caterina, you are young and so hot-headed. You must not worry about your future husband yet. We will not allow any of our daughters to be married against their will. You must know that. But we must settle Margarethe first and then Beatrice. Your time will come.'

Caterina followed her sisters up the large oak staircase to bed, filled with resentment that she had not been born the eldest sister. But as she climbed into her bed and pulled the curtains around her, she lay against the lace pillows and thought about Carlo Cavalcanti and what sort of life she might have with the man who sold silk to the Burgundian court.

CHAPTER 17

Antwerp
1490

Margarethe lay in her bed, propped up with cushions. She had flung the bed curtains open to let in some air. The room was humid, fetid almost, and she felt faint and weak. Early morning light filtered through the latticed windows in her bed-chamber. Pain was searing through her and in spite of herself, she let out a high-pitched scream.

'Madam, madam, calm yourself.' The midwife stroked her brow. Her voice was soothing, but her face told a different story. She was worried. The baby was stuck and Margarethe could not, however hard she tried, push any harder. Besides, the pain was terrible, unimaginable.

'I can't do any more,' she said after the last contraction as she collapsed onto her sweat-soaked pillows.

'I know, I know. You are doing well. I must examine you, I think.'

The midwife plunged her hand between Margarethe's legs. In agony, Margarethe let out an involuntary scream.

'Hush now, I know it's uncomfortable.'

'Uncomfortable!' shouted Margarethe. 'That was terrible. I've never felt such a thing before.'

'The baby is breach – I must turn it or you and the baby will die. You will never push it out the way it's lying.'

Margarethe wept silently and fingered her rosary. It was made of carved coral beads with a silver bead at either end. Cornelius had given it to her on the birth of their first child Jacob eighteen years before.

'I will turn the baby now. Take a deep breath.'

Margarethe took in a huge draft of hot humid air as the midwife plunged her hand deep inside her. Her fingers clutched at the rosary so tightly that the sharp carved edges of the tiny beads cut the flesh of her palm. She prayed under her breath. 'Pray for me, mother of God, now and in the hour of our death,' over and over again.

'There! It is done,' said the midwife with an air of satisfaction, wiping her bloody hand on her apron. 'I did one of those last week too.'

'And did it go well?' said Margarethe anxiously.

'Not on that occasion, no. Now, when the next contraction comes, you can push.'

Within seconds, the deep burning pain rose up through Margarethe's body and she pushed with all her might. Her entire being seemed to be on fire as she finally expelled the reluctant child.

The slippery infant fell into the midwife's waiting hands. She tossed the child upside down and slapped it firmly on the back. It wailed gustily.

Margarethe collapsed back onto the pillows and wept with relief and joy. The absence of pain was overwhelming. 'Is the baby all right?'

'Yes! A fine girl – a sister for all those boys.'

'A girl! Oh, thank you!'

At the age of thirty-nine, Margarethe knew that she was fortunate to have survived another birth. She and Cornelius were already parents to five sons. Two other children had been born – both girls – but they had died in infancy. This was then her eighth delivery, and she was grateful that it was over. She hoped fervently that she would never have to endure it again. She prayed too that this daughter would survive.

The midwife cut the cord; as was the custom, it would be burned later that day in the fire. The baby was bathed and swaddled. Margarethe's maid helped her to change her nightgown. Her bed was cleaned as best they could and the child was laid in her arms. Cornelius entered the bedchamber accompanied by Margarethe's dog, Lysbette, the granddaughter of her beloved Spitzke. The little griffon snuffled around the pile of soiled linen that lay by the bed before the midwife shooed it away. Gathering the linen up in her sturdy arms, she left the couple alone together. A fire had been lit in the hearth, casting a warm glow in the room.

'Is all well, my dear?'

'Yes, all is well, Cornelius. We have a daughter.'

Cornelius bent over the child and stroked her cheek.

'She is beautiful. I wonder what her brothers will make of her?'

'They will spoil her, I suspect.'

'And what shall we call her?'

'I would like to call her Maria – after my own mother. Maria Margret.'

Four days later, Caterina Cavalcanti received news of her sister's new baby as she sat in the drawing room of her house in Bruges. Her brother-in-law's letter spoke at length of the new baby's virtues – the child's blue eyes, and her full head of dark hair. Caterina had loathed childbirth and had refused to breastfeed any of her children. She had insisted on a wet nurse for each of them. To her, the thought that her sister had now given birth to her eighth child was horrific. Her sister, she felt, was too easily persuaded to do her husband's bidding, especially when it came to sharing his bed. Caterina had learned to be firm with Carlo and had often refused him entry to her chamber as a means of protecting herself from yet another pregnancy. It annoyed him, she knew, but she could always get around Carlo. They were so alike – sharp, manipulative and quick-witted. He had done well for himself and the family. He had left the Medici bank some seventeen years earlier and struck out on his own and he had made a great fortune for the family from his silk business. He travelled a great deal and those long journeys abroad gave Caterina respite from his incessant demands. She imagined that he took advantage of his freedom when he was away from home. She didn't resent it. As long as he returned from each buying trip with a length of expensive silk or a fashionable garment for her or the children, she was content.

Cornelius's letter continued with news of their sons and how well they were all doing; their eldest son Jacob was to travel soon to Portugal to collect the latest shipment of porcelain. Caterina was interested enough in her nephews' lives, of course, but she could never quite cope with the idea that her sister's children were in some way doing better than her own four.

She and Carlo had two daughters and two sons. They were attractive young people. The boys had inherited their father's dark Italian good looks and the two girls were fair-haired like their mother. But the boys lacked energy and she was envious of her nephew's desire to travel the world and increase the family fortune. She laid her brother-in-law's letter down her desk with a sigh. She would reply later that day. In the meantime, she must write to Carlo about a more pressing matter. He was in Italy on a buying expedition and was to leave Lucca, his final destination, within a week and return to Bruges.

Dear treasure, she wrote,

I ask you not to forget about my Italian coat, like the one Willhelm Imhoff brought his wife from Venice. Do not think ill of me because I always try to wheedle something

*out of you in every letter. I especially ask that you bring some
red and saffron coloured satin, if you can find an inexpensive measure or two.*

Yours ever,

Caterina.

*P.S. I have just received a letter from Cornelius. It seems
that Margarethe has been delivered of yet another child, a
girl, who they will name Maria Margret.'*

Back in Antwerp, the new baby was soon welcomed into the family. Four days after her birth, she was christened in the cathedral, accompanied by her father and her brothers. Jacob and Pieter stood as godfathers to the tiny girl.

A few days later, their mother felt strong enough to venture downstairs and re-join the family. She was anxious to spend as much time as possible with the boys, for Jacob and Pieter were soon to travel abroad to develop relationships with Portuguese merchants who would import their next big shipment of Chinese porcelain. The Portuguese and Spanish merchants dominated the direct trading routes to the East, and whilst some goods, including porcelain, could be carried overland along the Silk Road, it was a long journey and involved a complex sequence of intermediaries. The Portuguese had opened up a direct sea route to China the previous year, travelling around the Cape of Good Hope. They had returned with a shipload of porcelain from the imperial kilns and Pieter and Jacob were to make the journey to Portugal to secure the shipment. Pieter was only seventeen, and Margarethe was concerned that he was too young to travel so far, but Jacob and Cornelius had persuaded her that he was old enough, and ready and eager for the excitement.

Margarethe sat in the high-backed chair in the drawing room, her shawl wrapped around her shoulders, and the baby nestling contentedly in the little cot at her side. She sipped a little glass of wine while the boys laughed and teased one another around her. Their youngest brother Henryk was usually the butt of their jokes. A good-humoured boy of eight years of age, he had recently begun the study of Latin and had proved an able student. His elder brothers had never found learning quite so straightforward. They were better suited to a more active life. They were proud of their little brother, for he was the smartest of them all. But they were determined to rib him about it. Margarethe relished the time with her boys. She stroked her baby's cheek and laughed as the young men teased their little brother.

'Oh, leave poor Henryk in peace,' she begged, wiping tears of laughter from her cheeks. 'He is too good-natured. You'll see when you get back from your travels. He'll have grown big and strong and will not take any more of your ribbing.'

'Ha! I'd like to see that,' said Jacob. 'He's a thoughtful fellow, to be sure, and wise for his years, but he will never beat me with a sword, or a fist.' And he made as if to punch his little brother, who ducked nimbly out of the way.

Surrounded by her family, Margarethe gazed up at the Ming vase that stood on the mantle-shelf. It had protected them well. She had lost two babies, and that had been a tragedy, but it was so common for babies to die. And the vase was not magic, after all, she thought. She had never quite believed her mother when she had told her of its 'magical qualities'. But of one thing she was quite certain; she and Cornelius had had a successful and happy life. They had made a lot of money importing porcelain into northern Europe. Their sons were delighted to take the business on, and now they had a beautiful daughter. She fingered her rosary and prayed fervently that Maria Margret would survive.

The Ming vase glowed in the evening light, the flickering of candlelight reflected in its luminescent surface. The dragon seemed to dance gaily around its centre. That day she had written another entry for her mother's 'family history' and it lay now by her side, ready for her to put it back into its place deep within the vase. It was filled now with information about the family. Margarethe had taken the task on with enthusiasm and had drawn up a proper family tree. She had taken great pleasure in the task, as a sister was married or a child was born, decorating the names with little drawings and sketches.

Caterina had married Carlo and had four children. Beatrice had married too – also to a member of the Medici bank. He was called Folco d'Adoardo di Giovanni Portinari, and had been made acting manager of the Bruges branch of the bank some eleven years before. They had since moved to England, where he ran the London branch. It had been many years since she had seen her sister, but Beatrice was a faithful correspondent. She had five children of her own, although two had sadly died – a son at just three years of age and her youngest daughter, Magdalena, had been lost following their journey to London. The child had contracted pneumonia on the journey across the Channel and never recovered. Beatrice had written to her elder sister of her devastation, but she had somehow survived, and her remaining three children – two sons and a daughter – were in good health.

Lastly, little Katje had married a young man named Andreas, a cousin of their Uncle Daniele's wife, Annelise. They had met in Bruges after Daniele's wedding. He had been persuaded to return to Bruges for a short time to help their father run the business. In that first year, Annelise had pined for her home country, and her cousin Andreas had come to visit her and keep her company. He and Katje had met and the attraction was obvious. He was a furrier from a very successful family business in Sweden. Katje had returned to Sweden with him nearly a decade before and now had two sons. Daniele and Annelise had also returned to Sweden. Daniele had not enjoyed his time in Bruges. It reminded him too much of Venice; the narrow streets and canals were too claustrophobic for him and he pined for the Swedish countryside, where he was free to gallop through the forests with his dog at his heels. He and Annelise lived a simple but contented life in their country house outside Gothenburg. They had no children, but seemed happy enough.

All in all, Margarethe thought, as she rocked her tiny baby's cot, the family should be content with their progress in life. How much this had to do with the Ming vase she could not say. But she had lived up to her promise to her mother Maria and had taken great care of it. Maria and Peter were due to arrive in Antwerp the following day and Margarethe was excited at the prospect. Her mother was sixty-three now, but still healthy and strong. Her dark hair was threaded with silver, fine lines edged her clear aquiline eyes. Her father Peter was in good health, although recently he had suffered from gout, which made him irritable. Margarethe hoped that Maria would be happy with her newest granddaughter and pleased that she had been named for her. She resolved, as she gazed into the flames of the fire, that if her daughter survived to adulthood, she would give her the vase. Maria Margret would be the guardian of the magical dragon.

CHAPTER 18

Antwerp
1515

Maria Margret studied the maiolica bowl that her husband Antonio Corsi had just finished painting. Decorated in shades of vivid yellow, green, orange and blue, its bright colours shone out on that leaden February day. Antonio had been trained by his own father initially, but his talent had been really developed through his work with the famous potter Guido di Savino. Guido had moved from his home in Castel Durante, one of the leading centres of the Italian maiolica movement, to Antwerp some seven years before. Changing his name to Guido Andries, he married a local woman, Margriet Bolleman, and set up the first of several pottery workshops in the town. He and Margriet had five sons, all of whom would go on to be famous potters in their own right. A year or so after Guido had settled in Antwerp, he wrote to his old friend:

> *The people here are rich, my friend. They yearn for everything that is new and colourful. They have seen the porcelain brought in from the lands of the East, but only the very wealthiest families can afford such marvels. Everyone wishes to use beautiful pieces on their table. If they cannot have porcelain, they will buy maiolica. It will be successful here. Trust me. Make the journey. You will not be disappointed. Together we will be rich.*

Antonio, who had known Guido since they had been young apprentices together, made the journey to Antwerp shortly after receiving the letter. Born in Florence, he had started his apprenticeship in Venice before moving on to Castel Durante, where he met Guido. They were part of a group of potters who were determined to bring their extraordinary talent for creating useful and exquisite lustreware to northern Europe.

Maria Margret van Vaerwye had met Antonio Corso at a supper party given by her elder brother Jacob. She was twenty-one years of age; Antonio was twenty-five. They chatted easily throughout dinner and Maria Margret liked him immediately. He had an earthiness combined with an artistic temperament that she admired. Her experience of men was limited to her father and four brothers – all intelligent businessmen with a strong work ethic and vision, but not creative.

Antonio told her a little of his background. 'I was apprenticed to a potter in Venice when I was fifteen; I lived there for three years. It is a wonderful place. Have you been there?'

'No, but I long to go. My grandmother, Maria Haas, was originally from Venice. Her father Niccolò dei Conti was an explorer. He brought Maria back to Venice with my great uncle Daniele many years ago. She is dead now, sadly, but I am proud to carry her name. And I have one or two pieces of pottery that she brought with her from the Middle East and beyond. I could show you, if you like. We also have a beautiful Ming vase that her father brought with him from the lands of further India. I think she must have been a very special person for him to have entrusted it to her.'

Antonio was intrigued at this story of the vase and after dinner, Maria Margret took him to the drawing room where she showed him her collection of pottery.

Their courtship progressed, and the family was delighted when she announced to her father Cornelius that she wished to

marry Antonio. They admired him for his energy, talent and enthusiasm. Over the following months, they learned something of
his background and upbringing. His father had been integral to
the development of maiolica in Italy. He too, had been a famous
potter, who had made the journey to Valencia in Spain with a
merchant friend, Battista di Goro Bulgarini, and disguised in
poor clothes, he had masqueraded as a poor jobbing potter in
order to learn the secret of creating lustred pottery. Such pieces
had originally been made in the Middle East, where potters had
discovered that ceramic glaze could be rendered opaque white
by the addition of tin oxide. This white glaze provided a perfect
base for painting and the Islamic world had long exploited the
technique. The great lustred vases in the Alhambra in Malaga
were made in this way, and the Spanish potters were exporting
their works to the rest of Europe. Francesco di Marco Datini
– the 'Merchant of Prato' – had been importing large consign-
ments of lusterware into Florence for affluent families since the
early fifteenth century. Even the wealthy Lorenzo de' Medici of
the banking family in Florence had been impressed by a gift of
maiolica, describing it in a letter as "excellent and rare" pottery.

Jacob and Pieter liked Antonio well enough and were happy
to welcome him to the family. They were now in charge of the
family business, and had concentrated on three main imports:
pepper and cinnamon from the islands in the Indian Ocean, and
Chinese porcelain imported from traders in Portugal who had
opened up a sea route to China round the Cape of Good Hope
in 1498. Pepper was the most profitable commodity at that time,
and Antwerp – with its large port servicing hundreds of ships a
day – had a virtual monopoly on its import into northern Europe. As for Chinese porcelain, the brothers sold these pieces to
the great noble families of northern Europe and it made them
rich. The Chinese had a monopoly on porcelain production at
that time; many had tried to recreate the pale, translucent glazed

pieces, but without success. And so, they remained the preserve of the wealthy elite.

This marriage now opened up a new and lucrative business opportunity. Maiolica potters needed tin oxide to create the lustred finish on their work. Tin oxide was mined predominantly in Cornwall. Jacob and Peter imported the oxide and distributed it to potters in Antwerp and further afield. Before long, they had the monopoly in the Low Countries, adding to their already considerable fortune. And so the two arms of the family business – the rare and exquisite Chinese porcelain, and the lustreware from Antwerp – became inextricably entwined.

Antonio's workshop in Antwerp employed twelve staff. He was the foreman; beneath him were two throwers and three experienced painters, although Antonio also decorated pieces for special clients. Two kiln men made up the experienced staff, and beneath them were four apprentices, learning the various techniques. They produced many household items such as bowls, vases and plates, but also, increasingly, tiles, which the population of Antwerp requested to decorate their fireplaces and floors. They were not only attractive, but the tidy housewives of Flanders found them easy to keep clean.

Together, Antonio and Guido's fame spread far and wide. Guido was commissioned to provide floor tiles for a large house in England called 'The Vyne' and another set for a Cistercian Abbey in Flanders. Antonio produced a range of distinctive blue and white maiolica jars, which were quickly adopted by the surrounding hospitals and pharmacies for the storage of medicines. Each jar was hand-painted and labelled with the contents: Camphor for fevers, and cinnamon, nutmeg and cloves for digestion. One day, as she sat checking the ledgers for the business, Maria Margret was delighted to see a large order for pharmacy jars for the hospital of St John in Bruges, the hospital of which her grandmother had been patron. Her Aunt Caterina had now taken on that role and had ordered the jars for the hospital's new pharmacy.

Guido and Antonio's workshops were in Kammenstraat. This street soon developed a reputation and other well-known potters such as Jan Bogaerts and the Dmoelenyser workshop set up alongside them.

Maria Margret and Antonio's business went from strength to strength. Antonio bought the houses on either side of his workshop and he gradually created a large and comfortable family home around his workplace. Maria Margret took charge of the decoration. There were tiled floors, of course, and blue and white tiles in the fireplaces. The drawing room was arranged in the latest fashion, with costly tapestries on the walls and Turkish carpets draped over the large oak tables. The house was built around a central courtyard where Maria indulged her newly acquired passion for gardening. A small knot garden was created with box-edged flower and herb beds intersected by narrow brick paths inset with tiles. She would often sit there on a sunny day, watching the children play. They had five children in all – three boys and two girls.

As they grew, it became clear that the boys would follow their father into the business. Their eldest son, Cornelius, was a gifted painter. He would go on to be much feted, and travelled throughout his life to Spain, where he taught painting technique to Spanish potters, and on several occasions worked for the King of Spain. Their second son, Joseph, remained in Antwerp, and worked with his father. Their third son, Andries, moved to Delft, where he began to develop the maiolica business, specialising in blue and white decorative techniques. Maria Margret's two daughters both married merchants; her eldest daughter Beatrice, named after her mother's aunt, went on to marry one of Pieter's sons, Thomas van Vaerwye.

Beatrice had known Thomas all her life. Her parents' home and workshop was only four streets away from Pieter Van Vaerwye's large and distinguished home. He lived next door to his brother Jacob. The three families spent a great deal of time together; birthdays and holidays were always spent in the one another's company. It was fortunate that they all lived in large houses with grand drawing rooms where the young people could dance and mix easily. At least once a month, there was a party of some kind – a birthday, or a christening, or, as the children grew up, an engagement or wedding.

Beatrice had always liked Thomas. He was different from his brothers and sisters. They were all very outgoing and liked to play practical jokes on one another; they appeared to find life endlessly amusing. Thomas was quieter and a little shy. He was also the most academic of Pieter's five children. It was thought that he had inherited his intelligence from Pieter's younger brother Henryk, who was a Professor of Philosophy at the Catholic University of Leuven; he worked alongside the humanist Desiderius Erasmus, who went on to found the Collegium Trilingue at the University for the study of Hebrew, Latin, and Greek.

Beatrice and Thomas sought each other out at these family gatherings. They were often to be found huddled together in deep conversation. Beatrice, too, was a thoughtful girl. She was well read, artistic and musical. She had inherited her great grandmother Maria's turquoise eyes and dark hair. She was considered a beauty in Antwerp and many young men were disappointed when her engagement to Thomas was announced.

It was not uncommon for first cousins to marry at that time, and permission was happily given on both sides of the family. It would unite them even further, bringing the importers of porcelain and the maiolica potters into close alliance.

Thomas had no skills as a potter; he was an intellectual, not an artisan. His father and uncle had planned that he should take over the family import business. He had a fine mathematical brain and would be more than capable of managing the accounts. The work held little interest for him, but he could see that his future had been mapped out. A gentle young man, he did not argue or protest. He knew that it would be pointless. He would have preferred an academic life like his uncle's, but with a young wife to support, he followed his father Pieter into the import and export trade.

Beatrice's mother made her a gift of the Ming vase on her wedding day.

'It has been handed down through the generations, Beatrice, from mother to daughter. I was given it on the eve of my wedding,' said Maria Margret. 'My mother was given the vase by her mother. You are the fourth in line to inherit it. I hope it brings you good luck; that is the myth that surrounds it. The dragon is the symbol of good luck in China, and he has been lucky for me.'

The young couple settled into their home in Antwerp, close to the central market and cathedral. They were happy enough. The house was large and there was a garden where Beatrice liked to sit on sunny days. Her husband was attentive and gentle. He worked hard and learned the family business. He did not relish the prospect of travelling, but one of his brothers took on that role. What Thomas excelled at was strategic thinking; he could spot gaps in the market; he understood how the political situation affected his business; he was diplomatic and people trusted him; he made sound decisions and the business thrived.

Beatrice quickly became pregnant. But she lost two children before their son, Heinrich, was born weighing just a few pounds. He cried so lustily at his birth that Beatrice was confident he would survive.

Beatrice had another son and then, after the loss of a daughter, to her joy she gave birth to a second daughter. They named her Clara. She was small and dainty, with dark hair and her mother's bright blue eyes.

Their business went from strength to strength. Antwerp was the centre of international trade at that time and the family's wealth grew. Thomas traded with merchants from Portugal and Spain, importing porcelain, of course, but also sugar from Spanish and Portuguese plantations in South America and the Indies. Created on the backs of slave labour transported from Africa like heads of cattle, each man chained and lying head to toe with the next as if in coffins, they were taken to the sugar plantations in Brazil and the Indies. Sugar became the most significant commodity brought into the port of Antwerp and helped to make it the most important port in northern Europe. From Antwerp, the sugar was transported to sugar refineries in Germany, primarily in Cologne.

Antwerp, along with the rest of the cities of the Low Countries, was under the control of King Philip of Spain. He demanded high taxes from the wealthy merchants and over time they became impatient and eager to throw off the yoke of the Hapsburg Empire. Merchants like Thomas were educated and intelligent. They had vast wealth, and their knowledge of the world through trade had given them a profound insight into other cultures. Into this mix came the protestant religion, fanned out from Germany and Switzerland by Martin Luther and John Calvin. Appalled by the Roman Catholic Church's increasingly corrupt practices such as the sale of indulgences, these men were determined to bring the Christian faith back to its origins. With its emphasis on cleanliness, modesty, frugality and hard work, the Protestant faith began to take a foothold in the Netherlands, and Thomas was one of its earliest devotees. It appealed to his puritanical and intellectual nature. The idea that his relationship with God required the intercession of a priest had always irked him. He would rather make his own peace with God. He did not need absolution, especially one granted by a priest who might be corrupt.

In 1568 the people of the Netherlands rose up in revolt against Spanish control under the banner of William I of Orange. This was the start of the Eighty Years War, which ultimately would lead to the complete transformation of the Netherlands and the demise of its most important city, Antwerp.

The following fifteen years were challenging for the population of Antwerp. As the angry citizens demonstrated their anger at the Spanish, mob rule often broke out. Beatrice in particular was fearful as she did her best to bring their children up in this divided city. It seemed far removed from the city of her youth. She often thought back to the peaceful times she spent in the garden of her parent's home on Kammenstraat.

But now Beatrice often woke in the night to see flaming torches flickering through the latticed windows of their home as unruly gangs rampaged around the city. At such times, she would pace the bedroom, praying that God would save the family from harm. She even brought the Ming vase up to their bedchamber for safekeeping in case the mob broke into their home; she hid it in a cupboard in the corner of her bedroom. When at night her fear became overwhelming, she would get out of bed and take the vase out of the cupboard, stroking its cool porcelain exterior, as if by touching it she could invoke its magical powers.

One night Thomas was woken by shouts and screams in the road below. He sat up in bed and watched his wife tenderly touching the vase, beseeching the dragon for help.

'To whom do you pray, Beatrice?' he asked, startling her.

'Thomas, I had no idea you were awake.'

'I imagine I was woken, as you were, by that unruly mob outside. To whom do you pray? To God – or some magical, mythical figure?'

'I know you disapprove; I know to you it is heresy. But allow me a little belief. This vase has kept our family safe for many years. I simply seek a little comfort. I am fearful, Thomas, of what may become of us. How can we bring the children up in this dangerous place?'

'Come back to bed, Beatrice. All will be well. I have a plan for how we will escape Antwerp. You will see. You will not need to seek help from the vase.'

CHAPTER 19

Amsterdam
1580

Thomas supported the rebellion of the Prince of Orange. Over many years he and other merchants donated huge sums of money to the cause. But when Philip II of Spain threatened to blockade the port of Antwerp, Thomas made an important decision. He sold his house and moved the entire family to Amsterdam. If Spain was intent on destroying their independence and ability to trade, merchants like him would establish themselves in a city where they would be at liberty to continue with their business and free of religious persecution. Over sixty thousand people fled north to the fishing port of Amsterdam.

The wealth of Amsterdam in the 1580s was centred on two main imports: beer from Germany and fish caught in the North Sea. The fishermen of Amsterdam had discovered how to salt fish on board their ships and this had enabled them to travel farther and catch more fish than ever before. Now also firmly Protestant, they nevertheless were tolerant of residents who refused to abandon their Catholic faith as long as they were discreet. A few Catholic churches survived the Calvinist takeover, hidden away in private houses in the city. The philosophy of the Amsterdam elite was, 'If it's good for business, and is discreet, it should be tolerated.' People of all faiths were welcomed and the city had a flourishing Jewish quarter living peacefully alongside its Calvinist neighbours. Amsterdam's enthusiasm for trade finally helped to destroy the Spanish, who were now in firm control of Antwerp and the other southern cities of the Netherlands. Merchants in Amsterdam manufactured and sold warships to their enemy – the Spanish. Then, as the Dutch forces of William destroyed them in battles at sea, the Spanish saw their naval investment literally going up in smoke. Over time, this drain on Spanish funds enabled the people of the Netherlands to finally overthrow their oppressors whilst making them a huge profit in the meantime. In 1581 the northern states of the Netherlands formed an assembly called the States General. They became the only republic in Europe, and at its heart was Amsterdam, an economic powerhouse.

Within a few years, the city had grown beyond all recognition. Thomas initially moved his family into a wooden house, common at that time. It was not as substantial as the splendid brick house he had left behind in Antwerp, but it was serviceable as a temporary residence and he and Beatrice were just grateful to have escaped the dangers of Antwerp and have an opportunity to build up their business once again. They thanked God each day that their children, Heinrich, Friedrich and Clara, had all survived the war and the inevitable dangers of childhood.

Thomas was determined that the family would become one of the most important in Amsterdam. He spent the next decade establishing his business, developing a network of agents for his goods in Germany, France and England. He formed strong relationships with fellow merchants and became an important figure in the city's council. In 1590, Thomas purchased a new brick-built house – the first to be built on the Herengracht, one of the four main canals that curved their way through the city. Beatrice was delighted with the new house, where the only disturbance at night was the odd drunken sailor trying to find his way back to the docks. She often gazed up at the Ming vase, which had pride of place on the fireplace in the drawing room, and gave thanks for 'our safe deliverance from harm, and our success.' The fireplace was tiled with blue and white Delft tiles manufactured by her elder brother Joseph. He had fled from Antwerp with his own family and joined his brother Andries when Thomas and Beatrice had moved to Amsterdam. Between them the brothers developed a successful business in Delft, creating maiolica for the mass market.

There was talk amongst the leading merchants of Amsterdam of opening up direct trade routes with the Far East, which would cut out the Portuguese and Spanish. Thomas attended a meeting one evening held in a tavern in the centre of the city. He came back late. Beatrice had waited up for him and sat by the fire in the small parlour at the back of the house, sewing by the light of an oil lamp.

'Beatrice, my dear. You have waited up for me. I have some exciting news.'

'Well, sit, Thomas, and tell me all about it.'

'I have been shown, this evening, a document called the *Itinerario*. It was written by an explorer named Jan Huygen van Linschoten. It seems he sailed to the East Indies. His paper is full of the details. It made fascinating reading.'

'And what has this to do with us, Thomas?' his wife asked nervously.

'Well, I should have thought it obvious, Beatrice, my dear. It means that we are no longer to be bound by the monopoly the Portuguese have on the trade from Asia. Our time has come. We will soon be able to trade direct.'

The group had discussed that evening the relative merits of this sea route versus a new northern route that had recently been demonstrated by an explorer named Plancius. He had travelled to Asia across the top of Russia. This route had two distinct advantages over the sea routes of the past: it was shorter, and avoided the pirates who lurked in the Atlantic as well as any confrontation with the Portuguese who still dominated the southerly Asian trade route.

'We are to make some expeditions exploring this northern route, Beatrice. I have invested.'

'Will you have to go?' asked Beatrice anxiously.

'No. It is a young man's game. Michael Kaerel's son Johan is to go though. I met him this evening. He is a sharp and clever young man. I think he would be a good match for our little Clara.'

'You think so?'

'I do. Let's see how he gets on during the expedition. It will be hard, and one never knows if he will return. But if he does, I would like to introduce him to our daughter.'

The expedition went well and clearly demonstrated the possibilities of the northern route. But in the end it was agreed that the sea route around the Cape was still the most effective way of bringing goods back to Europe from Asia. Young Johan returned and a dinner was given by members of the VOC to celebrate the expedition. It was at this event that Johan Kaerel was introduced to Clara van Vaerwye.

The two young people understood from the outset what was expected of them. They were both dutiful and obedient. Johan was not especially tall, but he had a strong, sturdy build. He had light brown hair and attractive green eyes. Clara, who was dark and diminutive, liked him immediately. She was aware that at twenty-five it was high time that she was married, and was grateful that her father had selected a man with a good mind and a kind heart. Their wedding took place four months later and a house was purchased for the couple near Clara's parents' home on the Herengracht. The night before the wedding, Beatrice took Clara aside into the drawing room. She took the vase down from the fireplace.

'This is for you Clara. It has been in the family for so long, as you know. I often felt its power in those dark days in Antwerp;

I would ask the vase for help as the mob rampaged around our house. Your father disapproves, of course. His faith does not allow the worship of anything so idolatrous. And I do not really worship it, I promise you. But it has helped me from time to time. Given me courage. I hope it does the same for you.'

Clara took the vase and placed it in a cabinet in her husband's new study. She explained to him its significance.

'Well, if nothing else,' he said pragmatically, 'it is a lovely and valuable thing. I do not believe in magic, but I can see that it has proved an inspiration to your family over the years, with their trade in porcelain and the manufacture of maiolica. So I am grateful to your parents and proud to be its keeper. Thank your mother for me, will you? We shall keep it safe in the cabinet here. Let's hope it brings me luck next year when I go to Maluku. I shall be bringing spices back with me on that voyage, but there will be other subsequent journeys and I hope to develop our porcelain trade. Now the Portuguese hold on trade has been breached, there is no end to the wonderful things I shall be bringing you, dear Clara.'

The second element in the making of porcelain is feldspar. This is gathered up, broken into pieces and washed before being pressed into rectangular bricks. The kao lin (pai tun) and feldspar (pet un tse) bricks are then sold and taken down river to Ching-te-Chen. When the bricks are unloaded they are stored in dark caves. The pai tun and pet un tse are then mixed in equal quantities to produce the finest-quality porcelain. For lesser-quality porcelain, four parts pai tun are used with six parts of pet un tse. The mixing is done in a large basin and beaten with wooden spatulas; it is then kneaded. The work must continue day and night.

CHAPTER 20

Sheen
24th December 2015

Miranda and Georgie spent Christmas each year with her parents and Jeremy. With no parents of his own, he had effectively become part of their family and normally it was a jolly time, filled with games and crackers and food and fun. The routine was now well established. Jeremy would take tea with Miranda and Georgie at her house on Christmas Eve. They would eat Christmas cake and mince pies before loading up Miranda's old Volvo with the presents and suitcases. With luck they would miss the worst of the traffic and arrive in Surrey in good time for a restorative gin and tonic and a good dinner. Her parents were creatures of habit and so dinner was always fish pie followed by a trip to church for midnight mass, the only part of the ritual that Georgie had begun to rail against.

Christmas Day itself started in the kitchen with Miranda helping her mother prepare stuffing and a huge array of vegetables whilst Jeremy entertained Georgie with whatever board games could be found in the old games cupboard in the drawing room. Presents were over by eleven, ancient aunts arrived before twelve, and neighbours dropped in for drinks shortly after. The family would 'watch the Queen' before settling down in the large dining room, where they would tuck into turkey and Christmas pudding. The evening was spent in the drawing room playing charades and other games until bedtime. Boxing Day invariably involved a long walk, the eating of left-overs and an opportunity for Miranda and her mother to both put their feet up and relax.

Jeremy arrived as planned at three forty-five.

'Dear girl,' he said, embracing her as she opened the door. 'Here I am. Let's get this party started; where is my cake and where is my favourite girl?'

Georgie thundered downstairs and threw herself into his arms.

They sat at the kitchen table and Miranda took off the red-checked ribbon that she and Georgie had tied so carefully round the cake only a few days before. She had hoped to show the cake to Charlie in its pristine untouched state but he had left so suddenly.

'The cake appears to be up to your usual high standard,' said Jeremy, shovelling a large piece into his mouth. 'Delicious, Miranda. You really should go into business doing this. And the decorations are, as usual, fabulous. I presume your talented daughter created the stunning, if slightly psychotic, fantasy arrangement of woodland animals, ballerinas and footballers that I see before me?'

Georgie laughed and cake flew across the table from her overstuffed mouth.

'Georgie!' Miranda snapped. 'Manners – please.'

Georgie covered her mouth. 'Sorry, Ma,' she said. 'Yes, the decorations are all mine. I took everything out of the decorations box and just shoved them all on top. I had the animals on my cake for my third birthday, the ballerinas when I was four and the footballers I think came from my football-crazed years – age seven, from memory. Is that right, Mum?'

Miranda was staring out of the kitchen window into the dark garden beyond.

'Mum!' exclaimed Georgie.

'Sorry. I was miles away,' said Miranda.

Jeremy helped himself to another cup of tea and a mince pie. 'Georgina,' he said dramatically. 'I would like you to go upstairs and bring your suitcase down here, please. Can you do that for me? We ought to be getting off soon; don't want to be stuck in traffic all the way to Granny's.'

Georgie happily complied.

'Now, Manda,' he said gently as soon as heard Georgie's tread on the stairs, 'what on earth is the matter?'

'I'm just feeling a bit down. That's all.'

'Why?' asked Jeremy. 'You've got a wonderful daughter, a great best friend, we're off to have a lovely Christmassy time with your parents. Oh – and you've just got a fabulous new boyfriend.'

'Yes, you're right. I'm just missing him I suppose.'

'But you're seeing him on Boxing Day, aren't you?'

'Yes, that's the plan.'

'Well then, stop moping and go and get your bags, honey. Where are the presents for all those hideous aunts of yours?'

'They're already in the car. And they are *not* hideous aunts.' Miranda smiled.

Christmas passed much as usual. Miranda hoped for a phone call or at least a text from Charlie, but none came. She rang him on Christmas Eve but he didn't pick up. He was probably driving, she thought. She left him a voicemail message. '*Hi Charlie – hope Devon is fun. Really looking forward to seeing you on Boxing Day. Miss you. Bye.*'

On Christmas Day there was still no word. As the family opened their presents around the tree, their normally happy atmosphere was infiltrated by Miranda's growing sense of anxiety.

'Good heavens, Miranda,' thundered her father, 'do put that wretched phone thing down. You look as if you expect it to implode or something.'

'Sorry, Dad. I'm just expecting a call.' Miranda put her mobile down on a side table. Jeremy and Georgie exchanged worried glances.

But as another present was handed out – a boxed set of Hitchcock movies from Jeremy to Georgie – Miranda retrieved her phone and texted Charlie: '*Happy Christmas. Hope you're having a great time. We're all fine here. See you tomorrow! Xxx.*' It came back '*undelivered*'.

'Oh Miranda,' said Jeremy when she expressed concern over pre-lunch drinks. 'He probably has no signal. Have you ever been to Devon? It's in the dark ages down there darling.'

But Miranda couldn't relax. Christmas day came and went and she was increasingly irritable with everyone. Finally, Boxing Day arrived. She woke early, and reached for her phone. Was it too early to text? It was seven-thirty. She got out of bed and went next door to the bathroom. She checked her phone when she returned to her room. There was still no word from Charlie. Was he deliberately ignoring her? Perhaps he was ill or had had an accident. Her mind raced with possibilities. She knew she shouldn't text again. But she was unable to stop herself: '*Looking forward to seeing you later... what time?*' After all, it was not unreasonable to need to know what time he was intending to arrive.

She pulled on her dressing gown and went downstairs for breakfast. She put the kettle onto the old Aga and leant against it. Over breakfast, as the family began to drift into the kitchen, she announced that she was taking Georgie back to London before lunch.

'Oh Miranda,' said her mother, 'we get to see so little of you these days. And particularly of Georgie. Can't you go back tomorrow?'

'No, sorry, Mum. I've got something I've got to do this evening.'

They had planned to go for a walk before lunch, but Miranda was concerned it would delay their departure. 'The last thing I need is to get caught in traffic and be late,' she said exasperatedly.

In the end they left her parents' house at twelve o'clock and Miranda drove furiously back to London. She dropped Jeremy at the bookshop around two thirty. 'Thanks for a wonderful crimble,' he said, kissing Miranda on both cheeks. 'Have a good time tonight both of you... And give me a call tomorrow?'

'Sure, will do. Take care.'

As they brought their bags in from the car, Georgie said to Miranda. 'Where's the vase, Mum?'

'Oh, Charlie took it. Well, he bought it from me; he's going to put in a sale.'

'Oh,' said Georgie.

'You don't mind, do you?' said Miranda. 'You always said you hated it so much...'

'Yes, but it's funny isn't it? The place doesn't feel quite the same without it.'

'No,' said Miranda. 'Now go and unpack and could you take my bag upstairs too, darling? I ought to get on with cooking supper.'

'Sure,' said Georgie. 'What are we having?'

'I bought a bit of venison on Christmas Eve from that nice butcher that's just opened in the High Street. He was selling it cheap, as they were about to close for the holidays. I thought I'd make a nice casserole.'

'Hmm,' said Georgie uncertainly.

Miranda fried the pieces of venison with onions. She assembled the casserole and filled the pot with a bottle of cheap red wine and placed it on a low heat in the oven. She wandered into the sitting room and turned on the Christmas lights and the television to keep her company as she tidied up. *Dial M for Murder* had just started. She checked her watch. It was half past four and already getting dark. She pulled the curtains in the sitting room, half expecting to see Charlie's car pulling up outside the house. But there was no car. She wandered back into the kitchen and checked her phone. No messages.

She dialled his number. It went straight to voicemail. She hung up. Half an hour later, she dialled again. This time she left a message: '*Hi Charlie, it's Miranda. I just wondered what time you were planning on getting here?*'

At five o'clock, Georgie came back downstairs. 'Hi Mum, what are you doing sitting in the dark?'

Miranda sat in the gloom at the table, her head in her hands. The smell of venison casserole filled the kitchen.

'He's not coming, is he?' said Miranda dispiritedly.

'What time was he supposed to be here?' asked Georgie anxiously.

'He never said. He just said he'd come up on Boxing Day evening.'

'Well, it's not the evening yet. Come on, let's go and watch the telly.'

The two lay together on the sofa and watched the Hitchcock classic. As it finished, Georgie said to her mother, 'God, you can't believe people can be so cunning, can you? Do you think real people are ever that bad? Fancy planning all that.'

'Yes,' said Miranda, 'I do think some people are capable of that sort of thing. I think they call it psychopathic behaviour these days, don't they? Or sociopathic – people who have no scruples about getting what they want.'

Suppertime came and went. At eight thirty, Georgie reappeared in the sitting room. Miranda sat watching the television dazed and unblinking.

'Mum, do you think *we* could eat? I'm a bit hungry.'

'Sure, of course, darling,' said Miranda, leaping to her feet. As she served up the overdone casserole, she began to cry.

'Mum,' said Georgie, standing up and putting her arms around her mother, 'I'm sure there's some explanation.'

'Are you?' said Miranda. 'I think the explanation is that he has dumped me. I just don't think he's bothered to tell me yet.' And Miranda ran out of the kitchen in tears, leaving Georgie alone with a venison casserole.

CHAPTER 21

Sheen
27th December 2015

Miranda retreated to bed. She had had no word from Charlie; no text or call or message of any kind. The bracelet he had given her lay unworn on the bedside table. A reminder of something – what exactly?

She told Georgie that she was feeling unwell, but Georgie understood the real reason her mother couldn't face getting up. As she made herself a cup of tea in the kitchen, Georgie dialled Jeremy's number. 'Hi Jeremy, I'm a bit worried about Ma. The love-rat has not called. She's really broken-hearted. I don't know what to do.'

'I'll come,' said Jeremy. He arrived half an hour later and sat with Georgie in the kitchen. 'So, she's not got up at all?' he asked.

'No, only to go to the loo. And I took her a cup of tea a little while ago and a piece of toast, but she hardly said thank you, and you know what she's like about manners.'

'Yes,' said Jeremy. 'Yes, I do. I'll go up and see her. Oh and G,' he said as he reached the kitchen door. 'Well done for calling me. It was the right thing to do.'

Upstairs, he opened Miranda's door carefully. She appeared to be sleeping, her back to the door. But as he walked around the bed he saw that she was crying, tears pouring down her face, her phone lying next to her on the bed beside the Tiffany box.

'Manda, darling…' He lay down on the bed next to her.

'Oh Jeremy, I've been such a fool. I thought it was going somewhere, but now I think I was just a distraction.'

'Oh, I'm sure it was more than that,' said Jeremy as soothingly as he could. 'He wouldn't have given you that bracelet otherwise, would he? I mean you don't give presents to people you're about to dump, do you?'

'Don't you? Maybe it was to salve his conscience.'

'What? I'm going to dump her, so I'll buy her a nice gift from Tiffany's. How weird would that be?'

'It's not even from Tiffany's.' Miranda shoved the box with the bracelet inside towards Jeremy.

'Open it… Take a look. There's no Tiffany logo on the bracelet.'

'Since when did you become such an expert?'

'Since I checked on the Internet. All Tiffany pieces have the logo stamped on them, with the date. This is just a cheap fake – like him.'

'Oh Miranda – that's a bit harsh.'

'But true though. I just feel so… Used.'

Jeremy lay with Miranda for some time, cradling her in his arms until she finally fell asleep. Then he carefully moved her off his now dead arm and went downstairs. In the hall he noticed the vase was missing from the table.

'She's asleep now G,' he said, coming into the kitchen. 'I'll hang around if you like for when she wakes up. Shall we have coffee?'

'Sure,' said Georgina. 'Thanks Jeremy. I'm sure she appreciates you being here. I know I do.'

'Think nothing of it,' said Jeremy. 'Where's that hideous vase by the way? I noticed it's missing from the hall table.'

'Charlie took it,' said G, 'the last time he was here. Mum said he had bought it from her. He is planning on putting it into a sale sometime.'

'Did she want to sell it? I don't remember her saying anything about it.'

'I know. It was a bit strange. She's always been rather protective of it, actually. I didn't like it much, as you know. But whenever I made a rude comment about it she always sort of leapt to its defence.'

'So why sell it now?'

'I'm not sure. I think he sort of convinced her and then just took it. She said when he'd left that last time she wasn't really sure it was the right thing to do. I think she felt she'd been a bit manipulated, if that makes sense?'

'Georgie darling, did your mother ever think to find out exactly where that vase came from?' asked Jeremy.

'From her Aunt Celia,' said G.

'No, before that. Is it possible, do you think, that the vase might have been rather valuable perhaps?'

'Valuable? God, I hope not. We used to fling the car keys in it. How could it be valuable?'

'We are living in a world where the most unlikely things turn out to be worth a fortune. Now where does the love-rat work?'

'I'm not sure – an auction house in Hampshire, I think,' said Georgie.

'Right; do we know which one?'

'Mum knows, I think…'

'Georgie, get your mother's laptop and bring it to me. I think it's time we found out a little bit more about Charles Davenport.'

The Christmas and New Year holidays had fallen awkwardly midweek, and most businesses had opted to remain closed until the 3rd of January. Jeremy did the same with the bookshop over the Christmas period, which meant that apart from taking long, wintry walks in Richmond Park and popping into Miranda's each day to check up on her and Georgie, he had ample time to investigate the apparently opaque life of Charles Davenport.

'You would have thought,' he said to Georgie one afternoon, sitting in Miranda's kitchen eating leftover Christmas cake, 'that in this day and age, it would be possible to track someone down and know everything there is to know about them – where they live, the names of their family, their job history, the state of their bank account, embarrassing moments – but this guy has covered his tracks. Until I can get to speak to the auction house, I have absolutely nothing to go on. I'm not even sure he really is an auctioneer. His name is not on the list of associates there.'

'Mum did ring them and they knew him, I remember that. When she first got in touch with him about that book she sold him.'

'OK, so he has worked there at some point – maybe as a freelance. The thing is, G, I'm rather worried that he knows more about that vase than he let on. Let's go over what we know about it again?'

'Apart from the fact that it was a bit spooky and that Mum's great aunt thingummy left it to her, you mean?'

'Yes, apart from that. I don't even really remember what it looked like,' said Jeremy.

'Oh, that's easy. Mum took a picture a few weeks back and posted it on Facebook. I remember seeing it and thinking it was a weird thing to do.'

'Facebook? Really? That's amazing. G darling, I'm not actually on Facebook. Be a love and log into it or whatever you're supposed to do.'

'Oh Jeremy! Give me the laptop.'

Georgina logged into her Facebook page and from there to her mother's.

'There, ' she said, swinging the laptop round to face him. 'There's the photo.'

'Great, well that's something. Can you email that to me or something similar?'

'Sure.'

'I think we need to get in touch with an expert and find out what we can about this vase. If it is worth something, it can't just disappear. It will turn up somewhere at an auction.'

'Do you really think it's valuable?'

'Well, darling, it's the obvious conclusion to draw, I'm afraid. The love-rat disappears along with the vase. What other explanation is there?'

There was a curious snuffling sound and the pair looked up to see Miranda standing at the door to the kitchen wearing a pair of rather grubby blue pyjamas and some old hockey socks of Georgina's.

'So he's a thief as well as a lying bastard is he?' she said.

'I don't know,' said Jeremy gently, getting to his feet and drawing her into the kitchen. He pulled out a chair and guided her to it. She sank gratefully down, resting her head in her hands, as if unable to bear her own weight.

'I just think it's something we need to consider,' he continued. 'Georgie mentioned that he was going to put the vase into a sale of porcelain at his auction house in Hampshire at the end of January. I've been online and so far it's true. There is a sale, but I can't see any sign of your vase in that sale.'

'Well, he only took it down there on Christmas Eve, maybe they've not had time to put it in there yet?' Miranda suggested.

'Online?' said Jeremy. 'It would have taken them five minutes in this day and age. No, I think we ought to call them and find out if he ever actually took it there.'

'But won't they be closed?'

'I can but try,' said Jeremy.

'But he bought it from me,' persisted Miranda. 'I don't have any right to take it back surely; he gave me a cheque.'

'Have you cashed it?'

'No, I've not had a chance.'

'Did he give you a receipt?'

'No.'

'Good, then there's no proof that he owns it. What *we* have to establish is that the vase is *yours*. But first things first. Let me give the auction house a bell.'

It was a brief phone call. Yes, Charles Davenport worked at the auction house from time to time in a freelance capacity. Yes, there was a sale of Chinese and Japanese porcelain on January 23rd. No, a large dragon vase had not been submitted by Mr Davenport for the sale.

No, he had not been to the auction rooms on 24th December, or even been in touch with them for several weeks. And no, they did not know where Mr Davenport was.

'So,' said Jeremy, 'what does that tell us?'

'That he's a liar,' said Georgie.

'Or maybe he just didn't have time before Christmas?' suggested Miranda. 'I mean, we can't assume that he's up to no good.'

'Miranda,' said Jeremy exasperatedly, 'stop deluding yourself. They told me that he had not mentioned the vase to them, hadn't seen them in weeks. He was never intending to put that vase in the sale in Hampshire. He lied to you.'

'Maybe he's going to put it in a sale somewhere else then?' said Miranda.

'Now that is the first sensible thing you've said all Christmas,' said Jeremy. 'G, start trawling the Internet for sales of Chinese porcelain. Let's see what we can find out.'

The pieces are turned on a potter's wheel. The workers are divided into two groups – those who turn pieces of one foot in diameter, and those who turn the larger pieces. The wheel is a wooden disc mounted on a vertical axis, so it turns for as long as possible at a regular speed while the clay is shaped. As the potter shapes the clay, a boy drives the wheel with a rope on a pulley. The pot is then given to a third workman, who fits it into a mould to give it the required shape. There are two earthenware moulds – one inner and an outer one. The production of these moulds is a highly skilled task. There are only two or three workmen who are able to do it. The finished cups are placed in neat rows on shelves in the sun and around the walls of the potter's workshop. A fourth workman polishes each cup with a chisel, particularly around the edges, and thins it so that it becomes almost transparent. He moistens the pot as he works it, for if he lets it dry out it will crack. The pieces are now ready to be decorated.

PART THREE

CHAPTER 22

Amsterdam
1631

At thirty-three years of age, Hans Kaerel considered himself a success. He was married to a charming and pretty wife with whom he had three children and was the owner of a fine home on Herengracht, the most fashionable street in Amsterdam. Earlier that day, he had been appointed to the Board of Directors of the company his father had helped to establish – Vereenigde Oost-Indische Compagnie – the VOC. He had just one problem: a secret that had begun to tear him apart.

Hans sat in his private study at the rear of the house, checking his accounts. Meticulously tidy, the room was panelled in dark oak, with glazed bookcases built on either side of the fireplace. Hans' desk stood facing towards the door and his back was to the garden. The garden was his wife's domain and held no interest for him. Hans preferred to work in his study at night, after dinner, with the dark red damask curtains closed against the night sky. By the light of the oil lamps, the room was suffused with a warm, peaceful glow; the only sounds were the spitting of the fire in the grate and the quiet snoring and snuffling of his favourite dog Kuntze. The dog was a Kooiker, a breed much prized at the time. Intelligent and friendly, he was a good hunting dog. He was the perfect companion for a man such as Hans, who required total devotion from everyone around him. To say Hans was difficult would be incorrect. Exacting would describe his nature better. He was also a man of determination and quick intelligence. He knew what he wanted, and he was not to be crossed.

He could hear his wife Antoinette singing in the room next door. Unlike the rest of the house, which was dark and masculine, this little parlour of hers had been decorated in shades of pale blue, which reflected the sky on a winter's day; the floors were a chequerboard of russet and white tiles, covered with Turkish carpets. She had a couple of chairs, a small table also covered in a colourful carpet, and beneath the window, her beloved spinet – a gift from her husband on their wedding day. She played well and liked nothing better than to practice first thing in the morning. She refrained from playing in the evenings for fear of disturbing Hans' work. The fireplace was tiled with Delft blue and white tiles and above it hung a painting of a rural scene, exquisite in every detail.

Antoinette often stood at the large latticed windows overlooking the garden, which had been recently redesigned in the latest Baroque style, with box-edged beds set out in a geometric pattern filled with seasonal plants. Star amongst these annual delights were the tulips, purchased at huge cost. The tulip had become the latest craze in Amsterdam and was considered a symbol of wealth. Antoinette professed that her passion for the flowers was simply that she 'loved their beautiful colours and form.' But secretly, she was thrilled that her husband was able, and willing, to spend thousands of guilders to beautify her garden with this most fashionable of flowers. The tulips would only be in bloom for three or four weeks in April and early May. As soon as the first flower opened its petals, Antoinette threw herself into a whirl of social activity. Guests were served coffee, tea or lunch in the small pavilion that had been built at the bottom of the garden. From here, they had a perfect view of the spectacular display whilst the magnificent fountain that had been erected in the centre of the flowerbeds spattered water into a marble bowl at its base.

The drawing room at the front of the house was reserved for larger parties. It had views out over the canal and was lined with engraved and gilded leather panels specially imported from Venice. Turkish carpets in rich tones of blue and red covered the black and white tiled floors and the large oak table that stood against the wall. Chairs upholstered in blue leather were arranged around the room. When the candles were lit in the twin brass chandeliers that hung from the high ceiling, Antoinette thought it the most elegant room on the Herengracht.

The cabinets on either side of the large fireplace in Hans' study were filled with examples of fine porcelain, imported by generations of his family. One piece was particularly prized amongst the rest: a Ming vase, at least two hundred years old, that had been in his family since its creation. At least, that was the story he had been told by his mother Clara and grandmother Beatrice, who had inherited the piece from her mother Maria Margret Corso. Beatrice had married one of her cousins – Thomas van Vaerwye, the son of Peter van Vaerwye. Together they had moved to Amsterdam from Antwerp during the war with Spain in the early 1580s. Beatrice had then handed the vase on to her own daughter Clara when she married Hans's father Johan Kaerel.

And now it had come to him. He gazed up at the Ming Vase. It stood in pride of place on the top shelf. Other pieces were arranged on the lower shelves: a flask – bulbous at the base, with a narrow neck, that also featured a dragon chasing round the centre. There was a small Ming tankard; a wine jar that was decorated with charming scenes of Chinese courtly life, depicting slightly windswept ladies sitting with their children in a garden as a companion played the flute. A pair of blue and white bowls stood on the shelf below. He had given a similar bowl to the young painter

Rembrandt just the week before. The artist had recently moved back to Amsterdam, and when Hans visited his house he had been much impressed with the range of 'props' that Rembrandt kept in his studio storeroom. An extensive collection of porcelain, crystal claret jugs with silver necks and lids – some of considerable merit – were meticulously stored on shelves around the room alongside more bizarre items: weapons of all kinds, skulls of dogs, stuffed birds and game. The artist clearly had a passion for purchasing items that would one day be the centrepiece of one of his paintings. In the studio next door, where Rembrandt worked alongside one or two young apprentices, Hans observed the artist was painting a large Ming bowl he had sold to him the previous year. He thought the young men were capturing the bowl's detail beautifully, although there was no doubting who was the master and who the apprentice. Hans suggested to Rembrandt that it might ease the artist's persistent money problems if they effected a swap whereby Hans could provide one or two new pieces of porcelain in return for the painting. The artist had readily agreed and that painting hung now above the fireplace in Hans' study.

He looked back at his books, moving the oil lamp closer to the work. His eyesight was getting weaker, which concerned him. He would request a visit from the spectacle maker. He had commissioned a new ship, which he hoped to take to China that year. Laid out on his desk in tidy piles were the invoices from the shipwright. He had visited the shipyard earlier that day and had been impressed with progress. But it was an expensive venture and he needed to study and check the invoices carefully.

He had chosen a name for the ship. It was to be christened the *Vliegende Draek* – 'The Flying Dragon' – after the vase. He knew the mythology that surrounded the vase: whoever had care of it would have good fortune. His mother, however, disapproved of the name.

'It will bring you nothing but despair. You mark my words, Hans. Look what has happened to me. I had care of the vase and look at all the tragedy that has befallen me.'

It was true that his parents had had their fair share of tragedy. Clara had given birth to seven children and lost all but one. Three children died in their first year of life. When Hans was born she lived in terror that he too would be taken from her. But he survived, and when he reached the age of two years, she began to hope that her bad luck was behind her. She had three more children in quick succession, hoping for a large, happy family. But tragedy struck again four years later when her fourth child Karl died of scarlet fever. His sister Magda contracted the same illness and died weeks later. Her seventh and final child, Katje, mercifully escaped the illness. A beautiful child with long dark hair and bright blue eyes, her parents adored her. She was gentle and kind and had an extraordinary ability for one so young to intuitively understand what the people around her required. Her mother could hardly bear to be parted from her, even sharing the nursery with her at night. During the day, she dressed her, brushed her hair and spent hours playing with a collection of miniature household items she had collected for the child. In fact, she scarcely left the large nursery at the front of the house on the Herengracht.

As Hans grew from a boy to a young man, he observed this close relationship between his mother and little sister. He was not jealous in any way, for he too cared for Katje. She was a delight and adored her older, handsome brother. Besides, he was relieved that at last his mother had another child to whom she could devote herself. For the loss of so many of her children had made her neurotic and anxious. Until Katje's birth, she had tried to control Hans's life from the moment he woke until the time he went to bed. She was fearful if he ventured out of the house alone. In the winter months, when the canals froze, Hans and his young friends loved nothing better than to get out onto the ice and skate. Hans would wake in the morning and if the canal was frozen he would put on his warmest winter clothes and run down the oak staircase and into the basement where the kitchens and laundry were the domain of their kitchen staff Mitze and Saskia.

Saskia had been with Johan and Clara since they were first married and had cooked for them ever since. She was a sturdy woman with a kind round face and strong forearms. It appeared to Hans that she was in every way perfect – kind, calm and loving – and always with something delicious cooking in the huge range. Hans would go first to the kitchen to see if there were any sweet treats – a Speculoos biscuit perhaps, made with cinnamon and nutmeg for the feast of St Nicholas on December 5th. Then, stuffing the biscuits into his pockets, he would run to the boot room and find his skates, put on his thick woollen cloak and head off to the canal where he would meet his friends. But often as he emerged from the basement kitchens he would find his mother standing dourly in the hallway, her thin face contorted in anxiety.

'Where are you going, Hans? It is cold outside. You will surely catch a chill. Stay indoors with me and little Katje. We will do a puzzle together perhaps?'

Hans was unable to argue with his mother, but could also not bear the prospect of a day trapped indoors when the sun shone outside and the water lay frozen and inviting. At these times, he would seek his father's intervention. Fortunately, Johan was inclined to take the boy's side.

'Let the boy go, Clara – he wants to meet with his friends. You can't keep him cooped up in here all day.'

Clara would eventually relent and Hans would rush from the house before she could change her mind. As he raced down the large stone steps of the house on the Herengracht, his skates dangling over his shoulder, he was aware of his little sister watching wistfully from the drawing room window.

His young teenage years were spent in study and as much outdoor activity as possible. He was a good student, and his father was proud of him, but he was no academic. Johan was one of the original partners in the VOC when it was founded in 1602, and they needed young men who were prepared to travel abroad and protect and manage the Dutch trade in spices on which the company had been granted a monopoly. When Hans was eighteen, Johan formally introduced him to his partners in the VOC and they agreed that young Hans was to be sent out on the next ship sailing for the East to learn the business.

Clara argued desperately that Hans should remain in Amsterdam. 'Let him stay here, Johan, I beg of you. Do not send him away. He is only eighteen. He should go to university. He must be educated. Besides, so many terrible things could befall him. He could drown at sea, or die of one of the terrible diseases over there. You know how the young Baeker boy died of malaria on that trip. Please, Johan.'

But Johan was not to be persuaded and Hans was delighted to be sent away to sea under the command of Chief Merchant Jacob van Neck. He travelled to the spice islands of Malaku where they were to collect a shipment of pepper and establish a direct trading route between Holland and the islands. Hans was given the position of Chief Merchant's Assistant – answerable only to Jacob, himself. As such, he was one of the major officers on board and held a position of some responsibility. He was in effect the ship's secretary and accountant.

Their first voyage took them down the west coast of Europe and West Africa. They paused at the Cape to bring on fresh provisions before setting sail for Malaku, one of the islands off the coast of China that would eventually become known as the Dutch East Indies. Hans had been abroad for nearly eighteen months when he received word from his father telling him that Katje had died from tuberculosis. She was barely ten years old. Nine months passed before Hans could return to Amsterdam, on board a ship with a cargo of cinnamon and nutmeg. Johan confided in his son as soon as he arrived:

'I fear your mother has lost her mind. She never leaves Katje's room. She spends most of her time in the nursery, lying on Katje's bed, surrounded by the child's clothes and toys. If she bothers to get dressed at all, she chooses a simple black day dress and a black cap. She becomes hysterical if we even suggest she leaves the room. Mitze tried to persuade her to put some of Katje's clothes away the other day and I thought she would kill the poor girl. Go to her, but I warn you, she is much changed.'

Hans gently knocked on the oak door to Katje's room, but there was no answer. He slowly pushed it open. His mother sat in the small nursing chair, her hands in her lap, gazing at a portrait of Katje she and Johan had commissioned for her tenth birthday.

His mother had become almost unrecognisable – gaunt, pale, her blue eyes permanently red-rimmed from crying.

'Mama, I am here.' He knelt down at his mother's side and took her painfully thin body into his arms. She stiffened at his touch.

'So you are,' she said finally.

He followed her gaze towards the oil painting of his sister, set in an elaborate gilded frame. The girl was dressed in blue organza, her dark hair falling around her shoulders, her rosebud mouth smiling obediently. Her bright blue eyes looked wistfully at the viewer. It seemed to Hans that she was pleading with the observer in some way – to rescue her perhaps from the oppressive relationship in which she was bound with her mother.

'I am so sorry,' he said. 'I should have been here.' It was unclear if he was addressing his dead sister in the painting or his mother.

'Yes,' was all his mother would say.

Eventually, Hans went downstairs. He found his father in the study poring over columns of figures. 'Papa, I am so sorry. I should have been here.'

'Not at all, dear boy. You have your work, and thank God for it. Katje was the apple of our eye. She brought so much light and happiness to our lives. I miss her very much. But what could you have done? She was ill. She was never strong. It was always just a matter of time. At least, I thought so.'

Hans slumped in the chair opposite his father and wept.

'Dear boy, don't cry. There has been too much weeping in this house. You must go back to your work when you have had a chance to rest. This is no place for you now.'

'Really?' asked Hans. 'Won't Mama want to me stay here?'

'She will, but I won't let her. You cannot stay just to comfort your mother, Hans. You must continue with your work. I hear great things of you from Jacob. He has been most impressed. He says you have a great future. Your book-keeping is exemplary. You are good with the natives and the crew alike.'

'Well, I am delighted, obviously, but how will we tell Mama?'

'I've already told her. When you wrote to tell us you were coming home, I made it clear that she must not put pressure on you to stay. Losing Katje was God's will and we must accept it. "We must not punish Hans for our loss," I told her. "He must be allowed to travel and live his life." Besides, we need you to take on the business one day; you need to learn all you can now.'

'And what did Mama say?' asked Hans.

'The love of money is the root of all evil.'

Johan looked up at his son and winked. 'The first book of Timothy; chapter six, verse ten.'

Hans remained at home for three months. He helped his father with the book-keeping. He discussed business with other merchants at the VOC and spent any spare time with one or two of his friends who were still in Amsterdam. At home, in the evenings, the family would eat together in the large dining room at the front of the house. Now that Hans was home, his mother had agreed at least to come downstairs for the evening meal.

'Progress, progress,' said his father, handing Hans a glass of wine on the news that his wife would be joining them.

'It's good to see you here, Clara, my dear,' he beamed as she entered the room.

But his wife would not eat.

Saskia did her best to tempt Clara with imaginatively planned meals: 'Madam, I have a little salad to start – of nice leaves from the garden. It has a little oil on it, but is very fresh. Then we have a nice pair of pheasants, lightly cooked, very tasty.'

The men tucked in with gusto, but Clara simply manoeuvred her food around her plate, scarcely tasting it.

In the following weeks, the atmosphere became increasingly claustrophobic and depressing. Over a glass of port one evening, Hans suggested to his father that it might be time for him to return to the East. Fortuitously, the Governor-General of the VOC was soon to make a voyage to Jayakarta (as it was then known), where he intended to set up a permanent trading post. Johan agreed his son should be allowed to join him.

On hearing the news, Clara retreated once more to the nursery.

Hans left Amsterdam on the 7th of March 1619 – nearly a year after Katje's death. As his ship glided out of Amsterdam harbour, he felt the pressures of his family lifting from his shoulders. Hans stood on deck watching Amsterdam receding until the church spires and domes of the city were just tiny specks on the skyline. He breathed in the salty air as the seagulls free-wheeled around his head. He was free at last.

Hans enjoyed ship life. It was cramped of course, and he suffered terribly with seasickness if the weather was rough. As the assistant merchant, he lived a relatively comfortable life on board, behind the mast. This part of the ship contained the quarters of the senior officers, including the surgeon and the Reverend, together with any guests who were travelling on board. Hans had his own private cabin, but it was cramped, with a bed, a chest for his clothes, and a very small desk. He had a personal servant who would clean his uniform and tidy his cabin. Life on board was necessarily disciplined. The senior officers always dined together, with the evening meal served in the captain's saloon. Hans enjoyed the banter and chatter with the other officers. The wine and port flowed and the food was good, certainly at the start of each leg of the journey when the supplies were fresh. Before the mast, however, life was very different. These were the quarters of the lowlier ranks: seamen, artisans and soldiers, who had to endure cramped and often insanitary conditions.

In all, Hans was away for over four years. Towards the end of his tour of duty, he was promoted to ship's captain and put in charge of a large shipment that would be taken from the island of Manila back to Amsterdam. He brought with him a young girl named Mori whom he had rescued from a Portuguese slave trader. The trader had bought her from pirates, who had kidnapped her when she was just eight years old from her home village in the province of Goa. She was now fifteen and a Catholic. The trader made use of her and intended to sell her on when he was bored with her to the brothels of Batavia or possibly even Lisbon. She worked for him in every capacity – serving at his table, preparing food, doing his laundry and sharing his bed.

The merchant was named Carlos Fernandes. The Portuguese and the Dutch were at loggerheads over trade, but there was always a deal to be done if you were prepared to dine with the devil. Carlos invited Hans to dinner to discuss a shipment of pepper. Hans had been reluctant, but the price was good. His first sight of the girl had been as they sat before dinner on the large veranda overlooking the lush garden. Carlos called out, 'Mori, Mori, come here, you stupid girl. A man could die of thirst here.'

The girl materialised almost silently at his side. 'Sorry, master.'

'Well, bring the rum then!' he barked at her.

She returned with a bottle and two crystal glasses on a silver tray. Hans observed her fine long fingers trembling slightly as she laid the tray on the table between the two men. She was tall and slender. She wore a simple cotton dress and her hair was wrapped in a brightly coloured turban. She kept her eyes lowered and winced almost imperceptibly when Carlos the trader spoke to her.

'More rum, girl. Hurry with it. And where is our dinner? Serve it now.'

The large dining table had been laid meticulously with silver and linen; Carlos barracked Mori, finding fault with everything. 'Don't put the dish there, put it here! What is the matter with you? You are an imbecile. I should have left you with the pirates. You are not fit to live in a house. Are you stupid?'

The tirade continued. The girl was powerless and could do nothing but submit. She laid the dishes on the table with great care and only raised her eyes once as she served Hans with a dish of chicken. He was watching her intently, hoping some kindness would flow, unobserved, towards her. Her dark lashes flicked up momentarily, revealing large dark brown eyes filled with tears. She caught his gaze for a second before blinking; the tears spilled down her smooth brown cheeks. Hans resisted the urge to wipe them away with his finger.

Once the men were served, she withdrew and hovered in an ante-room. Clearly she had been instructed to remain, out of sight, in case Carlos needed anything. He drank heavily and soon after one o'clock he fell asleep, his head lolling on his chest, snoring loudly. Hans walked as silently as possible from the dining room and up the stairs to his own room. The girl was still lingering in the hallway. As he shut his door, he heard Carlos' rough voice, then a sharp slap. He heard her crying and had to fight the urge to rush downstairs and rescue her there and then. But he resolved to wait. He must not jeopardise his cargo, or her life.

The following day, he rose early. As he left his room, he noticed the girl slipping silently and meekly from her master's bedchamber. Her eyes were downcast as she passed Hans in the corridor. She appeared mute and yet he had heard her cry the previous night. She had a voice; she was simply unable to use it.

Over breakfast, he and Carlos made final arrangements for the shipment of pepper. Hans' ship was leaving that day and the shipment would be delivered within the hour to the port. He shook hands with Carlos and made to leave. But as he walked down the drive of the merchant's house, he cut back and hurried through the gardens of the estate. He found the girl hanging up washing in the kitchen garden. She pulled back in fear as he approached her.

He held his fingers to his lips: 'Shh… Please, I wish you no harm. But I cannot stand by and watch you being so abused by Carlos. He told me last night that when he is done with you he intends to sell you on.'

The girl's large, dark eyes widened in fear.

'Let me help you. I am leaving today and returning to my country in Europe – far from here and far from Carlos. You can have work in my house. I am a merchant, and wealthy. I will find suitable work for you – washing and cleaning. But you will not have to degrade yourself. Do you understand me? I am a good Christian. I will care for you.'

The girl said nothing, clearly assessing the situation.

'Mori, Mori! Where the hell are you, girl?' Carlos' voice carried through the house and out into the garden.

A look of panic spread across her face. 'Yes, I will come with you,' she finally whispered. 'When?'

'Meet me at the harbour this afternoon. We set sail on the evening tide. Do you think you can get away?'

'I will pretend to run an errand for him. I will get there some-how. Thank you.'

She turned to go back into the large plantation house. Hans heard a sharp slap as Carlos hit her once again.

The loading of the pepper took most of the day. When it was finished, the ship's Captain Jacob stood at the prow, ready to cast off and leave. There was no sign of Mori.

'We must make sail, Hans. The tide is with us.'

'Just a few minutes more,' begged Hans. 'I know she will be here.'

A quarter of an hour passed. 'We cannot stay any longer,' said Jacob at last. 'We risk losing the tide.'

'Go then,' said Hans, his eyes scanning the dockside.

As Jacob ordered the lines to be released from the harbour, Hans saw Mori running down the gangway. Her turban unrav-elled as she ran, revealing her long dark hair flying out behind her. She had a tiny bag clutched to her breast, as if in fear of los-ing it. She called up to Hans and waved at him.

'Wait, please…'

The ship's ropes had already been loosed and the gangplank pulled back on board; the vessel had begun to move away from the dockside. Hans rushed to the side of the ship and called to her.

'Jump, quick!'

The girl sized up the situation and the ever-widening gap be-tween the dockside and the ship; the emerald sea gurgling below. She ran back a few paces, tucking the small bag inside her cotton blouse. She rushed towards the edge of the dock and took a leap into the air, her legs pedalling as she did so, as if willing herself to reach the side of the ship.

Hans leant out as far as he could from the side of the ship and their hands connected in mid-air. He tightened his grip and she hung for a few perilous seconds over the dark, boiling sea before he could pull her to safety.

Finally, in front of him on the deck, she held her face in her hands and sobbed. 'Thank you... Thank you.'

'Thank God,' said Hans. 'Another few minutes and we'd have been away. Come with me. I'll find you a little corner, somewhere safe.'

As the master of the ship, Hans had a larger cabin than usual. It stood on one side of a sitting room that he shared with the captain. Next to his cabin was a small space that was intended as an office. It had a desk and a chair, nothing more. He ordered the desk and chair moved to the sitting room and had a small cot bed brought in for Mori.

'You will sleep here, all right? That way I shall be nearby and will make sure no one does you any harm.'

She was the only woman on board ship on that journey and the seamen noted the pretty girl with the long dark hair and slender figure. But Hans made it clear that anyone caught touching her would be flogged and left at the next port. The men muttered amongst themselves. They were jealous of the young man, for they were sure he was sleeping with her throughout the journey.

But Hans did not touch her. She was beautiful, certainly, and appeared willing and appreciative. But he knew he would be no better than Carlos if he made her his own.

When the ship finally landed in Amsterdam, Mori expressed her fears. 'What will people make of me here? You won't let them take me, will you, Hans?'

'No, I will not. I've told you. You will have work in our house. Good work. You are not a slave, Mori. You are a free person. Many of my contemporaries are involved in slavery, I know. But I do not believe it is right. I will pay you and you will be free to leave at any time. There are other people of colour here. Not many, but some of have found work in houses in this city. You'll see.'

His mother was in her bedroom when Hans arrived back home. She heard the clatter of horse's hooves on the cobbles outside; she heard Mitze call down to Saskia in the kitchens below. 'He's here!' She stood and looked out of the window. The bootboy, Michaela, was unloading chests and bags onto the steps of the large house. Hans climbed down from the carriage. He breathed deeply and looked around – at the house, the canal, up at the pale blue sky. He looked up towards his mother's bedroom and waved. He appeared thin, tired, but otherwise well enough, she thought. Clara waved back and her heart gave a little leap. He turned away from her towards the carriage and put his arms out to an unseen object within. He brought out a girl. She wore a black cloak with a hood. As he lifted her to the ground, the hood fell back, revealing dark hair, dark skin. The girl smiled up at him with an unwavering gaze. Clara heard him speak.

'Let's go inside and get something to eat. Saskia will have something wonderful. She always does.'

Clara walked uncertainly onto the large landing of the house. She leant over the oak banisters.

'Hans…'

He stood below her in the black and white tiled hall. He removed his hat, his cloak and gloves, handing them to Mitze. He looked up at his mother.

'Mama, I am here at last. I must eat something, then I shall come up.'

The girl looked up at the older woman – small, thin, erect and dressed entirely in black; she was an intimidating sight.

'Is that your mother?' she whispered, thinking of her own soft, round mother, lost so long ago.

'Yes, you'll meet her later. Let's go down to the kitchens and eat.'

They ate a pheasant pie that Saskia had just baked. Mori found the pastry heavy and difficult to chew; she had never eaten a pie before. But the meat was tasty and she was hungry. Mitze boiled up water to fill the large bath in Hans' room. Hans introduced Mori to the rest of the household.

'This is Mori. She will be helping us here in the house from now on. Make her welcome. Mitze, perhaps when you have filled my bath, you would show Mori to her room. She can have the little room in the attic I thought – next to yours. And could you let her have a little hot water too? There is a jug and basin in her room, I think. Put some soap in there for her, will you? We've had a long journey.'

Saskia and Mitze looked at each other over the Mori's head.

'What are you doing bringing that heathen here?' Clara demanded crossly when Hans finally went to see her. Any pleasure she might have felt at seeing her son once again after so many years had been spoilt by the sight of the dark-skinned girl.

'She is not a heathen, Mother. She is a good Christian – a Catholic, in fact. I know we are Protestant here, but she will be discreet. Besides, what would you have me do? Leave her with a man who abused her and used her? You are a good Christian, Mother, and have brought me up to be the same. How could I leave the girl to such a terrible future? She is kind and sweet and works hard. I'm sure Saskia and Mitze will soon have her trained up.'

Down in the basement, Saskia was also discomforted by the 'new arrival', as she persisted in calling Mori.

'Sir,' she asked Hans the next morning as she served up breakfast, 'what do you expect me to teach the new arrival?'

'She is called Mori, Saskia. In our language she would be called Maria. I expect you to teach her the routines of this house. But you might be surprised. She is also a good cook and could teach you a thing or two.'

At this, Saskia became alarmed. The thought that her place in the household might be challenged by this foreigner distressed her. 'But Sir, I have been here for nearly thirty years,' she protested.

'And will be here for the next thirty, I sincerely hope. Just be kind, Saskia. She can start with the laundry perhaps.'

The girl began to settle into the household routines. She helped Mitze with the laundry and became adept with the laundry press; she was meticulous about pressing Clara's garments; her sewing was quick and neat, so Mitze set her to work mending hems of petticoats and sewing on buttons. She was sent on small errands for Saskia and soon learned the layout of Amsterdam's streets and canals. As she wandered the cobbled lanes she would stop to watch a flock of geese flying overhead, and as she crossed over the canals, she would lean over the bridges as swans floated by in a stately fashion. Her room in the attic overlooked the canal, and if she woke early she loved nothing better than to sit on her windowsill watching the activities in the street below – the canal boats with their cargo travelling towards the market, laundry women carrying great bundles of linen from the large houses on the Herengracht. They reminded her of the women in her village in Goa taking laundry to the river each day. The room itself was small but cosy and she felt safe for the first time in her life. She had a bed, and a small chest in which she kept the clothes Hans had bought for her – two black day dresses to wear in the house, three aprons, three muslin caps, a selection of underwear that Saskia had helped her to buy and one dark blue day dress Hans bought for her that she was to wear on Sundays when she went to church with the family. She was very grateful for Hans' kindness.

'This is for me?' she asked when he brought the dress home.

'Yes, Mori. I wanted you to have something pretty to wear.'

'You are a very kind man,' she said, blushing.

Hidden amongst the new undergarments was her own tiny bag of personal possessions. These included a little rag doll that her mother Isabel had made for her. She had given the doll to Mori on her sixth birthday. It had been in the pocket of her skirt when the pirates invaded her village. She remembered how they had rampaged through the small settlement, killing old men and women, kidnapping anyone young enough to work. Pregnant women were slaughtered, some in front of their children's eyes. Most women were raped, some then taken, others killed – Mori's mother amongst them. Mori had been hiding under the bed when the men attacked her mother. She still felt shame that she had been unable to save her, but what could a tiny girl do against three violent grown men? When they had finished, they set fire to the house. She had run to her mother to try to save her and drag her outside, but Isabel was already dead; her throat had been cut. Mori, shocked and terrified, had run into the vegetable garden that her mother tended so carefully. She had been hanging up some washing as the men arrived; Mori noticed the chemise hanging on the line. She grabbed it and stuffed into her blouse. She had run then, as fast as her legs could carry her. She thought she had escaped, but as she ran into the forest surrounding the village, she stopped to look back. Behind her was a plume of smoke rising into the blue sky and on her heels a large bearded man, who grabbed her by her long dark hair and swung her round, calling out, 'I've got a live one here – looks in good condition. Think we'll take her.'

Somehow she had managed to protect the chemise and the doll throughout her long captivity. She took it out from time to time and inhaled the scent of her mother. In reality the scent had long gone, but it comforted her to have it and she was determined never to be parted from it.

As the Amsterdam summer merged into autumn, Hans began to believe that his mother had at last accepted Mori. She allowed the girl to collect her linen each morning, and had once even thanked her when it was returned, congratulating her on it being well pressed.

One afternoon, the family sat in the garden, taking tea. Clara had at last been persuaded by Johan to leave her bedroom and go outside in order to enjoy the late summer sunshine. Mori brought out a tray of porcelain cups and saucers, which she laid out on a table in the garden. Clara poured the tea and handed round a plate of Saskia's biscuits. She had a little colour in her cheeks for the first time in months. A starling flew into the garden and sat on the fountain. Soon it was joined by a second, then a third. Before long there were twenty, maybe thirty starlings gathering in the garden.

'How strange,' said Johan. 'It is time for the starlings to be travelling I think, but they seem to have been waylaid by our garden.'

Within minutes, a flock of starlings encircled the garden, swooping and wheeling, flying closer and closer to the family.

'I want to go inside,' said Clara, batting her hand at a starling that was flying over her head, grazing the top of her muslin cap. The family stood up to go inside. As they did so, they saw that the flock was growing in size. A huge column of starlings, like a tornado, was making its way across the gardens of the houses that fronted the Herengracht. Twirling and whirling about. Hans took his mother's hand and practically dragged her into the house. Johan was not far behind. They ran down the basement steps into the kitchen and slammed the glass door behind them as a phalanx of birds crashed into it. Hans ran up the stairs to the main house. Mori was already standing in the hall looking out through the windows on either side of the door. The column of birds now filled the sky; it was black with starlings. Clara went to the drawing room and shut the shutters against the sight. She called for Mitze to come and light the oil lamps. Mori brought a shawl for Clara, who had begun to shiver uncontrollably.

Hans stood in the hall looking out across the canal as thousands and thousands of birds moved as one against the evening sky.

'I've never seen anything like it,' he said to Mori as she came back into the hall.

'I have,' said Mori, 'when I was little. It's a bad sign. An omen.'

'Nonsense,' said Hans. 'It's just birds. They'll fly away soon.'

He was right of course, and within the hour the skies had cleared. As the sun set behind the garden, Hans tried to comfort his mother. But she had heard Mori in the hall and was worried.

'She said it was a sign – what of? Is it bad? I think it must be bad.'

'No, no,' said Johan. 'Hans is right. It's just a large flock of birds. Nothing more.'

The following day, Hans heard from the VOC that plague had been found in an Amsterdam family whose son had recently returned from Batavia, their major trading post. He was warned to be on his guard.

He kept the bad news from his mother of course, but did mention it to his father after breakfast as they worked together on papers in Johan's study.

'Do we think the boy brought it back with him?' asked Johan incredulously. 'Surely he would have shown signs on the journey.'

'Well, no other cases seem to have shown up yet. Let's wait. Perhaps it will be a minor outbreak. The family are in quarantine now.'

Five days passed with no further cases reported. Johan went to a partners' meeting of the VOC. He came back in a cheerful mood.

'Our profits are up, Hans,' he said gleefully. 'We will make a tidy sum on our investment this year. Four hundred percent has been talked of this evening.' He retired to bed.

The following morning, Johan woke complaining of being a little tired and lethargic. Hans advised him to remain in bed, but his father was determined to come downstairs and work in his study. But the following day, Johan was feverish, and was persuaded to stay in bed. The doctor was sent for and diagnosed a fever. Mori tended to him, bringing him water and a few little meals that Saskia had prepared specially for him. On the third day he got out of bed and stumbled badly. As he fell on the floor, he pulled a table over with him. Hans, hearing the commotion, rushed upstairs to see his father lying sprawled out on the floor of his room, rambling unintelligibly. The day after that, large blackish swellings began to develop, first in his groin, then under his arms and neck. Hans did not need to call the doctor to diagnose his father's illness.

He ordered his mother to remain in her room. The servants were to remain downstairs. The doctor was called for as a matter of protocol, and pronounced that Johan did indeed have the plague. The house was put under quarantine.

Johan struggled on for four days, but his symptoms grew worse and worse. Mori continued to tend to him. She gave him water and a little food when he could bear it, but seven days after he first felt unwell, poor Johan died.

CHAPTER 23

Amsterdam
1623

Two days after his father's death, Hans walked into his study to find his mother balancing precariously on a chair, struggling to open the glass doors of the display cabinet.

'Mother, what on earth are you doing?' asked Hans. 'You will fall. Here, let me help you.'

Clara pushed him away.

'I must destroy it,' she said.

'What? What must you destroy?'

'The vase. None of this would have happened if I had got rid of it years ago. First the babies, then Katje and now Johan. I cannot bear it any longer. It has to go.'

Hans lifted his mother from the chair and returned her delicately to the floor.

'No, Mama. You cannot blame an inanimate object. It is a simply a vase, nothing more. A thing of beauty and rarity. It has been in our family for over two hundred years. I have the family tree, filled in by generations – I keep it in my desk. It is a remarkable document, a testament to the extraordinary success our family has made of itself. Now, of course, I don't think that success has anything to do with the vase; it is down to hard work and determination. Neither is it responsible for the terrible tragedy of losing your children, or Papa's death. After all, throughout the generations children have died. Look, I shall show you here – one of Beatrice's sisters also lost six children. The generation before her lost twelve in all. Many more survived, but many were lost. No one has blamed the vase, and you must not either.'

Clara laid her head on Hans' desk and wept inconsolably. When she finally dried her eyes, she looked at him with anger.

'It's the fault of that girl you brought here then. That Mori, she's a witch. You must get rid of her. She brought the disease to this house.'

'Mother, no! It had nothing to do with Mori. You cannot think that. Father went to the VOC that day. I fear he caught it there. Three more cases were reported yesterday. All of them are associated with the VOC.'

Clara refused to be mollified, and Hans finally had to insist that there be 'no further talk of Mori leaving this house'.

Four weeks went by, with no one else in the household falling ill. Finally, the quarantine on the house on the Herengracht was lifted; Saskia instructed the bootboy Michaela to wash off the large letter 'P' that had been painted on the house's door. But Hans knew it was not the end of the matter. Amsterdam was in the grip of an epidemic. Five cases became twenty, fifty, then a hundred. Soon there were over a thousand. It was no respecter of class or position. Hans instructed the staff to be on their guard.

'We must limit our contact with everyone outside this house. I shall instruct the suppliers to bring all our food here and leave it in the stables at the back. We should avoid going to church; we can say our devotions at home until this terrible episode is over.'

But the episode became a full-blown epidemic, as cases kept on coming throughout that year and on into the following year and the next. By the end, over sixteen thousand people died of the plague – one sixth of Amsterdam's population.

In the summer of 1625, when no new cases had been reported for six weeks, the city authorities finally declared that the epidemic was over. As warm fresh air blew in off the North Sea, it seemed to presage a new beginning for those who had survived. The people threw open their windows, long shuttered against the disease. They began to mix with one another, to hold parties up and down the large houses on the Herengracht. It was at one such party that Hans met Antoinette. She was the daughter of a fellow merchant. Just eighteen, with fair hair and bright cornflower-blue eyes, she reminded Hans of a perfect china doll. Delicate, dainty and extremely pretty, she had a bright, sparkling voice and laughed frequently and easily. Hans decided, almost the moment he met her, that he would marry her. She would bring life and laughter to the house on the Herengracht, things which had been in short supply for many years.

The courtship lasted only a few weeks. The city's recent experience of death had made its inhabitants eager for life. Antoinette's father was delighted that his eldest daughter might make such a good match. So many fine young men had been lost over the previous two years and Hans was considered one of the most important members of the VOC. Hans did not love Antoinette, but he liked her and was grateful that she was prepared to marry him. He imagined that love would grow, over time. But his true feelings, he realised, were for Mori; it was she who had captured his heart. He realised that he had loved her from the moment he had met her. He had never acted on his feelings for fear of dishonouring her; of breaking his word to her. And because he knew that he could never make her his wife – his mother would never countenance him marrying an ex-slave. But when she came into his study in the evening with a glass of port on a silver tray and laid it silently next to him, he breathed in her scent and his eyes rested on her long delicate fingers and her slender forearms. He yearned to pull her towards him and kiss her. He had no idea if she reciprocated. He imagined she was unaware of his feelings.

Clara was delighted that Hans was to marry Antoinette. For the first time in many years, she began to look forward to a time when she might become a grandmother. And Antoinette did not disappoint. Within three years of their marriage, three children were born: a boy named Johan after his grandfather, followed by two daughters – Elisabeth and Cornelia, named after Antoinette's grandmothers, as was the custom. The nursery in the house on the Herengracht was redecorated. The portrait of Katje was moved to Clara's room and replaced with another of Antoinette.

'Mama,' she announced to her mother-in-law, 'I would like my children to fall asleep under the gaze of their adoring mother. I hope you understand. It is not meant as any disrespect to Katje.'

Antoinette had a knack of persuading people to do as she asked. She never raised her voice to argue, or even cajole. She simply made it impossible for people to refuse her. Hans was happy to oblige. He agreed to pay for the garden to be redesigned. He signed the invoice for the tulip bulbs. He concurred that her little parlour should be redecorated just as she liked. The nursery was altered to suit her and the children. In return, she carried each child uncomplainingly and gave birth quietly and decorously. Mitze was promoted to her personal maid and enjoyed the opportunity it gave her to have influence in the household. Mori became the downstairs maid. A new laundry maid was employed.

There was just one issue that Antoinette could not engineer to her liking: the presence of Mori in the household. She had long sensed an irritating attachment between her husband and the girl. It was as if there was a bond, a private unspoken understanding between them. And she did not like it. It excluded her and she was determined to excise it.

'Hans,' she said one evening after dinner as they sat together in her parlour. 'Hans, I wonder if we should consider one or two changes in our household staff.'

Hans looked up from his book. 'In what way?'

'I think Saskia perhaps needs some extra help in the kitchen. Her cooking is very adequate, but I hear that trained chefs are now very popular in houses like ours. She could assist and make breakfast and so on but perhaps the bigger dinners could be left to someone a little more... flamboyant.'

'Saskia has been here for over thirty years. I will not even think of replacing her.'

'Am I to have no influence over my own household?' asked Antoinette, smiling prettily at her husband.

'Well, what else do you wish to change?' Hans said, closing his book and placing it in his lap.

'Mitze is now my personal maid and is doing a good job, but I believe we need two new downstairs maids to really run the house properly. I don't think Mori is really quite adequate. Things are not cleaned properly, I've noticed. And she is not really up to the task when we have visitors. She appears awkward. People are embarrassed by her. It's not good for the business, Hans. I give a lot of my time to help arrange large supper parties for you, and it's too bad that things are spoiled by the inadequacies of our staff. My mother knows of two girls who have a lot of experience working in a big house in Amsterdam who would be perfect. They are sisters and do not wish to be parted from one another. It is rather sweet. If we were to take them on, Mori would really be quite superfluous.'

Hans looked at his wife intently. She did not catch his gaze, but continued to sew diligently. She displayed no emotion. Not a flicker of anger, determination, or venom. And yet, he knew that it was all there – under the surface. He could see that he was being presented with a choice – to lose Saskia or Mori. It was an impossible decision, and one that he was not minded to take.

'I will not lose Mori. You know that I rescued her from a terrible situation, and I promised her then that she would always have a job in my house. I will not go back on my word.'

'Good, so we are, at least, to have a new chef. I shall appoint someone and let Saskia know. And, I shall make Mori the nursery maid, with your permission? We will employ the new downstairs maids and Mori will remain upstairs with the children, where she will not be required to mix with our guests.'

Aware that he had been boxed into a corner by his clever wife, Hans was grateful that she appeared, at least, to have acquiesced on the matter of Mori leaving the household. He would see less of Mori if she was with the children all day, but she would be still be there – in his house.

The new arrangement appeared to go well enough, for a while. Mori adapted to her new position. She liked the children and did her best to care for them. But Antoinette was a demanding mistress and found fault with her work on a daily basis. Their clothes were not cleaned properly; the children's routine was wrong, and one afternoon, when Antoinette was downstairs in the drawing room entertaining friends to tea, she heard a piercing scream from one of the children. Rushing upstairs, she found Cornelia writhing on the floor clutching at her hand; Mori was crouched over the child, attempting to bathe the child's hand in cold water.

'What happened?' demanded Antoinette, pushing Mori out of the way.

'I… I put a log onto the fire. I turned away for a moment and Cornelia must have slipped.'

'Where was the fire guard?'

'I forgot,' Mori said through tears.

'Get out,' Antoinette shouted. 'Go to your room and do not come back down here.'

Antoinette called Mitze to come and care for the children while the doctor was sent for. The child's hand was treated. It would heal well enough, he said. But for Antoinette it was the last straw.

That evening, when the children were finally asleep, Antoinette went to see her mother-in-law.

'Mama,' she said, pacing the room, 'I wonder if I might seek a little counsel from you?'

Clara was always pleased to help her daughter-in-law. She was so grateful for the sound of children's voices in the house and loved her grandchildren desperately. Little Johan went each afternoon on his mother's instructions to visit his grandmother and sat on her lap and read from his book with her. It was the best part of Clara's day and she would do anything to keep Antoinette happy.

'Of course, dear Antoinette. Please sit down.'

Antoinette described the terrible "disaster" that had unfolded that afternoon. 'I really fear to leave them with her if I am honest with you, Mama dear. Hans will not listen to me. He insists the girl remains here. I would have thought he has done his duty by her. I know people like her can get work in this city. But why does it have to be in our house? I would like a properly trained nursemaid – maybe two – to care for the children. Does Hans not love his children?'

With her mother-in-law on her side, Antoinette knew that it was just a matter of time before she got her way. Her reasoning was unarguable. Mori presented a risk to their children. Within a week, Hans had found an alternative position for her, at the home of an artist friend.

Mori stood before him in his study, mute with disappointment and shame. 'You know I love your children. I would never do anything to harm them. It was a mistake.'

'I know Mori. And I trust you – implicitly. But Antoinette cannot forgive you. I am sorry. I have no choice. I have found a new position for you, with a good man. Emanuel is a talented artist. He will respect you. He lives in an interesting part of the city, full of Jewish merchants and tradespeople. I know there are many people of colour there. Perhaps it is for the best. You might even find a husband… Someone to care for you.' Even as he spoke these words, he felt a pang of regret.

Mori, who had sensed Hans' affection through the years, said nothing. She knew that a man like Hans, with all his wealth and position, could never really care for a fallen girl like her, a girl who had been abused by so many. She cared for him, but it was pointless to tell him so. And she was fearful of rejection, or disappointment. And so she agreed to leave the house on the Herengracht, taking, at Hans's insistence, all her clothes and possessions. He even gave her the little painted chest where she kept her belongings. Her things were moved on a small cart to her new employer's house. She was to assist Emanuel's cook in the kitchen and help his wife in the house. The house was not large, and easy enough to run. And Emanuel did indeed live an interesting life. He worked in his studio each day, alongside two young apprentices. They were amusing and liberated and thought Mori a beautiful and interesting subject. In fact, they often painted her, much to the annoyance of the cook and Emanuel's wife. She settled at the new house and enjoyed her work. But each day she thought of Hans and missed his kindness.

Antoinette was delighted. Two new maids were employed, in addition to two nursery maids. At last, she felt in full control of her household. She rewarded Hans by announcing that she was, once again, expecting a baby. Hans was pleased enough. His mother was thrilled. The pregnancy initially went well, but when Antoinette was four months pregnant, she began to bleed. She took to her bed and rested, but the damage was done, and a few days later, she lost the baby.

She tried to stay cheerful, as was her nature. But a deep depression took hold of her. She withdrew from all society and would see only her children. Even Hans was excluded. He asked a doctor to visit her, but he said there was little he could do. She would eventually recover, and Hans should just be patient.

Hans threw himself into his work. He had long planned a journey to China with a fleet from the VOC; he was intent on developing trade with the porcelain exporters in Canton. The wealthy middle classes of Amsterdam had developed a taste for the beautiful clear porcelain that the Chinese produced and Hans could see an opportunity for mass production. He was concerned for Antoinette's welfare in his absence, but his mother assured him that she would take care of her.

'You know what your father would have said, Hans. Business first. I will take care of Antoinette. I understand her pain better than you.'

Grateful, for once, for his mother's support, Hans finalised his travel plans.

He was away for two years in all, and stayed for the most part in Canton, where the porcelain for export was stored. There he chose thousands of pieces – bowls, plates, cups and vases. He also bought tea and silk. His family was often in his thoughts, and he wrote to them as often as he could. He received three letters from home – one from his wife and two from his mother. The children were progressing well, Clara wrote, and Antoinette was a little better. Hans also wrote to Mori, and was delighted when she replied.

My dear Hans,

I have been taught how to write by my employer. He is a kind man and I enjoy living here. The area is lively and I am allowed to go out one evening a week. I also attend a Catholic church; it is hidden away in the attic of a house on the Herengracht. I tell you this, for I know you will not reveal our secret. We do no harm wishing to worship in our own way. I went past your house yesterday, on my way to church, and I saw the nursery maid with the children. They looked well. Cornelia smiled at me and said hello. I was glad that she had forgiven me. They have all grown, especially Johan. He looked very handsome. Sometimes I visit

a little tavern nearby Emanuel's house. I have made some
friends there and think, perhaps, that you were right. It was
time to leave your house. But I am so grateful for all you
did for me.
  Your faithful servant,
  Mori.

Hans finally returned home, with a valuable cargo of porcelain. It would secure the family's wealth for years to come, he hoped. He was pleased to see that Antoinette was in better spirits. Time had done its work and she was delighted to see him. The children had grown, just as Mori had said, and hardly recognised their father. But Hans was patient with them and spent a little time with them each evening before dinner, reading and doing puzzles in the drawing room.

One afternoon, after a meeting with the Amsterdam chamber at the Oost Indisch Huis, he had arranged to visit his old friend Rembrandt, who was recently married, and living once again in Amsterdam. Hans walked down St Antonies Breeestrasse until he reached the Jewish quarter. Rembrandt had taken a house on Jodenbreestrasse. It was a large house, with room for a capacious studio on the top floor. It was less expensive than if it had been on one of the smarter canals, and he enjoyed the cosmopolitan atmosphere of the area.

As Hans approached the house, he saw a familiar figure. It was Mori; she was walking towards him, swinging a large basket of fruit that she had clearly just bought from the market. It was the first time he had seen her in nearly three years. Hans called her name. She smiled broadly as she recognised him and rushed over to him, spilling apples from her basket as she did so. Together they collected the fallen fruit.

'Mori,' he said at last. 'It has been so long. You look well. Are you well?'

'I am, Sir – very well indeed.'

'Thank you for writing. I did so enjoy your letter.'

'And I enjoyed yours. I have been studying. Emanuel says I have some skill for reading and writing, and he has lent me some books to read.'

'Good, good… Shall we… Can you spend a little time with me? It has been so long, and I have so much I would like to talk to you about. We could go to the tavern you wrote about?'

'I have to get back. The cook needs this basket of fruit. Emanuel has some customers to dinner this evening.'

'Of course… And I am on my way to friend's house, anyway.'

'Well, it was nice to see you,' said Mori, gazing up at Hans.

'Yes – look, maybe tomorrow? Is there a time when you can leave the house?'

'Yes, in the afternoon sometimes I can get away.'

'Meet me? In the tavern, over there…?'

'I will. Thank you.'

It was the first of many meeting in taverns in the Jewish quarter. Hans had a few acquaintances in that part of town - merchants and traders with whom he did occasional business. But no one from the VOC socialised there. No one in Antoinette's circle ever saw him in the company of the beautiful Indian girl. Somehow, now that he was no longer her employer, Hans felt freed from the bonds of duty. His desire for the girl grew and he could feel that she reciprocated. She said as much one afternoon as they walked towards Emanuel's house.

'I wish that we could spend more time together, Hans….'

The comment hung between them as they walked along the cobbled street, their fingers just touching.

'As do I,' said Hans at last. 'I shall arrange something.'

Hans took a small house on Prinsengracht. It was not large, but it was comfortable, and simply furnished. Before long, he and Mori were meeting there once or twice a week. He loved her, and she returned his love. Predictably, within a few months, she announced that she was pregnant. When she gave him the news, she stood in front of the fire in the little sitting room, anxiously twisting her hands. She was certain that he would abandon her.

'That is wonderful, Mori,' he said, beaming at her.

'But how – how can we go on?' she asked sensibly.

'I shall buy this house. You will move in and I shall support you and the child. I won't abandon you, Mori. I love you. You can simply tell Emanuel that you have found another position. I shall have a word with him. He needn't know anything.'

And so began Hans's extraordinary double life. He spent every night with his wife and family. In the mornings he worked, as usual in his study. After lunch he would go to the house on Prinsengracht. He bought Mori a ring, and they agreed she would tell her neighbours that her husband was a merchant who travelled abroad. He let himself into the house through the garden at the back so as not to draw attention to himself. Her pregnancy went well and she gave birth to a beautiful boy the following April. Hans suggested they call the boy Pieter, after one of his own ancestors.

'He was a German merchant, and the one who started our family business. He met his wife Maria in Venice and fell in love with her. They were very happy together. And now I have my own Maria.'

'But we cannot be married,' said Mori dispiritedly.

'I know, but it is as if we were.'

Each evening at six o'clock, Hans would reluctantly leave Mori and return to the house on the Herengracht. It was curious, he thought, that Antoinette never questioned him as to where he had been each day. The situation continued for a year, then another. Mori had a second child – a girl she named Isabel after her own mother. Hans loved his second family as much, if not more, than his first. He employed a serving woman named Brigitte to help Mori in the house. Although a good-natured woman, Brigitte had a natural curiosity about her employer's situation. She knew that things were not as they should be. It was only a matter of time before gossip began to spread along the canal.

The little family kept themselves to themselves. If Mori was in the garden at the back of the house playing with the children a neighbour would occasionally spot her and smile. She would smile back but never initiated a conversation. Of course, she went to the market and shopped for food. On one occasion, she met Emanuel's wife, Alicia, who enquired as to her new position. Mori was forced to lie.

When Hans arrived that afternoon, she wept. 'I feel that I am to be kept hidden. I am living a lie. I met Alicia today and I didn't know how to answer her questions about my "new job". I am grateful for all that you have given me, Hans, truly, but I feel so very ashamed each day. And so lonely. If you cannot come to visit me, I have no one but the children and Brigitte. And I know she is suspicious. She asks me often where you work, what you do...'

Hans was sympathetic but he was also worried. If word were to get out that he had a mistress, and worse, a mistress with children, his reputation would be destroyed, as would hers. Amsterdam was puritanical city, for all its worldliness. It welcomed people from across the world providing trade was involved. But in his private life, a man was expected to be above all suspicion. And there was another problem. Hans was building a new ship, 'The Flying Dragon', in which he planned to make another journey to journey to China. The last shipment of porcelain had made a huge profit and he had customers all over Europe demanding more. It would mean abandoning Mori and the children. He would ensure there was money to support her, of course, but she would be left alone for a long time.

That evening, as he sat in his study going over the figures from the shipwright, he listened to his wife singing in the next room.

His children were sleeping peacefully in the nursery upstairs. The fire crackled and his dog twitched in his sleep. He thought of Mori and her children, alone in the little house on Prinsengracht. He stood up and opened the glass cabinet next to the fireplace, carefully removing the Ming vase. He opened his desk drawer and found the paper on which his family tree that had been so carefully and meticulously completed by his forbears. From another drawer, he pulled out a large sheet of fresh paper and began to copy the family tree details. He found it absorbing work. The downstairs maid brought him a glass of port, but he hardly noticed her entering the room. Finally, his copying complete, he created a new entry; one that would appear on this copy alone. Next to his name he drew a line and wrote the word 'Mori' beside it. Beneath their two names he drew another line and wrote the names of his two children with her – Pieter and Isabel. The work blotted and dried, he folded it carefully and placed it inside the vase. He then put the vase back on the shelf in the glazed cabinet and locked it.

The following afternoon, he took the vase, hidden in a large bag, when he went to visit Mori. He played with the children. He ate a meal with her and as they sat in front of the fire in the little sitting room, he removed the vase from the bag and stood it on the table.

'What is that?' she asked.

'It is a vase that I inherited from my mother; and she from her mother. It has been in our family for over two hundred years. I would like you and the children to have it now. Family tradition has it that the vase brings good fortune to its custodian. I know you will look after it. It is very valuable.'

Mori touched the vase's smooth white surface, her fingers tracing the dragon. 'He looks angry,' she said.

'I know, but I don't believe he is. It was made for an Emperor. The claws there – just three of them on each paw – indicate it was intended for a royal person. I believe that one of my ancestors brought it back with him from China. I don't know who for, and I don't know why he never gave it up. Do you remember I told you about Maria and Peter who met in Venice? They brought it with them to Bruges, where they established a very successful business. Their children and their children's children went on to develop maiolica, using this vase as inspiration.'

'Your mother always said it was bad luck,' said Mori anxiously.

'My mother is wrong. The vase was not the cause of her troubles. I don't know if the vase brings good fortune or not. But it is valuable and it is an important part of my family's history. I want you to have it because I love you and consider you my wife. Here, look inside. There is a family tree here. You are part of it now, as are the children.'

'But Hans…' Mori began.

'Let me finish. I have to go away soon – on a long trip to China. It will be two years before I come home. I will make sure you have enough money. I have also written to Frans, one of my cousins. I have confided in him. He is a good man, a potter with his own large workshop in Delft. I have asked if you could go there and live with him while I am away. I would like Pieter to learn a craft. He seems a clever boy, and artistic. I think he has the skills to help us carry on that part of our family business. I import beautiful porcelain like this vase. But my cousins have taken their inspiration from pieces like this to create a whole new industry. The tiles around our fireplace here are made by them. The dishes we use in our kitchens are made by them. This is a huge industry and has helped to make that part of our family wealthy. If you are a good potter with a workshop of your own, you can be rich as well as lauded and admired for creating something of beauty and practicality. Pieter could work anywhere – England, France, Spain, Italy. The world will be his oyster. If you stay here, I fear for him… And you. It would be impossible for me to introduce him to the VOC. You must see that. But I will do right by him and Isabel, and by you.'

Mori's eyes filled with tears. 'How will I live without you? Could we not come with you, on the ship?'

'You know that is impossible,' he replied sadly. 'You will manage without me. You will be happier in Delft. Frans, my cousin, is a good man – a kind man. We understand each other. We both have overbearing mothers.' He gave her a smile, but she did not return it.

'In Delft you will be able to live freely . . . to make friends. You can tell everyone the story that you are married and your husband is away. I am not known there. When I return, then we shall see what the future holds. Perhaps you can come back here, or maybe you will be happier there. And Pieter will have started to learn his craft and enjoy it.'

'He is only five years old,' said Mori.

'I know, but in two years' time, he'll be old enough to start learning the trade. And for the next two years, being around Frans, watching his men at work, he will get used to it.'

'You think he should be apprenticed as a mere child? Not to learn to read, nor develop his mind? You think he is not clever enough?' Mori felt her eyes stinging with tears – of indignation, as well as sadness and disappointment.

'No, I think him very clever. But can't you see that I have a duty to ensure that he and you and Isabel have a secure future?'

'You talk as if we will never see you again.'

'Mori, you must know that is the last thing I would ever want. I know now that I love you more than anyone else. If I was not already married, you know I would marry you. But I am determined that while I am away no harm comes to you; that you are cared for. . . and happy. . . and have a future. I intend to return, but, you know, these journeys are not without risk. Do this for me, Mori. Trust me one more time. Have I ever let you down?'

The Ming vase is now ready to be painted with an underglaze of cobalt blue. Cobalt, or 'sumali' in China, is imported from the regions of West Asia. It is diluted with water and then painted onto the ceramic body of the pot. The potter must be very sure of his brushwork, for he cannot make any corrections. The designs have a soft, slightly out of focus quality. The high iron content in the cobalt results in a slight colour variation – dark specks of blue in some parts of the design, paler blue in others. This natural variation is referred to as 'heaped and piled' and is characteristic of early Ming. The base of the vase is given a six-character mark of the Xuande period. The vase is then ready to be glazed. The glaze is made of bright blue limestone. The limestone is transported many miles to Ching te Chen; it is heaped up in several layers with ferns and burned. The ashes are cleaned over and over again, and then mixed with porcelain clay, until they form a creamy substance or glaze, which is then applied to each piece.

CHAPTER 24

Sheen, London
2nd January 2016

Miranda, Jeremy and Georgie had arranged to meet at half past nine in the morning. Jeremy arrived promptly at nine twenty-five.

'Good, you're here,' said Miranda, almost pulling him in through the front door. 'I've been awake since about five this morning. Georgina found something on the Internet last night which I want to show you. I nearly rang you, actually, but it was rather late. I've not really slept since. Come into the kitchen.'

Georgie sat at the kitchen table with her mother's laptop open.

'Look at this,' she said to Jeremy.

SALE OF EARLY MING CHINA
Tuesday, 15th January 2016
Anstruthers, Hong Kong

A spectacular example of early Ming period blue and white china manufactured between 1426 and 1435 during the reign of Emperor Xuande.

Artist unknown.

The stark contrast of the blue subject matter against a
flawless white background draws the viewer to the piece.
The subject painted on the jar is a dragon with large teeth
and claws; he dominates and controls the jar,
as if the creator was trying to tell a story.
Also on the jar is the reign mark of the Emperor Xuande.

'Oh my God', said Jeremy. 'Where did you find that?'

'It's an online catalogue for an auction happening in Hong Kong in twelve days' time,' said Georgie.

'You are brilliant,' said Jeremy. 'Are we sure it's the same vase?'

'Well, the two pictures are identical,' said Miranda.

Georgie pulled up the two images side by side on the laptop.

'Bloody hell. What a bastard,' said Jeremy. 'It's bloody Ming! Do you have any idea what that means?'

'Not really,' said Miranda honestly. 'But the point is, Jeremy, how do I prove that it's mine? I mean, he paid me for it. He bought it. All right, so he duped me. But is that illegal?'

'You didn't cash the cheque and you didn't get a receipt. Surely, he would have to prove that he'd bought the item before he could offer it for sale. Otherwise it might be nicked? No reputable auctioneer like Anstruthers would take a piece like that knowing it was stolen.'

'Unless they knew it was worth a fortune and their share was going to be a fortune too,' said Miranda gloomily.

'Cynical,' said Jeremy. 'No, I don't believe that. Now, first things first. We have to approach this very analytically.'

Georgie and Miranda stared at him expectantly.

'Now, the first thing we have to do is to prove that you were, and hopefully still are, the rightful owner. And the only way of doing that is to contact that solicitor in Cirencester who dealt with your Great Aunt Celia's bequest. Miranda, you'd better give them a call. They won't want to speak to me. Secondly, we need an expert on our side. Someone who knows everything there is to know about Ming China. I'll do some research there and come up with a couple of names. We're going to have to have our wits about us if we are to catch Charlie out. The good news is that we already know what his game is. The thing is… Is he still in the country and is the vase still here too? It would be easier to get it back if it's still in the UK, obviously.'

'How will we find that out?' asked Miranda.

'Mum,' said Georgie excitedly. 'Didn't you get his address when you took that cheque from him?'

'Yes, I did. God knows what I did with it. I had it on a piece of paper somewhere.'

'Didn't you put it in your phone when you were going out with him?'

'No, I kept meaning to but I just never got round to it. And he never took me there or invited me there. We sort of existed here. His life at that house had nothing to do with me. Does that make sense?'

'Yes, it does. But either way, we need to find that address,' said Jeremy hurriedly.

'It was the The Manor, somewhere… Hampshire.'

'The "somewhere" being the crucial detail, darling,' said Jeremy, pacing back and forth across the kitchen. 'G, could you go and ransack your mother's room until you've found it? Miranda, you need to get on the phone to that solicitor. You've got his details somewhere, I presume?'

'Ye-es,' said Miranda uncertainly. 'I suspect his letter is still in my filing tray on the dresser. G, have a look, will you?'

The letter was duly found at the bottom of the tray, and as Jeremy filled the kettle, Miranda dialled the number.

'Hello, could I speak to the person who handled the estate of Mrs Celia Drake, please?'

There was a long pause before a man came onto the line.

'Hello, I am Charles Martin; I dealt with that particular estate. To whom am I speaking, please?'

Miranda went on to explain her circumstances. 'So, to sum up really, my great aunt left me several items in her will. I have your letter, which indicates that I was left some bits and pieces – "a variety of items that I might find either useful or aesthetically pleasing" – that is how you, or she, put it in the letter. But there was no actual list of the items. I do know what she left me, obviously – dishes, a quilt and so on. But, and here's the thing, I was left a vase – a blue and white Chinese vase. Someone recently persuaded me to part with it and rather recklessly I did. It turns out to have been rather valuable – Ming, in fact. I just wondered if you had any other details from the bequest that indicate precisely what my great aunt left me so that I can prove that the vase is legitimately mine. And any other information about it would be hugely useful – a valuation, perhaps, or how she had come upon it?'

'Oh dear, oh dear,' tutted the solicitor, 'Ming you say? Very valuable, then. I shall search the records and get back to you.'

Miranda put down the phone. 'It doesn't sound hopeful,' she said. 'Anyway, he said he'd get back to me. But I wish I could go down there really and meet him. Have a rummage through those records of his.'

'Found it!' shouted Georgina from upstairs. She came thundering down to the kitchen.

'Here,' she said breathlessly, putting the scrap of paper on the table. 'Here's the love-rat thief's address – you'd written it on a post-it and stuck it in your diary.'

'Oh, well done, G,' said Miranda. 'How did you think of looking there?'

'Instinct,' said Georgie.

'Right,' said Jeremy. 'Don't just sit there, look it up on the net.'

They typed in "The Manor, Chattleton, Hants" and pressed "Search".

The first Google entry appeared to be an advert from a letting agency for the house. Miranda clicked on it. The advert was six months old. She found a Google map of the house and clicked on "street view". The house was a large Georgian manor set in several acres of grounds. 'God, I can't believe I never did this before. I could have been stalking him all this time. This is a seriously beautiful house.'

Jeremy leaned in over her shoulder and peered at the laptop. 'Phew, it is, isn't it?'

'No phone number, but I could call the letting agency.'

'Go on then,' said Jeremy.

She dialled the number.

'Hello, Hemming and Partners.'

'Oh, good morning. I wonder if you could help me. I'm interested in a property on your books – the Manor, Chattleton, Hampshire. I wondered if it was still available to let?'

'Let me just check. I'm afraid that property has already been let.'

'Oh, what a shame,' said Miranda, 'I'm very interested. I don't suppose you know when the lease might be up for renewal, or if the present tenants are staying on?'

'I'm afraid I'm not allowed to give out any information about the present tenants, but I do believe the lease is coming up shortly.'

'Do you think you could keep me on file and let me know if and when it comes up, just in case the present tenants don't want to renew?'

Her details were duly noted, and Miranda hung up.

'That's quite a house isn't it?' she said. 'I mean, if he lives somewhere like that, he can't be short of a few quid.'

'First impressions can be deceptive,' said Jeremy darkly.

'Mmm…' said Miranda. 'Rather a large house to live in by yourself, isn't it? Not really a bachelor pad.'

'Oh Miranda,' said Jeremy. 'You think there might be someone living there with him?'

'Well, it's got to be a possibility, hasn't it?'

'Darling, you don't want to think about that.'

'Don't I? Maybe it's what I *do* need to think about. Maybe the love-rat is actually a two-timing love-rat or a married love-rat. I've had one of those before, so I'm familiar with the species. Look, you two, how do you fancy a bit of a day out?'

'Are you thinking what I think you're thinking?' asked Jeremy.

'Let's visit Hampshire and see if we can track him down at the house. Maybe we could drive on to the solicitors afterwards. They're not that far away – just an hour or so cross-country. What do you think?'

Jeremy exchanged a worried glance with Georgie.

'Mum, do you really think this is such a good idea? You've been so upset and I don't want you to be really hurt. You've no idea what you'll find if we go down there.'

'No, it's fine. I'm actually feeling much better today. I was very fond of him, maybe beginning to fall in love with him, but now that I know what his real motive was, all that's just evaporated really. And if there's a chance that we can track him down and retrieve the vase, we've got to take it. I'm not going to let that bastard steal my vase. Whatever we find at that house – a wife and six kids, a harem – I can handle it. So, are you coming? If you'd rather stay here, I understand. I know you've got schoolwork and stuff before the start of term.'

'Are you kidding? No way! Yes, I'm coming.'

Miranda called the solicitor back and arranged an appointment for later that afternoon to discuss Celia's bequest. Armed with his address, they locked up the house and set off in the Volvo.

The drive to Hampshire took just over an hour. During their journey, Jeremy called three of the porcelain experts and emailed them the image of the vase in the catalogue, plus Miranda's own picture of the vase on her phone. 'I think you'll agree that they appear to be identical. If you could give us some idea of valuation, it would be so helpful,' he explained. They promised to call back as soon as possible.

The M3 flowed smoothly and they took the turning towards Winchester. The A road turned into a smaller winding lane, which cut sharply through a deep, green valley lined with ancient woods and the occasional small red-brick village or hamlet. It struck Miranda with a certain irony that her first visit to her 'boyfriend's' house was being conducted in such strange circumstances. Had he not disappeared, perhaps she and Georgie might have been driving down here to spend a long weekend with Charlie. But as it was she felt like a stalker or a second-rate detective.

Georgie had taken charge of directions from the back seat. 'We should be there any time soon,' she said.

'Well done, G. I had no idea you could read a map,' said her mother proudly.

'Actually, Ma, I'm using the sat nav on my phone.'

The red brick mansion stood at the end of a long drive, set well back from the road. The entrance was through a pair of impressive metal gates hung on tall brick pillars topped rather incongruously – given that this was Hampshire and not the African veldt – by a pair of stone sleeping lions.

'Gosh, it looks even more magnificent in real life, doesn't it?' said Miranda, parking the Volvo a little further along in a small lay-by. The house and its grounds were surrounded by tall brick walls; they followed them back towards the gates and peered through, up the drive, hoping not to be seen. There was a brand new VW off-roader parked outside the house. Next to it stood an old Peugeot and a Land Rover. There was no sign of the Audi.

'Looks like someone's home,' said Jeremy. There was an intercom on one of the brick pillars and before Miranda could stop him, he had pressed the button.

'Hello,' said a disembodied woman's voice.

Miranda's heart sank.

'Hello,' said Jeremy. 'I wonder if I could have a word with Charles?'

'Charles?' said the voice. 'Are you a friend of his?'

'Yes, in a way. I've done some business with him in the past, and have something I'd like to show him. I happened to be passing and thought I'd see if he was interested.'

'Well, you've had a wasted journey,' said the voice.

'Oh dear,' said Jeremy. 'Is he not here?'

'No, he bloody well isn't.'

'I wonder,' said Jeremy, 'whether I might just come up to the house and perhaps I could show you the thing I was going to offer him; it's rather rare and beautiful.'

Miranda gesticulated at Jeremy, and mouthed: 'what are you doing? What thing?'

Much to her horror, the voice answered: 'OK. I'll buzz you in.'

The three walked up the long drive and knocked on the glossy black front door.

It was opened by a dark-haired young woman. Her blue eyes were red-rimmed and she looked pale and tense. 'Hello, I'm Callie. Do come in.'

She led them through to the kitchen at the back of the house. Miranda took in the sleek oak cabinets and marble worktops. There were tall French windows that looked out onto an impressive terrace, filled with teak furniture, which overlooked extensive grounds beyond. She glimpsed a tennis court and a swimming pool.

'Lovely house,' she found herself saying.

'Yes, it is. I won't be here much longer.'

A man wandered into the kitchen. He was much older than the woman, and wore tortoiseshell spectacles and a cashmere sweater.

'Callie – is everything OK?'

'Yes, Daddy – these people know Charles. They have something to show me.'

'Ah,' he said. 'Well, I'll go back to the sitting room. Call me if you need me.'

'Do sit down,' she said, and gestured towards the large glass dining table. 'Coffee?'

Jeremy was on the verge of saying 'yes', but Miranda intervened. 'No, no thanks – it's all right. We don't want to take up much of your time.' She had a sudden sense of sympathy for this wan girl, her dark hair scraped messily back from her face.

'So what do you want to show me?'

Jeremy took Miranda's phone out of her hand and found the picture of the vase. 'This,' he said.

'What is it?' she replied.

'Don't you know?'

'Why should I?'

'It's a Chinese vase – precise date unknown. Charles took it from Miranda here, just before Christmas. We wondered if the vase, and perhaps he, were here? Miranda rather wants it back, you see.'

'I see,' said the girl, gazing distractedly at the picture of the vase. 'Well, I'm afraid I can't really help you. The vase is certainly not here. You can search the house if you want to. And as for Charles, I'm afraid I've not seen him since about a week before Christmas myself. He was due back here on the 24th of December, but he never showed up.'

'I thought he was going to Devon for Christmas,' interjected Miranda.

'Devon!' said the girl. 'Why Devon?'

'Where his parents live,' said Miranda

'His parents! His parents are dead. And as far as I know, Charlie has never even been to Devon. Look, I don't who you are, or what you're doing here, but I think I should tell you something. Charles and I are engaged to be married, or at least we were. I don't actually know where he is. As I said, he was due back on Christmas Eve. I arrived here from London, and there was no sign of him. I've not seen or heard from him since. I've told the police but they say there's nothing they can do. I was scared something had happened to him, you see? But he appears to have just disappeared. His phone is dead and I simply can't get hold of him. Frankly, it's a mystery and if I'm honest, a total nightmare.' Her large blue eyes filled with tears.

'Oh, I'm so sorry,' said Miranda. 'You poor thing.' She instinctively got up and went round the table and put her arms round the girl.

'The thing is,' said the girl between sobs, 'I don't know whether to hate him or be worried about him. It's all just such a complete mess.'

'Can I ask you something?' said Miranda as the three stood in the hallway preparing to leave. 'Has Charles taken his passport?'

'His passport? I suspect so, why?'

'I just wondered if maybe he'd gone abroad?'

'It's a distinct possibility. He certainly took a bag of clothes with him.'

'Do you have any way of checking?' pushed Miranda.

'Why do you care so much?' asked Callie tetchily.

'Because he has something of mine that I'd really like to get back.'

'Do you mean he stole this vase of yours?'

'In a way – he convinced me to get rid of it when I wasn't really interested in selling.'

'He is certainly very persuasive,' said Callie. 'Look, let me check his desk, that's where he kept passports and things.'

The three followed her into the study and she opened the desk drawer.

'That's odd,' she said. 'The box where he kept his passport is open. He always locked it – he said to stop burglars – although I did wonder what he kept in there. There's no passport and no cash either…'

'So… Do you think he's planning a foreign trip?' said Jeremy.

'Yup! It certainly looks that way,' said the girl, slamming the desk drawer shut.

'If there's nothing else?' said Callie.

'No, and thank you,' said Miranda hurriedly. 'You've been very kind. I'm so sorry to have turned up at such an awkward time.'

'That's OK. And I hope you find your vase.'

She led them once again to the front door.

Miranda handed her a slip of paper. 'This is my name and phone number; should he turn up, could you call me?'

'It will be the first thing I do, I assure you,' Callie said sarcastically.

As they retreated down the stone steps of the house, she called out, 'And if you see the bastard before I do, tell him Callie sends her love.'

CHAPTER 25

Cirencester
2nd January 2016

Miranda pulled her Volvo into the car park behind Ciren-cester High Street. She bought a ticket and stuck it to the windscreen.

'Come on, you two, we've only got five minutes to spare before our appointment.'

Jeremy, Miranda and Georgie filed out of the Sheep Street car park and on to Castle Street. They turned left just before the magnificent parish church into Gosditch Street. The solicitor's offices were a short way down on the right-hand side.

Martin & Co was above a shop selling designer housewares. The entrance to the office was via a narrow doorway next to the shop. Miranda pushed the wooden door and it opened, revealing a narrow steep staircase carpeted with a cheap scuffed nylon runner. At the top was a small landing and a glass doorway etched with the solicitors' nameplate: Martin & Co. Miranda knocked on the door. A young woman with long brown hair braided in a plait down her back and wearing a green, knee-length woollen dress let them in.

'We're here to meet with Mr Martin,' said Miranda.

'Would you like to wait over there, please,' said the reception-ist, pointing at three shabby faux leather chairs lined against the walls. Clearly Martin & Co didn't like to waste money on un-necessary luxuries, thought Miranda.

Mr Martin arrived a few minutes later, bursting through the door. There was a sense of urgency and irritation about him, she noted: he clearly didn't believe in wasting time either.

'Ah, Mrs Sharp, you're here. Good. Oh, you're not alone. Is this your cousin?' he said, leading the way to his office and gesturing towards Jeremy. He carried a plastic shopping bag filled with bits of paper that he almost threw onto his cluttered desk.

'My cousin?' said Miranda. 'No, I don't have a cousin. This is my friend, Jeremy…'

'Oh? How odd. I took a call from your cousin – Manning, I think he said his name was – yes, Simon Manning, that was it. Do sit down… What do you mean, you have no cousin?' He fell silent and stared at the three visitors. It was as if he had run out of steam; the engine that had been motoring at full tilt since he blasted into the office had suddenly stalled. He looked accusingly at Miranda.

'I have no cousin, Mr Martin. And I don't know anyone called Simon Manning. What did this man want? Did he know me?'

'Yes, how peculiar. Carole!' he shouted through to his receptionist. 'Carole, bring us some tea, could you? I presume you'd like tea?' The three nodded pointlessly at this rhetorical question as he took up the narrative once again. 'Yes – most peculiar. He was interested in the estate of your great aunt. He appeared to know all about it, and so I presumed that he was… How peculiar. Oh, how embarrassing. I don't think I said anything indiscreet.'

'He knew about Celia?' said Miranda, astonished. 'But no one, only Jeremy here, and my parents knew about Celia, apart from…' She stopped.

'Ah,' said Mr Martin, peering over his half-moon spectacles. 'Apart from?'

'Charlie,' said Miranda to Jeremy and Georgie.

'No, he was definitely not called Charlie. I'd have remembered that, as I myself am called Charles. No, not Charlie.'

'Did he say where he was phoning from?' asked Miranda.

'From… No. I didn't speak to him long. He asked about the estate, he mentioned you by name and said he was your cousin, hence the confusion – ah, tea! Yes. Good. Carole, put it down here on the desk. Excellent… And biscuits. Do take one please, Mrs Sharp, and…' He looked blankly at Jeremy.

'Jeremy,' said Jeremy. 'Thanks I'd love one.' He handed the plate on to Georgie, who took two.

'No he didn't say where he was phoning from.' Mr Martin took a slurp of tea. 'And I did think it was a bit odd, because at the time of your great aunt's demise the list of recipients for her will was limited to the three charities and your good self. There was no mention in the will of another young person. Anyway, I'm afraid I told him that I couldn't tell him anything about the vase, as I was far too busy, and that if I had anything to say, I would say it to you this afternoon.'

He crunched down heavily on a chocolate digestive and chewed for a moment before taking another huge slurp of tea.

'He asked about the vase?' said Miranda.

'Yes, and as you had already rung about it, I naturally assumed that you must have discussed it with him in some way… But as I say, I was in a bit of a hurry and didn't really say much.'

'I see,' said Miranda. 'So you told him nothing about it.'

'No. Well, to be honest, I'm not sure what I can tell *you* about it. I was simply your great aunt's executor. I didn't even know her. It was a strange business. As I said, apart from your good self, and I presume one of your parents. . .' He looked questioningly at Miranda before continuing. 'She appeared to have no living relatives.'

'My mother, yes. She was my mother's aunt.'

'Quite so. But you were the only beneficiary named in person. No one else. The bulk of the estate was left, as you know, to three organisations. I had to sell the house and dispose of the furniture, which seemed a bit of a shame, as some of it was quite good, you know? I was surprised that she hadn't bothered to name individuals who might have liked some of those items. I arranged for it to be sold here in Cirencester through the auction house down the road. In fact, I bought one or two pieces myself – a rather pretty writing desk and a very attractive side table.'

'Yes. . . but what I am interested in, Mr Martin, is did she leave any instructions or information about the items that she left to me?'

'Yes – quite. That is why I was out when you arrived and was a few moments late.' He gestured towards the plastic shopping bag.

'I have a storage area nearby,' he continued. 'Clients' papers take up so much room, and one simply doesn't have space for it all here. Anyway, I had a box of bits and pieces from your aunt's estate that I didn't know what to do with. So they've been stored there. To be honest, I was considering getting rid of it all the other day, but then I got your phone call. I've not really had a look through it, but there might be something helpful in there.' He tipped the papers out onto his desk and gestured to them to take a look. There were old bank statements and out of date share certificates.

'I presume that all these accounts have been closed now?' asked Miranda.

'Oh yes. All closed and dealt with. Really it's probably all rubbish, but one feels responsible, you know.'

He handed a sheaf of the papers to both Jeremy and Georgie and the three began to work through them.

'Do you mind us doing this in here?' asked Miranda.

'Well, no, if you don't mind if I get on,' replied Mr Martin. He wandered out to his receptionist's office and started to dictate a letter.

It was Georgie who found it. In a self-sealing envelope that had resealed itself, and which was addressed to Mr Martin in beautiful hand-writing, was a list of instructions on the items that should be sent to Miranda.

'Mum, here's a note from Celia. Look.'

Miranda opened it and read the note penned in Celia's neat, rounded, feminine hand-writing.

Dear Mr Martin,

Further to my letter of the 12th inst. regarding the handling of my estate, I am writing to you with explicit instructions concerning my great-niece Miranda Sharp and the small bequest I wish to make to her.

I have ensured that the items I wish her to have are labelled with little pink stickers in order to avoid confusion. It is extremely important that the items are all sent to her recorded and carefully wrapped. Some of them are quite valuable, or of great sentimental value.

They are as follows:

A set of French flan dishes that I acquired early on in my marriage to Hubert. We were living in Amsterdam at the time and he bought them for me from a little shop round the corner from our house on the Herengracht. They are a little worn, but I think Miranda will appreciate them.

A Victorian carriage clock. I remember her admiring it one day when she came to visit me. I would like her to know that I did so appreciate her visits. I was rather lonely after my beloved Hubert died. I had one or two friends of course, but having never had a child, Miranda took on a great significance for me.

A leather-bound set of Dickens novels – I know she loves to read. And one can never be lonely with a good book.

A complete set of Walter Scott – not everyone's cup of tea, but I think she will like them.

An early edition of Jane Austin's Pride and Prejudice. Again, my husband bought it for me. He was always in and out of antique shops and second-hand bookshops. He said this was a good edition.

A quilt that my mother made for me. She was a wonderful quilter and the bedspread has been well looked after. Perhaps that is where Miranda got her talent for handicraft from. I'm sure that Miranda will appreciate it.

Finally, I am leaving her the Chinese dragon vase. It has been in my husband's family for many years. He always said it went back into the mists of time. The dragon has a rather angry appearance, but he is nevertheless quite beneficent I believe. He has gazed down at me from the mantelshelf in my bedroom for many years now. Hubert always said that it was a family tradition that the vase must be handed down from one generation to the next. I have decided that Miranda should have it. We have no children, and many of Hubert's family were killed in the war. I have no idea where any of his relatives might be now. Scattered across the globe, I imagine. And so I hand it to her… May it bring her luck.

Miranda sat in stunned silence, watched by Jeremy and Georgie.

'Well?' said Jeremy eventually, unable to bear the suspense a moment longer.

She handed him the letter.

'I don't know whether to cry, laugh, or be angry.'

'Why Mum? What's the matter? Is it bad news?'

'No darling… It's good news really; but I feel a bit sad that Celia obviously thought of me as a sort of surrogate daughter. I should have seen more of her.'

'But why angry?' asked Georgie.

'Because Mr Martin,' said Miranda, lowering her voice to a whisper, 'should have handed this letter on to me ages ago. I need to have a word with him.'

She stood up just as Mr Martin came bustling in.

'Ah… Good. Was it useful?'

'Yes,' said Miranda curtly. 'To be honest, Mr Martin, it is pretty crucial. It does explain that the vase my great aunt left me was rather valuable. It would have been very useful to have had this from the start.'

'Oh!' Mr Martin sat down at his cluttered desk and held out his hand. 'May I take a look at it?'

He scanned the letter.

'Yes…' he said after a few moments. 'Something of an oversight on my part. Not quite sure what I can say.'

'Well, at least we've found it now and it does make it clear that I am the rightful owner. So that's some sort of good news.'

'I don't suppose there were any photographs of the items Celia left, were there?' Jeremy asked.

'Photos? No I shouldn't think so. Sorry… I certainly didn't take any. I left all that sort of thing to my receptionist, Carole. She packed everything up and sent it on. I can ask her, though. Carole, could you come in here, please?'

Carole thought for a few seconds before replying to their queries about photographs. 'Yes, I think I took some pictures on my phone – you know? Just in case anything went missing.'

'And where are the photos now?' asked Miranda, her faith in Martin & Co now at an all-time low.

'They're probably on my computer. I'll have a look.'

Carole scrolled through the various files, eventually finding a folder labelled "Mrs Celia Kaerel". 'Here you go – pictures of all the items I sent you and also of her furniture that we sold.'

'May I have a look?' asked Miranda. Scrolling through the postage stamp-sized images of dining chairs, kitchen dressers, desks, kidney-shaped dressing tables and dinner services, she at last found a picture of the dragon vase, shot from two angles – one upright on a side table, the dragon's face in the centre of the frame, and another photograph clearly showing the markings on the base of the vase.

'Oh, well done! You took a picture of the base as well,' said Miranda incredulously.

'Yes, well it had some writing on it, so I thought I ought to.'

'Carole,' said Jeremy, 'I could kiss you.'

'Well, please don't!' said Mr Martin crossly. 'Well done, Carole – very thorough, as always. So, is that everything?'

'Yes, yes it is Mr Martin,' said Miranda. 'I think we have everything that we need.'

CHAPTER 26

Barnes, London
3rd January 2016

At ten minutes to nine o'clock, Miranda and Jeremy sat together in the shop, preparing to make the call to Hong Kong. She had assembled all the 'evidence' that she was the rightful owner of the vase, but was understandably nervous. Now that she had some indication that the vase might be valuable, the whole process seemed fraught with pitfalls and dangers.

'It's odd,' she had said to Jeremy the previous night when they finally got back from Gloucestershire. 'When I had nothing – financially, I mean – I was quite happy. But now that there is the possibility that I might actually be about to have a little money, it's terrifying. It's a bit like winning the lottery, but not being quite sure if you can remember where you put the ticket, you know?'

They had agreed to meet at the shop, as Jeremy was due to open that day. If she arrived by nine o'clock it would be two o'clock in Hong Kong and she would be able to speak to the person in charge of the porcelain sale.

She sat at Jeremy's desk, her hand on the telephone, her palms sweating. A cup of tea lay untouched beside her. 'Oh God, Jeremy, I feel sick. I'm not quite sure how to explain it,' said Miranda. 'What if they don't believe me?'

'Oh, for goodness sake, Miranda, just get on with it; how hard can it be?'

He dialled the Hong Kong auctioneer's number.

'Good afternoon, this is Anstruthers Hong Kong.' The voice was singsong, English, female.

'Oh, good afternoon, I wonder if you can help me. I would like to speak to the person in charge of the sale of a piece of Ming China – a vase – that you have in a sale on the 15th of January.'

'Putting you through,' said the singsong voice.

'Good afternoon, Michael Hennessy speaking.'

It didn't take Miranda long to explain her predicament. 'So to sum up, Mr Hennessy, this man misled me, I believe deliberately, about the value of the vase. He took it from me, without actually asking me, as it happens. He did leave a cheque for two hundred pounds on the hall table, but I've not cashed it. And I don't want to. It was when I started to try to trace him to get the vase back that I discovered he had put it in your sale in Hong Kong and that it is not just some cheap copy worth £100 or so as he said it was but the real thing.'

'Well. That's most disturbing, Mrs…?'

'Sharp – Miranda Sharp.'

'Mrs Sharp. I'm sorry I have to ask you this, but do you have any kind of proof that the vase is yours? Some kind of bill of sale, or at least a description?'

'I have no bill of sale unfortunately, but I have a photograph that I took of it on my own hall table. I also have a photograph taken by the solicitor who arranged my aunt's bequest, including the marks on the base. Finally, I have a letter from my aunt describing the vase and explaining that it had been in her Dutch husband's family for many years – "lost in the mists of time" is how she put it. Will that do?'

'Could you email all that to me, do you think?'

'Yes, I'll do it now. Then what?'

'If we can establish that you *are* the rightful owner, and that the vase was taken from you in error, or indeed fraudulently, then we must have another conversation and explore if you are still keen to sell the property, or if you would prefer to have it returned.'

'I see,' said Miranda. 'I'm not sure. I suppose if I'm honest it rather it depends on what it's worth.'

There was a moment's silence at the other end. 'That's a tricky one. The key issue is its provenance, you see. That's what matters and attracts buyers. But it could be worth a million or more.'

'A million what?'

'Sterling – at least that, if I'm honest. But I'm reluctant to say more. Am I to take it that you would like to proceed with the sale, on the 15th of January?'

'Well, yes, I think I would be interested.'

'Good. Well, first things first. Send over that information to me and then I'll get back to you as soon as possible.'

'Just one thing more,' said Miranda.

'The man who brought it to you, was he called Charles Davenport?'

'No, he wasn't.'

'Oh… Simon Manning, then?'

Silence.

'I take it that the silence means that was the name he gave you.'

'I really couldn't say, Mrs Sharp. It's complicated. But the good news is that the vase has not yet been sold and you have found us. Do you think you would be coming out for the sale?'

'Out to Hong Kong? No, I don't think I could afford to do that.'

'Well, you could go to our offices in London if that would work for you – on the day of the sale – and observe from there, or online – you know?'

CHAPTER 27

Hong Kong
15th January 2016

The saleroom began to fill up from nine-thirty. Proceedings were due to kick off at ten o'clock and there was a definite 'buzz' in the building. Michael Hennessy, dressed in his best auctioneer's suit – a dark grey striped three-piece made for him by his tailors in Savile Row rather than by their cheaper Hong Kong counterparts – had arrived earlier than usual, well before eight o'clock. He had been an auctioneer since his early twenties, but now, aged fifty-three, he had a feeling that he was about to make history.

The Ming vase had attracted a huge amount of international attention. There was no doubt it was genuine. The marks on the base of the jar were perfect, consisting of six characters said to have been made originally by the famous calligrapher Shendu. The symbol for 'Da', meaning 'great', looked like a man running, his arms outstretched, his front leg extended. One could usually detect a Ming forgery by checking this symbol. The forger invariably failed to get that sense of 'movement' that 'Da' required, as if the man were leaping forward over a stream. The lower half of the symbol on the top left was also tricky to get right. Shendu made it using just four strokes of the pen. Forgers, not quite understanding the significance of that economy, frequently used too many strokes. It was always a give-away.

Since Miranda Sharp had sent over the information about the vase's provenance, the fine ceramics department had been hard at work putting together expert opinion and endeavouring to discover a little more about how this Ming storage jar had come into the possession of the Kaerel family.

A genealogist had been employed at considerable expense to uncover the family's bloodline and had come to some remarkable conclusions. The Kaerels were one of the original families involved in the Dutch East India Trading Company. They had specialized in imports of Chinese porcelain from 1625 and had been crucial to the development of the blue and white porcelain export industry in Europe. But this vase pre-dated that. This was where the information became a little more complicated. Kaerel's great grandmother, Margarethe Haas, had been traced back to Antwerp. Pushing on further, they discovered that she had been born in Bruges. But the search had reached a fever pitch when a specialist in Anstruthers' art department uncovered a relatively unknown Dutch painter's portrait of a young couple believed to be Margarethe Haas and her husband. Not being considered of top quality, it had been languishing in a storeroom at the Rijksmuseum in Amsterdam. Called 'The Betrothal', it featured a beautiful young woman dressed in turquoise blue silk, her young husband holding her hand. A little dog lay at her feet. A Ming bowl filled with oranges stood on the chest at the side, and in the centre of the picture, on the mantle shelf, stood a Ming vase with an angry dragon chasing around its centre. It appeared to be identical to the one that Anstruthers had at that moment in their vault.

Hennessy had been ecstatic at the news. 'This is a game-changer, Antonia,' he said to the art historian. 'How on earth did you find it?'

'Well, it was odd. I had done some research for my PhD years ago, which was about the influence of foreign trade on art in the fourteenth and fifteenth centuries in the Low Countries. I had been to all the museums in Bruges, Amsterdam and so on, and to Venice and Florence too, of course. And I had a nagging memory of this picture. You know that the Flemish Baroque painters had a passion for mixing ordinary household objects – wine jugs, a dead pheasant – with more valuable items like Ming bowls filled with fruit, or whatever. I was interested in that juxtaposition of exquisite items, used in an everyday context, to demonstrate the enormous wealth of those Flemish cities. You know, how they'd arrange a bowl precariously on its side on a lovely linen cloth, with crystal glasses and wine nearby. Or a piece of Ming, used as a vase for flowers. It's a sort of decadence, I suppose. While I was visiting the team at the Rijksmuseum, they mentioned this picture. It was from the school of Jan van Eyck, who painted that marvellous painting of the Arnolfini wedding, also done in Bruges. Do you know it? But the brushwork in 'The Betrothal' is not so good. The quality of light is less luminous. And so it had been relegated to the storeroom. I think they bring it out occasionally for special Baroque exhibitions. They asked if I'd like to see it. I referenced it, in fact, in my final thesis. And to be honest, I'd forgotten all about it. But when you asked for help in tracing this piece, it came to me in the middle of the night. I'd seen that vase before. I've asked the team at Rijksmuseum for a JPEG of the painting and they are sending it today. We can put it online or use it during the sale.'

'Well done, Antonia, that's great work.'

'There's more. I don't know how we can use this bit of information for the sale, but I thought you'd like to know.'

'Go on,' said Michael Hennessy, leaning forward in anticipation.

'There's another painting at the Rijksmuseum. They acquired it many years ago, and although of quite a different style, they crossed-referenced it with 'The Betrothal'. It's a Chinese painting. But it features two women, one older than the other – perhaps a mother and daughter. They are sitting in a garden, fairly clearly in the Imperial Palace, in the Forbidden City, in Beijing. The garden is exquisitely painted, of course; blossom trees, birds and so on. And in the centre of the painting, sitting looking out onto the garden, are these two women. They are clearly not Chinese, even though they are dressed in traditional Chinese clothing, but their hair is loose – which was most unusual – and both have quite remarkable bright blue eyes, turquoise almost. The younger of the two looks so remarkably like the woman in 'The Betrothal' painting that some bright spark at the museum had a feeling they must be connected, perhaps even related. They are sending a copy of that to us too.'

'Do they know who painted it?'

'Well, this is the thing. It has all the hallmarks of the Emperor Xuande himself. You know, of course, that he was the only one of the Ming Emperors who demonstrated quite remarkable talent as an artist. He preferred subjects like animals and flowers. But he also did that wonderful picture of the two gibbons – do you know it?'

Hennessy nodded.

'Well, this picture of the two women is marked with characters that imply it was painted in the Hall Of Military Grace in 1435 – the year he died.'

'My God,' said Hennesy. 'Are you saying that the woman in the Chinese painting is the same woman as the one in the painting in Bruges?'

'Well, she can't be the same woman, as that painting was done in 1435, and the Bruges painting was done in 1469. But she might be a relation of some kind. She certainly looks very similar. It can only be conjecture, you know. But it might provide a theory for how the vase came to Europe. If these two women were part of a merchant family who travelled in the Far East, they would of course have brought back items from that part of the world; perhaps even items from the Palace itself. We could cross-check all the merchant travellers from Europe to China at that time and see if someone suitable comes to light?'

'Well, it's tempting Antonia, but I think not. It's too much of a long shot and I'm not sure we can prove anything from it. Besides, we're running out of time. I think we need to show the Chinese painting, and perhaps you could write it up for me and I'll have a think about how we can use it. But we can't, in all honesty, claim it has a connection to the vase. No, Antonia, you have done your work, and very, very well done.'

The saleroom was packed. Ranged down one side, at tables specially set up with screens and phones, were the dealers who would manage the online and telephone bids. The room was laid out with over one hundred gilt banqueting chairs. Coffee and tea were served in an anteroom, along with homemade shortbread biscuits. The auction house contrived to be a little bit of England in the heart of Hong Kong.

Potential bidders from across the world were ranged up ready to purchase the fabulous collection of porcelain that Anstruthers had assembled for the sale. But there was no doubting the star lot: Lot Number Forty-Two, the Ming vase, Xuande period, a previously undiscovered Ming storage jar in perfect condition.

Hennessy and a colleague, Jonnie Chambers, would share the auctioneering. This was to be a long process and they could only manage around one hour each. Chambers started the bidding off on the first lots, fielding telephone and online bids effortlessly with those in the room. 'Lot One: a remarkable example of Kraak porcelain; made for export to Holland in approximately 1620. What am I bid?'

Paddles with numbers were raised in the room. Young men and women fielding the phones raised their hands periodically.

'Paddle 1871, Sir,' said one pretty blonde employee.

'I have ten thousand Hong Kong dollars; fifteen thousand; ' said Chambers. 'Thank you, good swift bidding online, thank you for that, we appreciate the speed.' He nodded at the pretty blonde girl. 'Twenty-five thousand in the room... Just in time... It's now or never. Ah, another telephone bid, thank you... Thirty thousand... Are we all done now? Warning you, on the phone and online... Going once, going twice.' He smashed his gavel down hard on the lectern.

He rattled through the lots, the items gathering speed and becoming more and more valuable. 'Lot Twenty-Seven: one small Qing dynasty bowl. I have a bid with me here for three-hundred thousand Hong Kong dollars,' he said, staring at the screen on his lectern. 'Who will start me at three-hundred-and-fifty thousand Hong Kong dollars?' The bidding rose frantically to four-hundred thousand.

A dark-haired girl with an Italian accent raised her paddle. 'Sir, I have to translate...' Chambers looked irritated at this delay, as she proceeded to speak in fluent Chinese to her client on the phone.

'Carlotta,' said Chambers, 'do you wish to pay four-hundred-and-fifty thousand?'

Carlotta gesticulated towards the phone, where her client was clearly speaking rapidly to her in Chinese. She responded to him, a sense of urgency in her voice.

'Still with you,' said the auctioneer fractiously, tapping his fingers on the lectern.

A bidder in the room raised his hand.

'Four-hundred-and-fifty thousand,' Chambers said, 'in the room.'

'Four-hundred five... Against you,' he said, gesturing to the previous bidder, before turning to the Italian girl once again. 'Does your man want to bid at five-hundred thousand?' Carlotta nodded eagerly whilst speaking quickly and quietly to her mystery bidder on the phone.

'I must bring the hammer down sometime soon,' said Chambers in a languid manner, as if this was really the most irritating process to have to endure. 'Still with you,' he said, pointing to Carlotta. But another bidder in the room joined in the process.

'Five-hundred-and–fifty in the room.'

This went on for another five minutes until Chambers finally, and apparently with complete indifference, bought that particular lot to an end. 'With warning, I'm selling at six-hundred thousand.' He brought his gavel down with a flourish.

In Anstruthers' London offices, Miranda, Georgie, Jeremy and Miranda's parents sat together in a room that had been set aside for a handful of customers, whose bids were dealt with by a small team from Anstruthers with a hotline to Hong Kong. It was usual for those who couldn't get to the actual sale to bid online from home, but clearly one or two enjoyed the atmosphere in the saleroom and had come especially to London.

Miranda and her party sat at the back of the room with a member of the porcelain team from Anstruthers' London offices at their side. They drank tea and coffee and watched the sale unfold with fascination. Miranda had an overwhelming sense of anticipation. Her palms were damp and she kept fiddling with her mobile phone. 'When is our lot coming up?' she asked the young employee.

'It won't be long now,' he replied with the air of a young hospital doctor encouraging a mother in labour. He wore a rather tired blue suit, had floppy blond hair that fell over his eyes and a suggestion of acne sprinkled across his cheeks. He was probably no more than twenty-three years old.

'How long have you worked here?' asked Miranda, desperate for distraction.

'Oh, about six months – it's my first job after uni,' he replied enthusiastically.

'Oh, what did you study?' she asked, not truly interested in the answer.

'History of art,' he replied, predictably.

'Is it interesting, working here?'

'Oh yes, jolly interesting.'

'Do you like porcelain?'

'Well, I'm learning, you know?'

Back in Hong Kong, Chambers was coming to the end of his shift. Hennessy paced the edge of the room. He felt curiously nervous, rather as he had done when he first started as an auctioneer. Phone and online staff ambled in and out of the saleroom, materialising when a particular lot their client was interested in came up. It had the air of a busy market. The noise in the room was quite loud, with clients chatting and drinking coffee. Only those people who were actually bidding for a particular item were concentrating on the matter in hand. Everyone else appeared to be treating the event as a sort of glorified party.

At Lot Number Thirty, Chambers left the lectern and handed Hennessy the gavel. He got off to a good start and ploughed through the lots. 'Lot Thirty-Four – a very nice nineteenth-century porcelain vase from Guangdong province. I've got bids here… Of nine thousand Hong Kong dollars.' He looked around the room and spotted one of the Internet bidders waving her paddle at him. He checked the screen on his lectern.

'I've got a bidder in Taiwan on the Internet trying to get in… Fifteen thousand… That's a Taiwanese bid. Are we all done?' He paused to let the bidders in the room catch up. 'Ah, it's a telephone bid. It's in the room, on the telephone, against the Internet. It's going abroad then. Are we all done?' He smashed his gavel down.

The lots unfolded, fetching smaller or larger amounts of money. Lot Thirty-Eight went for over four million dollars; Lot Number Forty for over eight million. Finally they arrived at Lot Number Forty-Two.

'Lot Forty-Two', began Michael, his voice calm and cool. 'A rare example of early Xuande Ming China, signed by Shendu. We have provenance. The details are all in the insert in the catalogue and have been online. The piece was owned by the Kaerel family based in Amsterdam, who were part of the Dutch East India company who brought a huge amount of Ming into Europe. This piece pre-dates that. We have a painting up here on the big screens now, painted in 1464, of a merchant's daughter in Bruges. Her name was Margarethe Haas, and she is shown here with her betrothed, Cornelius van Vaerwye; it's the school of Van Eyck. You will see the vase – at least it appears to be the vase – in the centre of the painting. The piece came from the imperial kilns at Jingdezhen. Some of the finest examples of Ming China were produced at that time, under the rule of Emperor Xuande. The decoration is particularly fine, with the dragon motif – just three claws on the dragon, indicating it was a gift for a foreign ruler. So, what am I bid? I have bids here with me for thirty-five million Hong Kong dollars. Who will give me forty million?'

Jeremy in London leapt to his feet and shouted, 'Yes!' He glanced down excitedly at Miranda, who sat transfixed by the big screen in the saleroom showing Michael Hennessy on the stage in Hong Kong. 'Forty million!' shouted Jeremy. 'How much is that exactly?'

The young man from the porcelain department took out his phone and made a quick calculation.

'Nearly three-and-a-half million sterling; I'll get the guys round the back to put up an automatic calculator so you can see what it is in real money.' He disappeared behind the big screens in the saleroom.

The bidding went fast, the Internet and telephone bidders scarcely able to keep up with one another. They were constantly dialling clients. 'Hello, this is Maddie from Anstruthers. Can you confirm your name to me? We are on Lot Forty-Two now. Can you stay on the line? Bidding's at sixty million Hong Kong dollars now. Would you like to place a bid?'

Hennessy spoke clearly into the microphone on his lectern, his eyes constantly scanning his screen for Internet bids and restlessly searching the room and the line of telephone bidders. 'Seventy million on the Internet – bid nice and swiftly in Spain, would you, there's a bit of a time lag; seventy-five million, with me in the room – thank you; eighty million, it's a Hong Kong buyer with Geoffrey on the phone.'

'Ninety million, Sir,' called one of the phone bidders.

'Thank you,' said Michael. 'One-hundred million now though, with me here, flesh and blood.'

The bidding rose inexorably.

'Three-hundred million on the phone, with you, Carlotta.' He stared at the girl, who was frantically talking to her client in fluent Chinese. 'I've got three-hundred-and-fifty on the Internet, are you bidding again, Carlotta?'

It appeared that the bidding had come down to two clients: one on the phone and one on the Internet.

The room had fallen silent. The coffee cups had been put down on the carpeted floor and the hundred or so possible buyers sat in rapt attention as Michael Hennessy conducted one of the biggest and most expensive sales of porcelain that had ever taken place.

'Three–hundred-and-fifty million now, on the Internet. Are you bidding, Carlotta?' She held her hand up to Michael as if asking him to pause. She was clearly listening to her client. 'This is beginning to drag rather,' Michael said, with courageous insouciance.

Carlotta flapped her hand and almost shouted, 'Four hundred million.'

'Thank you,' said Hennessy calmly. 'Are we all done then? At four-hundred million Hong Kong dollars... Going once... Going twice.' He brought the gavel down so hard on the lectern that his screen rocked.

The room erupted into furious applause. Michael Hennessy leant on the lectern; he felt as if his legs were going to buckle beneath him. Jonnie Chambers sidled over to him and gently took his arm.

'Well done, old chap,' he said, guiding his friend and colleague to a nearby chair. 'A master class, if I might say so, in how to do it.'

The phone bidders were congratulating Carlotta, who was still attached almost umbilically to her mobile phone and her Chinese client. But she nevertheless accepted kisses on the cheek and pats on the back. Finally, her duty completed, details noted, she put down the phone. Michael came across to her.

'Well done, Carlotta. Good work.'

'Thank you, sir, and well done yourself. That was fantastic!' For the first time that day, she allowed herself a huge smile.

Back in London, Miranda sat in complete silence, clutching Georgie's hand. Tears rolled down her cheeks. Jeremy was virtually dancing round the room.

'I simply cannot believe it... Four-hundred million Hong Kong dollars; that's thirty-four million fucking pounds!'

'Jeremy!' said Miranda's mother. 'There's no need for that sort of language!'

'Sorry, sorry, but I mean it's unbelievable.'

'It certainly is,' said Miranda's mother, almost as if she disapproved of such reckless inflation.

'Say something,' said Jeremy desperately to his best friend.

'I don't know what to say,' said Miranda. 'It's just incredible. I can't take it in. It just seems impossible... Like a dream and I'll wake up tomorrow and I'll have an electricity bill that I can't afford to pay and nothing will have changed.'

'Darling,' said Miranda's mother. '*Do* you have an electricity bill you can't afford to pay? Why haven't you mentioned it before? We can help you; you can always come to us.'

Miranda looked kindly at her mother. 'I know, Ma, I've always known, but I wanted to do it myself. To show you that I might have married a useless husband, but I was all right. G and me, we're all right.'

Georgina stood up and hugged her mother from behind. She whispered into her ear, 'we're all right, Ma – you and me. We're more than all right – we're brilliant!'

'And to think that vase stood on our hall table all those months,' said Miranda. 'Me using it for flowers, and G knocking it with her coat each day. It could so easily have been broken, destroyed. But it survived. It's survived all those years; over six hundred years of people using it, painting it, plonking things in it. It really is a kind of miracle, isn't it? The dragon vase that was meant for a king landed up in Sheen with me and G...'

'Champagne!' said Jeremy. 'We must have champagne.'

The young man from Anstruthers leapt to his feet.

'Yes, of course. Please, how rude of me. I'll go and see what I can find.'

'Thank you,' said Miranda, 'and we must raise a toast to dear Great Aunt Celia without whom none of this could ever have happened.'

'And to Charlie,' said Georgie.

'Oh G, don't mention him at a time like this,' said Jeremy.

'No, because if he hadn't nicked it, we'd never have known it was valuable, so we have him to thank really, don't we?'

'Stolen, Georgina,' said Miranda's mother. 'Not nicked!'

The young man from Anstruthers reappeared with a tray of champagne for the sellers. He handed the glasses around.

'To Great Aunt Celia,' said Jeremy, raising his glass to the group in a grand gesture.

'And to Charles Davenport,' said Miranda. 'Alias Simon Manning, alias... Who knows?'

'Did Michael Hennessy ever say what had happened to him?' asked Jeremy as he sipped his Bollinger.

'No – but if I know Charlie, he got away somehow.'

The painter dipped his fine sable brush into the deep cobalt-blue underglaze. The vase, a storage jar intended for the palace, stood nineteen inches tall. Decorating it would take a great deal of skill, and the artist was not experienced in the painting of porcelain. He had done some good work on silk and paper; he had recently completed a charming illustration on silk of gibbons playing in a garden. The painting hung now in the bedchamber of his favourite wife. The gibbons were her particular playthings, purchased for her only recently, and he had completed the painting as a gift so that she could relish their playfulness even as the gibbons themselves slept.

The painting of porcelain was a departure. He knew that no errors were possible. The jar, which he was to paint, had been simply air-dried. Any paint that was now applied would seep indelibly into the surface. Once the design had been applied, the piece would be fired in the kiln. The painter knew that only after firing would the final colours be revealed. There was an almost magical alchemy that took place between the cobalt and the heat of the fire. Sometimes, after firing, the blue became dark and intense, almost black. At other times, the colour was paler, the colour of the sea or the sky. It was crucial that the painter applied the colours in such a way as to enhance the final design.

Around the top of the jar were four Kirtimukha, hideous monstrous faces that had their origins in Indian and Chinese mythology. The myth told of a monster who willingly ate his own body to please Lord Shiva. The god, pleased with the monster's sacrifice, gave it the name 'Face of Glory'; they were only used to symbolise the presence of a deity – perhaps at the pinnacle of a temple or, as in this case, on a piece of porcelain intended for a royal recipient. The artist was pleased with the Kirtimukha; in particular, he like the way their eyes bulged expressively from their hideous faces.

But the centrepiece of this jar was to be the dragon. And it was this that gave the painter the most cause for concern. He wanted it to appear animated and 'on the move' as it snaked through the sky, surrounded by little undulating clouds, its tail almost catching up with its face. Every part of the dragon must have an inherent energy. Its scales would be shaded with underglaze, dark through light, so they appeared almost to stand proud of the dragon's lashing back and tail. His three-pronged paws were tipped with just enough glaze to create a dark 'nail' bed from which the white sharp claw emerged. Its beady eyes were alert and all-seeing. Above all, the painter wanted the dragon to be free, flying through the sky for evermore, bringing luck and good fortune to all who saw him.

CHAPTER 28

Delft
1650

Pieter Kaerel sat in his workshop in Delft painting tiles. He had an order for over one thousand tiles to be sent to a house on the Herengracht in Amsterdam. The house was being refurbished and tiles were required for all of the fireplaces, around the range in the kitchen, and in the laundry room. Each one would be individually painted with a design slightly different from the other.

The finished tiles stood on shelves around Pieter's workshop. There were pictures of fishermen holding rods, hunters with their dogs and labourers resting beneath the shade of a tree – all pastoral scenes that reflected country life in Holland. There were fishing boats, and fishermen holding their catch aloft. There was even a galleon in full sail. Pieter had painted something similar for his own mother many years before. Their father had been a merchant who had died at sea, in his ship, *The Flying Dragon*, and he made the tile as small memento for her. It was the first tile he had created completely by himself without the help of his uncle Frans. His mother had wept when he brought it home.

But Peter's favourite subjects were animals: dogs running, dogs lying in the shade of a tree, cats snoozing, ducks splashing in the water, and geese diving, their feathered backsides uppermost, the water spraying out around them. He loved to paint horses, especially big field horses pulling a cart; he had even painted an elephant once – the image copied from a book that his mother had given him. All the tiles were meticulously decorated, their corners embellished with a simple flower motif that joined almost seamlessly with the tiles on either side, creating a flowing kaleidoscope of images.

The house on the Herengracht would also have a set of twelve tiles which, when joined together, created one complete scene. They depicted a large whale thrashing about in a choppy sea. This was a tricky job, for each tile had to line up exactly with its neighbour to complete the illusion. Pieter had already thrown away thirty-six tiles in his attempt to create this centrepiece.

Pieter's sister Isabel wandered through from the office next door. She had recently married a potter named Floris, and was pregnant with their first child.

'Hans, I am going now. I need to get back to Mama. Shall we see you a bit later?'

'Yes, yes. I'll be back in time for supper. I just want to finish this. I've still got over five hundred to go. I'm going to have to get Cornelius, and perhaps Floris, to help, I think. Do you think he'll have time? His painting is very good these days. They want these tiles by the end of the month.'

'I'm sure he can help. The job he's working on is almost finished.' She threw her cloak around her shoulders.

'It must be a huge house to need so many tiles,' said Isabel.

'Yes, they are a wealthy merchant family – part of the VOC. Oddly, we share the same name. Johan Kaerel – it's his house. Maybe we're related?'

'I somehow doubt that, don't you?' said Isabel.

'Yes, I suppose there are lots of people called Kaerel. See you later.'

Isabel arrived home just after dark. Her mother had already lit the gas lamps, and the house emanated a warm glow as she walked down the cobbled street.

'Hello, Mama,' she called out as she hung her cloak on the pegs by the door.

Her mother, Maria, emerged from the basement kitchen.

'Hello, Isabel. Supper won't be long. Are Floris and Pieter coming soon?'

'I expect so,' said Isabel. 'Pieter's just finishing a sequence of tiles for that big house in Amsterdam.'

'Oh? What house?'

They went into the sitting room. The fire was lit, and mother and daughter sat companionably together, their chairs facing one another.

'You know, the one on the Herengracht,' said Isabel, sitting down heavily. 'Gosh, I'm tired. The baby is getting heavy.'

'I didn't know he was doing a job there,' said her mother, picking up her sewing.

'I'm sure we told you. He's got the same name as us. Isn't that odd?'

'What do you mean?' said Maria.

'Kaerel.'

Maria smiled a little to herself. 'Oh, that's a coincidence, isn't it?'

'Do you think we're related?' asked Isabel.

'I doubt it,' said her mother. Maria looked up at the Ming vase that stood on the mantelpiece. It glowed in the flickering firelight. She thought then, as she often did, of Hans. His death, so many years before, had been such a terrible tragedy. The news of the ship going down in the Indian Ocean with the loss of all on board had been almost impossible to take in. For many weeks, even months, she had been sure that a mistake had been made; that he would turn up one day, walking down the streets of Delft. That he would return for her and the children.

After they had been sent away from Amsterdam, Maria's mind had been filled with so many different dreams of what their future might hold. She lay in bed night after night wondering what would happen when he returned from his travels. Her dearest hope was that he might marry her. But this would necessitate the disappearance of Antoinette. She would fantasise on these long, lonely nights that perhaps Antoinette might die. He would find a way of explaining the children to everybody. He could adopt them perhaps, passing them off as someone else's. But Antoinette did not die. Sometimes she dreamed of Hans writing to her from some faraway land, begging her to bring the children and join him. Together they would make a new start on some tiny island in the South China Sea. Or perhaps back in her homeland of India. But no letter came. What she never imagined was Hans dying; Hans drowning; Hans never coming back.

He was true to his word though and had made sure she was well provided for. She was able to buy a modest but comfortable house in Delft with the money Hans had given her. She changed her name to Maria; so many people didn't understand the pronunciation of Mori. It just seemed easier. Pieter and Isabel both learned to read and write. Isabel studied French and was delighted when Frans bought her a spinet for her tenth birthday; she practiced assiduously, and often played at their small family gatherings. Pieter worked hard at his apprenticeship and had real talent as a potter. By the age of twenty-one he had his own workshop and his own commissions. He had even been invited to England to lay a tiled floor at a priory in Hampshire.

Mori often thought of her own mother. She still kept the little rag doll and the chemise. The chemise had been carefully laundered and mended and lay in a drawer in her bedroom. The doll sat on the lace pillow of her bed each night. She had made a similar one for Isabel when she was a little girl, and was making one now for Isabel's child. Two sets of clothes for the doll lay on the little side table next to her chair; a blue dress edged in lace if the baby was a girl, or red trousers and a shirt if Isabel's first born was a boy.

She wondered sometimes about the myths surrounding the vase. Hans had said he did not believe that it brought luck to the person who cared for it. He told her it was simply a beautiful thing; a valuable thing; and something that should be used to inspire potters and painters. 'We make our own luck,' he had told her often. 'Remember that, Mori. You have made your own luck. When you decided to leave Carlos all those years ago, you made your own luck.'

It seemed to her that she had been fortunate in so many ways. Hans was right. She could have died with her mother so many years before. She could have been killed at any time by her captors, or by Carlos. Hans had rescued her and that surely was good luck. He had loved her and that had been her good fortune. And she had two beautiful healthy children who reminded her every day of their father. Surely, no one could have had more luck than her – little orphan Mori from Goa, now Maria Kaerel from Delft – householder, mother, soon to be grandmother, living a productive and happy life in a beautiful town in Holland.

CHAPTER 29

Coober Pedy, South Australia

Charlie opened his eyes. At least he was aware that his eyelids' muscles had changed position. The blackness that enveloped him was so total that it was impossible to know if his eyes were in fact open or closed. He put his hand out blindly and thrashed about. He located his phone, finally, and pulled it towards him. As he turned it on, a comforting glow emanated from the screen. He found the torch app and pointed it into the darkness. The bedroom walls had been whitewashed, and pictures – reproductions of Monets and Picassos – hung incongruously verdant on the walls, in a effort to disguise what was, in reality, an underground room carved out of the red, hot earth. For this was Coober Pedy, South Australia – a mining town in the heart of the Australian desert; centre of the opal mining industry and one of the hottest places on earth.

Charlie had arrived the day before, via Sydney and Adelaide. He had left Hong Kong the day he received a voice mail message from Mr Hennessy:

'*Mr Manning, this is Michael Hennessy. I wonder if you could call me at your earliest convenience.*'

This was followed by a second message, less unctuous, altogether more menacing in tone, one hour later.

'*Mr Manning. This is Michael Hennessy. I'm afraid there appears to be some rather major discrepancy with the Ming vase. I really must insist that you call me as soon as you get this.*'

By the time he got the second message, Charlie was at the airport. He booked a seat on a flight headed for Sydney that afternoon. He would have gone anywhere, but Australia seemed a good bet. It was civilized, they spoke English. He'd do well there. He removed the sim and threw his phone into the waste bin before he went through security. He paid for the flight on a credit card he kept back for emergencies. There was enough credit on it to last a few days.

In Sydney he checked into a small hotel in Kings Cross. Clean, comfortable, nothing special. He took stock. Miranda, it seemed had found him out and doubtless had by now claimed the vase. Her trip to the solicitor would probably have delivered some kind of proof of ownership. He wondered if Anstruthers, or indeed Miranda, would take it any further. Would they bother to report him; would Interpol be involved?

He resolved that he needed to lie low for a while. Going back to the UK wasn't an option – at least not yet. As he sat in a restaurant that evening, toying with a poorly cooked steak, he glanced at a magazine. An article caught his eye. An interview with a Russian opal miner named Vlad. Just Vlad. He had no surname apparently, surnames being superfluous in the opal-mining town of three and a half thousand disparate souls. Vlad had lived in Coober Pedy for over ten years. The reporter implied that the Russian had a past and it was not a past he chose to share with the readers of *Australian Life*. Back in the hotel lobby, Charlie looked Coober Pedy up on the shared computer.

The following morning he checked out, flew to Adelaide and then on by small plane to Coober Pedy.

As he walked down the airline steps behind the Chinese opal merchants flying in for their monthly buying trip, the heat hit him like a wall. He could scarcely breathe and felt sweat pouring down inside his elegant blue shirt; he was drenched by the time he reached the airport building. Grateful for the air conditioning, he grabbed his bag off the carousel and went in search of a cab.

'You here long, mate?' the taxi driver asked on the ride from the airport.

'Not sure.' Charlie gazed out at the shimmering red earth.

'You'd better get a hat,' said the driver, looking at Charlie in his rear-view mirror. 'Colouring like yours… You'll fry.'

The hotel was owned by a large woman known as Ma Baker. She'd lived in Coober Pedy all her life; she looked Charlie up and down as he signed the visitors' book.

'Here long? You a buyer or a miner?' she asked.

'Neither; not sure; playing it by ear.'

'You and everyone else here,' she said as she led him down a dark, almost circular corridor. As they descended, and went underground he realised that the air temperature had dropped dramatically.

'This is you,' she said, indicating an unremarkable white door. She unlocked it and held it open for him.

A room carved out of the earth, painted white. No windows. A large bed, comfortable looking. A melamine chest of drawers and a wardrobe stood incongruously in this airless curved cave. She pushed open a louvred door, revealing a simple bathroom.

'Nothing glamorous, but it's all there.'

'Thanks,' said Charlie. 'It's fine.'

Later that day, after he had slept a little in the room with the lights on, he had emerged into the hot, airless reception area.

'What can I do for you, Charlie?'

'Something to eat. Is there a restaurant?'

'Sure. Go down the high street – just there. Mac's bar on the left. They do a good steak, or a piece of lamb and some of the best wine you've ever drunk in your life.'

The restaurant was full, bustling. Charlie sat at a small corner table and ordered a bottle of Shiraz. Ma Baker was right. It was very good wine. A man standing at the bar looked down at him as he read the bottle's label. 'Good stuff, that Shiraz.'

'Yes,' said Charlie. 'I'm enjoying it.' He was aware that his accent stuck out like a sore thumb.

'You a Limey?'

'Yes,' said Charlie. 'You?'

'Originally, I'm from Europe, but you learn to fit in. Over forty-five nationalities in Coober Pedy. We come from all over, to seek our fortune. That your plan?'

'Might be,' said Charlie evasively.

'Or are you running away from something?' said the European, sipping his cold beer. 'Most of us are getting away from something… Or someone.' He gestured round the room.

It was full of men. That's what struck Charlie initially: the absence of women. Men in shirts, overalls, work clothes. He ate his steak and drank the wine. He stood up to pay and leave, but the European suggested that he introduce him to a few of 'the mates'. Reluctantly, Charlie agreed.

He sat at a table with four men. The European was called Mike; there was a man from Russia named Boris; a Serbian called Stefan and an Italian named Fabio.

'You hoping to stake a claim?' asked Boris in his thick accent.

'How easy is it?' asked Charlie.

'You'll need a permit. Stefan here got a big strike yesterday, didn't you?'

Stefan shifted uneasily in his wooden chair.

'Yeah…' he said monosyllabically.

'Tell you what,' said Boris. 'Come down with me tomorrow. I'll show you the ropes.'

'Really? Thank you.'

'Meet me here tomorrow morning at six. We get an early start.'

Ma Baker turned the generator off at night to save money.

'It will be black as coal if you wake up in the night, Charlie. I put a torch by each bed, so you can find the right place to piss.' She laughed. 'Generator goes back on at seven.'

As he stumbled about in the dark using his mobile phone to light the way to the bathroom, he checked the time. It was five forty-five.

He met Boris as planned just before six and they drove out to his 'claim', twenty minutes or so from the centre of town. He parked the old truck and led the way to the mine entrance.

'Here you are,' he said. He pointed at a rickety-looking metal ladder that disappeared into a hole in the ground.

'I'll lead the way, shall I?'

Descending the ladder, Charlie felt the atmosphere change from hot and dry to cool and damp. At the bottom of the ladder, Boris jumped the last few rungs with practiced ease.

'I'm setting a charge this morning.'

'A charge?' asked Charlie nervously.

'Yup… Going to blow it. Looking for a new seam of opal. Got a good feeling about it.'

He was fiddling with a small quantity of explosive that had been left in the corner of the mine.

'Shouldn't we… Go back up?' asked Charlie.

'No, mate. It's fine. We do this all the time. You just stay over there in that corner while I do the business.'

As Charlie stooped in a low corner of the mine, he was seized suddenly by a desperate desire to escape via the metal ladder. He hadn't come all this way, hadn't endured all the disappointment of losing the Ming vase, to be blown to bits by a madman called Boris. Suddenly all the planning and ultimately the failure of his scheme overwhelmed him. He had always been successful. He had 'acquired' so many beautiful things before and successfully sold them. He had made a lot of money. And he'd spent a lot of money too. Women, cars, houses. They were his weaknesses. He thought momentarily of Callie, sitting at the oversized island unit of their house in Hampshire. He thought of the hand-made shirts and suits left hanging in the cedar wardrobes in his dressing room. He thought briefly even of Miranda, and of Georgie. He had felt an unfamiliar sensation as he stole down the path from her house that day with the Ming vase tucked under his arm. Guilt. He had wrestled with his conscience that day and in the days that followed. But he had continued with the plan, had flown to Amsterdam, picked up a connection to Hong Kong, throwing his phone into a bin outside his hotel on the Herengracht. He wondered how many times Miranda had rung him. It was a shitty thing to do, to leave them both at Christmas. Callie and Miranda – both left waiting for him. He felt bad about that. Not his fault though; the sale was in January. Just bad timing.

He stood up, banging his head and grazing his shoulders on the damp, stony roof of the mine. He would have to stoop until he reached the ladder.

Boris was fiddling with something in the corner, muttering to himself. He had a bottle stowed in his pocket from which he swigged from time to time.

'Bloody hell, Boris,' said Charlie. 'You're not drinking, are you?'

The noise of the explosion brought men from mines all around. It was as if they were expecting it. They had all been waiting for the inevitable.

'That guy Boris – he's a crazy one. Too much semtex, too much vodka. It was just a matter of time.'

They never found the bodies. Bits of bodies, mixed with dark red earth, pieces of opal sticking to body parts.

'Jeez, he found a really good seam. Typical of Boris – to go out on a high.'

No one noticed that some of the body parts belonged to a tall, fair-haired Englishmen. Identity, address and destination unknown.

CHAPTER 30

Venice
May 2016

The speedboat roared away from the airport, bouncing over the waves. The driver was tall and dark; he wore beige chinos and a white T-shirt; mirrored Ray-Bans concealed his dark brown eyes, giving him the look of a young George Clooney. Georgie stood next to the driver, relishing the sensation of the salty air stinging her face. Jeremy lounged elegantly on the leather seats at the rear of the private taxi, sent by the Hotel Danieli to collect their VIP guests.

Miranda had never been to Venice before, but it had been on the top of her 'bucket list' for a long time. Once the money from the sale had gone through and the auctioneer's commission had been paid, she made a few charitable donations and set up a trust for her daughter. But there was still a great deal of money left over, and she was determined to do something more than just live a life of luxury. She felt that she had been the recipient of extreme good fortune, and it was her duty, even her privilege, to try to do something worthwhile with the money. She talked at length to Georgie about her plans, and to Jeremy too, of course, but her instinct told her that she should concentrate on helping people to help themselves in some way. It was a grandiose ideal and, at this stage, really just an idea, but she had started making lists of possible projects in a new leather notebook – one of the few new 'luxuries' she had treated herself to. She had taken advice, of course, and much of her time was now spent in a relatively enjoyable round of financial discussions, meetings with lawyers and plans made on the kitchen table. She had given Jeremy some money, which meant that he could concentrate on his writing. He kept the book shop open, but now employed two young people who worked there full-time.

Of course, she was not averse to the idea of some improvement in her own lifestyle. She got a few new clothes for herself and Georgie. She bought each of them a new laptop. But she had not yet thought of moving house. She had not even upgraded the old family Volvo. There was something comforting and reassuring in its presence outside her house.

The sale of the vase had caused a sensation, and the press had, of course, got hold of the story. She had endured several articles on the front pages of the tabloids, demands for interviews and so on. Inevitably, begging letters had begun to arrive. She read them all dutifully and sent a few cheques to people or organisations that she felt had a genuine need. For the most part, she managed to keep her feet firmly on the ground, and was relieved and delighted that Georgie seemed almost unaffected by their good fortune. She was too busy preparing for her GCSEs, but did admit that her new-found status as the daughter of a local wealthy celebrity had increased her popularity.

'It's funny, you know, Ma,' she said one day when she came home from school. 'I've never been the most popular girl, as you know. But suddenly everyone is inviting me to their parties, or trying to sit next to me. It's nice – sort of. But I know who my real friends are. They've not changed.'

'Well done, G,' her mother had said, passing her a cup of tea. 'Keep thinking that way. We've had a huge piece of good luck, but this money is our responsibility too, you know. It's not just a green light for us to "have stuff". I'm not sure what we ought to do with it yet, but together we can work on it and I'm sure we'll think of something. There are so many deserving causes, and so many deserving people, but it's vital that we make the right decisions. And the most important thing is that we try very hard not to let it affect our relationships – and it sounds like you've made a great start on that already.'

Miranda did, though, plan to use some of the money to travel, and the trip to Venice was the first of what she hoped would be several journeys exploring her family's history. The impetus was a final missive – a message from the grave almost – from Great Aunt Celia.

Three weeks after the sale had gone through and the money had been transferred to her from Hong Kong, Miranda was sitting in the kitchen writing a list of tasks for the day. The doorbell went, and upon opening it she found the postman holding a long, thin cardboard poster tube marked "special delivery". She signed for it and brought it back to the kitchen. She put it on the table and wandered across to the window. It was a chilly February day and the garden was encased in a white carapace of frost; the sky was a shade of the palest blue, verging on grey, that matched Miranda's new sweater. It was the most expensive sweater she had ever bought – two-ply cashmere, with long sleeves and a wide boat neck. It was warm and luxurious and gave her a guilt-inducing sensation of comfort and indulgence. The irony was not lost on her that as a semi-professional knitter, she could probably have made one for herself.

She flicked the buttons on her new coffee machine and returned to the kitchen table to open the parcel. Inserted in the top of the tube was an envelope addressed to her. Opening it, she found a letter from the solicitor, Mr Martin.

Dear Mrs Sharp,
    I am writing, in part, to apologise for the tardy return of this property to you. It was amongst your aunt's papers

*and during a further New Year's clear-out of my storage
facility, I discovered it propped in a corner. Upon opening
it, I realised that it was intended for you. You must think
me very disorganised. I do assure you that mislaying items
on behalf of clients is almost unprecedented. May I offer you
my sincerest apologies for this unaccountable error. There is
a letter from your great aunt which I have not opened, but
imagine will explain the enclosed.*

> *Yours sincerely,*
> *Charles A Martin*
> *Solicitor*

Inside the solicitor's letter nestled a second, smaller pale-blue envelope, addressed to Miranda in Celia's girlish hand. Miranda
ripped it open.

My dear Miranda,

*I have left a list of instructions for the solicitor – Mr
Martin. He is a funny little man, but seems competent. My
dear husband Hubert had a rather splendid firm of solicitors in London when we were younger, but alas, I fear that
the senior partner who dealt with the Kaerel family affairs
has gone to a better place, hence my using a local man to
deal with my effects.*

*The solicitor has a list of all the items I am leaving
you, which I trust you have read. I hope they have given
you a little joy, or perhaps even provided you with a little
income. I know how you have struggled since that husband of yours let you down. Inside this rather inelegant
poster container you will find my husband's family tree.
It was started, I believe, many, many years ago by one of
his distant relatives – Maria dei Conti. She returned to
Venice with her father Niccolò dei Conti, and her brother*

Daniele. The family tree has been added to ever since. Obviously, this is not the original, small fragments of which remained when my husband inherited it, but they were so delicate that he paid a professional to put the whole thing together as one continuous piece. It involved a considerable quantity of archive research, I seem to remember, as there were so many missing pages. The original fragments are in a museum somewhere... Amsterdam, I think? Perhaps stored there, or possibly discarded now as being of no interest to anyone other than the family. There are still a few missing people I am sure; the archivist did her best, but not every generation was as dutiful as the last in this project, and records are difficult to check as families spread out around the world; but it gives an indication of the extraordinary breadth of the Kaerels and their forbears. Thankfully, many of the women who kept this tree going were dedicated to the task and wrote small notes on their businesses or where they lived, and these were transcribed where possible. They were clearly a proud lot, the Kaerels and their ancestors!

Hubert's mother always said that the vase had been handed down through the generations of the family. I cannot say for certain that it was brought back to Europe by one of the people in the tree, but it is the most likely explanation; they were such a keen group of merchants and many of their dealings took them down the Silk Road. I am no expert, but I believe the vase dates back to the fifteenth century – the Ming period; that would suggest that dei Conti himself may have brought it back with him from his travels. It is said that he was one of the first explorers to visit China. Did you know that? After the great Marco Polo, of course. But it might have been brought in by one of the later generations of merchants. The only clue, however, is a line that

*was painted on the fragments of the family tree that we
inherited – a line that seemed to go from one daughter to
another, starting with Maria dei Conti herself.*

*We had the vase valued when we inherited it from Hu-
bert's mother, at one thousand pounds. I imagine it would
be worth a lot more now; perhaps even as much as ten thousand! I do so hope that it gives you pleasure, dear Miranda,
and if you feel you must let it go, then I do understand.
What, after all, is the use of something, however beautiful,
if one can't afford the heating?*

*I wish you well, dear Miranda – health, happiness and
love. As you know, I was never fortunate enough to have
a child, but I like to think that you, my dear great niece,
might think fondly of me now and look upon me as a loving, benevolent grandmother of sorts. Your grandmother,
my own dear sister, was so like you.*

With fondest love,
Celia.

As Miranda read the letter, a photograph fluttered onto the table.
It showed a young and very beautiful Celia – tall, fair-haired,
laughing at the camera. She held the hand of a tall dark-haired
young man. His other hand rested on the saddle of a bicycle that
leant against the low wall of a bridge straddling a canal. In the
background was a tall brick house with the classic stepped roof of
Holland and the Low Countries. She turned the picture over.
It said simply: CELIA AND HUBERT, HERENGRACHT,
AMSTERDAM 1937.

Miranda thought back to one of her last meetings with Celia,
in the house near Cheltenham. She had told her something of
their wartime experiences. Miranda had been spellbound.

'We had to leave Amsterdam at the start of the war. It was so
difficult living there. Hubert had a Jewish grandmother on his

mother's side, and he knew it was only a matter of time before the Germans found out.'

'Is that when you came to London?' asked Miranda.

'Yes – we were fortunate that my parents lived there and we had a place to go. So many others did not. Hubert joined up of course. As an engineer he was quite useful to the war effort. He was sent to the Far East but was taken captive by the Japanese. As it happens, his engineering background was rather useful – he ended up building the Burma railway…'

The old lady had fallen silent at that point, gazing at a photograph of her husband in a silver frame on the small mahogany table at her side. From Miranda's cursory knowledge of that period of the war, she knew enough not to probe any further. Another cousin of her mother's had died in Burma and she knew how brutal the prisoners' lives had been.

'It took a long time for him to recover, you know?' Celia continued eventually. 'Things were never quite the same again. But we were lucky in so many ways. Hubert got a good job and we travelled a lot. We even went back to the Far East – Hong Kong – for ten years. It was fun, you know? And in many ways, children would have made our life difficult. They would have had to come back here to boarding school, or Hubert would have had to work here in the UK. No, we were lucky that he survived at all really.' She gazed wistfully at Miranda, who sat on the faded linen chair by the fire in Celia's pale green drawing room.

Now, seated at her own kitchen table, Miranda felt slightly shell-shocked. Once again, she was touched at how fond her aunt had been of her, and guilty that she had not taken more trouble to visit the old lady, particularly in her later years. She remembered the odd Christmas, as a child, when her grandmother had still been alive. She and her sister Celia would retreat happily to the kitchen to wash up – one washing, the other drying. They were both always keen to be busy and useful, she remembered.

She looked again at the letter from the solicitor – dated the 5th of February. This parcel and the letter it contained should have been delivered, clearly, with her aunt's bequest, nearly a year before. She would then have known the value of the vase. Once again, she was struck by the incredible stroke of luck that kept the vase safe all that time. On its precarious journey to her house from the inefficient Mr. Martin's offices wrapped in nothing more than an antique quilt; the time it spent on the hall table, being brushed by Georgie's big coat; the flowers she'd put into it. Any one of these things could at any time have resulted in the vase's destruction. And yet somehow it had survived, and miraculously she had discovered its true value just in time.

She carefully pulled out the rolled-up tree and laid it out on the kitchen table, after first wiping away all the crumbs and butter smears left over from breakfast. She moved her coffee cup onto the dresser. God forbid that she spilt anything on this now.

Laid out, the tree measured over three feet. At the top was Niccolò dei Conti. Beneath him were his two children, Maria and Daniele. There was the name of his wife, Roshinara, and two other children who appeared not to have survived into adulthood. In fact, looking carefully at the dates, she realised that Roshinara, Magdalena and Dario had all died in the same year. Maria had married Peter Haas and had four daughters. Her eldest daughter Magdalena had married Cornelius. They, she now realised, were the couple in the painting that Anstruthers showed on the day of the sale. It was fascinating to discover what had happened to them; they had had eight children, two of whom had not made it to adulthood.

Fascinated, she read on through the generations. A delicate sepia-painted line ran down through the tree, through the names of Maria, Magdalena, Maria Margret, Beatrice and on and on until it arrived at Greta Kaerel, Hubert's mother. Hubert had been an only child and as he and Celia had never had children, it seemed the direct line had come to an abrupt end. What was the meaning of the line? Was it, as Celia had suggested in her letter, the line of inheritance?

An only child herself, Miranda had no one to consult, apart from her mother, who appeared to have little interest in the tree. 'Well, it's not really our family, Miranda,' she had said when told of the extraordinary parcel Miranda had received that day. 'It was really Hubert's lot – nothing to do with us.'

Miranda rolled the family tree carefully back up and put it away in her bedroom. But when Georgie came home from school, she took it out and laid it out on the sitting room floor.

'That's so cool,' was her daughter's verdict. 'I mean, granny is right. It's not as if these people are our actual relatives, but we are sort of related, aren't we?'

'Yes, G, I think we are.'

Miranda thought about the generations that had gone before her; she felt a bond with these women going back through time. Some had noted their occupations, or, presumably, their husband's occupations, next to their names: maiolica potter, merchant, importer, founder of the VOC. Later generations had diversified: landowner, banker, mine owner. Some had joined the professions: doctor, engineer, architect. The cities where they had lived – Venice, Bruges, Antwerp, Amsterdam, Stockholm, Gothenburg, Copenhagen, New York, Hong Kong, Sydney, Cape Town, London – were also marked, as if this was crucial to their identity. It read like a roll call of the development of the merchant classes from the Middle Ages to the present day.

'I'm sorry I didn't know Aunt Celia better,' said Georgie. 'I only met her a few times, at Granny's house.'

'Yes... I'm sad about that too,' said Miranda. 'I saw more of her when I was a child of course, when my own grandmother was alive. They were close – the two of them.'

Miranda took an old photo album down from the shelf and laid it on the coffee table for her and Georgie to look at. There were pictures of her in her grandmother's house in the country, playing in the garden, doing handstands and cartwheels. Showing off. Two elderly ladies sat in deckchairs gazing at her and laughing – her grandmother and great aunt Celia. They would have been no more than seventy then, but seemed ancient to her at the time. Behind them stood a tall, gaunt man, smiling faintly. He looked tired, exhausted almost. This must be Hubert, she thought. She had a distant recollection of him smoking his pipe, banging it on the edge of the table to empty the contents of the bowl. A sudden flash of memory came to her – Hubert doing magic tricks at the lunch table, bringing coins out from behind her ears. She had been fascinated. He must have died soon after. He'd had cancer, and looking at him she could see the illness was already there, already taking him away from his beloved Celia. Next to Hubert stood her own mother, looking on fondly at her only child. How like her own daughter she had been then. Tall, graceful, fair-haired, wearing a peasant skirt and cheesecloth shirt, she looked quite trendy; nothing like the grey-haired, elegant matron her mother had become. She wondered who had taken the photograph – her grandfather, perhaps? Or her own father? There were other pictures from that time: the family on a stilted walk round a park, the older members all gazing on fondly as Miranda fed the ducks, or played on the swing. There were pictures of her in school uniform, her in a Brownie outfit. As she turned the pages, she watched herself growing up through the lens of her father's old camera. Miranda in a long dress for the first time – on her way to a dance. Miranda with her arm through Jeremy's; he standing tall and erect, skinny and uncomfortable in his black suit and shiny shoes. Miranda in a pretty dress and hat, at a friend's engagement party.

Miranda's wedding to Guy. And there, at the edge of the family wedding portrait stood Celia. No Hubert – he had died by then. She smiled bravely for the camera, but Miranda realised it must have been very hard for her that day, looking on as her only niece married, setting off on her own journey in the world.

The family tree gave Miranda, and to some extent Georgie, a sense of their own history. They became fascinated by the cities where Hubert's ancestors had lived.

'We shall visit them all, Georgie – over time; would you like that?'

'I'd love it! It sounds amazing. Where shall we start?'

'Venice,' pronounced Miranda. 'It has to be Venice – where Niccolò came from. I've always wanted to go there. Your Dad and I were going to go for our honeymoon, but in the end we never did.'

Georgie squeezed her mother's hand.

'It's all right, G, I'm over him long ago. The only good that came out of our marriage was you and I thank God for you every day.'

And now here they were, approaching Venice from the sea, much as Maria dei Conti had done all those years before. Stepping onto the launch at Marco Polo airport, Miranda could see Venice in the distance. As the boat picked up speed they roared past the island of Murano towards the main island, skirting the northern edge of the district of Castello. As they motored round the tip with Castello on their right, the Lido – a long thin sliver of an island – far away to the left, they passed the island of San Giorgio Maggiore, with its magnificent church, its grey green cupola glittering in the sunshine. The boat slowed down as they got closer to their destination, the driver skilfully jockeying for position amongst the pleasure boats, motor taxis, *vaporetti* and gondolas. The cupolas of churches and spires of the *campanili* rose up amidst the russet and yellow roofs of the city.

And then the Piazza San Marco lay before them; a picture-perfect postcard of a place. The landmark buildings: St Mark's Cathedral, the clock tower, the Campanile and next to them the Doge's Palace, all unchanged since they were captured so spectacularly by artists through the years, so familiar and yet, to Miranda and Georgie, utterly new and exciting; their ancient exteriors at odds with the camera-laden tourists and the hawkers of cheap tat who filled the Riva degli Schiavoni.

The driver expertly manoeuvred the launch up to the landing point for the Danieli.

Once the boat had been made safe fore and aft, he helped Miranda, Georgie and Jeremy out of the boat and up onto the quayside. A bellboy from the hotel rushed to assist them, carrying their cases and gushing enthusiastically, anxious to demonstrate his mastery of English. Miranda had booked a pair of suites on the top floor and they were to be treated with kid gloves.

As the three walked into the imposing lobby of the hotel, Georgie looked around her at the impressive pillars that drew the eye to the intricately carved and painted ceilings. Collections of velvet chairs were clustered together in front of leaded windows. The overwhelming effect was of comfort and old-fashioned glamour. They registered at the desk that stood beneath the imposing oak staircase.

'Welcome to the Danieli,' said the hotel manager.

'Wow! What a place,' Georgie whispered to her mother. 'Not exactly Venice on a shoestring, is it?'

'No, G, it's certainly not that,' her mother whispered back. 'Not sure there's a useful "austerity" blog to be done from this place.'

Once installed in their apartment, with its bedrooms and en-suite marble bathrooms on either side of a large sitting room, Georgie opened the French windows and stood on the balcony, gazing out to sea. There was a knock on the door.

'That will be Jeremy,' said Miranda. 'Let him in, will you?'

'So, Jeremy – what do you think of this?' Georgie gesticulated wildly around the sitting room. 'Is your room nice too?'

'Yes my love, it's fantastic, and it's just next door. I too have a sitting room all to myself! Thank you so much, Miranda. A normal room would have been fine for me, you know?'

'It's my pleasure. A bit of luxury, I know. But I thought, just this once – we'd go a bit mad.'

They stood together on the balcony overlooking the lagoon. If they looked straight down they could see the Riva degli Schiavoni, full of traders and shoppers; slightly to the right they could clearly make out the church on the Isola San Giorgio Maggiore; if they leant over their balcony and peered far to the right, they could see the edge of the Piazza San Marco; and far away in the distance, the Lido.

'There is so much to see here. Where shall we start?' asked Miranda.

'With lunch,' said Jeremy firmly. 'Then we should just wander, I think. We can make a proper plan tonight over dinner. How does that sound?'

They spent their first afternoon getting their bearings, moving in increasingly large circles from the Danieli. They explored the dark narrow alleyways, emerging into sun-filled squares and piazzas. They drank freshly squeezed orange juice and dark coffee at cafés dotted around the city. They wandered into gloomy churches and gazed at frescoes and paintings. As the afternoon wore on, Georgie said, 'Ma, couldn't we go on a gondola?'

They stopped at the gondola station at San Marco and negotiated a price.

'My God,' said Miranda, 'it's jolly expensive.'

'Well we don't have to go,' Georgie said pragmatically.

'No, we can afford it, can't we? Come on, pile in.'

'Is there anywhere in particular you want to go?' the gondolier asked in perfect English.

'Not especially,' said Miranda, 'but maybe some of the smaller canals.'

Their journey took them first down the great waterway, the Grand Canal. It carved its way through the city exploding with traffic: *vaporetti* filled to bursting with tourists and locals going about their business; slick speedboats cruising slowly along the waterway, their inhabitants surveying lesser mortals on public transport with disdain. Gondolas bobbing along, the wash of the *vaporetti* creating eddies, the *gondolieri* expertly navigating the tricky waters. The buildings on either side impressed and excited – perfect examples of Gothic, Renaissance and Baroque architecture; Byzantine and Ottoman influences abounded everywhere.

Occasionally, smaller, more intimate properties nestled between larger, grander *palazzi*, with tiny gardens leading down to the canal, a wooden landing station positioned at the water's edge, a private speedboat rocking gently as the larger craft swept by. A cleaning lady shook out a carpet in one garden; clouds of dust flew around her as she banged it with a cheap plastic carpet beater; in another, a young man sat in a deckchair reading contentedly, in the shadow of the *palazzo* next door. He looked up as the family floated by. Georgie waved at him and he waved back before returning to his book. Everywhere were signs of humanity superimposed on a remarkable living, breathing architectural miracle. They floated beneath the Rialto Bridge, teeming with shoppers and tourists, and drifted on past the Fondaco dei Tedeschi.

'The merchant house,' the gondolier said, pointing at the building. 'For the Germans.'

He manoeuvred his craft expertly to the far side of the broad waterway and slipped silently down a side canal. The sounds and sights changed instantly. Gone were the tannoys of the *vaporetti*, the low gurgling of the speedboats idling along the Grand Canal, impatient to be out into the lagoon where they could open up the throttle and let rip. Here in the small waterways, it was mainly the silent gondolas that held sway. Just an occasional greeting between *gondolieri* interrupted the silence. Swans sailed past in stately fashion; birds flew overhead, heading towards the Riva degli Schiavoni and the open sea.

As their journey came towards its close, they found themselves on Rio dei Greci. They floated gently down towards the lagoon at the far end, and Miranda gazed up at the houses to right and left.

'That's a beautiful house, isn't it?' She was staring at large house, painted a shade of dark red, with eighteen windows overlooking the canal. A small speedboat was tethered to the wooden landing station. Adjacent to the house was a gated archway.

'Where does that little archway lead to?' she asked the gondolier.

'To the convent. That house backs onto the Church of San Zaccaria. The convent was next door.'

'Was?'

'*Si*, it's the local police station now.'

'How extraordinary,' said Miranda. 'Is there no call for convents anymore?'

'Venice was filled with convents, *signora*; now, not so much. The Church has less power and we have no need to banish our daughters to a convent life.' He smiled at Georgie and winked at her, causing her to blush.

The gondola floated under the bridge connecting the two sides of Riva degli Schiavoni and deposited the family at the landing station of the Hotel Danieli.

'Let's go and look at that church, shall we?' suggested Miranda.

They walked round the corner and found themselves almost instantly in the Campo San Zaccaria. The Church and convent stood side by side. But the convent, as the gondolier had said, was now a police station, its ancient exterior at odds with a pair of automatic sliding glass doors. Miranda rang the bell.

'Mum, what are you doing?' asked Georgie.

'Here, if you look through the doors you can see the convent behind. I'd like to see it. Wouldn't you?'

A bored-looking policeman buzzed the three tourists in.

Miranda, fumbling with her novice Italian, attempted to explain what they wanted. '*Vuolo visitare, il convento – e posso?*'

The policeman held up his hand and called through to a colleague in the next office.

'Yes? Can I help you?' asked the policeman in English.

'Oh, thank you, yes,' said Miranda with relief. 'I am interested in looking round the convent.'

'I'm sorry, but I'm afraid that won't be possible,' responded the policeman firmly.

'I am a writer,' continued Miranda. Georgie and Jeremy looked at her with surprise. 'And I am writing a history of this beautiful church and its convent. I would so appreciate the chance to look around.'

The policeman looked at his colleague, who gave a subtle nod of his head. 'OK, but only for a few minutes. We are busy, you understand?'

'Yes, yes I do. Thank you so much.'

He held his pass up to an electronic reader at the side of a second pair of glass doors, which slid open, revealing the pale apricot and cream interior of the cloisters. The family wandered through, accompanied by two police officers.

'May I take a few pictures?' asked Miranda, indicating her phone. 'For research?'

'*Si, si*, but no police.'

'No, of course.'

The cloisters stood around a central grass courtyard. Wooden doors intersected the white inner walls at regular intervals, presumably leading to the nuns' cells. A pair of elaborate carved doors led to an old chapel, now a small sitting room and café for the police – an incongruous mix of high church and fast food. At one point, Miranda wandered towards a heavy iron grille that led onto the canal – the Rio dei Greci. A policeman stepped in front of her.

'No, *signora.*'

As Miranda stood in the cool cloisters gazing about her, she thought back to the family who had returned to Venice from the East all those years before – Maria and Daniele with their father. In preparation for their visit to Venice, she had visited the British Library a week earlier and had been allowed to view dei Conti's diary. She had taken photographs of it on her phone and had since done some further research on the merchant explorer. She was fascinated by his extraordinary life. He had left Venice as a young man, barely out of his teens, and studied Arabic in Damascus. He had joined an Arabian caravan en route to Baghdad, sailed the Persian Gulf as far as Oman, where he learned Persian. He had crossed India, and on to present-day Sri Lanka. From there to Sumatra and thence to China. Leaving China he visited the Spice Islands – Sunda and Banda – before travelling to Vietnam and Cambodia. On his return journey he travelled via the Malabar Coast, across the Red Sea and to Cairo, where his disguise as a Persian merchant was uncovered. His life and that of his family were threatened, forcing him to convert to Islam. He then tragically lost his wife and two of his children and servants in an epidemic in Cairo. He arrived finally in Venice accompanied by just two of his children – Maria and Daniele. On his return he had begged absolution and had dictated his diary to the scholar Poggio Bracciolini. In all, he had lived a long and remarkable life.

But after reading the detail of Niccolò's journey, it was frustrating to know so little about his life once he returned to Venice.

What had their lives been like? Where had they lived in Venice? What had happened to Maria and how did she come to meet her husband Peter and move to Bruges?

A breeze blew in through the iron grille off the canal. She shivered involuntarily. Had Maria walked near this church, or taken a gondola down the Rio dei Greci? Had she seen what Miranda was seeing now? Venice in 1450 was no different really from the Venice of today. It was an extraordinary thought, that this distant ancestor of hers, this daughter of the Silk Road, may have stood where she stood, walked where she walked.

Their visit complete, their pictures taken, the three were ushered back out into the street.

'Well,' said Miranda, 'that was interesting. What a curious life the women there must have led. I can't imagine being locked up in that place, can you?'

'No!' said Georgie firmly. 'I can't imagine anything worse. Like being in prison.'

'I gather it was quite common,' said Miranda, 'for girls to end up in convents in the old days – if they were unmarried. Thank goodness Maria married. I'm glad her life didn't come to an end in a place like that.'

Back at the Danieli, they arranged to meet for dinner in the top-floor restaurant. The sun was setting over the lagoon as the three sat down, drinks in hand, to study the menu.

'Here's to you, Miranda,' said Jeremy, clinking his Bellini against hers.

'What for?' asked Miranda.

'For being the best friend a guy could have, and the best mother.'

'I'll drink to that,' said Georgie.

'And for not letting life get you down,' continued Jeremy. 'I was doing a bit of reading the other day about the significance of the dragon to the Chinese. You know, they consider it to be good luck. It got me thinking about that vase and the luck it's brought you – and me, come to that.'

'Yes, I know. I still can't quite believe it, if I'm honest,' said Miranda. 'And when I look at that family tree that Celia left me and see all those people, all those lives that were touched by the vase, it makes me think. I don't really believe in luck, but I do appear to have been the recipient of something quite remarkable – to be the last in a long line that stretches back in time to Niccolò dei Conti and his daughter and his daughter's daughter and so on.'

'All the way to me!' said Georgie. 'Surely I'm the last in the line, for now. And who knows, maybe I'll have a daughter too. And whilst I don't have a vase any more to hand on, we have the luck it brought us, don't we?'

'And with that luck, darling, comes our responsibility,' said Miranda. 'Remember that. We must do something worthwhile with our luck and not fritter it away. Remember all those who have gone before and what they achieved – all those businesses and children; all that pride they had in themselves. We must make that our legacy. The vase has gone back to its geographical home – back to China where it came from, where it belongs. But we carry its luck with us always.'

A NOTE FROM THE AUTHOR

This novel is based on the life of a real person – Niccolò dei Conti and his two children Maria and Daniele. Many of the 'characters' in the novel are based on real people, but the majority are not.

Niccolò dei Conti was an Italian explorer. Born in Choggia near Venice in 1395, he left Italy as a young man intent on travelling the world. He studied Arabic in Damascus before joining an Arabian caravan en route to Baghdad. From there he went by sea through the Persian Gulf to Oman, where he learned Persian. He crossed India and on to what we now call Sri Lanka. From there he travelled to Sumatra and on to the lands of 'further India', as China was then known. There is some disagreement as to whether he did get as far as China, but he certainly travelled to the Spice Islands and thence to Vietnam and Cambodia. Whether he actually met Admiral Zheng He is not known, but it is possible, as they were both in Sumatra at around the same time and dei Conti did write later of the immense power and capability of the Admiral's vast ships, which conquered the oceans on behalf of his Emperor.

Zheng He wrote of his own travels:

'*We have traversed more than 100,000 li of immense water spaces and have beheld in the ocean huge waves like mountains rising in the sky, and we have set eyes on barbarian regions far away hidden in a blue transparency of light vapours, while our sails, loftily un-*

furled like clouds day and night, continued their course as rapidly as a star, traversing those savage waves as if we were treading a public thoroughfare.'

In India, dei Conti met his future wife. Sadly, we do not know her name. But we do know they had four children who travelled everywhere with their parents. What an extraordinary life they must have lived. When Niccolò decided to return finally to Italy, the family travelled via the Malabar Coast, through the Red Sea to Cairo, where his disguise as a Persian merchant was uncovered. He was forced to convert to Islam in order to protect his family. This was a relatively common practice amongst European merchants in Asia at that time, and whilst it was an expedient thing to do, it was also an example of dei Conti's desire to learn 'at first hand' about the diversity of people and their religions. Tragically he lost his wife and his two youngest children, along with all his servants, during an epidemic in Cairo. What sort of epidemic is not known, but the plague, in all its forms – bubonic, septicemic and pneumonic – were endemic at that time. He finally returned to Venice with his two remaining children, Maria and Daniele, in 1441.

The plague island that I describe near Venice does exist. Poveglia was used as a quarantine island for victims of the plague and leprosy; between 1922 and 1968 it was an asylum. It is now deserted, and contains nothing more than the old hospital building and a chapel. The landing station is still there, but the gardens are now overgrown. It is currently the object of a battle between a property developer who wishes to turn it into a private hotel and the Mayor of Venice who wishes to preserve it for the people of his city. It is said that ghosts inhabit the island, and it can be hard to persuade taxis to take you there. I visited the island and it is indeed a sad and melancholy place. But I never encountered a ghost!

After his return to Venice, Niccolò lived another twenty-eight years to the ripe old age of seventy-four. In that time he was appointed a member of the *Maggior consiglio* in 1451; was elected procurator of the churches of San Francesco in 1453 and Santa Croce in 1460. But what he is truly remembered for is his diary, *India Recognita*, a record of his travels dictated to the humanist scholar Poggio Bracciolini, private secretary to the then Pope Eugene IV as an apostasy for his conversion to Islam. This diary was translated into a variety of languages, including Portuguese, Spanish, Dutch and English, and formed the fourth book of Poggio Bracciolini's's work, *De Varietate Fortunae – On the Vicissitudes of Fortune* – completed in 1448.

Sadly nothing more is known of his children and what happened to them. I have imagined their future in this novel; as the children of a well-known and successful merchant, it seemed to me that they would have continued with that way of life. Through their imagined lives, I have endeavoured to explore the extraordinary and rich tapestry of the merchant class in fifteenth, sixteenth and seventeenth-century Europe, as the cities of Venice, Bruges, Antwerp and finally Amsterdam became, one by one, the principal merchant centres of their day.

The following people referenced in the book did exist:

- Niccolò dei Conti
- Maria dei Conti
- Daniele dei Conti
- Emperor Xuande and his many wives and concubines
- Admiral Zheng He
- Polisena Cavorta – young nun who fell in love and ran away with
- Giovanni Valler

- Elena Marcello –nun of uncertain virtue in Sant. Angelo convent
- Antonio di Marco Gambello – architect of the re-designed façade of the San Zaccaria Convent.
- Willhelm Rumlim – German merchant in Venice
- Friedrich Diterichs – German merchant in Venice
- Tomasso Portarino – Medici Banker based in Bruges
- Carlo Cavalcanti – silk merchant to the Medici bank based in Bruges
- Folco d'Adoardo di Giovanni Portinari – Medici banker based in Bruges
- Guido di Savino – maiolica potter who became famous in Antwerp
- Margriet Bolleman – Guido's wife
- Francesco di Marco Datini – Merchant of Prato
- Desiderius Erasmus – humanist scholar
- Jan Huygen van Linschoten – Dutch explorer
- Plancius – explorer
- Jacob van Neck – VOC Chief Merchant

All the rest are fictional.

I have been aided in this novel by the work of many scholars and authors:

Lars Tharp, ceramics expert

The Book of Porcelain by Walter AStaehelin – a fascinating and beautiful book explaining the remarkable process of porcelain production in China in the 18th century.

Venice: A Documentary History 1450 –1630, edited by David Chambers and Brian Pullman

Court and Civic Society in the Burgundian Low Countries c.1420 –1530 by Andrew Brown and Graeme Small

The Web of Empire by Alison Games

Venice and Amsterdam by Peter Burke

A Companion to Venetian History, 1400 –1797 , edited by Eric R Dursteler

Maiolica, an essay by Timothy Wilson

My thanks to them and to the authors of all the other fascinating pieces of information I have discovered on this journey.

A NOTE TO READERS

Thank you for reading this novel. I do so hope you enjoyed it.

The 'stars' of this novel are, of course, the family at its heart. As I have said in my notes, Niccolò dei Conti and his two children, Maria and Daniele did exist. But I have fictionalised their lives on their return to Venice and created a large family of descendants. I am fascinated by family history, and have explored my own through various ancestry websites. I know it is of great interest to many of us – to understand where we come from; what our ancestors did for a living; what influenced their lives.

The other 'star' of this novel is, of course, the Ming storage jar. I have been fascinated by blue and white china ever since I was a young child and my mother gave me a miniature blue and white china tea-set for my dolls. I played with it for many years and as a teenager began to collect other – larger – pieces of blue and white china. I now have quite a considerable collection. As a young reporter working for the BBC, I was lucky enough to travel to Hong Kong and bought two large storage jars and a smaller blue and white vase from an antique dealer in the Hollywood Road – the centre of Hong Kong's antique district. They were not Ming of course, but had some age. I had quite a battle to persuade the airline to let me carry them with me inside the plane and not put them in the hold. They sit on the shelves in my sitting room to this day and have been an inspiration to me when writing this story.

I first came up with the idea for the novel eight or nine years ago. I was already writing my first novel, and had no time to develop this new story. But it continued to bubble away in my imagination. I collected bits and pieces of information, did some research about Niccolò dei Conti and was surprised when a press story emerged of a family in west London who had inherited a Chinese vase that turned out to be worth £39 million! It appeared that the story I had been harbouring all these years was true.

I began to write *Daughters of the Silk Road* as soon as my first novel was published and have spent a wonderful year exploring the various cities that feature in the story. I had been to Venice and Bruges in the past, but it was a new experience to see them through the eyes of my characters. It was wonderful to visit the convent of San Zaccaria (which is now a police station), and to 'find' the house on the canal where I like to think Niccolò and his family lived when they returned to Venice from the East. It was exciting to walk the pretty streets of Bruges and Amsterdam locating the houses where dei Conti's fictional descendants might have lived. And fascinating too, to visit Antwerp and be shown round a stunning house and workshop of a well-known book-binder. This house was the inspiration for the home of Cornelius and Margarethe.

I hope you have enjoyed reading my tale of the dei Conti family and their descendants. If you have, I would be so delighted if you could leave a review on Amazon for others. Also, if you'd like to keep up-to-date with all my latest releases, just sign up here:

www.bookouture.com/debbie-rix

Until the next time…

 @debbierix
 DebbieRixAuthor
 www.debbierix.com